THE DEVIL'S AGENT

BOOKS BY HANS HABE

PUBLISHED IN THE U.S.A.

Three Over the Frontier

Sixteen Days

A Thousand Shall Fall

Katherine

Aftermath

Walk in Darkness

Our Love Affair with Germany

Black Earth

Off Limits

PUBLISHED IN OTHER COUNTRIES

A World Crumbles

All My Sins (Autobiography)

THE DEVIL'S
AGENT

A Novel by HANS HABE

Translated from the German by Ewald Osers

NEW YORK

FREDERICK FELL, INC., PUBLISHERS

c. 3

Manufactured in the United States of America by H. Wolff, New York

Designed by Sidney Solomon

Published simultaneously in Canada by George J. McLeod., Ltd., Toronto

Library of Congress Catalog Card No. 58–8741

First published in Germany under the title Im Namen des Teufels, by Verlag Kurt Desch, Munich

H.R.

THE DEVIL'S AGENT

George Droste, an Austrian, becomes involved in the secret service of both Americans and Russians in post-war Vienna. When he decides to put an end to his activities, he learns that knowing too much is a dangerous thing.

Prelude

THE HANDS of the big gilt clock above the door leading from the terrace into the dining-room formed a right-angle: the time was almost three o'clock and most of the guests had gone. Only the man and the boy were still sitting over their coffee, deep in conversation.

It was an exceptionally hot summer day, but the terrace was in the shade and through the carefully closed windows the town in its heat haze wore an air of unreality. The motor-cars seemed to be gliding noiselessly along the Quai du Mont Blanc, as in a silent film. It was as if the slightly old-fashioned and highly exclusive Hotel Beau Rivage had seen to it that its guests should enjoy as tranquil and peaceful a scene as possible on that July day in 1955.

The man and the boy were talking English—the boy with an American twang, the man with just a touch of a foreign accent, though it would have been difficult to determine its exact geographical origin.

The man was in his middle forties and belonged to the type that was more apt to arouse the interest, and perhaps even the envy, of other men than rapidly attract the attention of women. He was tall and exceedingly slim, and his hollow cheeks below the strong cheekbones lent his features a half-feverish and half-muscular expression; his bony hands moved with lassitude, almost as though they were loosely and insecurely fastened to his wrists; his crossed legs might have belonged equally well to an overbred aristocrat or a fast sprinter. His chestnut hair, with its light dusting of gray at the temples, was carefully brushed back and thus emphasized the sharp outline of his perfectly regular face. Only his eyes—as is so often the case—had made themselves independent, almost as if in mockery over the ascetic appearance of their owner. Though hiding in their rather deep sockets, they had a bold and provocative glint: pale-blue eyes, full of life, humorous and a little mistrustful, without a trace of weariness, and a full ten years younger than the man they served.

The boy was probably about sixteen, and it was not merely his natural command of the English language which showed that he could hardly come from the same parts as his interlocutor. Though well-built, he was not tall for his age; he had broad shoulders, fair hair, and blue eyes—in appearance, bearing, and clothes undoubtedly a product of that American world which has absorbed most of the nations of the earth without, in the end, resembling any of them. An attentive observer, on the other hand, could not have missed the fact that the young American must have enjoyed a European education for more than a brief term; for he showed his vis-à-vis that well-mannered respect which the youth of America regards as an unnecessary, and indeed ludicrous, compliment to old age. But beyond mere manners, which the young man had evidently learned at a Swiss school, he seemed to have a genuine respect for his older friend: in fact, he was hanging on the man's lips with helpless—one might almost say girlish—admiration.

"I really don't know why the Swiss schools are so famous," said the boy, continuing their conversation.

"I think you've been quite happy here so far," said the man. He knew exactly what the boy was leading up to.

"Naturally," the boy hastened to agree. "But you must admit that I speak French fluently now, and that it is high time I learnt your mother tongue."

The man smiled. "And what objection is there to Zürich?" he asked.

"The objection to Zürich," retorted the boy, "is that it is almost as far from Vienna as Geneva is."

"You are mistaken if you think that I find it easier to be without you than you without me," the man replied seriously. "Especially after ten days' holiday such as this. I need a friend as much as you do. But believe me, the next two years will pass in no time. You know, time is a funny thing: the years in front of us seem unending, and those behind us so short. But one doesn't discover this till one gets old."

"Even Monsieur Lavasseur believes I would learn a lot more if I were with you," the boy insisted.

"Monsieur Lavasseur has spent his life in schools," said the man. "That's why he has so much respect for life. I have learnt too little, that's why I am impressed by schools."

"You see," the boy said triumphantly. "That's a sentence you don't find in the school-books."

"You are the most charming flatterer I know," said the man. "I'll think it over . . ."

He noticed that the boy's attention was suddenly distracted. And almost at once, lowering his voice, the boy said:

"Do you know the man over there?"

"No, why?" replied the man; but the boy thought it odd that George, as he called his foster-father, avoided casting even a quick glance at the solitary guest. Even when they made their way past the stranger's table the man stared straight in front of him, escaping the other's inquisitive glance.

Opposite the Brunswick memorial they took a taxi.

The man gazed out of the window.

"Till Christmas, then," he said, trying to hide his emotion. "You know, perhaps I'll come and collect you after all. I may well have some business in Switzerland just then."

The boy turned towards him and looked at him in alarm.

"But surely I shall see you at the station, George," he said.

And imploringly he added: "Am I not to see you off at the station?"

"Perhaps it would be wiser for you to stay at your school this evening," the man said. "You know, they don't like——"

"But it was all settled," insisted the boy, disappointed.

"Yes, indeed," the man said quickly, "but I shall probably not take the train after all. I'm thinking of hiring a car and driving over to Lausanne. . . . I really ought to visit an old friend there. I promised two months ago."

He looked at the boy and smiled. "Besides, you know how I hate those farewells at the station. I am a sentimental old fool, Johnny. Each time I find parting more difficult than the last."

"And yet it is much easier to depart than to stay behind," said the boy, attempting a precocious aphorism.

When, at last, they parted in front of the long, low château which housed the feudal school, the man managed to contrive things so that their good-byes came unprepared and almost as a surprise.

Back at his hotel, the man appeared to have entirely forgotten about his intention of hiring a car to take him to Lausanne. He locked himself in his room, wrote a few letters, paced up and down nervously, devoted far too much care to the packing of his case, and left the hotel only when it was time to go to the station.

The moment he handed his ticket and passport to the sleeping-car attendant he became aware of the man who had attracted Johnny's attention on the terrace of the Hotel Beau Rivage, but again he acted as if he were a stranger, and as if this second encounter were every bit as accidental as the first. But when, shortly after the train had pulled out of the station, the attendant inquired whether he wished to have his bed made, he declined: he sat down in the corner seat by the door and, without touching his newspapers, watched the door with the attention of a man expecting a visit.

The tinkle of the little bell which summoned the passengers to dinner had hardly died away when there was a knock at the door.

The man called out: "Come in," somewhat unnecessarily, for the door of the compartment had already opened.

"Good evening, Mr. Droste," said the man who entered the compartment. He was of medium height, with a healthy-looking figure and an unhealthy color to his skin. It was not easy to explain the plebeian impression which the man conveyed, for he was wearing a good, made-to-measure suit, a fine-quality white poplin shirt, a discreet tie, and carefully brushed shoes. Perhaps it was his hands—plump, red hands, with their fingers splayed out in proletarian fashion—that gave the lie to his natty elegance; perhaps it was merely the expensive and vulgar diamond ring which he wore, of all places, on the little finger of his right hand; or perhaps it was nothing of this at all, and it was simply that the whole man, in his good suit, had about him an air of disguise, just as if he were wearing some grotesque fancy dress.

"Good evening, Mr. Brown," Droste replied in English. "I was surprised to see you in Geneva." This time he avoided all unnecessary politeness and did not invite his visitor to sit down, for already Mr. Brown was settling himself comfortably by the window. "Shall we get down to business at once?"

Mr. Brown bent forward a little.

"You are to be given a new assignment," he said.

"I am on leave."

"It is hoped that you will cut short your leave."

"I am sorry," said Droste. "I propose to take a well-earned rest until January the First." His visitor's vulgarity stung him into using formal language.

"Your plan won't meet with much understanding," said Mr. Brown.

"I trust that it will," Droste replied politely. "During the eight years of my activity I have always felt gratified by the knowledge that agreements were honored." He gave a brief sigh. "Eight years without a day's leave. That makes eight months' leave."

"We don't work to trade-union rules," said Mr. Brown.

"Neither are they necessary in view of the excellent relations between employers and employees," said Droste. "Trade unions are the product of mutual distrust. Our work is based on trust."

Mr. Brown did not know how to take this. He said roughly: "So you refuse . . ."

Droste produced a flat, oblong silver cigarette-case from his inside jacket pocket and proffered it to his visitor.

"Mr. Brown," he said, "our relations—I mean the relations between the two of us—have never been very cordial. Or, to express myself more clearly, we've never been able to stand each other. That is why I would now ask you to convey my reply as accurately as possible, that is—without your own interpretation. I am not refusing to carry out an assignment which, so far, I do not even know anything about. I have merely no intention of cutting short my holiday, of which, for a number of personal reasons, I am in urgent need. I intend, during the next few months, to read some good books, to cultivate my garden, and to treat my stomach to the blessings of a domestic diet. I propose to spend the Christmas holidays with my son—whose attention, by the way, you attracted in a rather clumsy manner. Thereafter, on the first day of the New Year, I shall report for duty and resume my work in my usual conscientious way."

Mr. Brown had declined the cigarette and lit a cigar instead, omitting—much to his host's disapproval—to remove the golden band around the middle of the dark, delicious Havana.

"Cultivate your garden . . . !" said Mr. Brown. "We know very well where your house is."

"It isn't a secret, Mr. Brown. In fact, are there any secrets from you?"

"Your refusal might cost you dear," said Mr. Brown.

Droste smiled. "I don't think I am mistaken in saying that you are now exceeding your authority, Mr. Brown. I understand that, for yourself, you are uneasy at the thought of returning empty-handed. But I may assure you that you would find yourself in even worse disgrace if you were to annoy me by threats. Sleep well. You have no reason for spending an uneasy night." He rose and walked over to the window. "We are approaching the frontier. You had better withdraw."

Mr. Brown left without a word.

Droste let the window down and looked out. His temples were hot and the cool evening air was refreshing. Slowly the train drew into the frontier station of Bellegarde.

In Paris, on the following morning, he looked around in vain for his visitor of the night before, but he did not waste much time on his researches, so that he was not quite sure whether Mr. Brown had indeed returned home.

The next morning he took the Orient Express to Vienna.

He arrived at seven o'clock in the evening. The first street-lamps were alight on the Ringstrasse—much too soon—and, against a sky that was still pale blue, they seemed like stars in the daytime. As his taxi rolled past the Volksgarten, Droste remembered that it was Sunday: a Sunday crowd was streaming out of the park and there was a smell of hot asphalt, beer, and box hedges. He was glad to be home.

The vehicle crossed the city and took the road towards Nuss-dorf. Green garlands were hanging above the inn doors, and the

smell of beer gave way to that of wine. The rays of the setting
sun lay like gentle fingers over the vineyards behind the inns.
The decrepit old vehicle laboriously climbed up the steep road to
the Bisamberg.

It stopped at the end of a residential street. An active, elderly
woman, with cheerful red cheeks, was waiting for Droste—his
housekeeper Marie. She had stood there, waiting, for over an
hour in order to help him carry his luggage, for Droste's remote
house could not be reached by motor vehicles.

The church bell on the Bisamberg had struck nine when he
was left alone in his study. He lit his desk lamp, but did not sit
down at his massive writing-desk. Instead, he stepped out on to
the balcony. There was a deck-chair, and he sat down in it. Down
below glittered the lights of the city. The glow-worms danced
around his cigarette as though it were the queen of all glow-
worms. The peace around him was so deep that he was doubly
aware of his own restlessness.

So far he had been escaping his restlessness, but now he began, for the first time, to consider the consequences of his conversation with Mr. Brown. By now Mr. Brown would have made
his report and they would know that he was not prepared to
re-enter their services any sooner than had been agreed. He did
not think they would try to force him to rejoin them, but he
feared that his refusal might well arouse their suspicion. He had
been deluding himself that during the months of his absence
they might forget about him, and that afterwards they might
perhaps accept his final retirement. But now he began to count
on his fingers the months that were left to him: August, September, October, November, December. Five months in all. There
were still four days left before the end of July and, like a miser,
he added those four days. That made five months and four days.
After that he would have to see them and tell them that everything was over.

He was not afraid of that final, inevitable interview. It was the intervening days that he feared. Time had only one kinsman —Death. But Time was more terrible than Death. It was possible to make compromises with Death, favorable ones and less favorable ones. One could bargain with Death or one could cheat it. One could snatch a few days from Death, or even months, or years, maybe. In a man's fight against Death the whole of mankind was his ally: chemists, physicists, doctors and technicians— but against fleeing Time no one dared erect a dam, and the crumbling days had to be faced alone. One was moving towards Death only because one could not halt Time; there was nothing terrible in moving towards Death. What was terrible and certain was that meanwhile, on this fatal journey, one was losing Time. Morning was followed by evening, and night by day, and each new calendar was a prophecy of lost battles. Those with courage and those with faith believed that they would find life again after death; but no one was so courageous, or so full of faith, as to think he might find his yesterday again. "I have no time" was the most merciless sentence of humanity: for what could one have if one had no time?

Three months were lost—almost half the time that had been granted him. He had intended to make use of every minute of those months to write his memoirs and, at the same time, to construct that second line of defense behind which he hoped to withdraw. So far he had done nothing to build it, and he had not put his pen to paper. Had he begun to waver? Was he afraid? Had he not perhaps deliberately wasted the past few months so that there should be no time left to him for the necessary reversal?

He stood up. Panic seized him, the kind that seizes people who have got into conflict with the calendar and who believe that they must find their lost days in those yet to come. He crushed his cigarette with his toe and returned to his study.

From his desk drawer he took a black exercise-book which he had kept in readiness there for a long time. But before taking up his pen he cast a glance, as if to reassure himself that no one had touched it, upon the safe, which was built into the library wall, not conspicuously but not secretly either. Then he dipped his pen into the ink-well, and in a neat, almost calligraphic, hand he wrote on the first page:

This book belongs to my son Johnny. He is to open it on his eighteenth birthday—whether I am with him or not.

GEORGE DROSTE

Underneath he wrote:

Begun on July 27, 1955, on the Bisamberg, near Vienna.

And now no haste, he told himself. No haste, even though time is short. This must not become a book gripped by menacing fingers. I've got time, plenty of time . . . that's what I must remind myself of again and again.

He leaned back. He was still sitting thus, without having dipped his pen in again, when beyond the Danube, over the near-by Kahlenberg, the sun rose again.

PART ONE

I

Spy for East and West

CRIME DOES PAY.

This maxim, the realistic inversion of the current hypocritical assertion, comes to my mind every time when I climb, after a spell of restful gardening, the gentle slope to the delightful house that I have called my own for nearly a year. Or, to be quite precise—and I shall practise precision to the best of my ability in writing these memoirs—I must admit that this house, with its many gables and solidly prosperous appearance, has belonged to me since 1950, that is for five years, and that I acquired it at the time when the Bisamberg near Vienna, on whose slopes it is so gracefully enthroned, had still been part of the Soviet sector and the prices of properties and land had reached an all-time low. It had been part of my job then to foretell the probable course of international politics, and hence also of real-estate values, and I can hardly be blamed if I speculated no less skilfully on my own behalf, than on behalf of the powers in whose service I was.

If I were a professional writer, and therefore anxious to make capital out of this record of my experiences, my thoughts, and my very heartbeats—instead of putting pen to paper with nothing but the highest purpose—I should now keep my readers in suspense as to what I mean by "my bad deeds." If you come to think of it, the pleasures which men buy in a bookshop are rather absurd: they seek suspense—that is, a contraction of their blood vessels and hence an artificial disturbance of their circulation—and in the end they are even grateful to the author for having cut short their lives. While medical science is endeavoring to prolong the span of a man's earthly life with all kinds of wonder-drugs, mankind to-day is more afraid of boredom than of death, and thus the most marvellous inventions are doomed to failure simply because long life is incompatible with the artificial thrills that men must have. Needless to say, I shall not go out of my way to bore the reader—for otherwise he might put down this highly instructive book unread, and turn to some more obnoxious reading matter—but, on the other hand, I do not propose to keep him in "suspense" or to withhold from him, by all sort of tricks and sleight of hand, the solution of such problems as I am able to provide.

To anticipate therefore: I was and, technically at least, still am a spy—though of a rather special kind. Not because I drew a fairly considerable pay from East and West alike—a thing which other agents have done before—but because, unintentionally at first, and later with full deliberation, I have been deceiving my employers in the manner of a dishonest supplier who exploits his customer's ignorance by selling him useless or spoiled merchandise.

I have been an impostor as well as an agent, and my total lack of regret for having been either is not primarily due to the fact that it has been profitable for me. Naturally, the circumstance that I have so far pursued my work with impunity, even though with a few very close shaves, must influence my feelings to some extent. Human life consists of a series of episodes which are viewed in retrospect, so that the end influences not only the whole view but also any moral that may be derived from it. A man who deceives his mistress after a prolonged intimate relationship is thus inclined to judge the whole affair in the light of its sad ending, and he will regard the woman who has given him much happiness as the cause of his misery—a patent injustice, since life proceeds in a forward direction, whereas all subsequent viewing is done backwards. Similarly, most people regret their bad deeds not because they were bad, but because they led to a bad end; it follows, therefore, that more true repentance is found in jails, hospitals, and similar institutions, than in society drawing-rooms, government offices, or in God's good air, although there are a lot of people milling around who could well do with a little active repentance.

Nevertheless, my freedom from regret is not merely due to what has so far proved a "happy end," but also to my relationship to my victims. Though a gambler by nature, I have never liked card games and have always preferred the impersonal roulette wheel—probably out of some congenital soft-heartedness. Like everybody else I hated losing; but equally I disliked winning from fellow players who needed the money quite as much, if not more, than I. For the owners of casinos, on the other hand, I have never felt the slightest sympathy, and because I always earnestly tried to accumulate as many of their chips as possible I came to be regarded at Cannes, Las Vegas, and Estoril as quite a respectable winner at the tables. It was much the same thing with my career as an impostor: I owe my undisputed successes and my spectacular climb up the ladder of secret agents to the total lack of pity which, with a growing realization of what the game was about, I felt for those I deceived. For eight years I served the secret services: I came, first, to despise them and then to hate them. And if I have now decided not to deceive them any longer for the sake of my own advantage, then this is simply because I hope to damage them more by this frank record of my experiences than I could expect to do, in the present circumstances, through personal exploitation.

2

ʊʊʊʊʊʊʊʊʊʊʊ

Fulfilment of a Trust

AT THE RISK of anticipating, and at the even greater risk of presenting a deceptively favorable picture of my personality by relating the best deed I ever did, I nevertheless have to report how I came to adopt Johnny; for without this boy, now at school in Geneva, there would never have been this record of my recollections; a record that is not only liable but positively designed to tear the web, once and for all, between myself and my employers.

I met Johnny's father, Richard Grant, in Korea, where I happened to find myself on a special assignment at the peak of this bloody rehearsal-war. Richard, a man of only thirty-one, had been driven, like so many others, into the arms of the ever-lurking secret service by despair and subconscious suicidal tendencies. That the secret services are never short of people who are ready to undertake the craziest assignments is hardly surprising if one considers the large number of people who are prepared to smoke themselves to death, work themselves to death, or worry themselves to death. No matter how modestly people conceal their death-urge, it is often quite as powerful as their much-vaunted will to live.

During the last month of the Second World War, Richard Grant, then a parachutist operating in the Ardennes, had received the news of the senseless and tragic death of his beloved parents. No sooner had he returned home than his young wife, the mother of a six-year-old boy, faithlessly left him. It appeared, moreover, that his wife's unfaithfulness was by no means of recent standing, so that Richard Grant even suspected that little Johnny might be the fruit of his wife's adulterous relationship. This suspicion, by the way, was typical of his mental condition, for my acquaintance with the boy totally dispelled the doubts which Richard had sown in me, too, with the persuasiveness born of despair; the child and his legitimate father are as alike as two peas in a pod. Demobilized and desperate, Richard was unable to gain a foothold again in civilian life; besides, his more than usually exciting wartime experiences had taken him out of a rather humdrum job; and, finally, he was probably trying to prove himself, by daring and romantic feats, to the faithless woman whom he still loved and who cared nothing for his feats. So when the "dragnet"—as the recruitment branch of the intelligence service was called—began to concentrate on former paratroopers, Richard Grant dropped into its lap like a ripe plum.

I was myself badly shaken when I arrived in Korea, and in this condition of heightened sensibility I not only quickly discovered a kindred soul in Richard but was grateful to him for the support which I was able to give him. The straw, in my opinion, often needs the drowning man as much as the drowning man does the straw.

In that April of 1951, U.S. Military Intelligence was facing a serious crisis in Korea. The American Commander-in-Chief had just been relieved of his post and recalled to Washington, and his most loyal subordinate and later biographer, the Chief of Intelligence, had left the theater of war together with him. In the area of Yonchon and around the Hwachon reservoir a North Korean-Chinese offensive was brewing up, threatening Seoul, the capital. As always when the frontlines get crystallized and unfathomable, things are being prepared behind their invisible walls, Intelligence—being dependent largely on information from prisoners-of-war—was in the dark. In the present instance, however, both the precarious strategic position and the prestige of the new Command, and of the secret service imported by it, urgently demanded some convincing results. It was decided to charge some fifty agents with various reconnaissance missions and to "drop" them over different points of enemy territory. Some of the agents thus introduced into enemy country were to make their own way back through the enemy lines, with the help of maps and position plans, once they had collected their information; others were to be "picked up" by helicopters at certain points at a prearranged hour of the night.

In all such and similar operations, which are in no way out of the ordinary, the secret service divides its agents or spies into two categories, "expendables" and "non-expendables"—that is, those one is prepared to write off, and those one is not.

Here I must become a trifle technical. If a roulette player were to put a stake on each of the thirty-six numbers on the green cloth, and also on the Zero, he would be bound to collect a win from one of the numbers. Such a system, however, would be foolish in the extreme, since the chips placed on thirty-five out of the thirty-six numbers would inevitably be lost. Human life, however, being less valuable than roulette chips, is staked more generously. The greater the number of agents dropped behind the enemy lines, the greater the probability that one or the other will return with a few pieces of information; in other words, the secret service will gain, even if all the other human chips are lost in the process. Under favorable conditions it is estimated that in operations such as the one just mentioned about five out of every ten agents will make their way back to their unit. The situation in the Seoul area, however, was considerably more complicated, and no secret was made to me of the fact that of the fifty agents to be dropped, at least forty-five had been written off in advance. One of these was Richard Grant.

The briefing took place in a half-destroyed schoolhouse, or rather hut, in Seoul. The room was not unlike a doll's house or a stage set: one of the four walls had collapsed, so that the former schoolroom stood open on one side and provided shelter only against the lashing rain but not against the cutting wind. The blackboard was still in its place: it was covered with all kinds of signs and explanations, and there was a map hanging on it. There were also two or three pathetically small school desks, on which a few agents were squatting in their leather jackets; other officers were grouped in a semi-circle around the lecturing Intelligence major. A few hurricane lamps cast an uncertain light on the wet walls and the crumbling ceiling on which the silhouette of a huge rabbit was outlined: a stuffed, and no doubt here an exotic, animal that had survived on the desk of the teacher who had long fled or been killed. The major's explanations were accompanied by the dull rumble of the guns and occasionally punctuated by the loud crash of a bomb, which caused the major to frown angrily, just like a teacher who is interrupted by an unruly child.

I watched the faces of the men, in particular that of the man whom, in view of the intensity of our relationship, I felt entitled to call my friend in spite of the brevity of our acquaintance. Not for the first time, but with exceptional clarity, I realized the disastrous confusion which a subtly calculated lure of heroism is capable of causing in the human mind. If these men had been expected to jump from the second-floor windows of a building, every one of them would have refused; and yet their chances of coming through safely would have been vastly better than were those of their safe return from the country behind the guns. These Americans had never heard of Wotan, let alone of the elaborate comforts provided in Wotan's heaven for fallen heroes, and yet they seemed to differentiate between a pointless and a purposeful death, between what might be termed a private death (of which one was quite entitled to be scared stiff) and a public death (which one was in duty bound to face bravely). Admittedly their inner tension was betrayed by their faces, which appeared lined and emaciated in the flickering yellow light, giving them the appearance of skeletons sitting in a row, draped with uniforms, but their healthy fear of death had given way to an unhealthy fear of not showing a brave front. Once only, in the case of a bull-fighter, had I come across this curious distinction between fear of death and fear of death: I had seen him tremble like a child at the prospect of an appendix operation on the day after he had faced a *toro bravo* without batting an eyelid.

A sense of wretchedness came over me, the outsider, the only man in the nocturnal schoolroom who could have picked out the few who were not positively doomed. My own god-likeness, my knowledge of something which the others, those mortally affected, did not even surmise—all this gripped me so powerfully that for a moment I was tempted to break into the major's calm explanations and warn those about to be sacrificed, or perhaps even incite them to desert at this last hour.

Needless to say, I did not find enough courage for such a redeeming deed. I did not even betray my knowledge to my friend. I lulled my conscience with lame excuses, such as the argument that lists and maps were the puny works of man and that even the general who had given me the information could not possibly tell how the operation was likely to go. Nevertheless, even without any warning from me, Richard Grant must have had a premonition of his fate. Less than half an hour before take-off he took me aside and entrusted to me—in a jocular manner, of course, and concealing his anxiety behind terse, manly words—a few letters and photographs, including a letter to his son who was then twelve years of age. Vaguely, casually, and almost shamefacedly he asked me to look after Johnny in case he failed to return.

I do not wish to anticipate more than is necessary for the reader's understanding of this account. Johnny Grant, or more correctly Johnny Droste, now is a boy of sixteen, a good-looking lad, more than ordinarily endowed with the gifts of intellect and soul. Not only do I regard him increasingly as my own son, but he has also become in an ever-growing measure a friend—the only friend I have.

During my recent visit, however, when at last I rid myself of all self-deception, I realized only too well that I had been lacking in candor in my dealings with the boy, who is precocious in the best sense of the word, and mature beyond his years. I have been presenting his father to him in the halo of a false heroism; I have kept from him the circumstances which surrounded Richard Grant's death behind the North Korean lines on that April day in 1951. I have likewise carefully concealed from him my own past and the sources of my wealth, which he has come to accept as a matter of course, and, needless to say, I have not told him that, with a little courage and strength of character, I could have saved his father. Most children grow up with the most absurd ideas about their fathers anyway, but Johnny's case is even more alarming in that he has the romantically idealized picture of two fathers before him. In the course of the ten days which we spent at Évian-les-Bains, that pleasant place on the French side of the Lake of Geneva, ten brief days of unmarred beauty and harmony, I realized with alarm the boy's romantic inclinations, and more than once I hovered on the brink of a confession. Not only did I lack the courage to make it, not only was I afraid of breaking the spell of the few precious and irretrievable days of escape from my loneliness, but I also tried to convince myself that it was too early to expel the sixteen-year-old from his boyhood paradise.

Sooner or later the expulsion had to come. Are we not strangely made: capable of deceiving, cheating, and defrauding one person in cold blood, and doing everything in our power to present ourselves in the most favorable light to another? Man's eternal wish to be able to live his life twice over, the second time starting off with the knowledge and the lessons of the first, would not be so unattainable if we would only pass on the wisdom of our experience to our children instead of denying it to them with the lame excuse that it is better to "let them knock their own corners off."

In the train which bore me away from Geneva, certain events convinced me even further that I could more easily relive my whole dubious life from the start, without any emendation, than let my son —as I think I am permitted to call him—set forth on his own life's journey with the provender of false premises. At Christmas, when I hope to have concluded this record, I shall take the step which will put an end to my past life—or at least its last, decisive eight years— whether peacefully or violently I am, as yet, unable to say for sure.

3

∿∿∿∿∿∿∿∿∿∿∿

Murder in the Restaurant

I AM DESCENDED from an ancient dynasty of waiters.

As far back as the early part of the last century my great-grandfather Franz Droste is reputed to have been a waiter at the very popular Café Jüngling, which was then situated in the Jägerzeile, that favorite Sunday promenade of the Viennese. My grandfather Franz Droste the Younger served in the elegant restaurant of Meissl and Schadn on the Bauernmarkt, where he rose to the position of head waiter—admittedly only one of six but, as my father assured me, the most highly esteemed since he was in charge of the upper floor, which boasted an especially distinguished and aristocratic clientèle. My father George Droste, after whom I am named, worked his way up in the same establishment from the humble position of coffee-boy. In 1909, when I was born, he was the unchallenged doyen of the head waiters holding sway in the gilt-and-white dining-room.

I owe it to this long line of waiters and head waiters, but in particular to my father, that I started life with a certain advantage. Nearly all waiters acquire a sound judgment of people, and my father was sensible enough to instruct me, at an early age, in many a theoretical lesson about my future dealings with people. The belief that waiters judge their clients exclusively by the size of their tips, in other words—that their judgment of people is purely mercenary, is widely held but nevertheless slanderous. Needless to say, attentive service, like most things in the interplay of human relations, can be bought, but the man who has received it is mistaken in believing that he has also bought the respect and admiration of those ministering to him. All waiters—and this is what endears them to me—are in a certain sense realistic moralists, or moral realists: they exploit human weaknesses without allowing themselves to be influenced by them in any important degree. Servility, often attributed to waiters, does not consist in the selling of one's services, but in actually acknowledging some superiority in the purchaser of these services, or in one's employer. My father taught me to accept bribes without allowing my sound judgment to be blurred by the money received.

My father, George Droste the Elder—affectionately called Schorschi by the proprietors of the patrician restaurant right from his younger days—was a man of tremendously dignified appearance: tall, gaunt, with prominent, angular cheekbones, a narrow face, long hands unmarred by manual work, hands of such an aristocratic shape that as a boy I used to indulge in the pleasant speculation that some female ancestor of mine had perhaps not been over-fussy in the matter of marital fidelity. He wore sideburns, which gradually widened below his cheekbones, advancing almost towards the middle of his face, and lending it quite a unique appearance. This became even more marked as he lost his hair at an early age, and his bushy whiskers, springing as it were from a thin circlet of hair, formed a striking contrast to the shiny baldness of his head. It was typical of my father that, unlike his colleagues, he invariably removed his tailcoat—which, incidentally, he wore with an easy elegance—in the restaurant's changing-room. As he walked home in his light raglan overcoat—he wore the same coat summer and winter—the slim, rather pale man might have been taken for a belated reveller rather than a servant returning from a day's work. This mannerism alone shows that my father had none of that rigid class-consciousness which is the enemy of all progress and development: though devoted to his job he aimed at higher things.

Oddly enough his worthy ambition, which with self-denying solicitude he concentrated on his only child, did not at first meet with much understanding on my part. The blood of waiters, I have to admit, was flowing in my veins. I was completely fascinated by the spacious dining-room with its lavish stucco decorations and heavily gilt mirrors which bounded his kingdom and whither, on quiet afternoons, he would sometimes take me along in response to my urgent entreaties. I was positively obsessed by the idea of one day owning one of those fat black wallets with countless partitions, stiff with tempting white bill-pads and with even more tempting blue banknotes. My dream that some day I would mingle like him with the most elegant ladies and the most exalted gentlemen was not yet marred by the realization of the difference between the leisurely eating and the hectically rushing. In my intention to follow in his path I was deliberately or unconsciously supported by my mother, the simple homespun daughter of a fairly prosperous inn-keeper at Korneuburg, who adored my father uncritically and for that very reason was unable to understand his striving for something different.

I was seven years old when an event occurred which was to influence my life decisively. I remember, as if it were yesterday, how my father, usually calm and affecting a quiet reserve, arrived home that day with every sign of intense excitement and immediately related to my mother, in an unchecked torrent of words, the incident which, a few hours later, was screamed out by special editions of the *Neue Freie Presse* and the *Wiener Tagblatt*.

Count von Stürgkh, His Imperial and Royal Majesty's Prime Minister, unsuspectingly enjoying his luncheon in the upper dining-room that day, had been shot by a fair-haired young man who had, a few minutes previously, chosen a near-by table like a harmless diner, and even before the hastily summoned ambulance men could arrive on the scene the imperial dignitary had died in the arms of my anxiously helpful father. The assassin, a certain Friedrich Adler, had not attempted to escape, but on the contrary had demanded to be put under arrest, proclaiming ecstatically that his bloody deed might put an early and necessary end to the war which, as was known, had started with a similar bloody deed.

It is in line with a child's mentality, and perhaps also with my character, that neither the dead Count nor the assassin appeared to me as the real heroes, but that I saw the true hero in my father, who had witnessed the incident with a sang-froid no doubt greatly over-estimated by me. Children are powerfully attracted by strength, or what they regard as strength, so that even if they happen to witness an accident themselves they will be impressed not so much by the victim or the cause of the disaster as by someone able to apply rudimentary first aid or displaying sufficient presence of mind to ring for the ambulance. Consequently, whenever I and my friends played "Murder in the Restaurant," now my favorite game, I would invariably act the part of my father, compelling the other boys, with for once acknowledged authority, to take the lesser roles of the assassin and the assassinated.

But this was not what affected my future. Nor, for that matter, was it the fact that my father had suddenly become a person in the public eye, a man whose name and picture, although recognizable only by his characteristic whiskers, appeared in the papers. My mother—though reluctant to admit her pride—started an album, bound in wine-colored velvet, in which she meticulously pasted all newspaper cuttings and which was shown, in response to the awaited request and without the need for much persuasion, to the friends and relations who now began to visit us more frequently than ever before.

But, as I said before, it was not our sudden prominence—which anyway was soon forgotten over the collapse of the Empire, the end of the war, disorders and revolution—that had a formative influence on me, but what I can only call the odd behavior of my father. To the mounting alarm of my mother, our friends, and relations my father did not seem to share the general indignation over the young assassin's crime, and indeed began to make ever more frequent heretical remarks about what to him, too, was a hopelessly and irretrievably lost war: the assassination, no doubt a regrettable affair, would at least draw attention to the real state of things. The fact that my mother, who was shy by nature and disliked all public spectacles, was present in court during the trial was chiefly due to her fear—which she readily admitted—that my father might "do something foolish." He did not, however, "do anything foolish," and continued to serve the mighty with devout respect. But he spent more and more of his leisure away from home, at first, perhaps, only in political arguments over a glass of beer, but later at public meetings of just that political party whose leader was a certain Viktor Adler, the father of the assassin. My father, forgive my expression, was a Socialist.

I need hardly say that my youthful philosophy was in a hopeless tangle. My father, the man who ministered so efficiently to the needs of the powerful and at the same time enjoyed their intimacy, was, as indeed he should have been, my model and idol. But his own idol was now increasingly that young revolutionary in whose arrest he had been instrumental on that historic day. My father, like all head waiters—assigned by their very garments to that border-line position between "belonging" and "serving"—walked the narrow plank between respect and contempt for the socially exalted. But that his, and eventually my, hero should actually be a murderer—that, surely, is more than an everyday fate. My youthful panorama, in which right and wrong were constantly changing places like children playing blind man's buff, was further shaken when the Revolution not only immediately released the said Friedrich Adler but triumphantly raised him on its shield. My mother, who died of the Spanish influenza soon afterwards, tried to convince me to her last hour that wrong remained wrong, that nothing was ever achieved by brute force, and that some sort of order had to reign, even in a Republic. Yet Life's practical demonstrations proved weightier than her sermons, which the hard facts had long reduced *ad absurdum*.

My father had no difficulty now in dispelling my childhood dreams of tailcoats, wallets, tinkling crystal chandeliers, and elegantly dressed diners. He himself lost all joy in his profession, for he realized—though perhaps less clearly than I am formulating it here—that the result of revolutions is not that the waiters become the diners, but merely that the characters and the manners of the diners tend to coarsen. For many years he continued punctually to take the tram into town, to put on his starched shirt with accustomed care, and to return home at night, taciturn, in his ever more threadbare raglan—but disillusionment was consuming his thin body, and the vulgar circumstance that the diners were taking to calling out "Check!" instead of "Waiter, my bill, please," finally broke his tired waiter's heart.

4

The Prince, the Prima Donna, and the Major-General

I WAS SIXTEEN when, by my father's death, I was left alone in the world, and this may therefore be a suitable moment to focus a little more attention upon my own person.

I had shot up rapidly and was a tall youth. My silky brown hair I had inherited from my mother, while from my father I had my blue eyes which, at that time, were still innocently looking out upon the world. That I presented a pleasing appearance—or perhaps I should say, that I was intriguingly handsome—did not remain hidden from me for long. Not so much because I came to this conclusion myself, but because the fair sex began to show me their favor long before they could have been bewitched by my intellectual gifts. At the same time I was never one of those young people who attract the expert eye of aging women merely by their youthfulness: on the contrary, my appearance suggested that, though young, I was always ready to learn.

Let me say at once that, while not infrequently engaging a lively conversation with myself in front of the mirror, I was really far more concerned with the development of my intellectual faculties than my physical assets. The ease with which I absorbed school learning not only encouraged me but also gave me a gratifying independence of my masters, of whom I had no unduly high opinion. I did not rely on my innate abilities, however, but took care to sharpen my wits in constant rivalry with my class-mates—for instance, by making sure I got the better bargain in the swapping of postage stamps or in dealings in second-hand books.

In these circumstances I might have grown up as a young man content with himself and the world, had I not been seriously disturbed by my financial and social position. My father's little fortune, accumulated by honest hard work, had shrunk to next to nothing after the First World War since, contrary to his pacifist instincts, he had invested it in Imperial War Bonds; the devaluation of the currency mopped up what little had remained. After my mother's death my father had nobody left to talk to, and so he discussed with me the injustices of the political order—injustices which, moreover, he took personally. But since unwavering honesty seemed to me to be my father's most outstanding quality I was bound to conclude from his experiences that the State was deliberately bent on ruining the good citizen. Whether I was right in this opinion or not I do not know. But when he suddenly collapsed at the restaurant in the act of making out a bill, and when—as though death wanted to mock his life-long principles—he was brought home still in his tailcoat, so that his last journey was the first one in his despised professional clothes, I found that he had left me nothing but the house, though admittedly he had managed to keep that free from mortgage. My mother's family disposed of the house and the property at a not unfavorable price, but the carefully invested proceeds now had to provide for my keep and my further education. As a result, in spite of the security which the investment gave me for the next few years, I was a "poor boy" and my modest way of life caused me to feel my modest origins with redoubled pain.

The school, rather feudal for republican conditions, where my father had entered me thanks to the pull of an important client—a Secretary of State in the Ministry of Internal Affairs—and where I stayed until going on to the university, did not bring out my best qualities. During my years at school I was not, of course, able to deny my father's occupation as he figured in the records as "head waiter," but later I appointed him "restaurant owner," "hotel manager," and finally "hotel proprietor"—always careful to move no further away from the strict truth than was possible without losing sight of it altogether. That liars have a short memory and are bound to get caught up in their own web of falsehoods is the kind of moralizing text that, side by side with "The early bird catches the worm," is eminently suitable for display on kitchen walls but hardly merits serious consideration. Like many other liars, I too managed to train my memory adequately by the need to keep a lot of fabrications in my mind and reduce them to a common denominator. Fate did not treat me harshly, and hence not benignly: it withheld from me many a useful lesson and allowed me to triumph with my lies instead of punishing me for them.

Had I been able to embark on my intended career, or had I even been able to complete my course of studies, I should no doubt to-day be an ornament to my country's legal profession and an object of universal respect. However, as things turned out, I had to make up for the painful loss of such respectability by taking up other, rather less reputable, occupations. But my real career began only at the moment when, at my ancient and famous Alma Mater in Vienna, I made the acquaintance of a particular fellow student: Prince Benjamin.

The prince, then twenty-four and two years my senior, was a member of the ruling house of a small European Duchy which, thanks to the mineral wealth of its soil, the soundness of its banking firms, the excellence of its trout, its well-stocked shooting preserves, and its easy-going taxation policy, enjoyed a high reputation even among the great powers. Though only a distant relation of the ruling prince and likely to succeed to the throne only in the event of a mass epidemic among the princely family, my fellow student Benjamin was nevertheless causing much anxiety to his family and the Government of his native land—especially as that tiny country had always declined any musical-comedy publicity and regarded little Switzerland as an elder brother most worthy of imitation. Prince Benjamin was not exactly good-looking: he had what can only be described as an egghead, covered with prematurely thinning straw-blond hair, rather too prominent eyes, which seemed to be swimming in alcohol, and an untidily drooping lower lip. Yet in spite of his not over-attractive exterior Prince Benjamin behaved as if he had to enact, night after night, the tenor lead in the operetta *Old Heidelberg*—except that he lost his heart not to one Little Kate but, like a foolish butterfly, would flit from one fair flower to another. However, when these flowers included the wife of a highly respected Ambassador of a great Republic, which was, moreover, financially interested in the Duchy, and when the Vienna Government thereupon threatened to expel the pleasure-seeking butterfly in disgrace, the sorely tried family of the prince decided that its patience was exhausted. The prince's continued stay in Vienna was made subject to the condition that a tutor, or mentor, or companion, or what you will, was attached to him; and for reasons which it would be unnecessary to detail here I was honored with the appointment.

Unnecessary? Well, perhaps not entirely. From the first day of our acquaintance I had attached myself to the prince, or—as some said maliciously—thrown myself at him. In the whole of the republican university there was only one prince, only one member of a ruling family, only one living person that had stepped straight out of the pages of my childhood fairy-tales. Prince Benjamin did not really belong to the modern plebeian world, and his country seemed like a green island of the past amid the gray ocean of the present. I had no thought of a career when I attached myself to the companionable prince: I merely wanted to wine and dine with one of those gentlemen for whom my father had uncorked the bottle or served the meat. But when the princely offer was made to me I accepted without hesitation: the prospect of a select, insular existence seemed to me a confirmation of my own exceptional personality.

To say that no more unsuitable person could have been appointed to the post would be grossly unfair. I discharged my difficult yet congenial task to the complete satisfaction both of my ward and my employers, and not a breath of scandal surrounded the prince's fair name in the future. In spite of my extreme youth I had enough sense to realize that a tutor, just as a diplomat—and there is much that the two occupations have in common—must first of all gain favor with the person, or the powers, to whom he is accredited. My main concern was to win the trust, favor, and eventually the friendship of the prince under my charge and, like a good dog, to guard him without biting him. We soon became—and I like to include myself in this compliment—extremely popular guests of the Femina, a nightclub-cum-cabaret flourishing at the time; in the pleasant company of ladies we would attend the Krieau and Freudenau race meetings; we would spend many a gay weekend in the health-giving climate of the Semmering; we would occasionally indulge in the new wine at Grinzing or Nussdorf, or in some rather stronger alcoholic beverages at the various events of the carnival season, and—I have to confess—were counted among the honored regulars at Madame Rosa's secret establishment in the Rotenturm-strasse—but all in the most respectable fashion and without ever running foul of the many prejudices of our own society or the philistine regulations of the authorities. As a result I enjoyed the full confidence of the prince, who was anything but a fool and doubtless saw through me, but for that very reason appreciated me as a man who had tactfully steered him from the realm of dangerous escapades into that of conventionally permitted but none the less enjoyable adventures. When, for reasons connected not so much with his thirst for knowledge as his thirst for life, he decided to move on to the Sorbonne I accompanied him to Paris at the express wish of his parents and his Government, and in the years that fol-lowed I went with him to London, Rome, Berlin, and Madrid.

I need hardly say that my studies were soon sacrificed in favor of a mode of life which, though highly educational in a sense, was not exactly conducive to a legal education. When his father died and my friend returned to his Duchy, where, after some very awk-ward wartime experiences, he is now enjoying a well-earned retire-ment as a big landowner, industrialist, and father of seven princes and princesses, I possessed only few worldly goods. Thus, when the prince's family recommended me to a friend of theirs, a big man in the steel industry, I pitched my tent in the fair city of Cologne as his private secretary, assistant, adviser, and maid-of-all-work.

Before passing on to my not very heroic war experiences and hence to my memoirs proper, I feel I ought to explain why a man of my unquestionable talents, later to be so convincingly proved, had not up to his thirty-eighth year made a success in any but superior domestic situations.

I have never regarded domestic servants as inferior beings—not perhaps out of some democratic sentimentality, which is usually only another form of condescension, but because, being familiar from childhood with the innermost secrets of a servant's life, I have always been convinced of their practical wisdom. A man who takes employment as a servant lies down on a ready-made bed: he lives in a comfortable house that another has built or rented; he warms himself by a fire for which another has to supply the fuel; he shares in a luxury which he could never hope to attain himself, or only by a tremendous effort or a great stroke of luck, and he does so without the health-wrecking worry which the acquisition or preservation of wealth invariably entails. I was born a realist, prepared to accept the world as I found it, and I therefore never deluded myself that there exists anybody who is not a servant: teachers are the servants of principals, managers are the servants of general managers, generals are the servants of the general staff, heads of families are the servants of those selfsame families, mothers are the servants of their children, and God perhaps is worst off of all, being the servant not only of all mankind but perhaps also of the universe and its stars. Clever servants leave all responsibility to their masters: traveling light, they move from one place to another, from one household to another, loyal only so long as loyalty is no burden, and carefully choosing the people who will have to look after them. In this they resemble another animal, likewise despised and yet extremely cunning—the feather flea, which leads a pleasant and comfortable life feeding on the feathers of some busy bird, sharing, as it were, the good fortunes of what zoologists call its "host," but not unduly distressed in the event of the hospitable bird's death, when it will quickly find a new billet among the feathers of some other bird.

The steel magnate in the Rhineland was not the last bird among whose feathers I established myself. After leaving him—by which time he was barely able to fly without my help—I transferred my services to a singing bird. I sold them to Maria Gulbekian, the opera star, whom I had met at the house of my industrialist and who had held out to me prospects of higher remuneration and a more colorful life. I toured the world as the famous woman's private secretary—impresario might be a better word—and my principal duties consisted of assuring her that she was neither getting old nor losing her voice: both of these statements were untrue but nevertheless sweetened Mme Gulbekian's all-too-early middle age. When the beautiful woman, whose favor I had enjoyed in more senses than one, suddenly lost her life in a motor accident—a fortunate circumstance for herself, for she would not have got over the loss of her voice or her youth—I returned to my native Vienna and occupied, in quick succession, a number of posts which, in accordance with Austria's more modest conditions, were rather less profitable.

Austria's annexation to the German Reich and the outbreak of the Second World War brought about my first encounter with those secret services which were to become my destiny.

Among Mme Gulbekian's most ardent admirers there had been a Colonel in the German General Staff, a certain Christian Baron von Sensenöhr, who had been active in the illegal "black Reichswehr" and had therefore risen to some honors as soon as the shameful years of a peaceful Germany were over and his fatherland had recaptured its natural role of a military power. In 1939, I had just turned thirty: I was in alarmingly rude health; I had no difficulty in proving my Aryan descent; politically I was an unknown quantity; I had successfully completed my secondary education as well as several terms at the university and, since I could not be classified as indispensable, I seemed eminently suited to active service and a glorious hero's death. Naturally, I was not too keen on either, and without further hesitation I proceeded straight to Berlin to offer Colonel von Sensenöhr my—if possible unheroic—services.

Colonel von Sensenöhr had meanwhile become Major-General von Sensenöhr—a circumstance which I took as a good omen since in climbing a ladder one always gets further by holding on to the higher rungs. The Major-General received me with open arms. I soon realized that he was not in the least as his sonorous name and impressive career had led me to believe. In his late forties, he had a rather conspicuous *embonpoint;* he was short of stature, with shy eyes, soft features, and dark hair parted in the middle—all of which gave him the appearance of a peasant wench in uniform.

Throughout the war—in the course of which I rose from his honorary batman to the post of his A.D.C.—we spent countless evenings drinking together and talking about the life and tragic death of the woman who had evidently been the only, or certainly the great, love in Sensenöhr's life. I had known the adored woman far better than he, and was therefore able to supply little touches about her life and character which he eagerly absorbed.

However, I owed my promotion and safety not only to the General's sentimental affection for the dead *prima donna,* but to a far greater extent to his musical interests. Von Sensenöhr was an aesthete not only as far as the beautiful singer was concerned: he generally preferred Beethoven to Clausewitz and his tender instincts were reflected in the fact that his favorite instrument was the harp, that most feminine of all instruments, which he had learned to play by no means amateurishly but with surprising mastery. When he had taken off his boots and, still in his General's uniform but with his collar undone, began to operate the harp pedals in short woollen socks—a transfigured expression irradiating his round face as he wistfully listened to the dying notes—then even I felt my heart warming and I wished there were more Sensenöhrs in the world. But the harp, which my General loved like his better self, is, as everybody knows, a difficult instrument, not only to perform on, but also to transport. The General had to travel about a good deal, from headquarters to headquarters, from town to town, from front-lines to base, and it would not have been proper, let alone in accordance with army regulations, had he taken his gilt instrument with him on his journeys. This, therefore, was my job—and I discharged it with much skill and often at considerable risk, partly because of the Allied bombing but chiefly because of the total lack of musical understanding on the part of the military authorities.

Yet unfortunately, even with the best will in the world, risks can never be entirely eliminated in war. When my General was transferred to Intelligence, and I followed him, I little suspected what lay ahead of me. I performed my work not without some advantage to myself—for instance, I acquired such useful skills as the decoding of coded messages, the drafting of situation reports, the professional jargon used by spies and agents, as well as the primitive tricks they are so fond of using. At the same time I gave satisfaction to superiors who showed surprise at my adaptability and quick wit.

My quick wit, however, let me down badly in connection with the conspiratorial activity of my immediate superior, the selfsame Major-General von Sensenöhr. I had not the slightest suspicion of his leanings, even though it ought to have occurred to me that this gentle harpist could not in the long run find himself in tune with the rude trumpeters. I confess I was absolutely staggered when, one day in late July 1944, a bunch of S.S. men unceremoniously and brutally burst into our villa in Dahlem, which had so far been spared by the bombs, carried out a senseless and vandalic search, and put me under arrest without giving a reason. The full horror of the situation only dawned on me as, under the escort of two executioner-like characters, I marched past the library door just as one of the intruders sent his jack-booted foot through the strings of the harp. With a dying note the instrument collapsed on the floor.

The General, who meanwhile had been arrested at his desk at headquarters, luckily did not come to his end in the tragic manner which I, in my prison cell, regarded as his certain fate. He had belonged only to the outermost fringes of the conspiracy, not out of opportunism but probably because the conspirators had been reluctant to trust themselves fully to so dreamy and indecisive a person. I discovered later that, immediately following his discharge from detention, he had tried to seek me out in the most touching manner but I, my innocence proved, had long been posted to the Eastern front. It is true, of course, that I never got there. While my movement orders pointed eastward my own compass was steadily directing me westward. Thus I found myself in my familiar Cologne just as this tragically and pointlessly ruined town fell into American hands. As for my treatment during my detention as a prisoner-of-war, and later and most improperly as a prisoner-of-peace, I cannot really complain: I was soon promoted camp interpreter and granted all sorts of privileges by the Americans on the strength of their perfectly sound conviction that a man who speaks English fluently cannot possibly be a villain.

It was 1946 by the time I was released and returned to Vienna. A year later the events began to unfold which lend this record that general validity which—if they are to avoid the charge of presumption—the memoirs of an unknown person must inevitably claim.

PART TWO

5

Footsteps in the Dark

THE DATE—how can I ever forget it?—was May 28, 1947, a mild and promising spring evening, with a faint touch of summer in the air. After an unexpected, but most enjoyable, two-week holiday I was returning to Vienna from Baden.

I had spent the past fourteen days in the pleasant Helenental, a valley running in a westerly direction from Baden, between the rocky and somewhat over-dramatic scenery of the Schwechat. In the Middle Ages this had been a popular but rather risky trade route, as still witnessed by the ruins of Rauhenstein and Rauhenegg, formerly the castles of marauder barons, which picturesquely dominate the green valley. The ochre-colored manor-house of my former classmate, Baron Ferdinand Staub von Görwitz, was situated at the end of the valley, where the scenery loses its artificial, holiday-resort character and where, among cows, goats, chickens, and other domestic livestock, the visitor has almost forgotten the proximity of Baden, the town frequented for its sulphur springs for many centuries.

I must confess that I was somewhat surprised at the invitation of my schoolfriend, into whom I had run at the house of a mutual friend in Vienna a short while before, and whom I had not seen for some ten years. True, our relations had always been cordial, but they had never gone beyond the average kind of school friendship. Thus, I could not quite understand why Ferdinand greeted me like a long-lost brother, why he displayed such uncommon interest in my wartime experiences, and why he had insisted that I visit him. I knew that the prematurely bald, thin, and pasty-looking man

was a confirmed bachelor and that he probably suffered from boredom as much as from his gout-gnarled fingers. The Helenental,
where his family came from and to which, presumably for the sake
of the sulphur-bath treatment, he had returned, was situated like
the rest of Vienna's surroundings in the Russian Zone, which somewhat marred my pleasure at the unexpected invitation; on the other
hand, the food situation in the capital was still so precarious that the
prospect of enjoying a farmhouse diet for a few days soon silenced
my misgivings. As for the obvious question of how my schoolfriend,
the scion of a military family which had won fame and its title in
the Battle of Königgrätz, had contrived to keep up his residence
undisturbed in the Soviet Zone, without, moreover, complaining unduly about conditions there—that obvious question I omitted to ask
as soon as, jokingly, he promised me a diet of milk, butter, and
eggs for the duration of my stay, with a roast chicken or two to be
thrown in for good measure.

During the fortnight I stayed with him, however, nothing
really occurred to impair my well-being or arouse my suspicions.
My friend proved to be one of those tactful hosts who manage to
make their guests comfortable without overwhelming them. In
the evenings, we would discuss this problem or that in the most
friendly fashion, over a good glass of red Vöslau wine—and if he
carefully avoided the subject of politics I attributed this simply to
the unfortunate geographical situation of his estate in the Soviet
orbit. His charming sister, a widowed Countess Cosimano, who
could talk brilliantly about literature, art, and music, evidently
also preferred to leave the topical questions of the day untouched.
Only much later did it occur to me that my friend had several
times received callers, with whom he had spent some time in the
library behind closed doors, without my ever making their acquaintance; indeed, on one occasion, when I collided with two visitors
in the entrance hall, my friend even forgot to perform the proper
formality of introduction.

On the fifteenth day I decided not to outstay my welcome. I
had just begun to pack my bag when the Countess appeared in my
room with a parcel looking like a large box of chocolates. She
asked me casually if I would take it for her to Vienna and keep it
until a certain Herr Müller would call for it. Postal communica-

tions between the various occupation zones were functioning by then and there was no reason why the package, which evidently contained only papers, should be conveyed to Vienna by hand. But I didn't give it another thought. I placed the package between a shirt and a carton containing butter, eggs, and a small cake, and shortly afterward said my grateful good-byes to my friends.

It was seven o'clock on that mild spring evening when I boarded the decrepit old bus at Baden for Vienna. In the old days buses, trains, and trams had plied in great number between Vienna and Baden, carrying spa visitors as well as gamblers—for in addition to its sulphur baths Baden also possessed a casino—but now the rickety old vehicle seemed to be perfectly adequate for the public demand. Only two elderly ladies, dressed in velvet and clearly belonging to the newly poor, a man carrying a doctor's black bag, and a Russian soldier had taken seats on the bus—the ladies positively pressing themselves against the doctor, a thin wisp of a man in a threadbare overcoat, as though afraid of physical contact with the Russian. Nothing, however, seemed further from the mind of the young Russian peasant lad than interference with his traveling companions: on the contrary, he was sitting modestly in a back seat and fighting his nervousness by ceaselessly picking his nose. I may add, for the sake of curiosity, that I felt greatly reassured to see his massive forefinger first in one nostril and then in the other, since nothing links human beings so much as their little weaknesses, and because it is always comforting to find an otherwise terrifying fellow-being yawning, snoring, biting his nails, or even picking his nose.

I settled down by the window, two seats in front of the soldier, and as soon as the bus moved off after a great deal of waiting I surrendered myself to the kind of day-dreaming to which a well-lined stomach is so eminently conducive. During the past few days I had borrowed Arthur Schnitzler's story *Episode at Daybreak* from my friend's well-stocked and luckily unscathed library: as I gazed out of the hermetically closed windows, which had obviously not been cleaned for a long time, into the slowly descending evening my thoughts were revolving around Schnitzler's frivolous young Lieutenant Willi. Along the very road that I was now travelling, the Lieutenant—though in his more exclusive gig—had driven from

Baden to Vienna where, for the sake of some foolish ideas of honor, he had blown his brains out at daybreak. I also speculated about the very curious nature of progress: modern means of transport had considerably shortened all distances and it was no longer necessary to drive in a horse-drawn cab through half the night in order to get from Baden to Vienna; yet on the other hand these distances had vastly grown since Baden, in spite of its immediate proximity to Vienna, was now situated in an alien world which it was infinitely more difficult to leave than in the days of Lieutenant Willi and his light gig.

I was indulging in this kind of speculation about a divine justice which compels mankind to erect ever new obstacles along its ever more efficient roads, when I was roused from my thoughts by the noise of the bus rattling over the cobblestones of the deserted Wiedner Hauptstrasse in Vienna. In the darkness of Suttner Platz, in the Soviet Sector, the bus screeched to a halt. The two old ladies waited doubtfully until the Russian soldier had got off—a maneuver which must have been obvious even to him as he was the one farthest from the exit and had to squeeze past them to get out. The ladies alighted from the vehicle together with the doctor who, however, strode off rapidly in the direction of the Karlsplatz. I too set off, carrying my small suitcase, towards the Third District, where I was living in two rented rooms.

As soon as I turned into the poorly lit Rennweg, I had the disturbing impression that someone was following me close behind. It is, of course, never pleasant to hear a stranger's persistently echoing footsteps behind one's back in a dark street at night; and certainly in the Vienna of early 1947 one was not disposed to believe in coincidences, but on the contrary was always ready, whether one's conscience was clear or guilty, to assume the worst. Very soon I realized that it was not just my imagination playing tricks on me: my pursuer's footsteps grew faster or slower according to whether I was walking faster or more slowly.

I could not imagine why anyone should be following me. I should have breathed easier once I crossed from the Soviet into the American Sector, but I could not rid myself of the fear that seemed to permeate the air, and I almost began to run. The footsteps clung to me even as I turned into various side streets. Then just as I was about to reach my house the familiar roar of a jeep rose out of the stillness.

I quickly turned toward the street, determined to put myself under the protection of the Allies. But before I could signal the vehicle to halt, the car pulled up right alongside of me. From it leaped an American officer and, before I could say a word, grabbed the case which I was still carrying in my right hand. My pursuer did not, as I had expected, take to his heels but, on the contrary, came up to our group, turned to the U.S. lieutenant and uttered the simple yet, to me, quite incomprehensible words:

"Yes, that's him."

So that was me. Though at the time I could make no sense of that observation I later found it to be full of profound wisdom; for in the course of the next few hours I was to discover that everybody was indeed far better informed about myself than I was. Eight years have passed since that day in May, and it is only to-day that I can with conviction utter the words which the stranger then spoke with such casual assurance: "Yes, that's him." Yes indeed: that's me.

6

Mr. Smith as the Inquisitor

POLITELY but firmly, the lieutenant asked me to get into the jeep. He sat next to the driver while I squeezed into the back seat to- gether with my pursuer, a big hulk of a man in civilian clothes.

After a short ride, during which no one spoke and throughout which the officer clutched my case as if it were a jewel-box, the vehicle pulled up in a narrow street, off the Mariahilfer Strasse, in front of a small hotel which, like all second-rate hotels, made a third- rate impression. I was invited to follow the lieutenant.

On the second floor I was marshalled into a medium-sized room whose American office furniture—complete with steel desk,

swivel chair and, for my prudish taste, obscene wall-calendar—
made a strange contrast with the high, dark-brown hotel bed and
the old-fashioned lace curtain over the window into the area. As
though the new owners deliberately intended to mock the old hos-
telry, a folding army cot had been put up against the old-fashioned
piece which, in spite of its spiral-turned wooden ornaments, seemed
a perfectly passable bed; but this was somewhat offset by the fact
that on the swiveling, adjustable, and tiltable office chair reclined a
velvet cushion with a highly fantastical wool-embroidered tulip. On
the desk stood a steel lamp, practical and modern like the chair, but
this had not been switched on. A single bare bulb dangling from
the ceiling spread a proletarian light.

After nearly two hours, which gave me amply opportunity to
reflect on the unpleasant situation in which I found myself through
no fault of my own—the officer having withdrawn and bolted the
door behind him—the door was at last opened and the owner of
the swivel chair entered the room.

In his hand he carried a package which I instantly recognized,
even without the string, as Countess Cosimano's present to the
unknown Herr Müller.

The stranger settled in the chair with the tulip cushion and began to scrutinize me with evident but not necessarily hostile interest.
He wore an excellently cut light-gray flannel suit; though undoubtedly bought off the peg—for the two buttons on his sleeves were
hopelessly pining away for appropriate button-holes—this product
of the American high-class ready-made-garments industry could
easily compete with the best European made-to-measure suits.

My host was a gentleman of uncertain age, probably in his mid-
fifties; I am using the term advisedly, as both his appearance and his
manners were those of a gentleman. He was tall and slim, his snow-
white hair was parted and brushed against his long, well-shaped
head. His thin and rather long nose stood symmetrically positioned
in his face, like a straight exclamation mark, with hardly any widen-
ing at the base, so that one instinctively expected to find a stop underneath it; but instead, luckily, the line of the nose was emphasized
by a firm and expressive mouth. The rimless hexagonal glasses
through which he examined me for a long time did not, as glasses

often do, relieve the hardness of his features; on the contrary, they emphasized it by conveying the impression of two monocles.

"We may as well speak English since you are fluent in it, Herr Droste," he said.

"As you please," I replied.

"You occupy a furnished two-room flat at Number Eight, Dapontegasse?"

"I do."

"You are not, and never were, married."

"That is so."

"You represent the firm of Schlögelhammer & Co., wine merchants, of Bösendorffer Strasse."

This, too, I confirmed.

So far he had put his questions in the form of undisputed statements. But the next one was half statement and half question.

"And how long have you been working for the Soviet secret service?"

"I am not working for the Soviet secret service at all," I replied.

He cleared his throat, sarcastically rather than irritably, and continued his interrogation: "I suppose you didn't spend the past fortnight—or to be more correct, the period from May 13 to May 28 —on the premises of the Soviet secret service at Baden near Vienna?"

"I was staying with my friend Baron Staub at his place in the Helenental," I replied.

"How long was it from the time you last saw Baron Staub until you met him at the house of Ernst Vitztum on March 6, when he proposed that you work for him?"

"I hadn't seen Staub for ten or twelve years," I answered. "And he didn't propose anything, either at Vitztum's house or anywhere else."

The reader may believe me—and my son Johnny knows me well enough to realize that I have no intention of boasting—when I say that the inquisition to which the two-monocled gentleman was subjecting me failed to produce its intended intimidating effect on me, and was indeed beginning to give me some amusement.

And why not? Surely if the American secret service thought it necessary, for whatever reasons, to show an interest in Baron Staub, and hence also in me, it could have found no difficulty in discovering when and how we had met again after so many years; neither was my bachelor status a secret; and finally the information that Schlögelhammer and Co., wine merchants, had their place in the Bösendorffer Strasse could be gathered without particular acumen from any telephone directory. It was obvious to me from the start that my interlocutor was hoping to impress me by that expert knowledge of detail which frightens a scared man even further, because he assumes that if the authorities are so well informed about even his unimportant activities they must be excellently informed about the more important ones. In the course of my life, and especially during the war, I had often enough been in contact and in conflict with the authorities to know that such logic is most illogical: unimportant trifles are easy to find out and are therefore known to the authorities, whereas as a rule they lack all knowledge of essentials. Moreover—and this is an important point—I was innocent while being believed guilty; I could therefore get as much secret amusement out of my interrogator's ignorance as a guilty person who is believed to be innocent.

"Are you also going to maintain, Herr Droste," the American continued, "that you're not informed about the contents of this package and that you brought it to Vienna for mere courtesy?"

"I maintain just that, sir," I replied. "And a lot more. Since you're already anticipating all my answers, you've probably guessed that I will tell you next that the Herr Müller, who was to collect these papers from me, is entirely unknown to me."

"So the man's name is Müller," he said. "Just fancy: Müller."

"That's the name I was given," I retorted.

"And you don't know what's in these papers?"

"No, I don't."

"And you can't guess?"

"If it's true," I replied after some short reflection, "that my distinguished friend has sold himself to the Russians then these papers will probably contain directives for Soviet agents."

"What makes you conclude that?"

"If they contained Western secrets," I explained, "surely they would be smuggled from the Western into the Eastern Zone, and not the other way round."

"Shouldn't you have considered that before undertaking this dangerous mission?"

"I didn't regard it as a mission," I said.

"Would it surprise you, Herr Droste," he said, "if I told you that we're acquainted with your wartime activities in the German Military Intelligence?"

"Not unduly," I said, "considering that in the American P.O.W. camp, where I spent a lot of time, I was questioned on just this subject about two dozen times."

"But it's a curious coincidence," said the inquisitor, "that the Soviet secret service is particularly fond of using former German Intelligence people."

"Yes, I've heard it rumored," I said. "And I can't honestly say I'm surprised. The uncritical adulation of the expert happens to be one of the deplorable features of our age: just as a nose-and-throat specialist is allowed to continue his practice even though he may have personally treated Hitler's throat, so—if you will forgive my comparison—the professional cut-throats are similarly honored by amnesty and re-employment. Maybe the Russians have really picked me out of their card index, but I may assure you that this was done without my knowledge and agreement. I was, if I may put it that way, only a wartime-reserve Intelligence man; in peacetime I should prefer a more restful occupation."

The man in the swivel chair smiled. An attractive gentleness emanated from him: his carven features seemed almost paternal and he looked a little like President Wilson, who had also looked very paternal when, like a benign father, he had divided up Europe after 1918 like a birthday cake.

"I like you, Herr Droste," he said. "The Russians made a good catch when they got hold of you, and I'm a little ashamed that we didn't get to you first. If you'd care to add a little frankness to your sense of humor and courage, and tell us what payment your aristocratic friend has promised you for your services, we might perhaps be able to make a mutually advantageous deal. By the way, you may call me Mr. Smith."

He opened his desk drawer, took out a pack of American ciga-

rettes and politely offered me one. The search for a match, lighting
it, and the enjoyment of the first few puffs gave me time for reflection. There was a possibility that Mr. Smith was trying to trap me
into a confession, but I didn't think he'd stoop to such primitive
measures. I took his words as no doubt they were meant: as a proposition to join his own club in some capacity or other. The thought
crossed my mind that the most absurd consequences may spring, in
our absurd time and age, from the simple decision to venture a few
miles into the country for the sake of a roast chicken—but simultaneously I was aware that this was hardly the moment for such
philosophizing. To convince Mr. Smith of my innocence would
probably be impossible: his world was populated by agents and
counter-agents. Only with them did he know where he was; faced
with innocence he would be as helpless as an aged roué, at home
among demi-mondaines, would be with a virgin from the back-
woods. There was nothing to stop Mr. Smith, if I were to prove deaf
to his suggestions, from letting me stew either there or at an even
less suitable place for as long as he pleased; on the other hand, it
was not impossible that fate—fond as it is of appearing in the queer-
est places and in the strangest guises—might be smiling upon me in
this very hotel room, with its ancient, forgotten bed and its salacious
calendar. So, weighing my words carefully, I replied:

"It isn't easy to answer your question truthfully, Mr. Smith,
since there has been no talk between my friend and me about any
services. But it occurs to me—now that my suspicions have been
aroused—that the Baron told me he might help my firm open a
branch in the Soviet Zone. Thereby, as he pointed out, my meagre
monthly income of about three thousand Austrian schillings might
be trebled or quadrupled. How very foolish of me not to have
seen that his offer was not just motivated by charitable sympathy
and that beneath his cloak of helpfulness showed the cloven hoof
of the devil. For a lousy nine or ten thousand schillings he would
have expected me to serve those powers which, to judge by his
princely style of life, are rewarding him far more liberally! Of
course, I shall now decline his offer. I don't like being played for a
sucker, quite apart from my love of liberty which I do not propose
to jeopardize for the sake of a mere tip."

Mr. Smith got up even before I had finished speaking and began to pace up and down—a move which I didn't care for because I was no longer able to watch his face and could not tell how he was receiving my lies. That it was all lies, from start to finish, hardly needs saying; yet I didn't think they were in the least despicable since in this strange office truth was so clearly an article that was not in demand.

"Come now, ten thousand schillings a month is still good money, Herr Droste," said Mr. Smith, himself apparently an experienced buyer and therefore reluctant to see a price driven up. "You shouldn't reject the offer out of hand. You certainly shouldn't— not so much for the money but because it may be useful to keep up your business contact with the Baron. If, on the other hand, you feel inclined to work for me"—he said "for me," not "for us" —"you will have an opportunity of proving your worth in this Müller business. As for the financial terms, I've no doubt that a satisfactory solution will be found."

"Your trust honors me, Mr. Smith," I said with a little bow, "but as I've told you, I have no experience in this business of being an agent and I'd like to think it over a little."

Mr. Smith stopped in front of me. "There's no question of trust, Herr Droste," he said; "at least not for the moment. We Americans have a reputation for naïveté, but I always think the Europeans rather naïve in their reluctance to realize that they invariably come to grief through speculating on our *naïveté*. Do not therefore count on my trust, Herr Droste, and don't forget that your flat is in the U.S. Sector. Though not at all fond of Soviet methods, I don't like being made a fool of any more than they do. And as for this business of being an agent, there can indeed be no question of employment: at most, this is a test of a conditional nature. And lastly, there can be no question of thinking it over since for all we know Herr Müller may turn up at your place first thing tomorrow morning"— he glanced at his wrist watch—"or rather this morning, and neither we nor you would be served if he found your nest empty."

"I see," I said. "All right, then give me your instructions."

"Take this package," said Mr. Smith, evidently satisfied, "and give it to your caller without any comments. And just so you might not be tempted to play little tricks with us, let me add that you won't make any sense out of these papers. They are coded instructions and to the uninitiated they are mere gibberish. Confine your conversation with Herr Müller to a minimum, but slip in a remark that you would like to visit Baron Staub again as soon as possible. Your suitcase, complete with food parcel," he concluded, without smiling at the words, "will be handed to you as you leave here. I must ask you not to attempt to communicate with me once you have left this house. You will hear from me. Good evening, Herr Droste."

If the reader—as I am hoping—feels for me the sympathy that is usually accorded to the story-teller, regardless of his character or merit, then he would probably like to see me leave the dimly-lit hotel room and share in my sense of relief that this embarrassing adventure had after all come to a relatively painless end.

I am bound to admit, however, that I did not make a speedy departure, as would have been proper, but declared, regretfully, that I felt I must broach the financial question once more. During the next few days, I pointed out, I should hardly be able to follow my normal business, and besides, after Mr. Smith's convincing arguments, I was now aware of the dangers that lay ahead. I do not deny that the impertinence of my demands, though they were put forward in all modesty, might easily have excited Mr. Smith's anger and landed me in an awkward situation, but all my life I have preferred running risks to giving unpaid service to employers or enterprises. Finally, my sense of irony rose at the thought of leaving the building I had entered a few hours earlier as a prisoner with a cash payment in my pocket.

Mr. Smith, unfortunately, had little understanding for my perverted sense of humor. However, he did not seem annoyed in the least at my persistence. He offered me four thousand schillings if I wound up the Müller business without a hitch and subsequently submitted a written report. This seemed to me quite a decent figure for a start, especially as my monthly receipts from Messrs. Schlögelhammer & Co. did not amount to three thousand, as I had claimed, but only to half that sum.

In the dark hotel corridor my case was returned to me by a soldier, who led me to the front door and unlocked it in complete silence. The clock on the nearby church of St. Ulrich was striking three. A milk truck rattled over the deserted Mariahilfer Strasse. With an easy and carefree gait I strode towards my destiny.

7

The Charm of the Cyclamen

TWO days later, at 11 P.M., Herr Müller knocked at my door. That he arrived at this late hour, instead of coming in broad daylight, seemed to me rather foolish but was in fact more typical than I realized at the time. But in order to substantiate this claim I shall have to anticipate some discoveries that I did not make till later.

Only few spies can resist the temptation of acting like spies. Unhappy personal experiences, patriotic idealism, or special circumstances have driven many a person to take up an agent's career; but without a certain liking for adventure no one would stay in that profession for long. The agent may be admired but he is basically an immature personality, unable to reconcile or adjust himself to the laws of life; a pitiful creature with an inferiority complex, doubtful of prevailing in the ordinary daily competitive struggle and eager, therefore, to create for himself an unreal world of his own, whose laws he determines for himself. He is a fugitive from his own ego, feeling secure only in disguise; a drug addict, really, who can only keep his body and soul going by means of artificial stimulants. With the exception of a few artists, who create their work for the sake of creation and who cannot therefore be numbered among reasonable human beings, everybody, as soon as he has outgrown his childhood, chooses an occupation for the commendable purpose of making money and acquiring wealth or at least security. If this were not so the world would consist exclusively of streetcar conductors, detectives, trapeze artists, racing drivers, generals, and firemen—the occupations chosen by most children until they begin to understand that there is nothing more romantic than a well-padded bank account. The adventurer, however, forgets to grow up: like a child, he acts without an aim, out of pleasure in his action; like a child, equally, he does not foresee the consequences of his actions and he chooses crooked paths simply because he lacks the elementary understanding that a straight path is also the shortest.

Spies, for whatever reason they may have originally chosen their profession, are adventurers—that is, people who have not passed through the development that normally accompanies the process of getting older. This would not matter so much if their infantilism did not, in the nature of things, drive them right up to the edge of disaster. The ordinary adventurer as a rule only stakes, and loses, his own neck; but the adventurer of the spy species is occasionally trusted with hundreds of human lives. Clemenceau's remark that war is far too serious a matter to be entrusted to the generals applies even more aptly to espionage, which is far too deadly to be left in the hands of overgrown children suffering from arrested development. It is an infallible rule that the childish adventurer-spy, who does his play-acting with himself as an audience, will sooner or later be tempted to act in front of others. In the long run the spy will not be content with enjoying the romance of a job that is known only to him: he must tell others, or at least give them a hint, about what romantic business he plies. So that he ends up like that legendary monarch who spent a great deal of care on his disguise but, as soon as he was challenged, proclaimed with gratified vanity: "Never shall you learn my name—I am the Emperor Joseph II!"

Herr Müller, clearly also a victim to the cheap romance of his profession, appeared at my flat late on a foggy night—as behooves a good agent—and took charge of the Countess' package with an affectation of indifference that must have aroused the suspicions of the most guileless.

He was a mousy little man with horn-rimmed glasses whose snapped frame was held together above his prominent ears with a dirty piece of string. The man, as I realized at once, belonged to the Intelligence proletariat, that miserable crowd of spies who perform menial services for those in power and, more often than not, have to carry the can for them.

Herr Müller thanked me with exaggerated politeness for the cheap schnapps I had offered him, but declined a second glass, as if suggesting that the performance of his duties forbade him to indulge in such escapades. We conversed casually a few moments, during which I dropped the remark that I was thinking of visiting Baron Staub again soon, possibly the next weekend. In that case, Herr Müller replied promptly, he might give me a letter for the Baron, containing a few family photos of my friend which he happened to have had in his custody since the war. I was probably aware, he said, that Soviet censorship was still obstructing the most harmless correspondence between the different zones. I wasn't aware of anything of the sort, but I nodded in agreement. A few nights later, Herr Müller returned with an orange-colored envelope of medium size.

As soon as he left, the telephone rang. It was Mr. Smith, instructing me to appear at the Café Dobner on the Naschmarkt at three o'clock the following afternoon and to sit there studying the last page of the *Wiener Kurier* until a stranger addressed me. I was to hand him the envelope as soon as he explicitly asked for it.

Two weeks later I left for Baden. But first, I stopped off at Vöslau, a nearby village, to see a number of vintners, supposedly on behalf of my company. Then I called on the Baron and the Countess, explaining that my visit was no more than a little detour from a business trip. After a prudent interval, the Countess asked if I'd conveyed her little package, and only then did I pretend to remember that in my brief-case there was an orange-colored envelope which I had promised Herr Müller I would deliver to her. Now, finally, I yielded to my friend's pressing invitation to stop with them for the night. I decided to accept once more the hospitality of the Staub home and, for more than one reason, I was not to regret having done so.

I saw little of Countess Cosimano the rest of the day. She had accepted the envelope with a brief word of thanks and, without opening it, had absently put it down on the grand piano. But about a quarter of an hour later, when she thought I was engrossed in conversation with her brother, she left the room and took the letter with her. She returned later to announce that dinner was served.

We dined in the wood-panelled library where a solid mahogany gaming table in front of the fireplace had been tastefully laid with choice Augarten porcelain and Old Vienna damask, with three candles in tall, darkened silver candlesticks spreading a warm if inadequate light. Although the fire had not been lit the almost wintertime coziness of the room was more than welcome: in the afternoon a thunderstorm had broken over the Vienna Woods and the June sky had not cleared since. A fine drizzle was still falling, almost as if the heavens had spent their fury but had left behind a melancholy sadness in the atmosphere.

The servant problem, touched upon by the Countess a little while before, now gave me my chance for turning the conversation in what I hoped was not too obvious a direction.

"It is quite admirable, Countess," I said with a slight bow to my hostess and carefully subduing my voice, "the way you manage to preserve the past in this vulgar new world. In fact, I cannot conceive how, in a zone ruled by domestic servants running riot, you still manage to keep any ministering spirits at all."

The Countess and her brother exchanged a furtive glance but, as on previous similar occasions, they did not give a direct answer. Indeed, an awkward pause occurred in our conversation— almost as if I had tactlessly or thoughtlessly touched upon a delicate subject. Even after dinner the atmosphere never quite recovered, and at one stage the conversation took a positively depressing turn when the Baron casually remarked that most of our classmates were now dead and that it might be easier to organize a class reunion in heaven or hell than on the site of our old school in Vienna. Several times I observed the Baron's eyes straying across to his sister, past me and the flickering candles, with a weary and, I thought, frightened gaze: looking at my friend's gout-gnarled hands I could not help thinking that he was perhaps longing to take part in that class reunion in either heaven or hell—whichever applied in his case— as soon as possible.

I retired to my room early, at about half-past ten. Too late I remembered that I had forgotten to choose from the library shelves some bed-time reading matter. I have always been unable to go to sleep at an early hour. Since I'd forgotten to take something to read from the library I spent a long time lying on my back, and my thoughts began to revolve not so much around my accomplished mission but around the beautiful Countess.

The Countess was forty at the most. Of stately figure and darkish-blonde hair, she suggested in character and appearance the dry charm of those flowers which thrive better in the shade and the rain than in the sun and the warmth—the cyclamen, for instance, which are found near the edge of the forests of my native country, or even in the depths of the Vienna Woods, among the dead, yellow leaves of the trees, brilliant of color and yet of an autumnal transience. And just as the cyclamen—a half-extinct flower, by the way, and justly protected by the authorities—has about it something old-fashioned, its color recalling the favorite hue of our grandmothers' days, so there was something old-fashioned about the figure and movements of the Countess. The immaculate whiteness of her skin seemed to have been always carefully shielded from the rays of the sun by a graceful parasol; her softly rounded shoulders testified that she had never indulged in anything so vulgar as sport; and the full, womanly shape of her figure had never been deformed by any monstrous diet.

My thoughts, as I said, were revolving around the Countess with an intensity I did not understand when there was a knock on my door. Automatically I called out: "Come in!" And I became extremely confused on seeing the Countess enter—mainly because, not expecting to stay for the night, I had not brought any pajamas and was lying naked on the heavy farmhouse bed with its wooden canopy. I hurriedly pulled my white blanket up to my chin and muttered an apology.

"I could see your light," she said, entirely free from embarrassment, "and thought this might be a suitable opportunity for an undisturbed chat with you."

With these words she sat down, in her cyclamen-colored dressing gown, in an arm-chair which stood in the corner of the room, without the slightest notice of my discomfort.

Only a small bedside lamp with a parchment shade was burning in the rustically furnished room with its pleasant smell of untreated wood. Awkward as it was, I had to raise myself on my elbow in order to watch my visitor's features, which were almost entirely swallowed up in the shadows.

"*Cher ami,*" began the Countess—she was rather fond of sprinkling her conversation with French phrases—"the other day you took a package for me to Vienna and this time you brought me a letter from there. I hope you won't be annoyed if I were to entrust you once more with a letter. But first I must have your word of honor that anything I may tell you will remain between the two of us."

I have never quite understood the distinction—a childish one, as it seems to me—between a man's word and his word of honor, especially as it is no more honorable, though at times unavoidable, to break one's word than one's word of honor. So I unhesitatingly assured the Countess of my discretion upon my word of honor.

"It isn't easy for me," she began, "to give you an explanation, but I should find it distasteful to give you clumsy excuses or even smooth lies." She heaved a slight sigh, then brought out an oblong envelope from the pocket of her dressing gown, balanced it adroitly on the arm-rest of her chair and covered it with her white and attractively plump hand. "Besides, I am practically acting under duress. If you weren't clever I shouldn't talk to you like this; but since you are clever you would inevitably ask awkward questions in the end."

"You may speak quite freely," I said.

"You've already noticed," she continued, and I could see she was approaching her subject in a round-about way, "that this house, though it's in the Soviet Zone, is still untouched, unlooted, and is occasionally even peopled by servants. If, therefore, I were to ask you yet another favor you would put two and two together and would soon become suspicious. . . ."

"Countess," I interrupted her, "you are above suspicion."

"No, I'm not," she retorted, still in the same tone. "I'm nothing of the sort—no more than anybody else who lives in this vulgar world. Forgive me for speaking of my motives before getting down to my real request—but I'd like to prepare you so you won't be too shocked. In short, I have made certain compromises in order to preserve the things that have been close to my heart ever since childhood—no, I cannot really adduce as an excuse the circumstances that my life was in danger, at least not what is normally meant by one's life. But the danger of losing the kind of life which alone seems worth living," she added thoughtfully, "is that not the same as losing one's life? A refugee's life is to me an appalling prospect, and proud poverty, *cher ami,* is just a bad joke. The overriding thing for me is to hold what I have: for that end I would make any sacrifice."

"And your brother?" I asked. "What does he think of all this?"

"My brother," she said, with slight irritation in her voice, "is neither guilty nor innocent. Certainly, I won't claim that I'm doing this for his sake. He is totally incapable of any decision, good or evil, and it's not for him that I'm trying to preserve what we own. On the contrary, he is part of my possessions and must be preserved with them, unless he is to perish in the most wretched way."

The woman in cyclamen red became more likeable to me every minute—in the first place because I can never deny my admiration to anyone who pursues his aim ruthlessly, and in the second place because in the arrogance of her justification there was a touch of wistfulness, as if she realized that the belongings which she was defending with such gallantry were nevertheless doomed to perdition. I decided, and not only for selfish reasons, to meet her half-way.

"Your frankness does you credit, Countess," I said, "but you seem to be stopping short of complete frankness with me. You are wrong in doing so: I'm your friend. I conclude from your hints that the letters, which I have been guilelessly carrying, contained some secrets, and that you yourself, if you'll forgive my vulgar expression, are working hand in glove with the Russians. But even so, your intention of entrusting yet another letter to me hardly justifies your surprising revelations. Indeed, I should be repaying your confidence poorly if I failed to tell you that I suspect some undisclosed purpose behind your words."

"I'm obliged to you," said the Countess. "I did not expect anything else from you. I have been looking for somebody for several weeks: someone who'd be willing to undertake a journey for me, riskier and much more important than your excursions between Vienna and Baden. I've had my eye on you even during your last stay with us, but I still can't go into any details until my confidence is confirmed."

The situation was getting odder every moment. I was lying in bed naked, and in my excitement forgot about the blanket, which had slipped off my shoulders, exposing me from the waist up to the eyes of the beautiful woman. In spite of the dim light I could not fail to notice that she was eyeing me with an interest that went beyond the mere subject of her business proposition.

The rain was still tinkling against the window panes with a pleasant monotony. Outside, wrapped in the Austrian summer night, was the Soviet Zone. The seventeenth-century farmhouse furniture creaked now and again into our conversation. And in the blue chair, with the traditional fret-sawn heart in the back-rest, sat a woman who was trying to escape from the vulgar world by aiding and abetting it in the most alarming way.

I thought of Mr. Smith and what he would say to all this. And it occurred to me that being a double agent, a spy for both sides, must inevitably be part and parcel of the business of espionage: that spies alone, by virtue of their job, can cross the artificially erected frontiers in both directions and thus become the genuine mediators between two hostile camps. Had I not been working for the Americans, I reflected, I should not have made this second excursion into the Russian Zone; likewise, I should not be able to satisfy my own employers if I did not also accept the trustful offer of their adversaries.

"Countess," I said, "what you tell me surprises me and requires explanations. Supposing I understood your own motives— what makes you think I'd be suitable for an enterprise that is clearly risky, quite apart from the fact that I have none of the motives which are so cogent in your own case?"

For the first time it seemed to me that the Countess was smiling.

"My friend," she said, "your motives and mine are more akin than you think. You have repeatedly, and exquisitely, spoken of your love of money. Love of money, combined with the ability to spend it gracefully, seems to me quite enchanting. I am fighting to preserve something. You still have to acquire it."

"Are you promising me money?" I asked.

"Among other things. Besides, I had some treacherous dreams in your absence, George," she said, suddenly calling me by my Christian name. "Yes, most treacherous dreams."

"Dreams? What sort of dreams?" I inquired with interest.

"I saw you in full armor," she gestured slightly towards the window. "Up there, in Rauhenegg Castle. It was a marauder barons' castle once, where the proud knights were out for tangible gain. Your ancestors, George, must have been marauder barons and you have inherited that well-bred ruthlessness that is so agreeably conspicuous in our drab age."

"My ancestors, Countess Erika," I remarked, "were head waiters. And my unscrupulous nature, I fear, is not of chivalrous origin."

She dismissed my objection. "My instinct for masculinity is infallible, George. You're both a man and a gentleman, which is quite rare in this world of tadpoles. . . ." She rose to her feet. "You don't have to accept my propositions. In fact, they aren't really so important to me. But it's done me good to talk to you . . ."

"I will take the letter along," I said quickly. "Don't give it another thought."

I was already on the first stage of that journey whose route the Countess Erika was to confide to me in the course of the night. I felt a genuine affection for the woman who, envelope in hand, was standing by my bed. I sensed a romantic kinship between us and her vision of me as a marauder baron from Rauhenegg Castle appealed to me.

The moment she began to speak of my character I knew for certain, and with a pleasant certainty, that she would give me her instructions in the most agreeable circumstances; for experience has taught me that men and women almost invariably proceed from an interested and frequently sober introduction of their mutual characters to the introduction of their bodies.

When, therefore, as was only natural, I extended one hand towards the letter while placing the other round my beautiful visitor's hips so as to draw her down to me, this was done by no means from base calculation. Not only had I no intention whatever of demanding any advance payment for my professional services, but I thought on the contrary that a few happy hours would compensate the two of us in advance for the deception that was bound to follow.

Without any false show of resistance the Countess allowed herself to be drawn on to my bed. I dropped the envelope on to the blanket, thereby gaining the necessary freedom for both my hands; and while my left hand held her in a gentle clasp my right proceeded to divest her of her cyclamen-colored dressing gown. The Countess, who wore under her dressing gown only a charmingly old-fashioned and most becoming night-gown of fine cambric, buttoned up to her neck, disdained all undignified show of resistance —undignified, because it would have run counter to the nature of this majestic lady and hence been undignified if, even for a moment, she were to have lost her initiative, or if she were to have given the impression that she could be trapped into an indiscretion against her will.

It turned out to be a happy night, a night mixed with passion and businesslike sobriety, which lent her loveplay an unusual piquancy. The crescendo of our bodies had hardly abated into a gentle pianissimo when the Countess began to speak of my mission, which was to take me to Budapest, almost as if she realized that such an entirely unrelated subject was the most subtle way of renewing our passionate vigor. And even when her gently caressing hands allowed it to be understood that she wanted a renewal of our encounter, she still mentioned this detail or that about the precautions that would have to be taken in connection with my journey, abandoning this businesslike conversation only when she had unmistakably convinced herself that my affection had by no means been weakened by the sober intermezzo.

On the following morning I left the house early, since my bus was due in Vienna at half past eight. In our good-byes there rang a note of gratitude in which, as during the preceding night, the compact of two conspirators blended harmoniously with the conspiracy of two bodies.

8

ఠఠఠఠఠఠఠఠఠఠఠ

Mr. Smith Knows the Rate for the Job

A FEW HOURS after my safe return from Baden I had a telephone call from Mr. Smith—impressive proof that he was well-informed about my movements and that he correctly surmised that the Countess had again used me as her private messenger. Again Mr. Smith avoided giving his name, and again he wanted me to meet some stranger at a café. But I made it perfectly clear that I wanted a personal meeting with "Mr. S.," and that I would not hand over the letter to anybody else. There was a prolonged, annoyed pause, whereupon the caller asked me to meet "Mr. S." that same evening, between 7 and 7:30, in the garden of a certain Grinzing wine tavern. I was to make sure, by the way, that I got there without being followed.

It was a June evening of exceptional mildness, heavy with the scent of lilac which at this time of year so deliciously pervades my native city. In the narrow streets of the suburb of Grinzing, I convinced myself without difficulty that I had not been followed. The little streets were totally deserted in spite of the early hour, and the wine taverns which lined them had their traditional green garlands hoisted on long poles over the arched doorways: green signposts for the expert seekers of the new wine which had been dispensed for centuries among the ancient horse-chestnut trees in the old gardens and backyards at this time of year. But there was neither zither music nor singing, both of which, no matter how pleasant they may be, are apt, like water, to dilute the unimpaired enjoyment of the sparkling wine and are viewed by the really knowledgeable regular patrons of these wine establishments as an acoustic distraction from the pleasures of the plate.

I entered the wine garden punctually at 7:15. Only an old man and a young couple were sitting on the rough wooden benches—

the old man engrossed in his wine and the young couple in each other. The old man was a perfect replica of the late Emperor Franz Josef, with a bushy white mustache and bushy white whiskers, a huntsman's jacket, and a green hat. The young couple seemed very much in love: she looked as though she might be personal maid to a lady no longer able to afford a personal maid; he looked more like a student, of good family, perhaps only just back from the war, since my hurriedly averted glance revealed a make-shift artificial limb in the place of his right leg. I passed the obsequiously bowing owner of the place and sat down at a table in an alcove formed by thickly growing vines, a place for lovers rather than for sober deals between agents, but nevertheless an ideally secluded spot.

The owner had hardly placed a half-litre of wine before me when Mr. Smith came up the well-kept gravel path, greeted me with a friendly handshake, sat down beside me, and called for a second glass.

"The letter is in my pocket," I said. "But there are more important things to discuss first." I did not want Mr. Smith to think that I had troubled him personally merely for the sake of the letter.

I had made my opening remark in English, but Mr. Smith interrupted me at once and suggested we talk German—a language which he presently showed he mastered with a perfection that outshone my own linguistic achievements.

"I've been pretty successful with my first assignment," I continued in German. "I've been instructed to convey a short-wave radio to Budapest and to deliver it there to a certain address—I presume to the Soviet secret service. I understand it is a transmitter of handy size and of American make, and a model frequently used by American agents."

"So this time you've been officially engaged as an agent?" asked Mr. Smith.

"I think you'd call it that," I replied. "And for quite a substantial fee: an advance of five thousand Austrian schillings is to be handed to me tomorrow, together with the parts of the radio set and the appropriate instructions; a further five thousand awaits me in Budapest."

"You have accepted?" asked Mr. Smith.

"I believed I should be acting in accordance with your wishes," I replied with a slight bow.

"Perhaps," said Mr. Smith. "Although I must say your loyalty surprises me in view of the tempting offer by the competition."

, "I don't see why it should, Mr. Smith," I said. "I'm not exactly a coward, but neither am I a fool. How could I get out of the West without your sanction, or get in again afterwards? Besides, I presume that the capitalist United States can be more generous than the Bolshevik Russians."

"Have no illusions," Mr. Smith cut me short. "There is, as you may yet discover, a professional solidarity between the secret services. We make sure our agents don't play us off against each other and drive prices up. So you can dismiss the idea of our outbidding the Russians: we keep to the rate for the job just as they do. But please continue—I didn't want to interrupt you."

Though not at all pleased by his words, I gave him a detailed and truthful account of the Countess's instructions to me—except that my innate discretion and my upbringing prevented me from revealing the circumstances in which I had received those instructions. Mr. Smith, an excellent conversationalist, proved himself an equally good listener and heard me out to the end without interrupting.

"The set you mention," he observed then, "is certainly an American one and was indeed used a lot by our agents, and very successfully at that, although nowadays it is regarded as slightly obsolete and is hardly ever used. The Russians, always better at copying than inventing, have nothing to touch it for quality. They intend, I presume, to take it apart, ferret out its secrets, and then massproduce it. When that's done they will equip their agents in the West with this portable transmitter, and sooner or later, in its massproduced version, it will find its way back to me."

"Then you're denying the importance of my mission?" I asked.

"That depends," replied Mr. Smith. "The set is probably less important than the Russians think."

"What is important?"

"Maybe I'll tell you later," said Mr. Smith, "when we've reached an agreement—provided we can. Through a peculiar set of circumstances you've been entrusted with an assignment which requires expert handling. But let me put you straight on one or two points, even though this is hardly the time for a short course in six easy lessons. Some of the remarks you've dropped have convinced me that you've no more than an amateurish idea of our work. You seem to believe quite seriously that in working for both sides you have discovered a comfortable escape from the dangers of the espionage business. But believe me, that's not a new discovery: espionage for both sides is the most trivial form of espionage. The statistical fact is that some ninety per cent of all agents invariably work for both sides. This is in the nature of the business. Since courage isn't the most conspicuous characteristic of agents, they insure themselves against the risk of discovery by a timely disclosure to the opponent, or at least they offer him their services at the moment they're caught red-handed. That's why an agent, once discovered, is as good as worthless: we assume that from that moment on he is working also for the other side."

"I notice, Mr. Smith, you are treating me to the first of the six easy lessons," I said.

He ignored my remark. "To come back to your case, Herr Droste. You can't just stroll out of the Western Zone with a suitcase full of radio parts. If you did, it would be immediately obvious that you were in collusion with us. You must therefore, without any help on my part, have yourself smuggled out of the West—and back in again. In other words, you'll have to take the full risk. To me, you only begin to be of any use once you have taken these risks. Whether or not you do take them is up to you."

I felt that we were getting to the point. "And what are you offering," I asked, "if I decide to go along with you?"

"I've no intention of making a convert out of you," smiled Mr. Smith. "The secret service is not the Catholic Church. But if you follow my instructions and your mission is successful, then I can promise you something that, with a little imagination, you might call a career with prospects."

"Supposing," I said, "I did find it worth my while?"

"Then let's come to the point," said Mr. Smith. "You described your mission as important. I'll grant that it is, but for different reasons than you think. Without wishing to lecture you, I'd like to explain a few general principles. No doubt you remember from your own past work that every Intelligence organization has three tasks to perform: the collection, the transmission, and the analysis of information. What you may not realize is that the first of these three is by far the most simple. Take a straightforward example. In the last war the Germans had hundreds of agents in Africa, mainly among the pro-German Arabs, whose job it was, among other things, to keep the Germans informed about the arrival and departure of American naval units, troop transports, and submarines. Since there are no such things as underground harbors or collapsible warships, our naval movements in the ports of Algiers, Tunis, or Dakar did not remain hidden from even the most moronic Arab street urchin. The collection of information, therefore, was— as it is in most cases—child's play. Spies, my dear Herr Droste, are nearly always excellently informed—but the espionage services very rarely. The transmission of information, and especially the timely transmission, invariably meets with insuperable difficulties. In other words, a Counter-Intelligence service able to prevent the transmission of information to the enemy will discharge its task far more effectively than one that concentrates on the preservation of secrets —which is usually a hopeless job anyway."

I nodded eagerly. Mr. Smith seemed pleased.

"The Russians," he proceeded, "have hundreds of agents in the West, but their operations do little damage so long as we manage to control the transmission of their information. Secrets, if you wish to call them so, are fed from Vienna, or via Vienna, into Hungary and thence to Moscow every day. Eastern agents are daily entering the West from Hungary. Through what channels does the information reach the East? By what routes are the agents brought into the West? These are the questions that interest me. That, Herr Droste, is why I don't much care what you take to Budapest. *How* you do it, and by what route you return to Vienna—that is what I want to know, and that is what I want an accurate report about, complete with names, details of means of transport, and official and unofficial helpers."

He signalled the owner and settled the bill. "I'll go now," he said when the owner withdrew. "You stay here for another fifteen minutes." He unobtrusively pocketed the letter for Herr Müller, which I had passed to him under the table.

"I'll have the letter returned to you tomorrow morning," he concluded. "For the rest, follow minutely the instructions which the Russians will give you, and above all act as if your neck were at stake if the Americans caught you. As soon as you have the set you'll hear from me." After an almost imperceptible pause he added: "You'll receive the same sum as the Russians are paying you. I don't blame you at all for inflating the sum by fifty per cent for my benefit. You couldn't know the rate for the job. From now on, I feel sure, you'll repay frankness with frankness."

He shook hands with me. "Good luck!" he said. He almost sounded as if he meant it.

I was left alone in the wine garden, with a great many questions unanswered. Why had Mr. Smith given me his confidence after such a short acquaintance? Why had I accepted the risky mission? Who was Mr. Smith? Who was the Countess? In this game of the wolves, in which I'd been trapped, was there still a purpose or had the game become its own purpose? Was it worth joining in the game? Could deadly danger be outweighed by money? Did I have to deliver what I'd promised, or could I deceive the cleverly devised machine? Was I still driving—or was I already being driven?

There were two empty glasses in front of me. Mr. Smith had been gone for fifteen minutes. I rose and left. From a nearby garden I heard snatches of the wandering minstrels' songs in the soft night breeze.

PART THREE

9

To Meet Little Red Riding Hood

I ARRIVED in Budapest at six o'clock in the evening, after a twenty-four-hour journey. I took an ancient taxi to the Hotel Astoria, where the porter took charge of my false passport, made out to a Georg Derek, businessman. I was assigned a spacious and not unfriendly room on the second floor.

About half an hour after I had checked in, a man appeared at my door who introduced himself as Akos Horvát, and said that he had come to collect the safety razor. Horvát was the name I had been told in Vienna, where I had also received my false passport, my instructions, and my advance of two thousand five hundred shillings. I had also been instructed to hand over my black leather case to a man asking for a safety razor. Thus, with a sense of relief, I handed over the case to my visitor and regarded my mission as completed. I had no idea that it had just begun.

Instead of leaving, Horvát sat down, uninvited, on the ancient gray-green settee in my room. He was a peasant type, short and thick-set, with a close crop of black hair, a thick mustache whose ends were brushed upwards, and a pair of shrewd eyes which darted about the room like a couple of mice. He wore a suit of coarse, heavy cloth, despite the hot weather, and a pair of laced boots. Yet his speech and choice of words were fluent and educated.

Horvát handed me an envelope from which a few clean pengö bills were peeping out. I assumed, naturally, that this was my fee but Horvát corrected me: this was merely a little something to help me enjoy myself during my stay in Budapest; it had nothing to do with my fee, which I would receive in full, as arranged, in my own currency at the proper time.

Though pleased and not at all reluctant to spend a pleasant evening at the expense of the Soviet secret service, I felt somewhat disturbed by the fact that Horvát had no instructions whatever about my return to Vienna. In spite of his rustic appearance he seemed surprisingly well versed in city lore. Within a minute, he had written down for me the names and addresses of various restaurants, cafés, and night clubs, as if he belonged to the local tourist information bureau instead of the secret service. I thought it a good time then to ask how long I was expected to stay. The lively little mice in Comrade Horvát's eye-sockets came to a halt, regarding me with surprise and, it seemed to me, a touch of pity. Why be in such a hurry to leave Budapest? he said. The date and details of my return would be told to me in good time. Meanwhile, he added, I ought to make the most of Budapest's excellent cuisine and give no credence to the Western fairy-tales that my freedom of movement would be in the least restricted.

When Comrade Horvát left with the suitcase, I looked into the envelope he'd left behind. For once the banknotes failed to have their usual cheering effect on me: a quick calculation convinced me that the sum was too big, evidently intended for a lengthy stay. When I went down to the lobby and demanded my passport back, my suspicions were confirmed: my passport, the clerk informed me, had been handed to the alien's department of the police, in accordance with regulations, and would be kept by them for the time being.

Armed with the brief manuscript-Baedeker of the obliging Comrade Horvát, I stepped out into the street which bore the name of Louis Kossuth, the Hungarian freedom fighter, and had, rather subtly, not been renamed. I intended to have an excellent meal and an equally excellent glass of wine, to think over my awkward situation and consider what my next steps ought to be. First of all, however, I wanted to take a little walk—partly to renew my acquaintance with Budapest, where I had spent several weeks with my harpist-General during the war, and partly to investigate the truth about my freedom of movement.

Although the Hungarian capital had been occupied, or to use the official term "liberated," only two years before, and although the country was not yet ruled by an openly Communist Government but by a Coalition Government whose benches appeared to be equitably shared by the puppet masters and their puppets, a very noticeable change had nevertheless come over this once lively and gay city on the Danube. I have seen Russian towns, but they never struck me as nearly so depressing as the newly peoples-democratic Budapest on this fine summer evening. The towns which have grown under the hands of the Communists have an up-and-coming air; they have a vulgar and newly-rich look which makes them doubly distasteful to me, but they never filled me with the sorrow I experienced in the occupied-liberated cities which have so clearly come down in the world, almost as if their new masters were preserving the glories of the past as a deliberate mockery.

The streets were poorly lit, and the shop windows not at all. The great mansions in Louis Kossuth Street stood like aristocrats turned to stone, aristocrats who had seen better days and were now ashamed of their threadbare clothes of flaking mortar. The massive semi-nude caryatids supporting their arches and balconies—almost deliberate symbols of a capitalist exploitation of labor for the most frivolous of purposes—seemed utterly out of place and suggested those agonizing nightmares when one walks naked through the streets. In the display windows of what used to be the most elegant shops in Central Europe the dummies in their tasteless standard dresses seemed to be making apologetic gestures, just as if the wax figures felt the humiliation of the garments they had been made to wear. The time was not yet nine o'clock, but a great silence hung over the city center, so great that the rattle of each passing car was clearly audible on the dance-floor-like smooth asphalt of the streets, and the tinkling of the canary-yellow trolleys sounded as irritable in the empty streets as the wailing sirens of an ambulance in a deserted landscape. When I reached the Danube embankment after a short brisk walk the moon was standing above the royal palace on Castle Hill, on the far side of the river, high and aloof. One could not tell from here that the palace had been entirely burnt out; only through the hollow dome, with its thin gnawed ribs, did the pale moonlight filter, and in St. Gellért's imploringly raised hand the cross, which used to be illuminated, showed no light. The Buda side of the city, from which the Russians had conducted their siege, was one vast heap of wreckage. Half of the suspension bridge was sagging so grotesquely into the glittering water that it appeared as if the huge stone lion at the bridgehead was bending down to the river's edge to drink from it. The big hotels behind me were likewise mere façades with no buildings behind them; only in one of them a dimly lit café had been installed. Here, too, I had the impression as if the *nouveaux messieurs* had deliberately created a graveyard in which the coffins were not tidily buried but where the bones were allowed to litter the ground and the corpses to stink to high heaven. Lonely, but certainly unwatched, I strolled down the Danube Promenade, the corso that I had known resounding with gypsy music, along the river in which swam the silvery reflection of the moon but from which, at the same time, rose the summery smell of decay—almost as if the Danube, flowing through the impoverished city, could see no reason why it should behave more decorously.

Among the addresses given me by my "guide" was that of an establishment named Füzfa. I decided to go there, partly because its combination of restaurant and nightclub appealed to me, and partly because it was the only one in the list that I did not know.

The place was immediately next to the Opera, and its name in purple neon letters was visible a long way off in the darkened Andrassy Avenue, once Budapest's most spectacular thoroughfare.

The impression of being faced with a caricature of the past, which I had received on my nocturnal promenade, became even stronger when I entered the restaurant. The new establishment was equipped with old furniture, uniformly deep red in color and uniformly plush in material. Small boxes with semi-circular openings were grouped horseshoe-fashion around the room, strongly suggesting a film set intended perhaps—by a producer unacquainted with Paris—to represent the famous Maxim's. A waiter in a grease-stained but perfectly fitting tailcoat conducted me past the gypsy band to one of the boxes and, among a flood of Hungarian courtesies, urged me to take a seat.

Sitting in my red-plush box and enjoying first a crisp golden perch-pike, followed by a delicately pink and tender chicken immersed in paprika sauce, I began methodically to think out my position.

The components of the transmitter had been handed to me in Vienna by the same Herr Müller, who had also collected the Countess' second letter. On his last visit the colorless little man had displayed a less inhibited and almost jovial manner. A few hours later, in the middle of the night, I had a visit from Mr. Smith and two other Americans. The two experts—for that, I suppose, was what they were—were busy on the set till daybreak, while Mr. Smith and I got through a bottle of Gumpoldskirchener wine in pleasant conversation.

On the following morning Herr Müller brought me a false passport of very genuine appearance and left me exact instructions as to where, when, and how I was to cross the zonal border. If I had not been so inexperienced, the fake passport and the over-elaborate instructions would have made me suspicious even then. After all, if the Russians were involved in the business—and quite obviously they were—there was no conceivable reason why I should make an illegal entry, complete with false passport and involved precautions, into a Hungary they dominated. However, Herr Müller dispelled my doubts by pointing out that surely I had to return to the West and would then have to face an investigation if I did so under my real name. I accepted this explanation and set out on my journey. I was passed on from a truck driver in Vienna to a bricklayer in Eisenstadt, and then a peasant near Strass-Somerein, almost like a nicely wrapped parcel, until I found myself on Hungarian territory where, after a walk of three miles, I reached the nearest railway station without incident. The journey, in the details of which Mr. Smith had expressed himself chiefly interested and which I therefore carefully committed to my memory, went off very smoothly—except for the footslogging part, which was not altogether to my taste, seeing that I have always been a passionate supporter of modern means of transport—so smoothly, in fact, that I began to ask myself why the Communists had not entrusted one of their own people with so well-organized and unexacting a trip.

Now the answer was beginning to dawn on me. If the Russians were detaining me merely in order to convince themselves that I had handed over the components of the transmitter complete and undamaged, then I had nothing to fear, for Mr. Smith's engineers had minutely examined the set but had altered nothing. Another solution seemed more likely and filled me with serious misgivings. If the Americans were interested chiefly in discovering how the Russians organized the smuggling of human beings—the most highly explosive commodity circulating at that time between East and West—out of Vienna and into Hungary, then why should the Russians be less interested in how a person could, against his wishes, get out of the East and into the West? In vain did I persuade myself that I was jumping to conclusions: as always when one develops a theory based on fear everything now seemed to fit into the pattern of my anxieties. The Russians, I told myself, had equipped me with a false passport and got me into Hungary without passing their frontier posts so as to make it impossible for me to return to the West by the legal way. If they held on to my passport I would be entirely at their mercy; or at least, if I wanted to return to Vienna, I would have to look around for an illegal way out myself. They could therefore blackmail me or force me to escape, and then they need only watch me in order to discover the long sought-for escape route of other refugees. Then there was the surprisingly large sum of money which the genial Comrade Horvát had given me. Was it not perhaps designed to tempt me rather than serve my enjoyment? True, I should not be able to tell for a few days whether my suspicions were justified, but meanwhile I had to admit that the more innocent explanations which I turned over in my mind did not stand the acid test. The crowded restaurant, with its fiddling gypsy band, seemed to me no more than a comfortable corner of the vast trap into which I had so foolhardily walked.

If the Soviet secret service had indeed given me my large purse so I should use it to finance my escape I was determined to disappoint them. I was going to take Comrade Horvát's good advice literally. My first step was to order a bottle of 1927 Hungarian Törley champagne, the best year for this wine, and before long my attentive waiter returned with it, properly chilled.

No sooner had he uncorked the shapely bottle and set before me one of those slender glasses that used to be manufactured only in Hungary in the old days, than a blonde consequence of my grand-seigneurial fancies appeared at my table. This peoples'-democratic nightclub hostess, who sat down beside me without further ado, differed from her Western colleagues merely in that her shiny black-silk dress had obviously been made before the war. She was not exactly fat but possessed those full charms which are so delightful to young men in their puberty, when they are anxious to make the acquaintance of the unknown in as generous a measure as possible. I will not deny that she was quite appetizing in her rosiness, but the degree of her attraction depended on the size of one's appetite: in other words, she would seem more charming to a starving man than to a gourmet. For the rest Piroska—that was how she introduced herself—looked rather like an enormous doll which, through some oversight at the factory, had been stuffed with enough sawdust for two or three dolls. Her massive breasts—Piroska, by the way, meant Little Red Riding Hood, as she hastened to explain to me—were not only pushing out of the low, oval *décolleté* of her evening-dress, but seemed to be trying to push each in front of the other: forced toward one another without a restful valley between them, the two mountains appeared engaged in a race as to which should jump out of the dress first.

If my mesmerized stare was focused on these competing mountains, the reason was not some belated attack of puberty but the fact that from Piroska's massive—but, as I have said, quite appetizing—neck there dangled into her bosom a gold cross of downright improper dimensions. Although I had experience enough in these matters to know that ladies of the most ancient profession frequently display a piety that surprises the layman and possibly offends the believer, this Christian demonstration on the part of a peoples'-democratic nightclub hostess nevertheless astonished me.

Our conversation, conducted by Piroska in the most charmingly illiterate German, was at first about humdrum topics, connected with the restaurant which, for no obvious reasons, bore the rustic name Füzfa, meaning willow-tree. Even so, it was noticeable that my buxom companion made the most uninhibited derogatory remarks about the guests.

The conversation took an interesting turn when Piroska asked if I had known her native city before. When I told her I had, she immediately began to compare the wretched present with the golden past. She had a store of exceedingly distasteful episodes of the time when the Russians were laying siege to the city, and made no secret of her indignation over their sexual unrestraint. If, as I was inclined to believe in my suspicious frame of mind, the Soviet secret service had picked on Little Red Riding Hood to sound my real feelings, the girl certainly was not doing anything to provoke me into indiscreet remarks. Indeed, my suspicions had almost disappeared, and even my earlier anxieties were beginning to seem groundless, when, almost abruptly, Piroska declared that she could not "stand it in Budapest any longer" and had been trying for months to get out of this "prison."

"My dear," I thereupon felt obliged to ask, "aren't you talking a little incautiously? After all, I am a stranger."

"I'm a good judge of people," she replied easily. "That's part of my profession. I can smell a Communist," she continued, sniffing the air with her little *retroussé* nose as though she really wanted to discover some Communist odor. "Besides, the Bolsheviks would have to lock up the whole of Hungary, since, with only the exception of the big-shots, everybody wants to get out. Do you think I could find a job in Vienna?" she asked, thus dismissing my objections.

"Well, there are a few nightclubs again in Vienna," I replied hesitantly. "But do you really see a serious possibility . . . ?"

"My father confessor is willing to help me," she said. "The priests are the only people left with any courage. Are you a Catholic?" Without awaiting my reply she continued, "Do you know that there are more people going to church nowadays than there used to be? The services are always crowded, and they"—she pointed into the restaurant—"can't stop it." Then she added, "But don't we want to make ourselves more comfortable?"

"By all means," I said, but I did not quite get her meaning.

"Why not order another bottle, honey," she asked, as if my readiness to make myself comfortable entitled her to a more intimate form of address.

Since, as I have said before, I had no intention of being miserly with the secret service's money I signalled to the waiter and met my companion's request by ordering another bottle of 1927 Törley. With the familiarity shown to waiters by nightclub hostesses who have been with an establishment for some time, Little Red Riding Hood now turned to him with the request that he might give us "a better box." Though I could see nothing wrong with the box we occupied, I followed the knowingly smiling waiter and Piroska along a narrow passage behind the boxes and up a steep flight of stairs to a single box, well above the level of the restaurant floor. Presently Piroska, with rather too much archness, pulled a red curtain across the dove-cot-like entrance, so that we could neither be seen from the restaurant nor see the diners there, but could still wallow in the wailing strains of the gypsy music. I made some complimentary remarks about the band, but the girl maintained that it, too, was "no longer any good" since the best gypsies had been enlisted for the harvest work and the present leader owed his job solely to his excellent Party connections.

No sooner had the waiter uncorked the new bottle of champagne with a joyful but very plebeian noise, than Piroska, who was again very modestly sitting opposite me, resumed the tale of her father confessor. He was only thirty-three, she said, and had studied in Rome, where he had constantly been in and out of the Vatican. Apart from Hungarian, he could speak six languages—not counting Latin which, of course, he spoke fluently. He was a handsome man and the women were all running after him, but I was not to get this wrong: the man was a saint. Even so, he was concerned as much about the bodily as the spiritual salvation of his flock, and that was why he was doing everything to help good Christians get to those parts where they were still allowed to be just that.

With little Red Riding Hood's admiring account of her father confessor we had got through half the second bottle and I now cast a glance—surreptitiously, as my natural politeness demanded even in the company of ladies of easy virtue—at my wrist watch. The time was half-past one in the morning. Down in the restaurant the *joie de vivre* of the Government officials and black-marketeers appeared to have reached a climax: rather noisily they were singing those gypsy tunes which, provided only they are sad enough, invariably make the Hungarians cheerful.

Piroska had noticed my discreet gesture and misinterpreted it.

"But I am talking a lot of nonsense which doesn't interest you a bit, Georgie," she said. She had asked me my Christian name right at the beginning, as indeed is the proper thing for a nightclub hostess, and it was only natural that she should now use it in an intimate diminutive.

She pushed the table, which stood between us, away a little,

walked round it with mincing but, in spite of her bulk, not ungrace-
ful steps, and immediately, eschewing all further formalities, sat
down on my knees. She was either much lighter than I had assumed,
or else she possessed that skill of making herself lighter than in fact
she was. As her erotic vocabulary was evidently confined to the word
"comfortable," she invited me to make myself "comfortable" and
assisted me in this by undoing my tie and caressingly sliding her
fingers between the buttons of my shirt. Although I pride myself on
being a *gourmet*—the French are clever enough to differentiate between *gourmet* and *gourmand,* the connoisseur and the glutton—I
must confess that by now, possibly under the influence of the alcohol
consumed, I was no longer entirely unsusceptible to the advances of
my appetizing Little Red Riding Hood. These advances, by the way,
were of that peculiar Hungarian nature which makes me doubly
sorry that unfortunate circumstances have erected a barrier between
East and West. Only Hungarian women—and a considerable international experience entitles me to make this pronouncement—have
the knack of making every situation so "comfortable" that a man
really gets the illusion that even the most daring erotic actions are
designed solely for the achievement of greater "comfort." The most
striking illustration of this theory was provided by our "more comfortable" but still extremely cramped and confined box at the
Willow-tree. Piroska, still sitting on my knees, discarded all superfluous garments. Next, she relieved me of all those that might re-
strict my freedom of movement and finally, she gently pushed the
table aside so as to be able to lean over it the more easily—but all
this was done not with any jarring matter-of-factness but with that
solicitous affection with which the womenfolk of less civilized lands
put their men's slippers by their arm-chairs or run the bath water for
them on Sundays. Her loving guidance had no vice about it, but on
the contrary was almost imbued with that domesticity and hospitality with which other women take a guest's arm to take him into the
living-room or in to dinner. I must also record that I was pleasantly
touched by the tactful manner in which Piroska, before my closer
approach, turned her head apologetically and, with a quick but modest gesture, took off the gold cross which she wore round her neck.
Only when she had thus put off her better self did she nod her

round doll's head at me, in token of her cordial rather than passionate readiness.

An hour later, when we had each consumed a final glass of
Barack, an excellent apricot brandy, I should have returned to my
hotel in the most serene and carefree frame of mind if my Little Red
Riding Hood had not made an apparently trifling slip—the kind
that is made sooner or later by most agents and spies and which, according to circumstances, may cost them their neck, or merely their
liberty, but at any rate the confidence of their chosen victim. Piroska
declined to accept the appropriate sum of money which I presented
to her in the most chivalrous manner possible, and maintained that
a renewed visit would give her far greater pleasure than my cash
present. As I stepped out into the dark street of the sad, unfamiliar
city, whose darkness was no longer relieved even by the purple
neon lights of the Füzfa restaurant, there was no doubt left in my
mind that I had had some fun on my first night in Budapest at the
expense of the Soviet secret service—though not in the sense that I
had hoped for.

10

To Wear the Livery of the Devil?

FIVE DAYS had passed since my arrival in Budapest, and with every
hour of my unsolicited stay my suspicion deepened that I was being
held in the Hungarian capital for some mysterious, or at any rate
some rather unhealthy, purpose.

The desk clerk at the hotel, whenever I asked about my passport, merely shrugged his shoulders, no longer even troubling to
give me a plausible explanation. My funds, which I had been deliberately spending in the most liberal manner, were almost totally
exhausted. There could be no question of my meeting the inevitably

approaching hotel bill. Another thing that annoyed me was that, from the morning following my arrival, I knew that I was—as the underworld expression is—being "shadowed." Indeed, from that moment onward I was unable to take a single step without being followed by a man in a light gray double-breasted suit. When I stepped out of the elevator in the morning he was there, waiting, in the hotel lobby, hiding behind a newspaper. Within a matter of seconds he would enter whatever restaurant I had chosen to take a meal in. And when I attended a performance of *Countess Maritza* —which, notwithstanding its aristocratic setting, was still a reliable standby of the Budapest musical-comedy stage—I found him comfortably ensconced in a seat in the orchestra, one row behind me.

When on the evening of my fifth day I still had not heard anything from my employers, I decided upon a course of action that appealed to me chiefly because of its originality.

Having consumed an excellent dinner and enjoyed a bottle of very pleasant Badacsony wine at the Kis Royal Restaurant—a place that can be highly recommended in spite of its somewhat reduced circumstances—I looked about for my "shadow." As behooves a shadow, he had taken a table just behind me and was busy eating a modest meal, appropriate no doubt to his position as a Government employee. It was a warm summer evening, the horse-chestnuts were in full bloom, and dinner was being served in the garden beneath the rich green foliage. My friend, too, was sitting at one of the neatly laid garden tables and had just lit a malodorous cigar when I approached him and, skipping the formality of introductions, sat down beside him.

"I must ask you, sir," I said, "to pardon this most improper trespass on your privacy, but, if I am not mistaken, we have now spent five days in each other's company and are in something like the position of passengers on an ocean liner who get to know one another without formal acquaintance. I don't wish to make any trouble for you with your employers, who no doubt instructed you to stick close to me, but you really should change your suit from time to time and not wear such a conspicuous red tie which, in any case, testifies to your political loyalty rather than your good taste. As I say, I don't want to put you in any embarrassing position with your employers—indeed I should be glad to do anything I can to get you a raise—so please don't interrupt me, but listen to me carefully. It isn't that I don't like your enchanting city," I continued, with a sweeping gesture, "after all, how could anybody fail to like it? Nor am I in any particular hurry to return to Vienna. As a place for a summer holiday, I've got to admit, Budapest is in many respects preferable to Vienna, whereas my native city may perhaps boast of certain advantages during the winter season. The real point of the matter, my dear sir or comrade, is simply that my cash is exhausted and that I can hardly hope that the legendary Hungarian hospitality will also apply to hotel managements. Would you have the kindness, therefore, to report to your superiors that I shall be compelled to move from the very pleasant Hotel Astoria into some shelter for down-and-outs unless my empty coffers are replenished by tomorrow. I should now, with your permission, take my leave," I concluded, "if it weren't for the fact that I have a little confession to make. The bill which I have run up here exceeds my funds, and it seems to me that for obvious reasons it would be unwise to allow me to become the object of a scandal. I would request you, therefore, to settle my dinner bill: I had one chicken soup, one stuffed paprika, one salted gherkin, one portion of pancakes, and one bottle of Badacsony—no, no bread."

I should like at this point to dispel the possible, but utterly mistaken, impression that I am a man of exceptional courage. Indeed, in the course of these memoirs I hope to have repeated opportunity of proving the very opposite. The palm of glory is awarded for courage rather too thoughtlessly. The best proof of this is the expression "absolute contempt for death" which is often used to praise courage of the highest order—just as if contempt for death were something glorious instead of being downright silly and presumptuous.

In reality most, though not all, feats of heroism are performed for the sole purpose of escaping death or some other impending unpleasantness—respectable actions, no doubt, but no more than the normal result of a sound instinctive reaction innate to most people. The polar explorer who survives in the eternal ice, the man under sentence of death who escapes, the officer holding out at a lost post until relief arrives—all these make popular heroes, and the public are only too apt to overlook the question of what else these heroes could in fact have done than act heroically? Much more interesting than the courageous, to my mind, are the cowards. It is they, contrary to widespread belief, who are the exception, for they lack those reflexes of self-preservation with which nature has equipped the majority of human beings. Courage therefore—and I shall come back to this point in greater detail—has nothing to do with character. It is a kind of reserve which is drawn upon, almost automatically, in the emergence of difficult situations. If it were otherwise there would be no wars, since ninety-nine out of every hundred soldiers would desert; the war-lords, on the other hand, proceed from the correct calculation that, in order to make heroes, they need only create the most impossible situations imaginable.

Having been driven to my courageous act by pure necessity I spent an uneasy night, disturbed by nightmares.

On the following morning, shortly after seven, I was awakened by a telephone call from Comrade Horvát who, suddenly emerging from concealment, instructed me to be ready an hour later. Outside No. 12 Rákoczi Street, not far from my hotel, a black car, a Hotchkiss, would be waiting for me and would take me to my destination.

At the appointed hour, outside No. 12 Rákoczi Street, waited indeed a high limousine, which suggested an aristocratic wedding conveyance rather than the fast car of a secret service organization. A broad-shouldered man of unpleasant exterior—the plain-clothes men of all countries are as much alike as twins—opened the door for me and, with an expressionless face, got in beside me. After my very first question he made it clear that he was unacquainted with the German language, or indeed any other language in current use. No further word passed between us as the elegant Hotchkiss, coughing slightly like an elderly count, bumped its way criss-cross fashion through Budapest—evidently for the sole purpose of making orientation impossible for the stranger.

After touring the streets for about forty minutes we found ourselves in a residential neighborhood which, though by no means conversant with Budapest's town plan, I immediately identified as situated at the foot of the Swabian Hill, and which, if I had been disposed to do so, I could have found again without much difficulty and after no more than a brief search. At a crossroads our residential street was suddenly barred: three or four soldiers stood in front of a road block, not unlike a customs barrier, which they opened only after my escort had duly produced his papers. The car then proceeded through several streets which bore no name plates, past prosperous-looking houses which had been vacated by their owners. In front of a big yellow villa in the rapidly outdated *art nouveau* style of the early part of the century the procedure with the identity papers was repeated, but from the gestures of an officer, I gathered that we were expected. And then—there was no doubt about it—I was in the study of the Chief of Hungarian Intelligence.

It was not out of discourtesy that the Chief did not rise to greet his visitor. He was a person of such colossal dimensions that every movement was clearly an effort for him. He probably also suffered from asthma, for he breathed heavily, frequently stopped short in his speech, and at times snorted audibly through his nose.

The Chief, as I had privately christened him, spoke German fluently, though not quite faultlessly, and certainly seemed to understand even the finer nuances of the language. I might add that on his desk there was a family photograph showing a blond woman with two children who were not unlike their father; otherwise there were no pictures in the cool, sober room—not even one of those portraits of Lenin, Rákosi, Stalin, or some other celebrity to which, during my six-day stay in Budapest, I had become quite accustomed.

With a good deal of effort the Chief leaned forward over his desk and pushed a box of long, dark Russian cigarettes across to me.

"Take a seat and have a cigarette," he said jovially. "How do you like our Budapest?"

"Very much, thank you," I said, a little taken aback by his conventional inquiry.

"Did you know Budapest before?" he asked, still in a conversational tone.

"Yes, I spent a few weeks here in the war."

"Quite so, quite so," said the Chief, as if he had just remembered an old acquaintanceship. "Of course you were A.D.C. to General Sensenöhr at the time. Well, a few things have changed around here since then."

That was something I could not deny. At the same time I noted with some amusement that the methods of all secret services were evidently alike: just as my American friend Smith had done, so the Soviet Chief was now trying to impress me by his knowledge of unimportant data.

"I want to congratulate you, Herr Droste," he continued, rubbing his ear-lobe. "You have successfully come through several tests. You'd be no use to me if you hadn't spotted the agent who was shadowing you."

He laughed noisily, with a great deal of self-satisfaction and very little breath.

"The fact that you have done nothing to leave Budapest without our knowledge," he continued when he had recovered, "likewise speaks in your favor, Herr Droste."

"Why should I?" I interposed. "You made sure I enjoyed the most generous hospitality."

An expression of disapproval appeared in his inflated face. "You don't have to like it here, Herr Droste," he said. "Personally I prefer agents who are not subject to fits of political loyalties. You were in the war yourself and know that volunteers, as a rule, are no good. We've got plenty of good Communists; what I'm looking for is good agents. Let's come to the point—But before I give you any further instructions I would like you to know that I am prepared to reward your further services with two hundred dollars, which you should be able to convert with considerable profit in the black market on the other side."

I bowed to indicate my agreement, even though I was a little disquieted over the colossal magnitude of the sum. Moreover, the matter-of-fact manner in which the Chief referred to further instructions, without in the least troubling to find out if I was prepared to undertake any further jobs, deepened my uncomfortable feeling that I was a prisoner, even though my prison bore all outward appearances of comfort.

"At the Füzfa Restaurant," continued the Chief, "you made the acquaintance of a young lady who told you a thing or two about her father confessor. You will go to that restaurant again tonight and tell the young lady that you are in serious trouble because the authorities have unexpectedly impounded your passport. Besides," he added, puffing, "you'll be speaking no more than the truth. Get her to take you to Father Peter Zombory—that's the man's name—and tell him that you have come to Budapest on business, but that you are now under suspicion of being a spy and are about to be arrested. Allow it to be understood, without actually saying so, that you are employed by an American firm in Vienna and that you have collected here certain information about Hungarian economic matters which are not without importance to the Americans. The Father," he added almost casually, "is a spy for the Vatican. Ask him, if need be implore him, appeal to his conscience as a Christian———" Here the Chief interrupted himself, fought for breath for a minute, and then continued, "As I said, appeal to his conscience as a Christian. Ask him to hide you, and if possible to get you across the frontier. Once he has agreed to do so you'll get my further instructions."

The long speech had left the fat man exhausted. At last, determined to take a risky course, I launched out on a lengthy speech myself.

"Sir," I said, "I am surprised by your attitude. First you commend my intelligence, and the next moment you seem to underrate it considerably. That my young friend Piroska—I hope I am pronouncing the name correctly—is an agent of yours I have of course realized from the start. This splendid young lady declined to accept my payment for a job conscientiously done—a thing none of her harmless colleagues would do. Why should I now present myself to Piroska as a would-be escapee instead of co-operating with her as a colleague? But that's not the main point. At Baden near Vienna I was entrusted with a mission which was certainly not one of the easiest, and I think I may boast that I have discharged it to everybody's satisfaction. Nothing was said in my agreement about any further, possibly far more tricky, assignment, nor did I expect that, through the confiscation of my passport, I should be coerced into accepting one. Why, sir, do you force me to undertake a mission without first finding out whether I might not voluntarily undertake it—though, of course, for an appropriate fee? Return my passport to me and give me my train ticket. If I am still prepared to stay here and help you discover the secret channels of Father Zombory —you'll notice I have remembered the name—then you will have gained an agent instead of having made use of a will-less and unwilling tool. As for the two hundred dollars," I concluded, "that will be all right—not so much because of the amount, but because my predilection for—if you'll pardon the bourgeois term—security inclines me to prefer a regular employment to a non-recurrent haul."

Throughout my speech the Chief had not ceased to massage his left ear-lobe with his right hand—an operation which cannot have been easy for him since his arm, short in relation to his obese body, had to circle his massive front. He showed no intention of cutting me short, however, and I began to think that this unattractive mannerism, which had once or twice caused me to interrupt myself, was a token of benevolent approval.

"Herr Droste," he said, "without knowing it you have passed another test. I like you. I like you exceedingly. You probably know that it is not customary to confide to agents more than is strictly necessary for the discharge of their immediate task, but I will make an exception in your case. The reason why you are not to take Piroska into your confidence is very simple: she is unreliable. She is also working for the Russian secret service."

"I thought . . ." I interposed.

"Don't think too much! I know exactly what you are thinking, and you're thinking wrong. Our political relations with our Russian brothers are excellent—but politics and Intelligence work are two entirely different things. A good Intelligence service must have good experts on its staff, just as a good factory. A good factory wants to outstrip others by producing better articles. There is no such thing as co-operation between rival secret services, neither here nor in the West. You remember this! But you needn't worry, Piroska knows that you are our fish and won't do anything to get you hooked by the rival firm. For the rest, you may put your mind at ease. We shan't pick you up either at the hide-out which Father Zombory will find for you, nor during your escape. We merely want to know where Father Zombory makes his spies disappear to, and how he gets them out of the country." He lit one of the dark cigarettes but stubbed it out again after two or three laborious puffs. "As for your passport," he continued—and now he looked like a very brutal gypsy baron—"that would be no use to you anyway, since we could always arrest you at the frontier. The fact that I am keeping it is therefore a sign of my trust in you. I believe you if you say you wouldn't make use of it." He pushed his chair away from his desk, indicating that he was not interested in my reply, and with a considerable effort opened a drawer. He took out a few banknotes and concluded: "This is just for your expenses. Your fee in dollars will be sent to you."

I took the money. "You will allow me to point out," I said, realizing that any opposition would be useless, "that there is a sum of two thousand five hundred Austrian schillings still owing to me for the conveyance of the radio set."

The Chief pulled his chair up to the desk again, pushing the drawer shut with his belly.

"You'll get that before your departure," he said.

The black Hotchkiss took me back into the city. The aristocratic vehicle swayed slowly across the proletarian suburbs. Through the grimy windows I looked out into the dusty streets where half-naked children were playing in the midday sun. Since my escort had not in the meantime learnt any useful language, and since the driver again thought it necessary to waste as much gas as possible, I had ample opportunity to contemplate my situation and examine my reactions.

The Chief's words of praise and his lucrative offers did not deceive me for a moment. I realized that I had been shabbily rewarded for my services, that I had been deceived about my true mission, and that I had in fact been lured into a trap from which there was no other way out than the one prescribed to me. But were matters different with Mr. Smith? His appearance and his manners were smoother than the Chief's. The picture of a career voluntarily chosen by myself, which he had painted for me, had seemed more civilized—but he, too, knew perfectly well that I should have no choice and that, having taken the first step, I should be compelled to take the next.

If at that moment I first decided in my mind to deceive both secret services, though as yet without any clear idea of how this was to be achieved, then this decision was due—for the moment at least—to my refusal to be deceived by them. Just because they thought me more stupid than I was I decided to be cleverer than they.

Another person might have reacted more naturally. He would have tried to free himself from his fatal entanglement instead of fleecing those he condemned. But I cannot say it emphatically enough, I was not out to fight an evil thing. Besides, I did not then suspect the full measure of its vileness. A person who has recognized an evil and does not want to submit to it unconditionally has a choice of three possible courses of action, of which the conventional world recognizes only two: that of avoidance and that of opposition. The third one, the one not conventionally acknowledged, is that of opposition through association. The half-hearted, the passive, and the submissive put on a monk's habit, they hide from the Devil and are praised for it. The bold, the active, and the impulsive put on shiny armor and engage the Devil in mortal combat. They, too, are praised for it. The third put on the livery of the Devil and speak in his name. They are damned, even though they are the only ones who have realized that Knowing comes before Knowledge.

But these, at the time, were only my feelings and not my thoughts. I did not leave the jungle. I advanced into it with what weapons I had.

II

A Secret Service with a Difference

WHENEVER I THINK of Father Peter Zombory, whom I met through the good offices of my Little Red Riding Hood from the Füzfa Restaurant, I picture him as a character in a black-and-white film. He was a man who defied description in terms of color. His face was white, translucent, drawn with extraordinary nobility—one of those faces that have to be seen in profile to be fully appreciated. Only in profile did his long, curved nose of Savonarola-like contour achieve its full effect, as did the knife-edge line of his mouth which, for all its sharpness, was very expressive. The Father's hair was black, but not simply of that dark hue commonly referred to as black: it was deep raven. Brushed smoothly against his narrow skull, his hair seemed almost like a little black-velvet cap above his high, veined forehead. His eyes too were dark—so dark in fact that the pupils did not show against the deep brown irises and, looking into his eyes, one often had a sense of gazing into a fire of black flames. The Father's age was difficult to guess, but he could hardly be more than thirty-two or thirty-three, judging by the youthful—one might almost say athletic—suppleness of his body. His snow-white hands, gleaming from among the black of his simple priestly garment, were reminiscent of those in El Greco's praying figures—hands of which I am never sure whether they are devoutly extended towards the All-Highest or profanely eager to draw the God-head down to ourselves.

The Chief's assertion—incidentally, I did not discover his name till much later—that Father Zombory was a Vatican spy did not seem to have been very far from the truth.

Throughout many years the Vatican secret service has been the only one that occasionally filled me with something like respect—not because of its particularly ethical aims, which in fact differ only very slightly from those of other powers, but because the Vatican's organization is not marked by that gross disproportion between effort and result which has reduced all other secret services *ad absurdum*. The agents of the Holy See, scattered as they are over the whole globe, receive no pay for their special work and do not therefore feel impelled to justify their existence at every step. They make no reports unless they have something to report, and if they do make a report they show remarkable accuracy. Secret services such as the Hungarian one, with which I had just been in contact, and others as well, have to justify their expenditure and must therefore put up a show of highly mysterious activity, as instanced by the circumstances surrounding my meeting with the Chief. The Holy See, which altogether never admits the existence of a Vatican secret service, does not require this complicated and costly *mise en scène* for the deception of the taxpayer or his representatives. In the priests, monks, and nuns who are for ever touring the world, inconspicuous and not answerable to anybody, the Vatican has a far greater number of informers than any secret service, including the American or the Russian, could ever afford. These agents of the Holy See, moreover, do not suffer from romantic delusions, nor do they revel in the part of spies. What is more, contrary to the widely held romantic view, a travelling nun can collect far more information than some alluring beauty who may from time to time succeed in seducing her victim but rarely in gaining his confidence. Another point is that the agents of the Vatican, because of its theoretical interest in world affairs rather than an active participation in them, are able to practice a certain objectivity in judging events and situations, whereas other spies will try to color the information they have obtained in accordance with the tastes, hopes, or aspirations of the recipients of that information. Furthermore, the Holy See has only one secret service and not several competing espionage organizations. And, finally, it only very rarely uses outsiders as occasional spies. It is therefore at an advantage over other secret services, in much the same way as a big landowner who has his own laborers to till his fields is in a better position than one who has to hire migrant labor.

I had described my alarming situation to Piroska in the most heartrending tones and urgently appealed for her, or rather her father confessor's, help. After first getting in touch with him she instructed me to meet her at the Father's monastery, off Váczi Street in the suburbs, on Sunday at four in the afternoon, but I preferred to misunderstand the time and to call on Father Zombory just before three. Instead of representing myself to the priest as an Austrian businessman and merely hinting that I had been doing intelligence work for the West, I told Father Zombory my whole story, expressly emphasizing that I had come to Budapest as an American agent, though on a Soviet assignment. I also enlightened the Father about the part played by the pious nightclub hostess and concluded my account as follows:

"Now you know everything, Father, and I am asking you to get me out of this country—but without danger to yourself and in such a manner that I will not be forced to give the Soviet secret service a report that would make me a traitor."

The priest had listened to me attentively. The monastery cell in which we sat—the Father on a plain bench and I on one of the two ascetic chairs—would have been very like a prison cell if the only barred window of the high, bare, and whitewashed room had not looked out on a garden in full bloom, drenched in the warm sun of the early summer afternoon. The Father was sitting below a plain crucifix carved from light-colored wood, which hung solitarily on the wall, and a sunbeam with millions of dancing little motes lay between us, so that the priest seemed to be much farther away from me than in fact he was, on the far side of a barrier of streaming light.

"My son," said Father Zombory, "let us leave aside, for the moment, the question of whether I have in fact the possibilities which you mention, and whether, if I had them, I should be prepared to use them for your benefit. What proof have you that you are what you say you are, what proof have you of the truth of your story? Might you not easily—I am not suggesting you are—but might you not easily be an *agent provocateur,* sent to test an awkward representative of the Church?"

"You are asking concrete questions, Father," I replied, "and you are entitled to expect a concrete answer. But how am I to know whether I am what I say I am? What does anybody know of himself? I have told you I am in American service, and I have not concealed from you that I am also in Soviet employment. But I could not tell, let alone prove to you, why I should regard myself as an American rather than a Soviet agent. But supposing I were an *agent provocateur,* why shouldn't I follow the course mapped out for me by the gentlemen of the Hungarian secret service? I could have told you a plausible story, one that was perhaps more plausible than the truth—after all, that is what makes lies so convenient: that they are often superior to the truth in plausibility. But if you were to ask me whether I had spoken to you so frankly because I had suddenly heard the voice of conscience, I should not be able to answer you. People speak of the voice of conscience as if it were some voice familiar to us, something like a mother's or a brother's voice which we recognize instantly, even through a closed door or from far away. But it seems to me that the voice of conscience might be anybody's voice. In fact it is easily confused with other voices, with the voice of fear, for instance, which warns us not against what is evil but against what is dangerous. Or the voice of experience, which springs not from repentance but from the consideration that some unpleasant event may be repeated, or, finally, the voice of prudence, which today calls for a moral action but tomorrow may call for a highly immoral one, if what we call prudence deems it advisable. Which of these voices was it that spoke to me? I don't know,

Father. I only know that I am unable to continue with this dishonest game."

"You are a clever man," said the priest, "clever and dangerous. I say dangerous, because by reflecting about yourself you manage to turn black into white. The reason why more good men are found among the ordinary people than among the likes of you is not that the unintelligent are born virtuous, or that the virtuous are born unintelligent, but that the intellect, like an ingenious attorney, exculpates vice and lets it loose again upon the world, like an acquitted criminal. 'Blessed are they that are poor in spirit,' my son—and why? Because the poor in spirit are left alone with their wicked deeds, because they cannot call upon their intelligence to dispel the pangs of their conscience. If you will open the book on the table over there at the marker, you will find underlined a maxim of Jacques Maritain, the French philosopher, whose wit I admire more than I respect his principles. *'Le diable est pur parce qu'il ne peut faire que le mal.'* " The Father quoted in French without a trace of accent. " 'The Devil is pure because he can do only evil!' The French are fond of appearing blasphemous through striking formulations, but this sentence is not so blasphemous as it may seem. The philosopher does not claim that the Devil is pure although he does evil, let alone because he does evil, but because he does only evil. The accent is on the little word *only*. Good and evil are each a unit within themselves, and they are exclusive. When the Devil tempts a man he does not let him become evil, not wholly evil, because then the tempted person would himself become a devil and thereby pure: but the Devil does not suffer competition. What he desires is confusion, which is the same as uncleanliness, impurity. God created day and night, but dawn and dusk, twilight and gloaming He did not create, they arose without His doing from the fatal intermingling of light and darkness which God divided from one another on the first day of Creation, long before Man was made." The Father folded his hands and regarded me fixedly. "The Devil," he continued, "knows that all evil is done at dusk and at dawn, in the twilight and in the gloaming. Who am I? What is right and what is wrong? What is good and what is evil? Whose voices are they that I hear? These, my son, are vain questions, questions that flatter our vanity because they sound so wonderfully humble. But in fact they are diabolical questions, prompted by the Devil in order to confuse us."

"Do you, then, deny doubt altogether?" I asked.

"I deny that we are unable to tell good from evil," he answered. "The Devil is allowed to do only evil, so that the evil may become visible for what it is. God created visibility. You are saying, or at least suggesting, that you cannot see the right road. But that, my son, is deception, or self-deception. What in fact you are doubting is whether you have the strength to choose it. The road is clearly visible, only your decision is in the twilight."

It was my turn to guide the conversation back to its starting point. "Does this mean," I asked, "that at least you concede that I am not an *agent provocateur?*"

A smile fluttered round the priest's lips, as fine as the lips themselves. "I believe," he said, "that you have not decided to be an *agent provocateur.*"

"But it does not mean that you will help me?"

"Oh yes, I might," he said. "On condition that you make the decision."

I turned to the window. The quietude of the Sunday lay over the garden within the four plain monastery walls and its effect on me was heightened by the occasional impatient tinkling of the streetcar bells. This sunlit paradise, with its docile tulips, its blasé roses, and its wind-swept pinks, this garden lovingly tended by gentle hands, was situated within a city that had suffered a siege not long before, that had been defended by strangers and attacked by strangers, a city that was now swarming with spies and policemen, where brute force was aspiring to power, and where men's souls were in the same untidy confusion as the debris of the wrecked buildings. The longer I stood there, meditating, gazing out into the garden—across which a little monk was now quietly strolling, engrossed in his breviary—the more I began to wonder whether the man in the monastery cell belonged to that peaceful garden or that world outside the tall gray walls, and what the decision would be like towards which he was urging me.

But no matter which world the black-and-white man belonged to, whether his cell was the secret headquarters of the troubled world or, on the contrary, a refuge from its troubles, it was obvious to me that I was to be recruited, just as I had been recruited on that day when the beautiful Countess entrusted her first letter to me at Baden. She had touched me in my chivalry or my vanity—it was difficult to say which—just as Mr. Smith, good judge of character that he was, had later touched me in my greed. The Chief, in turn, had recruited me by force and cunning, and this priest now appeared to be about to appeal to my moral sense, or perhaps even to my fear of the hereafter, holding out to me eternal bliss with the same liberality as the Countess had her white body, Mr. Smith his green dollar bills, and the Chief my coveted liberty.

I wanted to ask a few questions to discover the Father's intentions—realizing that it would be a strenuous but exhilarating experience to pit my wits against his—when there was a knock at the door and a monk, opening it slightly, put his shaven head through the narrow crack. Although he spoke Hungarian I understood at once that he was announcing Piroska.

The very sight of her filled me with a lively amusement that came as a welcome relief after the seriousness of the past hour. She wore a black dress which could hardly be surpassed in modesty, its widow-like monotony relieved only by the gold cross which was again suspended from her—now chastely covered-up—neck. Her black straw hat, under which her striking hair had now been tamed into the most decorous style, I can only describe as touching: it was the kind of headgear that country girls arriving in the big city purchase somewhere near the station in the belief that it will make them look like fashionable city dwellers. The black cotton gloves, which Piroska did not take off throughout the ensuing proceedings, added the final touch to her disguise as the provincial widow travelling to town to visit her husband's grave.

Piroska made her entrance in the best theatrical manner. With quick steps she walked up to the Father, took his hand, and with a bob that was more like a genuflection, bent over it and, before the priest could stop her, pressed it ardently to her lips. She then greeted me with such dramatic pity as if the fiend already held me in his grasp, and as if she had come in the nick of time to save me from my tragic fate. Had "the unfortunate," as she called me, not been followed on his way to the monastery, she asked? Had I really found my way to the rescuing angel safe and sound? Had I told Father

Zombory the whole truth and frankly revealed my desperate situation to him?

A good quarter of an hour passed before Father Zombory was able to say even a few casual sentences. While I leaned against the wall by the window and Piroska finally sat down on the wooden bench, exhausted—sitting, moreover, in such a chaste and upright way that I found it difficult to recall her in a more relaxed posture —the Father was pacing up and down with measured tread, his long, white, El-Greco hands lying, finger-tips touching, flat on his chest.

Now that he began to speak I could hardly believe my ears. He had, he said, listened to the story of my plight and had decided to get me out of the country. However, he added, this was the last time he would be able to help anybody, for he himself would not be staying here any longer. He could trust his faithful and devout daughter, his good Piroska, and could therefore reveal to her that he himself intended to escape in a few days' time—together with me. It had cost him a long and hard struggle, he added, to make up his mind to leave his flock, but he had been basely betrayed and was now left only with the alternative of escape—extremely risky though it was —or the cruel dungeons of the Soviet secret police.

It is always the most difficult thing for an actor to be convincing, at the same time, to an intelligent and a stupid audience, and the Father clearly did not find it easy to make the part he had chosen equally credible to his two rather different spectators. However, I had the impression that he was not concerned very much about my applause and that, on the contrary, he was, in a way, taking me into his confidence by acting for Piroska's benefit alone. I did not for a moment believe the story about his escape, but that made me admire even more the mastery with which he acted his part in front of the girl, and that without even once looking at her.

If it was the Father's belief that Piroska, while quite ready to betray me or anybody else in cold blood, would on no account endanger his own life, then his gamble proved a brilliant calculation.

He had hardly finished speaking when she jumped up, threw herself down at his feet, clutched his knees, and implored him with tears not to try to escape, for the love of Christ, but to hide out in some safe place. The Father gently lifted her up and, deliberately misunderstanding her words, began to reassure her: he was most touched, he said, by her devotion to him but he felt sure that another spiritual guide would look after her with the same solicitude as he had tried to give her. No, exclaimed Piroska, that wasn't it at all, the Father would by courting death if he tried to escape, especially if he were to join forces with me, a dangerous spy, whose escape the authorities were determined to prevent at all costs. And how, asked the Father, registering a degree of astonishment that severely taxed his histrionic talents, could she possibly know these things? At this point Piroska again fell on her knees, frantically clutching the priest's soutane. She beat her breast, tugged at her cross, covered her eyes with her arm, and generally acted as if the Devil had indeed taken possession of her. She herself, she alone, she screamed, beating her fist against her bosom, had betrayed him. It was she who had brought me here to lure the Father into a trap—but she had never suspected that he would himself want to escape and she could not now bear the thought that they might intercept him on his flight and kill him. Only now that he himself was in mortal danger did she realize the monstrosity of her actions and she would do penance, any penance which he or the Almighty God might choose to impose on her. The little black straw hat tumbled off her head; she tore her hair and tried wildly to catch the Father's hands in order to smother them with tears of repentance and contrite kisses.

To me the scene was part cruel and part grotesque, rather like a fit of madness, and I expected Father Zombory to cut it short. However, experienced actor that he was, he seemed resolved to play it out to the end. When Piroska had somewhat calmed down and, with my help, was sitting again on the chair by the table, he subjected her to an interrogation which would have done credit to the Holy Inquisition itself. Who, he questioned her, had instructed her to insinuate herself into his confidence? When, and in what circumstances, had she been recruited for her vile activities? Where, and how often, had she made her reports to her employers, and what had she told them? He then switched the trend of his questions to me and I noticed that he had admirably memorized my own evidence and was now carefully confirming every point of it. He was standing before her, tall and slim, occasionally raising his arms, as though holding the Cross up to the Devil, and it was of the Devil, the torments of hell, the wailing, and the gnashing of teeth that he spoke to her in the most fiery language whenever her urge for confession appeared to flag for a moment. The unfortunate girl, quite unequal to such an assault, was sagging more and more. Without the accustomed make-up she had looked somewhat faded and unhealthy before, but now her skin had assumed a cheesy color, and her round doll's eyes disappeared entirely under her tear-swollen lids.

The possibility of escaping hell-fire after all, but even more so the conviction of having snatched her beloved Father from certain death, eventually calmed Piroska's disturbed soul. Hastily she picked up the little black straw hat, which was lying on the floor like a dead bird, and stood there holding it awkwardly in her hand. As she stood there, helpless, in the middle of the small room, she reminded me of nothing more than a big black cow which had lost its pasture and could not find its shed. When the Father began to say a few encouraging words to her she burst into tears of gratitude, but eventually summoned enough strength to walk out of the cell.

"You will leave your hotel at seven o'clock to-night." The Father addressed me as soon as the girl had left. Not by a word, a gesture, or even the slightest hint did he refer to the scene we had witnessed. "Don't take any luggage with you whatever. Do you possess any papers or documents which might be valuable?" When I assured him that I did not he continued, "Go out for a stroll. Make sure you are not followed. If you are not quite sure you will return to your hotel and await further instructions. But if you are sure you are not being shadowed you will enter the church in St. Christina Square between eight and nine. You will buy a candle there and light it in front of the statue of St. Stephen in the right transept. The rest will follow. Before you can be taken across the frontier you will spend a few days—I cannot tell you how long—in a safe place. At that place you will meet several people who will be waiting, like yourself, for transport across the frontier. Among these people there is a woman on whom you will focus your entire attention. Before your departure you will write out a detailed report for me about that woman. Is this all clear?"

"Not entirely, Father," I replied. "An unknown place . . . a strange woman . . . a report . . . A few precise details would be useful."

"First of all, my son, let's get you to safety," said the Father, now in a paternal tone. "You'll know the rest in good time."

"And yourself?" I asked, just to confirm my surmise that Father Zombory had invented the story of his escape merely for Piroska's benefit.

"My place is here," he said, putting his hand on my shoulder.

I made my way back to the city center on foot. The afternoon sun stood brilliant in the western sky. Soon, I thought to myself, dusk would fall. Dusk—when all outlines dissolve, when trees look like human beings, human beings like shadows, and shadows like trees; when solid things turn into silhouettes and silhouettes are piled up into mountains; when the remote distance suddenly towers up before us and near objects seem to slip out of reach; when everything loses shape and substance, and intermingles, and turns obscure and incomplete—the dusk which Father Zombory hated so much.

But did he really hate it?

12

〷〷〷〷〷〷〷〷〷〷〷

Enter Nora

WHEN I RECALL the week which I spent in Budapest after my visit to Father Zombory, people and events fade away before the figure of Nora Güldendag, and it almost seems as though I had never met them, or as though the events had never taken place; as though, in fact, they were no more than shadows behind the woman who was to be of such decisive importance in my life. Memory is unfair: it colors events in accordance with their outcome and it measures people with a yardstick which at the time of our meeting them did not yet exist. But as my personal interests are not necessarily identical with those of the reader, who is entitled to expect at least some measure of completeness in this account, I propose to continue with my chronicle up to my meeting with Nora Güldendag. After that, I fear, my story is bound to get somewhat out of perspective anyway.

On returning from the monastery in a pensive frame of mind I found my old friend Comrade Horvát, waiting for me at the Hotel Astoria, to be fully informed about the circumstances and outcome of my interview.

The agent's unexpected visit suited me very well. Indeed, I do not know how I should have acted without Comrade Horvát's unwitting help. I had to get to work skillfully. I told Comrade Horvát that I would make my escape with Father Zombory's help in the very near future, possibly within the next twenty-four hours. No purpose, however—I added—would be served if he had me watched, since the suspicious priest had sworn not to stage his hocus-pocus unless he was certain there was no danger in it. Likewise, the cunning Father had not given me any details of my flight. I would get his instructions at the very last moment and it was very doubtful, therefore, whether I should be able to contact him, Horvát, or his employers in time. Thus, I explained, if I happened to be whisked out of the country without an opportunity of getting into touch with him, the best thing would be for the secret service to contact me in Vienna, where I would then, naturally, give them a full report on my escape, my helpers, and all geographical and personal details. In Vienna, moreover, I added realistically, still anxious to gain Comrade Horvát's confidence, I should expect to be paid the outstanding amount of my fee.

Although I was not then familiar with secret-service machinery, I knew enough to realize that my rustic-looking visitor was not authorized either to approve or to reject my plan, and that he would first have to climb the whole ladder of the secret bureaucracy. In the meantime, so I hoped, I should have vanished from the orbit of the Hungarian secret service. Finally, and above all, if my plan succeeded I could subsequently, in Vienna, supply to the Soviet secret service a report in which truth and fiction were blended entirely according to my own taste.

I left my hotel as soon as the agent had gone. I made sure I was not being followed, and at a quarter past eight entered the touchingly simple, almost rural-looking church in St. Christina Square.

I bought a candle and lit it in front of the statue of St. Stephen—
and immediately found myself in very holy company. An elderly
priest with a benign pink face approached me and inquired if I
wished to confess. I affirmed eagerly, convinced that the good man
was concerned not so much with the salvation of my soul as that of
my body. And indeed the question of speaking my confession into
his ear never arose. No sooner had I knelt down in the confessional
than the priest whispered to me to follow him to the presbytery in
a few minutes' time. In its coach-yard a gray taxi would be waiting
for me. This vehicle, which was not really a taxi, would take me to
a certain place where I should only have to say the word "Sanherib"
to whoever opened the door in order to be immediately admitted.
The priest made me repeat the word which, evidently to his surprise,
I did not find difficult to memorize, recognizing it as the name of
an Assyrian king of Biblical repute.

I may save myself the detailed account of my removal to a
Budapest convent, that of the Gray Sisters of the Sacred Heart,
which was situated on the outskirts of Budapest. The journey was
neither exciting nor exceptional. I would only record, for the sake
of accuracy, that I did not arrive at my destination till midnight
because the journey, operated as it was by invisible hands, involved
so many stops that even the most persistent pursuer must have long
given up the zig-zag chase as a bad job.

Advance notice must have been given of my arrival, for Mother
Martha, the Mother Superior, was still awake to receive me.

She was a quiet little woman, and only a very shrewd judge of
people—and perhaps not even he—could have guessed her exceptional character and history. Like the other members of her Order,
she did not wear the habit which an unthinking imagination associates with nuns, but a plain gray dress with a small, starched,
striped collar, and a minute white cap was perched on a luxuriant
head of hair. Indeed, a layman would have taken her not for a nun
but for a hospital nurse. Her age was difficult to guess, but was
probably no less than fifty and no more than sixty.

The Mother Superior received me in the poorly lit visitors' room
of the convent, an oblong room with walls papered in gray, its
spinsterish severity strangely relieved by a dark-red piano. She did
not catechize me about myself or my plans—in fact she did not

even ask a casual question—but proceeded straightaway to inform me, in the manner of a friendly boarding-house keeper, about the other "guests"—she actually used that term—whom I would meet in the morning, and about the domestic routine, the times of meals and their rather modest nature. With an almost roguish smile, which betrayed her sense of humor, she warned me of my room-mate, a certain Count Dezsefalvy, whose manners she described as "boorish." I should be wise, she thought, to pass over in silence and without taking offense his frequently insulting remarks. With the other two male guests, Brother Francis and Mr. Vass, I should no doubt get on well, especially if I could see my way to playing an occasional game of chess with Mr. Vass, or to listening patiently to the friar's musical exercises. It would depend on the length of my stay—which she herself did not know—whether I would meet Nora Güldendag, a lady of whom Mother Martha had nothing special to report, apart from the fact that she was ill in bed, and unlikely to leave her room during the next few days.

The next morning, roused from sleep by the convent gong at six o'clock, I had my first sample of the Count's rough manners. During the night, luckily, he had not heard me come in—but that only made him the more indignant, on finding the second bunk of the truly ascetic room, no more than a pace away from him, occupied by another man. The Count was about sixty, bear-like in manner but in appearance more like a bird of prey, like a vulture that has spent a long time looking in vain for carrion. This impression was heightened by his thin, reddish neck which, during the day, seemed to lose itself in a high starched collar. I was presently to discover that being addressed by the Count at all was an exceptional honor; this had clearly been due to his surprise and was not to recur. The Count, clad in checked knickerbockers and an old, rather short, jacket, spent his time wandering, taciturn, through the cool rooms of the convent: now and again he would sulkily inspect the kitchen or, talking only to himself, he would burst into angry denunciations, not only of the new rulers but also of his friends, who were being damnably slow about delivering him from his undignified situation.

While I could never penetrate the haughtiness with which the Count surrounded himself, I made friends very quickly with Mother

Martha's second guest, Paul Vass. He was a man of colossal physique, clearly of peasant origin. His full mane was yellow rather
than white, just as his bushy mustache suggested that it had been
fair not so long before. His short, broad fingers were always slightly
bent and splayed out, as though a lifetime's calluses prevented
them from being closed together. He invariably wore a brilliant
white shirt without a tie, black boots up to the knees, and the black
suit worn by Hungarian peasants on Sundays. Yet Paul Vass was a
man of remarkable education: he quoted Goethe and Baudelaire,
his favorite poets, in the original languages, and in our night-long
conversations he referred to Hegel, Fichte, and Kant.

The Count, the peasant leader, the impostor—this strange trio
was made into a foursome by Brother Francis, whom the Mother
Superior had briefly mentioned on the previous evening. He was a
little man, with short thin legs, countless anxious furrows on his
forehead, and fine, translucent ears, conveying the general impression of a sad dachshund—an impression which belies all
theories of physiognomy, as I have rarely known a more cheerful
person than the Franciscan. That his cheerful nature was not always
manifested in the most agreeable form was hardly his fault: he just
happened to play the piano with far more ambition and courage
than skill, and he was no doubt firmly convinced that his musical
performances helped to relieve our boredom. The rest of us were,
to a greater or lesser extent, seriously worried about our futures—
but not the little monk. He differed from us also in that he kept
strict silence about his past life and his present troubles. Nevertheless, it came to my ears that this was not the first time, or even the
second time, that the Franciscan friar had found asylum in the
convent, both *en route* out of and into Budapest, so that I was
probably not far out in concluding that Brother Francis was one of
the travelling agents, or couriers, of the Holy See.

The first forty-eight hours of my stay at the convent of the
Gray Sisters passed without any noteworthy incidents—apart from
the letter which was handed to me by a nun on the first morning
after my arrival, and whose contents, though not surprising, rather
alarmed me.

The very circumstances surrounding the delivery of Father
Zombory's letter were exceedingly strange. The chubby-faced and,

in a rustic sort of way, pretty young nun who handed me the letter
asked me to read it carefully: she had been instructed by the writer,
she added, to take charge of the letter again, once I had read it. In
his short letter, phrased almost in the form of an order, Father
Zombory instructed me to devote my undivided attention to a certain Nora Güldendag who was, like myself, staying at the convent
of the Gray Sisters, pending transportation to the West. She was
under serious suspicion of being employed by Soviet Intelligence, a
suspicion which Mother Martha refused to acknowledge. He, Father
Zombory, had yielded to Mother Martha's insistence and had agreed
to convey Nora Güldendag across the frontier, but it would be my
task, so far as was in my power, to keep an eye on her and, in particular, to ascertain whether she maintained, or tried to establish,
contact with the outside world. Likewise on the forthcoming "journey"—as the Father put it—I was not to let her out of my sight.
If, and when, I had anything suspicious to report, I was to take the
bearer of this letter, Sister Giselle, and her alone, into my confidence.

   Forty-eight hours, as I have said, passed before I laid eyes on
Nora Güldendag, and whenever I caught sight of the chubby-faced
Sister, who seemed to seize every opportunity to hover around me, I
felt tempted to send a brief message to Father Zombory about the
Swedish woman's not entirely unsuspicious illness. I do not know
why I failed to do so—except, perhaps, out of respect for Mother
Martha, about whom I learned a great deal more in those two days
—mainly from Paul Vass—than the Mother Superior, ever anxious
to prevent the conversation from turning upon herself, would have
thought proper.

   When we all assembled in the visitors' room in the evening—
the Count, the peasant leader, the Franciscan monk, and myself—
I was forcibly reminded of those convalescent homes or water-cure
places which look back on a century-old tradition in my native
country. We sat in wicker arm-chairs, on the gray walls hung three
cheap oleographs representing saints, as well as a crucifix, the center
of the room was occupied by an oval table covered with dark-red
velvet embroidered with wool, and by the window stood that in-
congruous wine-red piano which provided the monk with his musical ecstasies.

Late at night we talked to each other, not about our physical ailments, like the inmates of a home, but about our personal troubles, and very soon the conversation turned to the sisters ministering to our needs and in particular to Mother Martha, just as if they were the nursing staff of the establishment and she its medical superintendent.

It was thus that I learned that in the time between the wars, when Hungary had been ruled by a dictatorship mitigated by *joie de vivre* and corruption, the little Mother Superior had been elected a Member of Parliament—the only female member of a religious Order—where she had soon made herself unpopular, both with the easy-going circles of the Right and the oppressed Liberals, by her ultra-clerical views and super-conservative speeches. During the Second World War, when the Arrow Cross movement—an imitation of the Nazis—came to power and threw open Hungary's frontiers to the German troops, everybody expected that the radical nun, who had in the past made many an unfriendly reference to the wealthy Jews of Hungary, would readily join them. But how little did they understand Mother Martha's character! Not only did she organize the Catholic Resistance—riding her bicycle all over the country, preaching, agitating, and conspiring—but she actually took it into her head to save the Hungarian Jews from extermination. Hundreds of persecuted found asylum in her convent in the course of the years; she prevailed upon a Swedish diplomat to make out false passports for the unfortunates; and those refugees who succeeded in getting across the frontier brought with them the story of the little woman who, pistol in hand, had faced the S.S. men trying to enter her convent and forced the bewildered invaders to retire. But this was not the last surprise. When the Russians laid siege to Budapest and occupied a convent on the right bank of the Danube, which belonged to the Mother Superior's Order, the little woman rowed herself across the river, between the enemy lines and through the artillery fire that was bursting over the river from both sides; she demanded to see the Russian commander and got him to release her charges. Such deeds could not remain unknown. A popular legend sprang up around them, and when the capital was at last liberated from the National-Socialist terror the new Premier's first call was on the Mother Superior of the convent of the Gray

Sisters of the Sacred Heart. Mother Martha was offered a ministerial post, which she promptly declined. She did not trust the peace that had come upon the bayonets of the Soviet troops.

When someone who is disrespectful by nature suddenly experiences respect, then it will be of double measure—and it was probably my admiration for this exceptional woman that restrained me, throughout two days, from calling upon Sister Giselle's services as a messenger. But on the third day—to be perfectly frank—I should undoubtedly have performed my sorry duty, even if only for the sake of self-preservation, if an event had not taken place which put me out of reach of that temptation for all time: I made Nora Güldendag's acquaintance.

It was early afternoon, I had taken a stroll in the convent garden with Mother Martha, who seemed to have singled me out for her special affection from the start. Mother Martha had been called away and I slowly returned to the visitors' room, which was reached from the garden by a few steps. The Count was again sitting in one of the wicker nursing-home chairs, reading his old paper. The peasant leader was engrossed in a game of chess with himself. The monk was torturing the wine-red piano. But leaning against the piano, almost as if she really enjoyed the pitiful rendering of a Bach cantata, was a tall, slim woman.

Nora Güldendag wore a simple gray dress with a white collar, so that for a moment I thought she must be one of the Sisters of the Sacred Heart. But as soon as she advanced towards me with a friendly smile and extended hand I realized my mistake. The first thing I noticed was her small, regular, brilliantly white teeth. Next I saw her soft brown eyes, her silky light-brown hair, her high cheekbones, and her small, almost imperceptibly upward-tilted nose. After that I became aware of her walk. She was rather tall for a woman and came almost up to my forehead. As her well-shaped hands and her feet were likewise on the big side, she seemed to be trying to cover up her tallness—and this lent her walk and gestures a pathetic awkwardness, almost a bashful, maidenly touch. Altogether, if I may be forgiven the overworked and abused word, there was a "chastity" about Nora Güldendag which captivated me completely and which I can only now begin to explain. She seemed chaste because she concealed everything that was beautiful about herself, instead of, as is more normal with women, emphasizing it. She seemed to feel ashamed of her fine figure, her winning smile, and even her warm eyes. What she could not conceal or cover up was her voice, and, indeed, I often used to ask myself—indulging in that favorite pastime of lovers—what it was that had first made me her slave, whether my eyes or my ears had first responded to her, whether in fact it had been a case of love at first sight or love at first hearing. I cannot, as is customary, liken her voice to music for it was not a musical voice and did not flatter the ear alone. In fact, I am beginning to wonder whether I was right in speaking of an acoustic sensation at all. There was something corporeal in Nora's voice, it was there to touch, velvet-soft, like a delicate white skin, and equally exciting. It did not hang in the air like a musical note but rather like a light-footed ballerina.

I am aware that this description of Nora Güldendag is bound to confuse the reader, and will perhaps even fill him with anger and irony. I may as well warn him, here and now, that I shall have to cause him this annoyance many more times—every time, presumably, when reference is made to Nora Güldendag. The story of my love does not, as it does, perhaps, with other people, fit harmoniously into the story of my life: indeed the story of my life is likely to make that of my love seen implausible, just as the story of my love must cast doubts on the story of my life. If only I were a novelist—as I often wish I were—and entitled to invent and suppress characters, I should never allow the path of my hero George Droste to cross that of the woman Nora Güldendag—because from the moment of their meeting I should no longer be able to make my hero act true to character and display that consistency which, unfortunately, the reading public seems to demand. My heart is trying to hold fast to reason. It fails in the attempt and—like the clown who chases after the circus horse, clutching at its tail, and eventually tumbles into the sand in the ring—the result is a clumsy stammering. And, like the clumsiness of the clown, it may well cause nothing but laughter. Too soon, at the very moment of introducing Nora, I have forgotten my part: the cynic has turned sentimental, the philosopher has turned foolish, and the man of experience has turned childish.

But just because this chapter is about Nora Güldendag, I cannot resort to those tricks of the trade which, in putting down my recollections, I am beginning to learn. I suppose I ought to disclose only gradually, and after piling up suspense, whether Nora Güldendag was in fact a Soviet spy, as Father Zombory supposed, and what reasons she had for coming to Budapest. But I cannot build up or sustain an atmosphere of tension at Nora's expense. Permit me, therefore, to reveal straight away that she was no spy, neither in Western nor in Eastern service. And although I prefer to tell her story later, as it was gradually unfolded to me, I may as well say now that in my report to Father Zombory, compiled four days after meeting Nora, and entrusted to the ever-hovering Sister Giselle, I listed a good deal of compelling proof for Nora's innocence, although in fact I possessed no such proof.

During our flight together I did indeed not let her out of my sight—but not by any means because I was conscientiously fulfilling the Father's orders. Just as, from the moment of meeting the Chief of the Hungarian secret service, I had resolved to deceive the Eastern secret service, so I was now setting out, though for entirely different motives, to deceive one of the secret services of the West. If ever there was an ironical fate then, surely, it was mine. My existence of one perpetual lie began with a white lie: for the sake of a woman I began to lie, and she was to be the only one never to forgive me my lies.

13

〰〰〰〰〰〰〰

Danger at Dawn

WE WERE all in the convent garden, with the exception of the Count who, as a former big landowner, disliked all contact with nature, when Mother Martha appeared and in a calm, matter-of-fact manner invited us to get our things together and get ready for the trip. She allowed us twenty minutes for this operation and I noticed that Sister Giselle, who was bustling around us with excessive helpfulness, did not let any of us out of her sight even for a moment.

In the convent yard a medium-sized delivery truck was drawn up, the white letters on its side spelling out *Hungaria Mosoda. Mosoda,* as I was told, meant laundry, or dry cleaners. We said a hurried good-bye to the good Sisters and settled down in the empty van, needless to say on the floor, but not without a few very outspoken remarks by Count Dezsefalvy about the discomforts of our accommodation.

It was dark in the truck; only through a minute window in the back of the driver's cab did a narrow strip of light penetrate inside the fast-moving vehicle. There were five of us: Nora, the monk, the Count, the peasant leader, and myself. What bound us together was fear, but as there were five of us this fear took five different forms. The merry Brother Francis had become quiet. I heard him muttering and assumed he was saying his prayers. The taciturn Count was talking incessantly. It was as if, after treating us so haughtily at the convent, he was now courting our favor—as if our favor could have helped him. Perhaps he regarded Vass, the peasant leader, as the strongest of us, for he was continually asking him pointless questions.

We had driven like this for no more than half an hour when the vehicle halted.

During a flight, which is all movement, stopping is unbearable. We looked at one another, without being able to see each other properly, and no one dared to speak. I was sitting next to Nora, my knees drawn up, and my hand, seeking for support on the floorboards, touched her hand. She did not draw it away, indeed, it seemed to me that her hand, like a frightened bird, was tremblingly seeking shelter under mine. Why did I experience in the presence of this woman a sense of shame—a sensation quite alien to me? My hand did not shake, and that was why I felt ashamed. The woman by my side was bound to assume that I was full of calm and assurance, whereas, in fact, as a double agent, I was the only person in the dark vehicle who had hardly anything to fear from discovery.

From outside came the disputing voices of two men, and we all thought our truck had been stopped by a police patrol and the driver was trying to convince the police of the innocent nature of his cargo.

The Count's nerves gave way. He asked: "Why don't they let us out?"

Vass quickly clapped his big peasant's hand over the Count's mouth.

At last the double door at the back of the van was opened. The rays of the afternoon sun fell into our darkness.

"You must change here," said the driver in broken German. "I got you out of the city, but in the country my laundry-truck would attract attention."

As we got out we immediately noticed another vehicle waiting for us—an open truck of somewhat rustic appearance. We were in a farmyard. There was a homely smell of dung. Two young peasants were trying to pull a horse out of a liquid manure pit. A dog was lying in the sun yawning. Nothing could be more reassuring than this picture of undisturbed everyday life.

We climbed up on the truck. It was loaded half-way up with hay, in which sat two peasants and a peasant woman. I don't know whether my fellow escapees had enough leisure to notice how this well-functioning operation had evidently been carefully planned, down to the minutest detail, by the powers in whose hands we were; but I observed how the three people silently intermingled with us, so that we no longer represented a conspicuous townish group to anybody happening to walk or drive past us. Brother Francis was covered up with hay, so that only his small shrivelled head peeped out, and his cowl was not visible. Just as the Count had been, a little while before, so the monk was now the most embarrassing fellow escapee—and since it is only pious talk that danger makes for unity, we should no doubt all have been happier if the monk had been conducted across the perilous frontier without us.

A young peasant of comfortingly indifferent appearance at last climbed into the driver's seat and the truck, which must have been scrapped as unroadworthy even before the war, moved off with a little cough.

Towns through which the war has passed need years to find peace again, but the countryside, where peace is at home, recovers it instantly. From time to time Russian army vehicles raced past us; twice we saw a clanking military train carrying tanks; in a few villages there was clear evidence of billeting—but nobody seemed to care about our old truck. The Russian soldiers, those terrifying Ivans of the big towns, were here for the most part sitting on horse-drawn carts, or driving a cow in front of them, or sitting by the door of farmhouses smoking their pipes. Looking into their faces, one had the impression that all they wanted was a piece of their native Russian countryside.

"Why didn't one ever think of living like this?" said Nora.

"Shall we still think of it tomorrow?" I asked.

"Perhaps not," she said softly. "But it's a pity to forget it. One doesn't realize till too late how simple everything could be. . . ."

"One ought to be afraid more often," I said.

The Count was all the time watching the monk, who had made a slight movement and lost a little of his hay, so that his brown habit was now a trifle more visible.

"For God's sake, stay in that hay," the Count exploded at the monk. "As it is, the Russians looked at us most suspiciously in the last village." He turned to Vass. "Do you suppose they have telephones in these villages?"

"They didn't take any notice of us," said Vass. But he too was watching every farmstead we passed. "One could hide out in any one of these houses," he said suddenly.

The idea was infectious. We scrutinized each farmhouse as it fell back behind us, and every one of us seemed to be asking himself for how long one could find asylum there.

Gradually darkness descended upon the scenery. In the light of the dying sun the dust looked like blue glass.

"Why doesn't the driver put his lights on?" asked the Count. "They'll stop us yet for some silly trifle. What do you think, Mr. Vass?"

"He probably knows what he's doing," replied Vass.

"They're sure to stop all vehicles at night," said the Count. He was making pessimistic remarks in the hope of hearing them optimistically refuted.

The two peasants and the peasant woman said nothing. One of the men passed round a piece of bread and cured bacon. We were grateful for the matter-of-factness of the gesture.

At last the driver switched on two weak lights. At the same time the vehicle left the main road just outside a small village and turned down a narrow lane. It jolted over the hardened mud, churned up during the last rain.

Abruptly the vehicle stopped. None of us dared make a move. At last a voice called out:

"*Kiszálni!*"

We climbed out.

In the beam of the headlights—which hardly deserved this name, being little brighter than carbide lamps—we saw an apparition. Apparition is the only word—for the man in the dim light was as unreal as a specter. He was a young priest who seemed to have sprung up in front of our truck from nowhere. He wore a billowing black cloak, and in his hand, like the shepherds in the Bible, he carried a plain, rough-carved staff.

The two peasants and the woman who had been our escort greeted him with "Praise be to Jesus Christ," and he answered "Praise be to Him!" Then they walked past him and the darkness swallowed them up for good.

"Follow me!" said the young priest. He was, as I was told later, the son of a peasant from Burgenland, the part of Austria adjoining Hungary, and spoke German more fluently than Hungarian.

We had left the truck behind. We walked along in twos. I held out my hand to Nora. She took it and did not let go of it again.

We first crossed a wood, and then followed a narrow path through what seemed to be a boundless field of maize. The priest walked ahead with a sure step. Now and again farmhouses, peasant cottages, and small thatched shacks appeared on either side behind the tall ears of maize. Our guide gave them a wide berth. Friendly oil lamps were burning in the tiny windows of these houses, and the care with which the priest avoided them was doubly disquieting. On the horizon a half-moon rose slowly. Out here in the Hungarian plain the moon did not suddenly appear in the sky, like the sun it slowly climbed up from the ground—not, however, as the sun promising a new day, but menacing and eerie, like a handle-less sickle.

Sharply our guide altered course: he was now making straight for a farmhouse. He stopped outside and called out loudly:

"Pista bácsi!"

An old man carrying a hurricane lamp came out of the house. The two talked softly in Hungarian; then the peasant invited us to step in.

The family—the old man, his son, his daughter-in-law, and the couple's three grown-up sons—were having their meal. A big bowl with soup and potatoes stood in the center of the table; everybody had only a spoon which they used to eat out of the common bowl.

"We are two kilometers from the frontier," said the priest with a smile. A radiant calmness shone from his young, sun-tanned face. He pointed to one of the three lads at the table. "Károly will get you across the frontier. You'll start out towards three in the morning. I must ask you to obey Károly's instructions most carefully. Now I should advise you to lie down and try to get some sleep. You will be called in good time."

We nodded our agreement. Only the Count, feeling that safety now lay no longer with Vass but with the priest, said,

"But surely you are staying with us, Father?"

Everybody laughed.

"You are in good hands," the priest said indulgently.

He took the lantern and led the way across the yard into a barn. In the barn he put the lantern down on the floor.

"Put it out, please, as soon as you have more or less settled down," he said. "No need for a light to show from the barn."

We made ourselves comfortable in the stacked hay while the priest left us. Only the Count remained standing by the lantern.

"I'll put it out," he said.

Without waiting for our consent he blew it out.

I had settled down in the hay next to Nora Güldendag.

"Are you comfortable?" I asked softly.

"Yes," she said, quite close.

"Try and get some sleep," I said. "You will need it."

But we knew we would not get any sleep. Directly above the corner where Nora and I had settled down was a small window in the thin wall of the barn. A beam of moonlight came through it.

"Let's change places," I said. "The moon is shining into your eyes."

We got up. She took my place and I took hers.

"Thank you," she said softly.

She was not sitting upright, but neither was she lying down. It seemed to me that she chose this uncomfortable position because she thought it improper to lie down in the hay with a man.

"Have you no blanket?" I asked.

"I have a shawl," she said, "but I am not cold."

"But you will be," I said. "After the moon has set and before the sun rises is always the coldest time."

"You talk like a boy scout," she laughed softly.

I stood up and opened her small suitcase. In the light of the moon I immediately found her black knitted shawl. I spread it over her.

For a while there was silence. Then the monk, the only one to have found sleep, began to snore. Silence was as infectious as fear. It was a good thing he snored.

The Count, who was sitting upright next to the peasant leader, said, "You don't think they'll forget about us?"

I had deliberately moved away a little from Nora. I lay down on my back and stretched out my arm. I could not reach her with my arm stretched out. But, I reflected, if she, too, were to stretch out an arm our fingertips would touch.

She was now lying on her back. She extended her arm toward me. Our fingertips touched.

I said, "Are you superstitious?"

"No," she said.

"You are not afraid to make plans?"

"I've long given up making plans," she said.

"I was going to ask you," I said, "where you'll stay in Vienna."

"We are not yet across the frontier," she said.

"So you're superstitious after all!"

"I shall stay with a friend," she said. "A Countess Tydings. On the Ballaria."

"May I call you up some time?" I asked.

"Now you are making plans," she said.

We pretended that our fingertips had met by accident. But we did not move for fear our hands might part and chance might not lead them together again. Our hands no longer belonged to us. They were like two beings in love, facing one another hesitantly, uncertain whether to turn away from each other or come closer together. We waited for what our hands would do.

"The poor Count," whispered Nora. "He is so afraid."

"And you?" I asked.

"I don't know," she said.

"You ought to be afraid," I said.

"Why?"

"If one is fond of life one is afraid to lose it."

She made no reply but her hand crept a little nearer to mine. Immediately my hand advanced toward hers. Three of my fingers were now lying on three of hers. Not only had my hand cut itself off from my body, but every finger had made itself independent of my hand. Three beings in love were uniting with three other beings in love.

"Please be quiet now," we heard Vass' voice trying to reassure the Count. "Try to get some sleep."

"Herr Droste isn't sleeping either," said the Count. "He is still whispering."

"Follow Brother Francis' example," said Vass.

As if trying to live up to his role, Brother Francis snored even louder than before.

"I am whispering," I said softly to Nora, "because I don't want to disturb the others. But I think I should be whispering even if we were alone."

She made no reply, but I could feel she was turning her head towards me. I too turned towards her. I felt as if her head rested on my arm. I was careful not to move my hand. It occurred to me that I had held her hand all the way to the farmhouse. But at that time our hands had still belonged to our bodies.

"Now the moon is shining into your eyes," she said. "You can't go to sleep like this."

"I shall sleep in Vienna tomorrow," I said.

"You are not afraid either," she said. It almost sounded as if we shared a secret.

After a while she said, "I am glad you came to the convent. I am being selfish. I should have been afraid on my own."

"I am glad about everything that's happened," I said.

Love and fear had wrestled with each other, now, as once before during this escape, both were overshadowed by shame. This proud, pure woman was turning to me for security—to me, the most insecurely drifting of the lot, the spy who had entered the convent on false pretenses, who participated in this flight as a bogus escape, and whose very fear was a sham.

We did not talk any more. She closed her eyes, as if sleeping. But she was not asleep. From time to time she opened her eyes and I hurriedly shut mine. I do not know how long we played this game.

The moon had set. Nora straightened up.

"Now you are cold," I said.

"It'll soon be dawn," she said. "Always the coldest time . . ." She laughed softly.

From outside came the sound of hard steps.

"Get ready to start off!" called the young peasant lad, entering the barn.

We were on our feet at once. He closed the door.

"We must go in two parties," he said in German. "I shall lead one party and my brother the other. Three of you will come with me, the remaining two will go with my brother. Those with me take the shorter but the more difficult route. The lady and Brother Francis had better go with my brother."

Nora and I exchanged glances in the darkness.

"I would rather go with you." She turned to Károly.

Everybody was looking at her.

"It's the more difficult route," repeated the peasant.

"I'll be glad to go with your brother," the Count spoke up.

"Very well then," said our guide. "In that case you"—he pointed to Nora—"and you two"—he pointed to Vass and myself —"come with me. Brother Francis, you'll stay here with the other gentleman. My brother will come to collect you in ten minutes. What I'm going to say now applies to all of you. Don't take a single step without my brother or me. There are mines and signal rockets under the barbed-wire barrier along the frontier. The barrier is eight meters deep. We shall take you to a point where the wire fence has been cut. When you have crawled through you will be on the other side. Get under the trees at once. Don't step out of the wood until a searchlight beam has just swept over you. The light comes from a watch-tower. It is manned by one of our people —but if he sees you he'll have to open fire all the same. The moment the searchlight beam has swept over you you will move on, going straight ahead. After about three minutes you will reach the Western sentry posts." He paused. "I am sorry, but you'll have to leave your luggage behind. Will somebody repeat what I have said?"

Vass repeated the peasant's instructions. A few minutes later we were on our way to the frontier.

We were advancing in single file: our guide, Vass, Nora, and I.

I said: "I would not have parted from you either. Only I did not dare to say so."

She did not turn.

Behind us, in the east, the sky was turning gray. I had to think of Father Zombory. How had he put it? "The Devil knows that all evil is done at dusk and at dawn, in the twilight and in the gloaming." In the day-time the forest held no terror; and even at night there was no terror in it. But it was full of terror in the pale twilight of dawn. Anything that resembles human beings is frightening, I thought. The trees are frightening because they now look like human beings. I recoiled from the trees which had suddenly got between Nora and myself. The boulders in the forest were like kneeling women, mourning, with gray shawls over their heads. The sentries up on the watch-towers, it occurred to me, did not know that George Droste was a spy for both sides.

Our guide halted.

"I shall be back here again in ten minutes," he said. "I must make sure that the watch-tower is manned by one of our people."

We were halted again, and in our stationary condition the dangers again seemed to multiply. Time, too, multiplied. Our frontiersman, who had promised to be back in no more than ten minutes, had not returned even when twenty minutes were gone —and it is impossible to convey quite how long those twenty minutes seemed to last.

"Do you suppose they've caught him?" asked Vass.

"If he doesn't return, shall we find our way back?" asked Nora.

"He told us not to budge," I objected.

"It must take him a while to make sure that his people are on sentry duty," whispered Vass. He was comforting us and himself.

"It's getting lighter," I said.

"But it's still too dark to see anything," said Nora.

"We ought not to talk," I said.

A fresh morning breeze swept through the forest, carrying with it inarticulate sounds. The rustle of the leaves sounded like human voices.

Somewhere a dog barked.

"Bloodhounds," said Vass.

"Some farm dog or other," I said, trying to comfort my companions and myself.

At the same instant our guide appeared.

"Quick!" he commanded.

At the woods' edge we were suddenly facing a high barbed-wire fence which we had not seen before. We had had no idea we were so near the frontier.

"Down on your stomachs!" whispered our guide. "As soon as you've crawled through the hole run over to those trees. Directly ahead, in a straight line. These are mines to the right and left. You know the rest."

Now we noticed that the tall fence had been cut at its lowest point. A semicircular opening had been made, like a mousetrap.

Vass was the first to crawl through the hole. Then came Nora. She was the slimmest of us and was through in no time. She hesitated before getting up and running forward. I hurriedly pressed our guide's hand. Then I too forced my way through the barrier.

The moment I reached the wood on the other side the beam of a searchlight swept over the fields. In the gray dawn the beam seemed like a wan shaft of sunlight.

"Now!" I said, and took Nora's hand. Our hands intertwined as if they had known each other for a lifetime.

Three minutes later, having advanced in a straight line, we ran into the first Western sentries.

14

An Offer from Mr. Smith

MY FIRST few days back in my native city were devoted to the drafting of my reports for the American and the Soviet secret services. Both of them had honored me with their unflagging attention: Mr. Smith rang up as soon as I was back and summoned me to his office—a circumstance I regarded as a sign of his confidence—and Herr Müller turned up at my flat within twenty-four hours and urged me to complete the account of my escape as quickly as possible.

To draft an Intelligence report which is a complete fabrication in many particulars, and totally misleading as a whole, is not a very difficult task, provided certain psychological and political facts are remembered. And I can think of no better way of inflicting damage upon the secret services than by enlightening my readers—among whom there may well be some would-be spies—about the methods to be followed.

The young man intending to choose the career of an agent without wishing to expose himself to dangers which—let him be quite clear about this—would not help his advancement in the least, ought to realize first of all that the principal purpose of all secret services is to confirm the mighty in those intentions which they are in any case determined, for political, military, or personal reasons, to pursue. The agent who deludes himself that he can influence the course of political events or of military operations by his reports is a vain fool; an Intelligence chief who believes he can turn the wheel of history is a suicidal lunatic. A person enrolling as an agent accepts the post of flunkey: to contradict his employer, or to presume to lecture him, is to risk his job. The simple fact that the State pays for the secret service and not the other way round ought to be sufficient to stop an agent from sending in reports which might be felt to be awkward by his superiors. If over many years I have succeeded in serving my bosses to their complete satisfaction by reports which were frequently pieces of imaginative fiction, then this was due solely to my early realization that governments, as a rule, do not wish to learn anything new from their secret services, but finance them merely so as to get from them confirmation of the correctness of their own decisions. The successful agent must have a sure instinct, political acumen, and a quick brain—not as the layman may think, in order to discover the opponents' intentions, but to discover the intentions of his employers in good time. Whenever politicians propose to adopt some new policy or other, and whenever strategists work out some new plan of action, they invariably refer to Intelligence reports by way of justification. It would therefore be a poor secret service that could not, at such a moment, come forward with convincing evidence in support of any proposed line of action.

At the time of my own employment as an agent, for instance, the West was anxious to find the aggressive intentions of the East confirmed by its secret services; the East, at the same time, wanted evidence of the warlike preparations of the West. I should have been regarded as an idiot, or maybe even a traitor, if my reports had contradicted these preconceived ideas.

All this is not to say that Intelligence is of no importance or has little influence—after all, the High and Mighty are invariably dependent on their flunkeys. Statesmen, politicians, and generals know very well why they want to make sure of the maximum possible influence upon their secret service—but they desire this influence not in order to be more accurately informed, but because it is up to the secret service which piece of evidence it supplies out of the multitude of information at its disposal, and whether it supplies it rapidly or reluctantly, convincingly or in an implausible form. Just before some international conference, for instance, the secret service of country A will have received a number of reports suggesting a stiffening in the attitude of country B; needless to say, it will also have a number of equally unauthentic reports predicting a more conciliatory attitude on the part of country B. It is for the Intelligence chief and his advisers to decide whether to serve the aggressive or the conciliatory trends in their country, which reports to submit, and which to dismiss as irrelevant, to which persons their files shall be opened, and to whom they shall remain closed. Thus, while most of my colleagues were hard at work to ferret out the enemy's intentions, I confined myself from the start to watching the lips of those on whose word I depended. Secret-service work favors the opportunist—which is why Mr. Smith was not far off the mark when he once commended me as "a born agent."

Another important point in the drafting of espionage reports is to remember the international *ésprit de corps* which characterizes the secret services. A young agent who has just completed a journey from X to Y in enemy territory, without incident, and has, as a result, collected some more-or-less useful information, would do himself and his employers a poor service if in a fit of youthful enthusiasm he were to speak truthfully of the enemy's inadequate security measures, which enabled him to collect such information. After all, when a boxer has won a fight his manager does not go about announcing that the victory had been easy and practically a walk-over—on the contrary, he will crack up the experience and skill of the vanquished in order to magnify the importance of his man's victory. Similarly, the managers of secret services have no incentive to present their opposite numbers as stupid amateurs; they have, in fact, every reason to emphasize the abilities of their opponents. All this, my dear young spies-to-be, is particularly true today, when the secret services have long lost their original purpose. Nowadays they deal not with any guileless individuals on the enemy side, but almost exclusively with professional enemy agents, so that we may properly speak of boxing matches within the same weight-class.

In the course of my career I have met many an unhappy agent who never suspected that the only reason why he had got stuck on his low rung, or even been dropped a rung or two, was that he had discharged his tasks—though successfully—much too quickly, too simply, and too easily. One cannot, of course, expect the directors of Intelligence services to encourage their agents

openly to invent highly romantic reports and to glorify the rival
service: an agent who lacks the tact to understand these unspoken
wishes of his employers is a poor servant and deserves to remain a
proletarian among spies for the rest of his life.

My tact, congenital to me, just as my opportunism, told me
from the start that the secret services were chivalrous organizations
which did not belittle the other side behind their back but—on
the contrary—spoke highly of them. If I always gave much space in
my reports to the perils I had faced, to my own shrewdness and
bravado, as well as to the gallantry and subtlety of my opponents,
then this was done not for self-aggrandizement but in the clearly-
perceived interests of my employers, who were thus enabled to make
an impressive show with my reports in the very highest quarters. For
this reason I also avoided, right from my first reports, to present
my findings as final—much as a victorious boxer must think of his
next purse and, immediately after the knock-out, begins to consider
the possibilities of a profitable return match. A good agent must
know that the secret services are perpetually in financial difficulties
—for it is nowhere easy to fit them into the official budget—and
that it is up to the spy, an agent, also, in the commercial meaning of the term, to present his firm's past business to taxpayers and
their representatives in a way that will induce them to invest further
capital.

This little manual for the drafting of totally fabricated, or at
least highly colored, Intelligence reports would not be anything
like complete if I failed to add one further point. Human trustfulness—you may take it from me—is every bit as boundless as human
distrust. Anybody building up on trustfulness or distrust must act
like a wise husbandman who bears in mind not only the quality
of his seed but also the nature of the soil where it is to be planted.
A seed of lies will yield the most splendid harvest provided the
soil in which it is planted is favorable: before uttering a lie or
committing it to paper it is therefore necessary to consider the soil
expertly and judge whether it will accept or reject it. If the secret
services received nothing but authentic information, well-substan-
tiated reports, and genuine secrets their archives could be housed
in the tiniest room. But, in fact, the secret services not only lend a
willing ear to liars like myself, but they even owe them a lasting

debt of gratitude, since lies alone can fill those vast steel safes which in turn are necessary to justify the secret-service budget. Thus, while most shamelessly lying to the secret services throughout the past eight years, I was at the same time contributing a not inconsiderable share to their existence. It is not therefore surprising that I met with an almost boundless trustfulness everywhere.

I might add the final point that an agent's report, while it does not have to be accurate in its subject matter, must be absolutely accurate in its detail. If, for instance, an agent reports that a certain foreign diplomat has revealed to him a secret in a slightly intoxicated condition at the Perroquet nightclub in the Boulevard Montparnasse in Paris, then that diplomat, as well as the agent, must have really been at the Perroquet on the night in question, the nightclub must really be situated on the Boulevard Montparnasse, and the diplomat must in fact have drunk more than one glass. Whether he did tell the agent a secret, or anything at all, is irrelevant.

Espionage, therefore, is not an indoor sport. An agent cannot sit at home: he must be acquainted with the places, the people, and the circumstances about which he reports—because it is this superficial knowledge that impresses his employers, and it is only through his ignorance of such unimportant, and hence easily checked, details that he can be unmasked as a fraud.

My natural bent for my new profession was clearly revealed in the two reports which I drafted during the first few days after my return to Vienna and which were the fruits, not of long experience, but—as it were—of my instinctive grasp of the problem.

The report for Mr. Smith did not cause me much of a headache. After all, Mr. Smith knew of my relationship with his Eastern opponents and I was therefore able to interlard my fiction with quite substantial doses of truth. I described in detail my impressions of Budapest, always anxious, of course, to paint Eastern poverty and discontent in the strong colors which please the American eye. I reported my conversations with Comrade Horvát and my interview with the Chief; however, I did not just casually mention the address of the secret-service villa, but I laid due emphasis on my ingenuity in establishing its location, which I moreover illustrated with a sketch plan. I revealed Little Red Riding Hood as the Soviet

agent she was, but allowed it to be understood that only my be-
witching charm had enabled me to make this discovery. On the
justifiable assumption that the activities of the Vatican secret service
were not unknown to the American Intelligence, I painted a faithful portrait of Father Zombory and Sister Martha, and concealed
no particular of the return route, which the Catholic underground
and my own skill had opened up for me.

In this wrapping of truths and half-truths I was entitled to hope
that my lies, too, would carry enough credence. Instead of betraying
the people who had smuggled me out of the Western Zone into
Hungary I concocted an account which, on the one hand, was con-
sonant with the romantic aura of Intelligence work and, on the
other, was designed to increase the respect felt for the enemy's—
i.e., in this case the Soviet—secret service. My report mentioned a
farmhouse with a trap-door, a blindfolded walk of several miles, a
forest which looked like any other forest, and, lastly, a beautiful
young peasant woman who lived on the Austrian side of the
frontier but spoke only Hungarian. Since I knew exactly how we
had been conducted out of the East into the West it was a reasonable
assumption that the drill was much the same in the opposite direction. I therefore listed a lot of details about my "escape" from the
West, but in such a way that all concrete data were missing. My
information was like the signposts that are often found in the
mountains, with perfectly clear arrows and precise distance in
kilometers, and it was impossible to prove that I had scattered
mine at random over the landscape and that they led nowhere.

Compiling the report for the Soviet secret service was far more
tricky, for Herr Müller's behavior confirmed what my logic had
warned me to expect—namely, that my rather hasty departure had
caused a certain amount of suspicion.

I described how, shortly after my last meeting with Comrade
Horvát, I had been addressed in the street by a priest, who had
taken me in a taxi to a convent. From there a black limousine had
conveyed me to a castle about fifty kilometers from Budapest, and
at that castle, which had no contact with the outside world, I had
met Count Dezsefalvy, Mr. Vass, and Brother Francis, and spent
a week with them. During that time—I rather liked this touch—
we had fed on U.S. Army rations. One night we had boarded a

vehicle which I had been able to identify as a Soviet army truck. This truck, I continued, had evidently been stolen by the American secret service because its driver could speak only English. We had been met, I stated in conclusion of my extensive report, by three Americans who had guided us through a forest, which looked like any other forest, to a point on the frontier where the barbed-wire fence had been considerably cut over a width of about four feet.

As will be seen from this brief summary—which, needless to say, does poor justice to the vividness of my imagination or the elegance of my style—I managed to mix a pretty potent cocktail of fact and fiction also for the Soviet Intelligence. There was no reason why I should have suppressed the names of my travel companions, who had all arrived safely in the West, indeed, the disclosure of their names was the only thing that could lend verisimilitude to an otherwise worthless account. My psychological subtlety was fully demonstrated in my description of the three fictitious American agents, as well as by my account of the imaginary conversations between the Count and the renegade peasant leader. The agents I described with much the same objectivity as is displayed in Soviet text-books, where Chicago gangsters are represented to the eager Soviet schoolchild as typical Americans. My imaginary conversations between the Count and the class traitor, on the other hand, fully supported the Marxist theory that all opponents of the Communist system are absolutely indistinguishable.

The fee which Herr Müller brought me a few days later showed that although I had gambled with the trust of the Soviet secret service I had not this time lost it.

It will at once be detected that, while listing in my report for the Soviet secret service the names of all my male fellow escapees, I had omitted to mention Nora Güldendag. This discretion was due not only to my feelings for Nora but also to my respect for her life, whose outlines were beginning to take shape before me.

Nora Güldendag was the wife of a Swedish diplomat—the same who had so bravely supported Mother Martha's work during the German occupation of Hungary. Nora, too, had at that time given every help to those in trouble, and had more than once

got into considerable difficulties as a result. A few days before the
Russians began their siege of Budapest, Nora's husband, Legation
Counsellor Gunnar Güldendag, had driven out into the country
to take some Swedish Red Cross food supplies to a group of his
protégés hiding in a monastery near Lake Balaton. From this daring trip the diplomat had failed to return. At first it was assumed
that at this twelfth hour he had fallen into the hands of the S.S.
divisions retreating towards Budapest and Vienna, but this theory
could no longer be upheld after the German surrender. Gunnar
Güldendag might, of course, have got mixed up with the fighting
lines and died a civilian hero's death—but for a number of good
reasons Nora had refused to accept this possibility. There remained therefore only one explanation: that the Russians, for
reasons unknown, had taken him prisoner and deported him. The
Swedish Government, the Red Cross, and a number of neutral
organizations at first took up Güldendag's case; but all was in vain
and Güldendag was still missing. However, it was not in Nora's
character to accept defeat without a fight. She stayed behind in
Budapest, first with the official support, then with the tacit approval, and finally against the express instructions, of her Government. She toured the country, at first with an official pass, but later
without the permission of the authorities; she intervened with the
Western missions, with the Hungarian authorities, and with the
Soviet military headquarters, and eventually made herself unpopular with all of them. Her travels through the dismembered
country, still bristling with arms, aroused the suspicions of the
secret services. The new masters of Hungary regarded her as a
Western agent; the Western Intelligence services, equally distrustful of a woman so resolutely taking her destiny into her own
hands, felt convinced that the Soviets had gained the Swedish
woman for themselves by threats or promises. Though reluctant
to give up the struggle, especially as she had discovered first one
and then another promising clue, Nora was eventually compelled
by circumstances to leave the inhospitable country—and since she
no longer possessed a passport and the authorities refused to give
her an exit permit, she decided to resort to Mother Martha's help.

    I have said that I omitted to mention Nora in my report to the
Soviet secret service not only for personal reasons but also because

of the respect which the story of her life had exacted from me. But there was a third motive for my exceptionally correct attitude. In Nora's company—I cannot put it otherwise—my conscience seemed to awaken, that strange being within us, that odd personality which we can never quite make out: at times almost like a Rip van Winkle, unroused by the most violent shaking and prodding, and at others so frantically active and ever alert.

Need I say that Nora had no suspicions of my true character, let alone about my Budapest mission? She believed me to be an honest businessman from Vienna, who had travelled to Hungary in the best faith and there, through no fault of his own, had got into trouble with the Soviet secret police. When I visited her in Vienna, at the flat of her friend, the Swedish Countess Tydings, the conversation, as was natural in the circumstances, drifted to spies and espionage, and Nora made some contemptuous and indeed angry remarks about the "snoopers and tale-bearers" who had "done more harm in the world than poison or the assassin's dagger could ever do." My conscience, when she was about, was not yet so roused as to make me reveal myself to her and share with her my secret, but it was no longer so soundly asleep that I could have made her one of my victims.

Besides, I must confess that after my first call at the house on the Ballaria, when admittedly we were alone for only a minute, I went home with a distinct sense of disappointment. The dead are perfect, little as they may have been so while alive; how much more difficult, then, to vie with one who, even in lifetime, must have been something like that legendary knight Bayard, the "chevalier sans peur et sans reproche!" During our escape, or perhaps even at the convent, I believed I had observed in Nora a germ of affection for me; but now my confidence gave way to the gloomy realization that I was not even a dead man's rival: his rival was the respectable Herr Droste who did not exist. When I walked out of the flat where Nora was staying I felt that George Droste was every bit as much a missing person as Gunnar Güldendag had been these past three years.

It is quite possible that my life would have taken an entirely different turn there and then, had it not been for an occurrence which gave my career a decisive twist and separated me from Nora for some time to come.

About ten days after my arrival in Vienna I was once more summoned by Mr. Smith to the hotel where, in very different circumstances indeed, I had first made his acquaintance.

"We'll come to the point at once," he said, offering me a cigarette. "What would you say to a trip to America?"

"America?" I said, scarcely mastering my amazement. "I should be less surprised if the idea had been put to me by the Russians."

"This isn't a mission," explained Mr. Smith, obviously enjoying himself. "At least, not in the usual sense. Would you be prepared to go to school for a few months?"

"You mean I am to attend a spy school?"

"That's rather too popular a term," said Mr. Smith, adjusting his rimless glasses, which still looked to me like two sharp monocles. "Still, call it what you like. But I see my proposal surprises you. Perhaps you think it improper that a man who has just successfully graduated from a university should be sent back to primary school. Am I correct?"

I did not dispute it.

"I have a dislike of amateurs and amateurishness, Herr Droste," he began again. "Too many people are doing things they don't know how to do, and before you know it you have a hierarchy of amateurism, with incapable people in turn employing incapable people. At the same time the amateurs are distinguished by especial zeal: they are enthusiastic about doing the things they don't know how to do. Hence the dynamism of the amateurs, and hence, also, their deceptive initial success."

"Are you referring to me, Mr. Smith?" I asked, with a smile.

"Guessed it in one," replied Mr. Smith, with courteous brutality. "I have studied your report; I have studied it with much care. It is the report of a dangerous, because highly gifted, amateur—which, by the way, is not a contradiction in terms. You didn't do badly in Budapest—not badly at all. You saw and seized your chance. But to seize one's chance is in itself amateurish: one must control chance. I have no wish to discourage you by demonstrating to you, point by point, the mistakes you made; or by proving to you that you allowed the very best opportunities to slip by and that you failed at the vital moment. I am not denying that you describe what you saw with a certain brilliance—but you did not see what you ought to have seen."

I sat there like a schoolboy who has the faults in his essay pointed out to him. I was not in the least surprised that Mr. Smith should have found certain gaps in my report: a lot of skill had gone into that report to make Mr. Smith regard as a beginner's mistakes what in fact were the subtleties of a swindler! Even so, I felt it necessary to object.

"Mr. Smith, I am quite convinced that I am an amateur—there's no need for you to prove it. But that doesn't mean I have made up my mind to become a professional———"

"Oh yes, you have," interrupted Mr. Smith. He was no longer the remote elderly gentleman, he was giving me that hearty commercial traveller's sales talk at which the Americans have been past masters ever since they wheedled what was later to become New York out of the Red Indians for the price of twenty-four dollars. "You cannot deceive me, Herr Droste," he said, "and it would be a pity if you deceived yourself. You are a born agent—I knew that the first time I saw you. The question is merely whether you want to remain an amateur, waiting around for casual offers and doing casual jobs, or whether, instead of gambling in a game of chance, where you must lose in the long run, you would not rather play a game of skill, in which you'd have excellent chances of winning. I should advise the latter—mainly for financial reasons to which, I believe, you are not unamenable."

"My earnings to date . . . ," I objected—but Mr. Smith cut me short.

"Your earnings to date have been the wages of an unskilled worker," he said. "And for a lower-class spy, if you will forgive my saying so, they weren't at all bad." At this derogatory phrase he literally sniffed his nose, almost as if a bad smell were really rising from his coffee cup. He put the cup down on the desk and continued: "On the other hand, you have an opportunity of going to America, admittedly without salary but with all costs paid, and of getting what you might call your degree. I can't promise you that you'll pass the examinations which you will have to take like

THE DEVIL'S AGENT

anybody else, but I should be much surprised if you did not land a First. Don't ponder over it too long; it is, as they say in business, a unique offer."

"I am flattered, Mr. Smith," I said, with a slight bow towards the desk. "Though a beginner, I am not all that amateurish as to belittle the blessings of a good schooling. Besides, what could be more tempting than to turn one's back for a while upon this inhospitable spot and make the acquaintance of your United States of Canaan, flowing with milk and honey? At the same time, I hardly suppose that my enrollment at the Alma Mater would be unconditional—and as for future possibilities——"

Again Mr. Smith interrupted me. "You needn't trouble, Herr Droste," he said. "I'll be glad to answer your questions. Your enrollment is subject to two conditions: discretion and exclusiveness, both of them self-evident. In other words, what you learn you keep to yourself, and if at a future date you do any work, you do it for us. Your chances are unlimited. It is one of the peculiarities of our *métier* that the number of applicants is extremely high, but that of usable labor exceedingly small. Agents are like actors, the mediocre ones are exceptionally badly off, and the good ones exceptionally well off. I can't make a contract with you, Herr Droste, but that is as much to your advantage as it is to ours. I may, however, tell you that your journeys, your training and, of course, your pocket money will cost the United States about eight thousand dollars, save me the laborious task of converting this sum into your native currency. We are wealthy and for that reason we are careful with our money, we don't invest eight thousand dollars just for the fun of it. Besides, you will have long guessed that I have a very definite job in mind for you. An interesting and a profitable job. You pass your examinations, Herr Droste, and you won't look back."

He rose. I too got up.

My indecision was not acted. It was tempting all right to leave Vienna, that poor, mangy Vienna, that fairy-tale dream that had come to an end, and to make the acquaintance of the powerful, victorious States. I absolutely believed Mr. Smith that, if I decided to take up this new career, I should not get stuck in mediocrity. During the past few weeks I had got used again to a life of luxury, and the prospect of having to return to hum-drum and trivial worries was downright appalling. On the other hand, my experiences of the last few weeks, surely not the worst in an agent's career, had left their mark on me, and I was not at all clear about the relation between danger and reward. But more than anything I was thinking of Nora: she knew nothing of my pangs of separation. I should find parting with her rather painful.

"How long will you give me to think it over, Mr. Smith?" I asked.

Instead of looking at the calendar he glanced at the electric clock. "I shall expect you at ten, tonight," he said.

First Interlude

BY SEPTEMBER 4, 1955, George Droste's memoirs had reached the point to which the reader has now followed them. The day was a Sunday. For two months Droste had worked almost without a break, even on Sundays and holidays, and he was feeling the need for a few days' rest.

The weather favored him. When he woke up about eleven o'clock the sun was shining into his bedroom—a late-summer sun, taking passionate leave of the hot season.

Droste had a bath, took his time over getting dressed, and had Marie, his old housekeeper, serve a refreshing light brunch on the shady terrace outside his study. He then ordered a taxi and drove down into the city, past the rich green of the vineyards on the Bisamberg. Like a country bumpkin who only rarely visits the big city, he made sure he did not miss anything. He enjoyed a leisurely cup of coffee on the narrow terrace of the Hotel Sacher, where he looked at the Sunday papers, but not without bestowing his admiring glances on the women in their light summer dresses—Americans, Frenchwomen, Englishwomen, and beautiful Viennese—who entered and left the café.

He dined at the Park Hotel there, beneath thick trees which were floodlit green, and listened to the agreeably muted music that was coming from a nearby garden restaurant and to the tinkling of the passing street cars, which he could not see. The time was just after nine when he glanced at his watch, and as he suddenly felt a longing for a chat with his son Johnny he decided to make for home and place a call to the Geneva boarding-school.

Shortly before ten o'clock he paid off his driver and slowly climbed up to his house through the now chilly evening air.

His housekeeper was standing on the doorstep.

"A gentleman's been waiting for you ever since six o'clock, Herr Droste," she reported. "I couldn't get rid of him."

"You haven't taken him into my study?" Droste asked with a frown.

"No, he is waiting in the living-room."

Droste immediately recognized the man who rose to meet him. He had encountered him several times in recent years—first in Africa, then in Korea, finally in Berlin and Paris. And as the man changed his place of residence, so he also changed his name. He was, Droste believed, an Albanian by birth. He was still a young man, slim, with dark hair, of markedly Balkan appearance and Balkan manners—which need not be taken as necessarily unpleasant. His feminine smoothness, his *outré* fashion-plate elegance, and his importunate politeness had always amused rather than annoyed Droste.

"Ahmed," said Droste, "—if I may still call you so—what are you doing in Vienna? I'm sorry I kept you waiting so long."

"I had no appointment," said Ahmed, polite as ever, "and it is for me to apologize. Unfortunately, I have to leave your beautiful city again tomorrow, and on no account did I wish to deny myself the pleasure of seeing you."

He was speaking French, like his host.

"What can I offer you?" asked Droste, urging his visitor to sit down.

"Your charming housekeeper," said Ahmed, pointing to the table, where a half-emptied bottle of Gumpoldskirchner was standing, "has looked after me. I might almost say: has spoilt me. Your cellar does you credit, *cher ami.*"

"And what brings you to Vienna, *cher ami?*" asked Droste.

He did not for a moment believe the visit to be accidental. "Or am I forgetting my manners by asking such a question?"

"On the contrary, quite on the contrary," said the Albanian. "Your question makes my mission easier for me, George. For the sake of our old friendship I should hate to deceive you even for another minute about the true purpose of my visit."

"Yes, indeed, our old friendship," said Droste. "Do you remember that charming little French chick for whose favors we competed at Oran?"

"You shouldn't remind me of her." Ahmed smiled. He slipped his fingers up his jacket-sleeves—a mannerism of his— and energetically pulled down the cuffs of his cream-silk shirt which had threatened to disappear from view. "You shouldn't remind me of the occasion," he laughed. "As always, you cut me clean out of the picture."

"And the mission you have mentioned, *cher ami?*" asked Droste.

The young Albanian frowned—which produced an odd effect as his high swarthy forehead was anyway lined by many wrinkles. A new fold was now squeezing itself between two existing ones.

"We are worried about you, George," he said. "We were sorry when you retired—you know that. You were a master of your craft—there's no denying that. You are still young and active, what a pity that you should have felt so soon the urge to retire on your laurels. Still, you must admit that we have made no attempt to enlist you again. . . ."

"*A votre santé! Cher ami,*" said Droste, raising his glass. "I've always liked the respect shown to retired workers in the Soviet Union," he continued with a smile, "and I hope there is no intention of disturbing my retirement."

"*Au contraire, au contraire,*" Ahmed hastened to declare.

"On the contrary, we should like you to enjoy your retirement more completely than you are doing now."

"I don't quite understand," said Droste.

"Old friends ought to be frank with each other," said the visitor. "Your retirement was a great loss to the service, George, but we are not quite so badly informed as you may think. We are aware that you are working on your reminiscences, diaries, memoirs, or whatever you wish to call them, and it seems to us that this isn't really a suitable occupation for an ex-agent."

"I really don't know what you are talking about, *cher ami*," said Droste.

"Oh yes, you do," retorted Ahmed. "Memoirs are a curious business. Writing one's memoirs is all right for people who have been failures. You remember when the English asked Napoleon if he was going to write his memoirs on St. Helena he replied: '*J'ai confiance dans l'histoire.*' Only those who have no confidence in history must write their own memoirs. It's a job for retired generals, deposed heads of Government, aging actresses, and all kinds of *passée* prostitutes. Discreet autobiographies aren't worth writing, and the indiscreet ones are *au fond* the biographies of others, to whose lives and story the author has no right." Again he fished his shirt-cuffs out of his sleeves. "As a matter of interest, George, how far have you got with your work?" he asked abruptly.

"I am afraid you are misinformed, Ahmed," said Droste. "*Entre nous,* it wouldn't be the first time."

"Don't make my mission more difficult for me," said the Albanian. "It really isn't meant to be so unpleasant as you seem to think. You might have guessed this from my last question."

"You asked me how far I had got with my work."

Ahmed took a sip from his glass. "Just so. We can understand that after you've spent several months on your work you don't just want to drop it into the waste-paper basket. The waste-paper basket," he laughed, "would in fact be a highly explosive depository for that kind of work. In short, Moscow offers you a certain sum, perhaps a not inconsiderable sum. . . ."

"I can't sell what I haven't got," said Droste.

"You are being stubborn, *cher ami*," said Ahmed. "There's no need to demur! The best patents are those that are never exploited. I believe it was one of your ingenious fellow-country-men who invented the ever-lasting match, but he was wise enough to sell his invention to the Swedish match industry, which paid him a better price than he could ever have earned with his perpetual match. The Soviet Intelligence, of course, would live down your memoirs, so you mustn't expect a fortune for the buying up of your patent. Nevertheless, the figure of twenty-five thousand dollars was mentioned to me in Moscow— as you see, we still pay in dollars."

"You're tempting me to write that autobiography, or reminiscences, memoirs, or whatever you call it," said Droste, "but I am afraid you want to see a manuscript that I cannot produce."

"That is your last word?" he asked.

"Most definitely," replied Droste with a polite smile.

The Albanian put his glass down on the table. New ripples appeared between the corrugations on his forehead.

"You remember Knut Arwed who was fished out of the Tagus near Lisbon?" he asked suddenly. "Or that German—I think his name was Stämmle—who vanished from the Kurfürstendamm in broad daylight? I feel positively sick when I think of the mutilated corpse of little Jean Pottier. Or of our mutual friend Lotti in Rome——"

"Spare me the reminiscences, Ahmed," Droste interrupted him. "Those men were traitors. . . ."

"A man who writes his memoirs is a traitor," said the Albanian. He rose abruptly, and his shirt-cuffs disappeared in his jacket-sleeves for good. "I did not take on this mission by accident, George," he added, a little more mildly. "I used to be your friend, and I believed myself to be acting in your own best interest. I hope you are aware what the failure of my mission must mean to you."

"The loss of twenty-five thousand dollars which would have been extremely useful," said Droste, his tone unchanged. He too stood up. "As I said, I wish I could help you. . . . May I call you a taxi?"

"No, thank you. I have a car."

"Best of luck, Ahmed," he said, "and look me up when you're in Vienna again."

"You know as well as I do, George, that we are not in the habit of repeating our offers," said the Albanian.

He ignored Droste's hand. A moment later he had vanished into the darkness, where his car appeared to be waiting.

Slowly Droste climbed the hill to his house again.

"Tomorrow morning at eight, as usual," he said to his house-keeper, who was waiting for him in the door.

"I thought you were having a little holiday, Herr Droste." Old Marie sounded disappointed.

"I'm afraid I have no time for a holiday," said Droste.

He looked at his watch. It was too late now to place a call to Geneva.

PART FOUR

15

~~~~~~~~~~~~

Secrets of an Espionage School

UPON MY ARRIVAL at the airport of Washington, D.C., four days after my interview with Mr. Smith, I was taken over by a U.S. Army sergeant who loaded me on to a truck, just as if I were a consignment of wine newly arrived from Europe. But since all the canvas flaps had been let down I saw about as much of the American capital as a packing-case would have done. When the metropolitan street noise—to which, coming from a traffic-starved Vienna, I was particularly sensitive at the time—died away after a few minutes I assumed that we had left the outskirts of the city. The fact that our journey took about two hours did not, however, cause me to jump to any conclusions: after all, I was in the hands of the secret service and for all I knew our destination might have been just behind the airport. I discovered subsequently that this was not the case and that we had been streaking purposefully straight through the State of Maryland. Now and again, for the sake of mystification, the secret services are sometimes even prepared to save fuel instead of wasting it. Throughout the journey I was very much aware that my driver belonged to Intelligence: he was watching me continuously in his driving mirror, no doubt to make sure I did not spy out the secrets of the motor highway through a gap in the tarpaulin.

My watch stood at twelve o'clock when we passed through a gate, guarded by troops, and through a high barbed-wire fence. A few moments later we pulled up at an exceedingly pleasant country house. The sergeant jumped down from his cab and assisted me out of the vehicle. He also put down my luggage on the well-kept gravel drive.

By the entrance stood a group of seven or eight men who appeared to have been waiting for me. They wore the greenish-blue overalls known in the U.S. Army as "fatigues"—perhaps because officers and men usually fatigue themselves in these suits. I noticed that above his left breast-pocket each man wore a narrow leather label on which his name had been stamped. Only the one who immediately came over to me seemed to prefer to remain anonymous. His label simply said "Commander."

The Commander was a short, lean man with narrow shoulders, an almost concave chest, and a sallow face. I have always found that men resemble either animals or plants, so that, if only you look at them closely enough, you can liken them to cats, or oranges, or giraffes, or apples. This lean little man resembled an animal as well as a fruit: he was a cross between a fox and a pear. His face tapered towards the top, from his jaw upward, so that his forehead seemed narrower than his cheeks. Indeed, it would not have surprised me to find his head ending, above his reddish fair hair, in a thin stalk. In profile his head looked similarly pointed— only now its shape was that of an isosceles triangle, from his ears to the point of a very straight and very long nose. His small, deep-set eyes radiated a crafty intelligence, so that I was instantly reminded of that Maître Renard, in La Fontaine's fable, who parts the stupid old raven from his piece of cheese without much difficulty or fuss.

"Welcome!" said the Commander, in a cordial tone. His voice came as a surprise, it was deep and sonorous. Before I could introduce myself he said quickly: "You are the last of the class which has just assembled here and which consists, for the moment, of twenty people. These are some of your colleagues." My colleagues grinned. "You will choose a name for yourself—will you give me a false name quickly, please?"

"Lehmann," I said promptly.

The Commander nodded, satisfied. "Very well, Mr. Lehmann. You have an hour to get into your kit. Meanwhile you will consider who you are. I should point out to you that throughout your stay in camp you will not only keep the name of Lehmann but will also have to keep up in all circumstances—I repeat, in all circumstances—the identity which you will now invent for yourself. I must warn you in fairness, that your instructors and colleagues, and anybody else you may come in contact with, will do their best to prove that you are not the person you say you are." Again my colleagues grinned. "In other words, it would not be advisable for you to pretend that you are an Arab sheikh—because you couldn't keep up that character or background against our doubts. One other thing. From time to time, for instance in our theoretical lectures, either I or one of your instructors will call out 'Maximum.' This means that we are speaking to each other as instructor and student, and not as the actors of some part or other. But even then, and of course also *vis-à-vis* your colleagues, you will always remain Mr. Lehmann. And now"—he turned at random to one of the men—"Mr. Green will show you to your room. We shall expect you at one-thirty, in lecture-room Two. Good luck!"

Green, a clean-looking American boy of no more than twenty, led me into the house.

It was a spacious, rambling country house, built of red brick in the English style, with steep gables, pleasantly overgrown with green creeper, with leaded stained-glass windows on the ground floor, and with heavy, iron-studded, mahogany doors between the rooms. The obvious guess was that the building, which was situated in the middle of extensive grounds in the fertile State of Maryland, either belonged to a patriotic millionaire, who had put it at the disposal of the secret service, or else had been requisitioned from some gangster, who had made a quick fortune but had then got into trouble with the tax authorities.

As my colleague Green informed me—he was not, by the way, an exceptionally friendly person—apart from the twenty students there were only half a dozen instructors and the Commander in the house. I was the more bewildered when I saw what the Commander, no doubt ironically, had called "my room." It was not a room at all, but a ghastly dormitory, with five army cots lined up next to one another, so close that I could only hope my neighbor would not partake of any malodorous food for supper. And when I found out that all the accommodation allowed me for the contents of my travelling case was a tin locker, reminiscent of those inadequate luggage lockers at railway stations, and that we should all have to share a shower, in a room of prison-like proportions, I abandoned all hope that the food, at least, would be good.

It was not till several hours later that I had occasion to sample the camp cuisine—and then it was a most pleasant surprise. At eight o'clock that morning, on the plane, I had been served one of those meals with which air line companies endeavor to atone for their multifarious sins—such as delayed departure, late arrival, lack of ventilation, cold, heat, air pockets, and landings in the most unexpected places—but since then I had not had a bite of food, and my stomach was angrily rumbling in a language which, luckily, the secret service did not understand. With that insulting air of knowing the ropes, invariably adopted by older boys to "new boys," even if they have only been at school for an extra day, Green handed me a greenish-blue fatigue uniform, urging me all the time to hurry up so we should not be late for the lecture.

The written entrance examination—for that was what it turned out to be—was personally conducted by the Commander, but the rest of the instructors were all present to invigilate us. We sat at little writing tables, placed rather far from each other, and on each of them there was a fat set of questionnaires all ready waiting for us. We were given two hours to fill in the forms.

I should like to deal at some length with the contents of this questionnaire and with the way in which I answered it, for in the course of my two-hour entrance examination I discovered a number of things which were to determine the rest of my time at the espionage camp.

The questionnaire, which—I am not exaggerating—contained some four hundred questions, represented a dupes' trap of colossal magnitude and quite incredible primitiveness. One glance at the innumerable sheets of paper was enough to reveal the real purpose of the test, since not even a genius with a prodigious brain like Pascal could have answered anything like four hundred questions in one hundred and twenty minutes, it was quite obvious that the idea was to discourage and confuse the candidate. From his reactions, the teaching staff would then be able to judge whether he had got lost in the jungle of the inquisition, or whether he had coolly and boldly left those questions unanswered which were the most difficult and would have wasted most of his time. I realized also that the secret service had denied me my lunch, not out of any lack of hospitality or misplaced meanness, but in order to get the candidate into a thoroughly disgruntled mood.

A quick glance through the first two dozen questions further convinced me that the school was interested not so much in the proper answering of the questions as in the testing of the candidate's character. What annoyed me most about this was the assumption that a person of moderate intelligence would not immediately spot this intention after the most cursory perusal of the questionnaire. Very well, I said to myself, I'll give you what you want. Consequently, when I came to the question asking me to name the ten greatest men of all time, I avoided such names as Napoleon, Caesar, or Alexander, because I felt sure that American democracy would frown upon such despot-worship. Instead, I neatly put the name of Abraham Lincoln in the empty space on the right-hand side, deliberately disregarding the more obvious George Washington for fear it might earn me the odor of opportunism. Asked what form of death I should choose if I decided to commit suicide, I promptly answered "Revolver," since masculine pride probably looked down on poison as a woman's weapon, and the cutting of one's arteries was no doubt regarded here as unhygienic. Among the ten books which I should take with me to a desert island I naturally named the Bible, which enjoys an excellent reputation also in espionage circles, as well as the collected works of Siegmund Freud—the latter on the assumption that these tests were probably evaluated by psychologists who would have a soft spot for a fellow-practitioner.

I took the greatest possible care over my biography. I called myself Richard Lehmann, teacher of German language and literature at a Vienna secondary school. I mentioned my impecunious youth and a subsequent legacy, as well as my travels as the secretary for a foreign millionaire. I stated that I had been a wartime-reserve-captain in the Wehrmacht and that I was single. Generally speaking, I tried to give proof of my imagination on the one hand, while, on the other, guarding against too severe tests of it and crafty leading questions.

When the questionnaires had been collected we all sat down,

together with the Commander and the six instructors, in the mess, to a meal whose excellence I have already mentioned and which, after my lean years in Vienna, I enjoyed heartily.

The meal gave me a chance to observe my colleagues. As the conversation was conducted in English I established without much difficulty that of the twenty men sixteen or seventeen were certainly American; one of the foreigners declared himself to be a Frenchman—which undoubtedly he was—and the other did not even try to conceal his origin: his yellow skin immediately gave him away as a Chinese. He called himself Lu Wang and was a small, muscular man with a donnish pair of spectacles. He immediately struck me by his excellent manners and clever conversation and subsequently became my most valued acquaintance in the camp. I was, without any doubt, the oldest of our class—a circumstance which I did not like at all and which gave me a kind of inferiority complex and a sense of having been slow in "moving up." Also, it made contact with my colleagues more difficult. The young man Green, who sat next to me, in particular seemed to be out to increase my uneasiness by treating me with a kind of mock reverence, just as if I were not in my late thirties but in my early seventies. When the conversation turned to wartime experiences he inquired whether my remarks referred to the First or the Second World War, and even when I calmly replied that during the First World War I had still been a schoolboy he did not let go of me. This time he wished to know what rank I had held in Hitler's "army of pigs."

The only reason why Bob Green—I never discovered his real name—is receiving from the outset rather more attention than the rest of my colleagues is that I cannot possibly give here a full account of my eight weeks' training course—much as I should like to and interesting as many of its features were—but that I must confine myself to the description of the principal characters and events. Twenty-four hours after my arrival in camp our number had shrunk to sixteen: four, who had failed to pass the entrance examination, disappeared without farewell, and of the remaining sixteen three, and possibly four, were certainly not acolytes but clearly belonged to the staff of the secret service. One of these was Bob Green.

"Clearly"—that word brings me to my main theme. Young Green was the kind of actor who would not have been allowed at the Burgtheater of my native Vienna, let alone at a more naturalistic theatre, to play even that much-ridiculed part of "My lord, the horses are saddled." Long before our first day ended at the transformed millionaire's mansion, or gangster's retreat, it was clear to me that the only purpose of the handsome, typically American boy with the crew-cut and baseball movements was to make my life a misery, and hence find out how I would get on with a thoroughly objectionable roommate, table companion, and fellow student. Needless to say I tried to get on with him. No matter whether he placed a wet brush under my sheet; whether he mocked me for my German accent; whether, as if by accident, he spilled a bottle of green ink over my clean shirt; whether he bragged of his successes with the fair sex whom I was "too old to understand"—I treated him with invariable paternal indulgence, but without irritating him by condescension.

More or less everything in the camp was as transparent as Bob Green's acting—which convinced me that the espionage services must rely on rather poor human material and that, though failure at the school was evidence of a total lack of intelligence on the part of a candidate, the successful completion of the course was by no means a warranty of a person's suitability. A few examples will, I hope, prove my point.

The written entrance examination was followed by a number of physical tests. We were taken up into the steep hills behind the estate and suddenly found ourselves on a rocky cliff below whose edge a thin but opaque canvas had been fixed. The instructor in charge told us to jump off the cliff. We were to break through the sheet and hurl into unknown depths. A few of us hesitated for several minutes and some refused altogether. Only Lu Wang, the Chinese, and I jumped immediately—he, possibly, because he was a man of more than ordinary courage, but I, simply because it was again "clear" that the United States had not brought me all the way from Vienna to Washington, and thence to the camp, at considerable expense, so that I should break my neck on the first day. The enterprise, as I expected, proved perfectly safe and emboldened me to pass various similar tests in the most gallant manner.

It was much the same when the Commander—after repeated calls of "Maximum," indicating that this was an entirely unofficial affair, quite outside the normal school routine—invited us all to his birthday party. This was held at his private apartment, which was furnished in excellent taste and with every modern comfort. Had there been only beer and whisky, both of them national drinks in America, or at most a bottle of brandy, maybe then I would have been fooled. However, champagne was served in seemingly unlimited quantity, admittedly without vintage year but the product of the reputable French firm of Moet et Chandon— and this convinced me at once that the Commander had at least one birthday during each training course, in order to test his pupils' reactions under the effect of a drink with which they were not familiar. I enjoyed the champagne thoroughly, having always been on a footing of mutual sympathy with that excellent beverage, but limited myself to the minimum in my consumption of American whisky, called, for no obvious reason, Bourbon. In fairness to the educational methods of the secret service it must be admitted that the liquid test proved effective in the case of two or three of my colleagues—at least in the sense that at the end of the jollifications, at two in the morning, they had to be carried back to their dormitories in a sorry state.

Objectivity requires me also to report another instance which proved that, while falling far short of full success, the school did not entirely fail in its purpose. One of my alleged colleagues was a fair boy of about twenty-two, with blue eyes and a milk-white skin, with delicate movements, and a voice like a bell—a strikingly handsome boy of mild manners, who was popular with all of us, though he would have greatly annoyed my fellow-Viennese, the philosopher Otto Weininger, who is well known for his horror of all feminine traits in men. Although a blind man must have seen at once that young Peter had been placed among us as a decoy for possible homosexuals, one of the candidates, otherwise not at all suspect, found it impossible to resist his charms. Thus, after what the Statute Book calls "an act of gross indecency" had taken place in the shower-bath, and, moreover, in a particularly repulsive form, the two men were removed from the camp—young Peter, of course, only until the beginning of the next training course, when he would return in his part of decoy.

Very soon we switched over to what was called "practical tasks."

One of the instructors, for instance, took me to an empty room and informed me that this was the hotel room of a Communist big-shot in a Hungarian provincial town. He himself, the instructor, would in this practical test act the part of the proprietor. The proprietor, I was told, had informed me, a Western agent, that in the room, though in an undisclosed place, there was an important document in a sealed envelope. I would have five minutes to find that document. After five minutes something would happen which would force me to make an escape from the Communist-occupied hotel. The instructor-proprietor withdrew, stopwatch in hand, without telling me whether the main thing was to find the envelope or to prove my skill in escaping. I devoted the first couple of minutes to a topographical and strategic survey, and in particular established that there could be no question of escaping by the window. The remaining three minutes I spent in a systematic search for the envelope. I did not find it, presumably because it was not in the room at all. After exactly five minutes the door burst open and the "proprietor" called out: "Follow me! You must flee! You've been found out!" Outside in the corridor he hurriedly turned to the right while I, after a moment's hesitation, began to run in the opposite direction. By so doing I brilliantly passed the test, much to the surprise of the "hotel proprietor," whose surprise in turn astonished me. On entering the room he had uttered the words: "Follow me! You must flee! You've been found out!" not in a whisper, but in a loud roar, making it obvious to anyone reasonably alert that the "proprietor" was a traitor, that his shouts were designed to betray me to the Communists, and that nothing would therefore have been more foolish than to follow the way he led.

Such tests, designed to be instructive, we had by the dozen— but space prevents me from discussing them in detail. However, they all had certain characteristics in common. To begin with, these tests and training courses, elaborately thought out by psychologists after years of experiments, were all based on the utterly false psychological premise that a man can be ordered to be afraid or to put himself into a state of panic—which, of course, is just as impossible as relieving a frightened man of his fear by a simple word of command. I very much doubt that I should have acted with similar sang-froid in a Communist-occupied hotel in Hungary as I had in the make-believe hotel room of our training establishment. The pupil's imagination is bound to fall short of the psychologist's inventive power, and his reactions in situation "X" minus Fear and in the identical Situation "X" plus Fear are as different as night and day.

Secondly, these practical exercises invariably presumed a set of circumstances which, awkward as they were, were lacking in realism. We were taught, for instance, how to write secret messages on the shell of an egg with invisible ink, and it was explained to us that as soon as the egg was hard-boiled the writing would become perfectly legible. These highly entertaining instructions reminded me of my mother's cookery-book—one of her few possessions which I had saved through all wartime hazards, and which I had often dipped into with a sense of relish during and after the war. At a time when people spread margarine on their slice of bread I used to get great fun and much comfort out of such directions as: "Take a pound and a half of butter." This invisible ink was a most amusing toy, but I found it hard to imagine that, say, in a prison in Prague I should be able, without attracting attention, to demand a raw egg, or that my liaison-man could embark on a journey to the West with his pockets stuffed full of raw eggs. Nor did I think that the Bolshevik post office could be trusted to convey such a cargo undamaged. Thirdly, these tests were designed to increase our self-assurance, or, in other words, to lead us to overestimate our own profession. To a man who passes on a cookery recipe in code form, this recipe becomes a secret document and this "Secretinism" becomes proof of intelligence. Fourthly, the Commander and the instructors seemed to display that delight in romantic fiction, in "a story," which I was to find in nearly all secret-service personnel: they did not reflect that lying is not a sport which can be learned or perfected by daily practice. In their delight in the fairy-tale they were increasingly losing sight of reality. And this brings me to the story of my final examination at the espionage school.

The examinations were held separately for each student, and I assume that each of the candidates got a different task.

I was roused from restful sleep in the middle of the night and taken to an empty room. There an instructor, who had been waiting for me, revealed to me my highly delicate situation. As an agent of the West I had been arrested in an unspecified East European country. I had been taken to a prison camp and was now awaiting my chance to escape. But being a conscientious spy I did not wish to leave the camp empty-handed. Through a chain of circumstances I had found out that among the camp commander's papers there was a document of value to the West. This document I had stolen from the camp office in an unguarded moment—or rather, I had been about to steal it when I was caught red-handed. "Now," the instructor informed me, "you will be put before a summary court. Your salvation depends on whether you can or cannot think of a plausible story. Only one other thing: you cannot refuse to answer the tribunal's questions. You will be picked up in fifteen minutes from now." With these words he locked the door behind him.

Exactly fifteen minutes later I was roused from my meditations by two men whom I had not seen before. The time was after midnight and the big house was in complete darkness. The two Martian-looking characters played their part of Eastern police bullies with a positively impassioned realism: they pushed me down the stairs, dug me a few times in my ribs, and lastly, when I did not hurry sufficiently, treated me to a few lusty kicks. This, as was clear from my treatment, was my solemn final examination.

There was complete darkness in the cellar of the manor, into which I had been bundled. I stood motionless for about ten minutes, uncertain whether I was alone in the room. I had an uncanny feeling of being surrounded by lurking human beings. Then, all of a sudden, I was in the blinding glare of a searchlight trained upon me. The light was so strong and so painful to my eyes that I could not see the men sitting behind it, though from their voices I judged that there were four or five of them. I did not know any of the voices and only heard the questions which beat down on me in the most rapid and most brutal manner. At last the chairman of the tribunal came to the point.

"And how do you explain your presence in the Commander's office, you bastard?" he asked, in a most insulting tone.

"I refuse to answer," I said.

"You can't refuse to answer," said the voice behind the search-light, and its companions joined in with a number of further obscenities.

"I refuse to answer," I repeated.

"You've got to answer," shouted the chairman of the tribunal; but there was some uncertainty in his voice as if he was not sure whether he ought to have me executed, in his role of chairman of the summary court, or, with calls of "Maximum," remind me of my instructions, in his capacity of examiner at the secret-service training school.

After some more refusals, which I did not justify in any way, I allowed it to be understood that I could not tell the truth even though it would clear me completely of all suspicion; for if I did I should expose a lady whom I greatly admired and should still not save my forfeit life. Only after a further bombardment of sneers, questions, and threats did I consent to come out with that "truth" which I had worked out during my fifteen minutes' reflection time.

"I am in love with the Commander's wife," I confessed in a low, broken voice. "She knows that I am not an American agent and that I am totally innocent. Like myself, she is convinced that I shall find justice in the end and that sooner or later I shall be released. We want to get married then. She is also aware that her husband has been deceiving her for many years. His mistress' letters, which contain convincing evidence, he had hidden among his papers in his office. It was these letters I was trying to find when I was apprehended. That is the truth, so help me God."

Nobody answered. I heard the men whispering among themselves. Then, for the first time, came the familiar voice of the school Commander.

"Maximum!" he said, in token that the cruel game was over. "I am sorry, but you have failed your examination. Please come and see me in my apartment in ten minutes."

I was not surprised that my story should have failed to impress my examiners. I had been summoned before the mock tribunal without appropriate background information, I kept telling myself. For all I knew, the fictitious camp might have an unmarried commander with whose wife, consequently, I could not have an affair. Moreover, in real life a tribunal like this would be presided over by the camp commander himself, and it would not therefore be advisable to remind him of his erotic lapses. In short, I had no reason to be particularly proud of my improbable and romantic "story." The only point I refused to see was that I should be more stupid and less imaginative than the majority of my colleagues. And surely we would not have been trained for eight weeks merely so that every one of us was failed in the end.

It was with such thoughts that I reported at the Commander's apartment. It was now two o'clock in the morning.

For the first time since my arrival he shook hands with me and led me to his study, which was simply but pleasantly furnished in the American colonial style.

"Brandy?" he asked. "Or would you prefer a whisky?"

"Which ever you've got handy."

He went to a small circular table on which stood a cluster of bottles. He poured a brandy for each of us, returned to his desk and sat down facing me.

"Well," he said with a friendly smile, which made his foxy face quite attractive, "I did not want you to have a sleepless night. I got to like you during the past eight weeks and I am very sorry you failed your critical examination. You can't know that this is what happens to about eighty per cent of all candidates. You will understand that in our final selection we cannot be too careful. But one should never argue with one's fate. Who knows but one day you will be grateful to us for our severity."

I nodded in agreement. "Frankly," I said, "there is one point I don't understand. During the past eight weeks I have learnt a great many things. Is it not incautious to send me out into the world with this knowledge?"

The commander knit his narrow, pear-shaped brow. "Useful as this knowledge is, nothing of what you've learned here is un-known to the enemy Intelligence. If you were to desert to the enemy tomorrow you would learn much the same things at his schools and, just as probably, you would fail your examination there."

"So you think I'm a hopeless case?"

"Are you very disappointed?" he retorted.

"I am more surprised than disappointed."

He gazed meditatively into his glass. "Disappointments," he remarked philosophically, "are a matter of being hardened to them. You look to me like a man who has hardened himself. Have you ever suffered a similar disappointment before?"

The alarm bells rang within me. Rapidly I took stock of my situation. Eight thousand dollars invested; my superior intelligence; intimate acquaintance with the secrets of the school; at least fifty successful tests against this single failure; the nocturnal invitation to the Commander's room; drinks and a cozy atmosphere; but above all, the still unabated interest of the head of the establishment—all this added up to a warning not to relax the vigilance I had been practicing for the past eight weeks.

"Yes," I replied, after a little thought. "A similar, though perhaps not quite so drastic, disappointment. I was a young and exceedingly ambitious teacher at the time—I think it must have been my first term. At the Vienna grammar school, where I took one of the lower grades in German and History, we had a Ministry Inspector come one day—this sort of thing happened about once or twice every year. We had been doing the Minnesingers, and nearly all my pupils were excellently informed about such poets as Walther von der Vogelweide, Wolfram von Eschenbach, Dietmar von Aist, and von Kuerenberg. But as bad luck would have it the Inspector, a schoolmaster himself and a shrewd judge of boys, picked on the one boy, a certain Jochen Jeremias, whom I had utterly failed, in spite of all my efforts, to teach anything at all about the civilization of courtly chivalry." I laughed. "Young Jeremias, I'm afraid, was neither courtly, nor chivalrous, nor civilized. Not to put too fine a point on it, he was a moron. But the Inspector considered him a typical product of my teaching methods and—I hardly need tell you the rest—I got a terrible dressing-down in front of the assembled staff, almost as if I were every bit as stupid myself as Jochen Jeremias."

I wanted to embroider my pretty story a little further, and to point a few psychological parallels, but I was not given the chance. The Commander leapt up, very nearly upsetting his brandy glass, came up to me, shook me by the hand and declared: "Herr Droste, you've passed your examination; you've passed it brilliantly!" And remembering that he was indeed dealing with a model pupil, with a man who was top of his class, he uttered the word "Maximum" to confirm that the course was now definitely at an end. "Needless to say," he added, "you also passed the first final examination out there with flying colors—but that was less important than the one you have just passed so brilliantly. Even under the impact of your disappointment and the unfairness of the pretended examination result, you acted true to your assumed character; you remembered that you had not in any way been absolved of your pledge to remain the teacher Lehmann. Let me congratulate you! I am extremely sorry to have to let you go—I'd much rather keep you here." He was almost moved as he poured us another round. "I am afraid you're not going to get much sleep tonight," he said. "You must leave the camp in a few minutes, without seeing your colleagues again. You will find comfortable accommodation at the Mayflower Hotel in Washington. An official, who will introduce himself as Kenneth Kenneth, will give you further instructions in a few days' time."

An hour later I was on my way to Washington in a comfortable car, with—for once—no blinds obstructing my view.

We arrived at six o'clock in the morning. The heavily gilt hotel lobby with its tall mirrors had a disenchanting effect, like a woman caught awakening, her hair not done, nor her face made up. Porters in green aprons and charwomen with grief-lined faces —normally hidden from the eyes of the hotel guests—were busy unrolling carpets, operating vacuum-cleaners, and scrubbing the floor tiles.

Strange, I thought to myself as a yawning bell-hop escorted me to the lift, I could envy even those people. It seemed to me that there was no one I did not envy.

16
ᐧᐧᐧᐧᐧᐧᐧᐧᐧᐧᐧᐧ

Emergence of a Professional Spy

I WOKE UP in a difficult frame of mind. I had slept for only a few hours and the hangover-like fatigue which had suddenly hit me, like an ill wind, upon arriving at the hotel, had not evaporated. As I pulled the heavy curtains and, standing by the window in my pajamas, looked down on to the busy Connecticut Avenue, the colorful scene failed to divert me; on the contrary, it merely fed my dull anger. Even the hearty breakfast, a meal which usually refreshes me instantly, did not taste right.

At that moment the telephone rang. Irritably I lifted the receiver: it was Mr. Kenneth Kenneth, inquiring curtly how soon I could be ready. For a moment I was tempted to tell him that I was ready now—ready to turn my back on him and the whole of his silly, smug crew. But then I glanced at my watch and, in a matter-of-fact way, informed him that just before 1.30 would suit me. Mr. Kenneth Kenneth, another of those people whose name was not his name, seemed to hesitate for a moment, no doubt a man who needed an hour and a half to get ready for new deeds was a little slow for his taste. But in the end he said, "O.K." and after exactly an hour and a half the black bird screeched again to announce the arrival of the car.

A taciturn driver in a black limousine took me to a building in the Administration district, a building immediately recognizable as a temporary wartime structure. Gray, and with a makeshift air, like a big house of cards, it was wedged in between the more solid houses and official buildings. Its name was "Q Building," from which mysterious appellation I concluded that this must be Intelligence headquarters. The receptionist laboriously made out a pass for me and, for good measure, pinned a circular disc with a number to my lapel. He then directed me to Room 301A on the third floor.

The interior differed from other office blocks only in so far as the doors bore plain numbers, instead of the customary name-plates or designations of departments. The men and women I encountered in the corridors, who seemed to me to be putting on a great show of self-important bustle, all wore little enamelled discs with numbers on, like myself, or else discs bearing numbers as well as their photographs; evidently the ones who also displayed their likenesses on their chests or bosoms belonged to the permanent secret staff.

A blonde secretary, whose ripe charms were almost improperly advertised by her enamel-mounted photograph—she wore the round disc much too low, in the place where on her well-rounded breast one would suspect a further small roundness—immediately conducted me to Room 301A. Her boss, she said, was awaiting me.

He was a man of about forty-five, who betrayed his military-college training at the first glance and who looked both uncomfortable and disguised in his double-breasted suit. His speech, too, was soldierly and impersonal, the manner of a commander baldly explaining to a junior officer a tactical situation and the resulting necessary action.

On the staff of the British Embassy in Washington, the disguised civilian began, there was a Third Secretary by name of MacMahon, whose range of duties considerably exceeded those of a common-or-garden Third Secretary at an Embassy. Mr. MacMahon—the double-breasted colonel slid a photograph of a handsome young Englishman across his desk—was engaged on "atomic matters." For some reason or other the British regarded him as an expert in this field, and nearly all information supplied to Britain by the U.S. Administration passed through his hands. In reply to my question as to what he meant by "atomic matters," my interlocutor was evasive. All I need know, he said, was that the Americans were keeping their British allies informed about the latest developments in atomic research and about certain vital military experiments, and they had no intention whatever of allowing the results of such research and experiments to fall into the wrong hands. But that, he explained, was just the point. There was a justified suspicion that MacMahon was either a Communist agent himself, or that at least he was in the hands of a female Communist agent. The girl—again the anonymous officer slid a photograph across to me—was a dancer, or crooner, or some sort of entertainer at the Golden Girl, a New York nightclub, on the corner of Sixth Avenue and 52nd Street. At least once every week the Embassy Secretary made a trip to New York, where he visited the nightclub and, no doubt, also the private apartment of the lady in question. Another frequent caller, not at the nightclub but at the girl's apartment, was Lieutenant-Colonel Nikolai Sobrin, the Assistant Military Attaché at the Soviet Embassy in Washington and undoubtedly a secret-service man. Putting two and two together, my informant remarked, it was to be assumed that MacMahon took the information he obtained in Washington to New York, and left it there with the girl, who then passed it on to the Soviet agent. However, continued my informant, Intelligence was not content with such simple arithmetic. The young lady was drawing a pay of fifty dollars a week at the Golden Girl, plus a commission of about forty-five dollars on drinks consumed by customers—this made a hundred dollars, which was certainly not enough for the purchase of a mink coat, an electric washing machine, an expensive television set, and a pale-blue Chevrolet convertible. But even that was not all. Intelligence had been successful in intercepting two telegrams sent by the young lady to MacMahon's private address within one week—again my interlocutor slid a pair of photostat copies across the smooth top of his steel desk—and these clearly suggested an agreed code. "Red still not arrived, please wire three hundred dollars, love Maud" read the first of them. The other, handed in forty-eight hours later, reported: "Thanks for money, Red arrived, all my love, Maud." My interlocutor thought it hardly necessary to point out that, in addition to being an American first name, "red" was a color with political implications.

"Your job, Mr. Droste," the military gentleman concluded, "will be to prove this Maud guilty. Let's get this clear, you don't have to watch or to observe the lady." He uttered the last word with puritanical distaste. "That's been done amply. Nor do we

want to pump her for secrets. It's not likely she has the least knowledge about atomic matters. There's no doubt she's just a letter-box.
At the same time, it's no good your telling us that we are right—
we know that already. You've got to make that woman's acquaintance, gain her confidence, visit her apartment, and either trap her
into a confession or convict her irrefutably. We need evidence,
cogent evidence, evidence that's sufficient to convince our British
friends."

He was about to get up, but remained seated when he saw that
I was not yet satisfied with his instructions.

"I have a few questions, sir," I said.

"Go ahead," he said, a little irritably.

"First of all, I think I am right in saying that this is a not altogether straightforward business and, to be quite frank, I am surprised you should entrust a beginner with it."

"Not a bad point," he said appreciatively. "From the dossier
which I am going to give you in a minute you'll see that the girl
who calls herself Maud Leoni is really called Grete Prochaska"—I
did not get the name till much later, for he pronounced it as if it
were some Estonian river—"and that she comes from your native
Vienna. You will convey to her the regards of one Fritz Benkhoff
from Vienna, about whom the folder will give you full information."

I bowed, mentally as well as physically, before such painstaking
groundwork.

"My second question, sir, may seem to you impertinent—but I
do not suppose you expect your agents to be unthinking machines.
In short, why don't you pass on your information to the British
Embassy or to the British Intelligence service, which surely have the
same interests as you?"

The colonel's impatient frown showed that he certainly did regard my question as impertinent.

"I don't know why I should answer your question," he said,
"but I don't mind telling you. You are a beginner, Mr. Droste,
even though you've been described to me as an exceptionally
efficient beginner, and that's why you don't seem to know yet that
diplomacy and Intelligence work are two entirely different things.
As the man concerned is a foreign diplomat we should not be

authorized to take any action without first communicating our suspicions to the State Department. The State Department would, at a guess, take several weeks, or even months, making up its mind whether it should face the British Foreign Office with such a monstrous accusation. The Foreign Office, for its part, would be most reluctant to admit to our State Department that it had sent us such a doubtful character as Mr. MacMahon, let alone entrusted him with the handling of top-secret material. But even assuming that the Foreign Office in London were willing to pass the whole matter over to M.I.5 or M.I.6, the British secret service would of course go all out to prove the diplomat's innocence. British Intelligence would be bound to act in that way, not only for patriotic reasons but because they don't want to make trouble for their own Foreign Office. At most, MacMahon would be transferred to some place like Afghanistan. But it is unthinkable that the British would allow themselves to be shown up as such dolts that they can't spot MacMahon's machinations until they have their attention drawn to them by our secret service. In consequence, we've got to face both our own State Department and the British with a *fait accompli*. This is the more necessary as it would give us some influence in future on the selection of British diplomats for posts in America. As you see, British and American interests run parallel only on the very highest level—and we're not concerned with that here. Is that clear?"

It was indeed clear. However, I felt it necessary to ask a personal question, even though I did not think this would relieve me of the envisaged assignment.

"As you are no doubt aware," I said, "I was enrolled in Vienna by Mr. Smith. He hinted that he had a job for me there. Is he——?"

"Of course," my interlocutor interrupted me, at the same time demonstratively rising to his feet. "Of course he is fully informed. My secretary will give you the file and a thousand dollars. One thing more. Your contact is a Joe Brown, a dealer in second-hand cars, Number 2040 Broadway. You will memorize the name and address. Any questions you will take to him exclusively. Likewise, if you should have any major expenses, he will be at your disposal upon submission of a detailed expense account."

"The lady might be expensive," I remarked.

The colonel in civilian dress shrugged his shoulders and saw me to the door.

On the threshold it occurred to me that the assignment might be more dangerous than my informant had led me to believe. "In an emergency, can I turn to the police?"

"The F.B.I.?" The colonel was as horrified as if I had suggested connecting a burglar alarm to Al Capone's headquarters instead of the police. "You must be out of your mind, Mr. Droste! We have managed to keep the F.B.I. out of it so far and we shan't put them on the track just as we are about to pull the thing off. You're working for Intelligence, Mr. Droste, not for the police!" After this sharp lecture he continued in a calmer voice, "You will take a room at the Astor Hotel on Broadway, in your own name. You are a wholesale wine merchant from Vienna. I hope a fortnight will be enough for you to achieve the kind of success that I can report to higher quarters. Good-by!"

Thus, without having seen much of the nation's capital, I left Washington for New York at six o'clock in the evening.

There I was in my comfortable Pullman coach, outwardly a distinguished foreign traveller but in fact a pawn in the cold war between East and West, on my way to trap a woman spy or to empty a "letter-box," in a strange city, and no more convinced of the righteousness of my mission than, presumably, the blonde "letter-box" herself.

I did not feel like studying the dossier; besides, I had been taught that it was not advisable to do such things in public places. My thoughts therefore reverted to Nora Güldendag—where, in fact, they had been when the telephone shrilled on my bedside table and I stopped thinking and started acting.

During my eight weeks in camp, while summer declined into autumn, I had been observing myself constantly. I had tried to assess my feelings for the far-away woman coolly and objectively, and I had more particularly watched whether time, as I had expected, would gradually dim the beloved picture. But time is capricious and unpredictable, and subject not even to its own laws. Sometimes years will seem like days, and at another time hours will seem like months. Time is no more reliable than the vain device with which we measure it—the clock. A clock alone will not tell us whether it is morning or evening; it will mislead us by being fast and deceive us by being late; it will stop for a while and start again; it will run down while time runs on, or run on while time stands still. Time and oblivion, people say, go hand in hand, but this readily accepted adage underrates the importance of the human personality, which is for ever at war with time and on whose strength the outcome of the struggle depends. There are feelings, it seemed to me, which weary in their struggle with time, which turn wrinkled and sear, like our miserable human skins. But there are also feelings which are not so miserable and which do not go limp, even when our whole body has long shrunk to the bones. There are, in fact, feelings which, for better or worse, ceaselessly rejuvenate themselves so that they trot alongside time, just as the New Year skips alongside the decrepit Old Year, on the covers of calendars. I knew that it was too early to speak of "time;" after all, very little time had passed since my parting with Nora. It had been a new feeling then—and it would not have surprised me if this feeling had since gone with the wind of time. But it had resisted it; indeed it had grown stronger, sturdier, and healthier in the rough weather. I knew that I was not deceiving myself. Maturity means acquaintance with one's own feelings. Just as parents proudly report of their infant's instantly recognizing some friend or other when he knocked at the door, so maturity means the ability to recognize instantly any caller knocking, from within, at the door of our consciousness. It seemed to me that my maturity had begun.

I got the friendly old Negro with the white jacket, a real Uncle Tom out of my battered boyhood book, who was in charge of my Pullman coach and who kept offering to shine my shoes—for these comfortable coaches with the swivel chairs are the only place where, for a few brief train hours, the modern American can transfer himself back into his long-vanished feudal era—as I was saying, I got that solicitous attendant to bring me writing paper and an envelope, and began a letter to Nora. Since leaving Vienna I had been in the hands of the secret service and expressly bound to silence. But I had told Nora that I would be going to America and there was no reason any longer why I should hide from her. While I was pondering how to explain to her my long silence I gazed out into the evening. The first frost had painted the trees in bright colors. I thought that of all seasons I liked the autumn best because it was the most individual. At other times all trees were either green or bare, but now each wore its own dress, proud among the multitude.

It was with such meditations that I began my letter, fully conscious of how ill these flights of poetical fancy suited me and how much they belonged to the great deception which I was in duty bound—and, who knows, even willing—to practice upon the woman I loved.

The train thundered over a railway bridge and screamed through a tunnel as, just before reaching New York, I stuck down the envelope. Even before looking out for a porter, or taking a taxi into the strange city, I had sped my letter on its way across the ocean.

17

Shades of Mata Hari

DEAR JOHNNY, dear reader: the grotesque story which I am about to recount is, you may believe me, as typical as any in the thousand-year-old history of the secret service.

How many stories have you not read with a delicious sense of thrill: of bold agents and beautiful women spies, of breath-taking chases after secret plans, maps, chemical or physical formulas—adventure stories crammed full of black briefcases, stolen documents, and photographed letters! Siding, in your bedtime reading, with one spy against another, you no doubt believed that whenever your favorite agent boarded a train world history was travelling with him. I am now going to tell you the story of Grete Prochaska, who called herself Maud Leoni, at the risk of spoiling your future delight in those hoary fairy-tales which, if indeed they contain a grain of truth at all, are launched into the world by the secret services themselves, or by their lackeys for the sake of their greater glory and your confusion. Believe me, the secret services have their advertising managers and publicity agents, just as the soap manufacturers and the owners of tobacco plantations, and once you have swallowed enough of their subtle advertising slogans you will seriously believe that the secret services are either threatening or protecting you, whereas in fact their magic powers consist solely in conjuring the money out of your pocket into theirs. Of a thousand missions that you learn about, some nine hundred and ninety-nine end more or less like my assignment with Maud Leoni; but the one which ends differently is of such tragic significance that you would never wish to hear of spies or secret services again if it were truthfully reported to you. But more of this later.

I suppose that you will have already formed a picture of the Golden Girl nightclub. But your picture is false. It was not the kind of place one sees in spy films: clouds of cigarette smoke hanging in the air, suspicious characters with small mustaches sitting about at small tables, a greasy head waiter who is sure to "know something," and, finally, a girl dancer, announced by drum rolls, wearing a skintight evening gown and providing both suspense and musical interest. The Golden Girl was a perfectly respectable place of entertainment, of medium size, patronized chiefly by small-town Americans up in the big city. They, however, did not get their money's worth: the chief attraction was a short, fat comedian from Hollywood, whom I, personally, found most amusing, but who did not of course live up to the name of the place.

It is true that Maud Leoni, one of these girls, was billed as an international attraction, a "Viennese singer," but she was not—as one would have expected of the heroine of a spy story—the star of the programme. She was, in fact, the second number on the bill, and she sang a few light songs in French, Italian, and German without warming up an audience which found it difficult enough to understand the American spoken in New York.

It cost me a sizeable tip—naturally I was keeping a very careful and somewhat imaginative account of my expenses—before the head waiter consented to take my card with a few lines to the performer. A little while later he brought me a note from Maud,

containing the bare suggestion that I should have lunch with her
at the Golden Girl the next day.

The graceful blonde girl, who proved exceptionally pretty at
closer range, gave me a big smile, and an attractively firm handshake, and invited me to sit down by her side by vigorously slap-
ping the upholstered seat—rather like a dog-lover giving the command "sit!" to her pet, or like a nice old aunt encouraging her
favorite nephew to make himself comfortable at her side. The gesture, as I discovered later, was typical of Maud. She was the image
of the sweet Viennese girl, the type so lovingly perpetuated by
Arthur Schnitzler in his *Countess Mitzi* and in his working-class
children. She was twenty-three or twenty-four, with a most delightful little *retroussé* nose, indeed, everything about her seemed to be
provocatively upward pointing—her tiny nose, her usually pouting mouth, the little curls on her head, and her small, firm breasts.
She had a charming way of blushing—not so much about what was
said as about her own words; sometimes she even blushed while
walking along, as though she knew that the language of her hips
was more piquant than that of her lips. But above all, she was obviously a good-hearted creature—the type one could imagine as
keeping several pets, or paying for the education of a poor nephew,
or selflessly helping some unfortunate young man in his sexual
difficulties.

She was extremely pleased to learn—as in fact she already knew
from my card—that I had been sent by Fritz Benkhoff, whom she
had supposed to have died in an Allied prisoner-of-war camp. In
the course of our conversation I came to the conclusion that Intelligence had indeed made me the messenger of a dead man; this
filled me with a sense of discomfiture which I found hard to suppress. Fritz had evidently been a girlhood love of hers, or rather
a childhood love, an early dancing partner, or perhaps her first
lover, whom in her memory she had since invested with such idealized features that the impression I got of him was one of those
composite photographs in which "the most Grecian nose," the
"deepest eyes," and the "most intelligent forehead" are pieced together to produce one face.

I soon realized that Maud identified her childhood boy-friend
with her distant native city, which she had left a year ago and

which was already beginning to be transfigured in her memory. Nostalgia is a strange disease, comparable, perhaps, to malarial fever, which comes in sudden attacks, shakes the sufferer like the Biblical pestilence, disappears without trace, is regarded as cured, then strikes again, and—even when there has been no attack for a long time—continues to be present in the blood. Maud Leoni, at the moment I met her, was just going through one of these violent attacks, made worse, no doubt, by my presence and my reminiscences. I cannot deny that I took cold-blooded advantage of her sick condition.

The very same evening I took Maud—her duties did not start till half-past ten—to a Viennese restaurant on 79th Street. The place was situated in a semi-basement and called itself Beautiful Vienna, an appellation which was bound to strike anybody not himself a sufferer from nostalgic malaria as a piece of irony. On the walls was a colorful panorama representing a kind of potted version of "beautiful Vienna," the Giant Wheel was placed right next to St. Stephen's Cathedral, and the Vienna Woods abutted on the Imperial Palace. The lively proprietress spoke English with an unmistakable Viennese accent, but her Viennese on the other hand was heavily interlarded with American expressions and she insisted, even in her German conversation, on calling me "Mister."

I was beginning to think that I had taken Maud to the wrong kind of restaurant—but nothing could have been further from the truth. She consumed the transatlantic Schnitzel with an excellent appetite, rested her pretty little head in her palms, sighed till her bosom rose and fell, and, when an old Rumanian burst into song, even let some big tears spring from her blue eyes and trickle down her rosy cheeks.

It really was boundlesly mean of me to exploit so ruthlessly the fact that in Maud Leoni's bosom beat the heart of Grete Prochaska. On Monday I had treated her to Wiener Schnitzel and guitar music at the Beautiful Vienna; on the following day I gave her Apfelstrudel and zither music at the Stefansturm Restaurant; and on Wednesday we went to the Johann Strauss, where we ate a goulash which lacked just that gravy which, at the Beautiful Vienna, had been poured over the Wiener Schnitzel.

Several days passed in a partly patriotic and partly gastronom-

ical friendship and I came to know Maud's past as well as if I had
grown up with her—but I was not a step nearer to my real purpose. Twice, in the afternoons, she had driven me in her smart
pale-blue Chevrolet out into the open country, to the Hudson
River, whose forest-clad banks reminded her of the Danube; in the
evenings she wore a silvery wrap of real mink, and every time I
met her she wore a different dress—to make no mention of her
charming little hats, whose sophisticated triviality betrayed the
skill of an expensive milliner. But still she had not dropped the
slightest hint about the sources of her inexplicable wealth.

Since it is my duty to report how I succeeded after all in discovering Maud's secret I am afraid I shall have to trouble the
reader—very much against my better instincts—to accompany me
into my charming compatriot's bedroom.

On the fifth or sixth day of our acquaintance Maud called me
at my hotel and asked if I was not getting tired of restaurant fare
and if I would not prefer to have dinner at her apartment. It was
Sunday, she explained, and the Golden Girl was closed anyway,
and although she made no claims to great culinary prowess, she
thought, nevertheless, that she might manage an Austrian dish or
two. I accepted with pleasure and presented myself on her doorstep not only with a bunch of yellow roses but also—as I hope I
may be allowed to mention with a pat on my back—with three
bottles of Gumpoldskirchner wine.

Maud received me with a blush and a chaste kiss which matched
her get-up exceedingly well. Over her black-silk dress she was
wearing an apron of such minute proportions that it looked more
like the kind of bib tied round children's necks; and as the
charming young creature stood on tiptoe to breathe a kiss on my
lips she looked exactly like the lady maids in Viennese operettas
who, feather-duster tucked under arm, also invariably stand on tiptoe, bending forward and pushing their behinds out, whenever they
surprise their masters with a caress.

But if Maud had perhaps merely acted the soubrette part of
the lady's maid, there was nothing of the musical-comedy about
her cooking. The Russian eggs, which ought to be called Austrian
eggs anyway, the golden-brown roast chicken, and the cucumber
salad, with its sprinkling of red paprika, were no more than a

prosaic prologue to a Linzertorte which, crisp and yet moist, interlaced with a thin but tasty layer of jam, as with a narrow ribbon, would have done credit to the most famous pastry-cook of my native country.

Need I say that these delights—washed down by our native wine and accompanied by an excellent gramophone playing the oldest and the latest Viennese waltzes—that these delights of the palate and the ear soon aroused, as is inevitable with insatiable human nature, an appetite for further, different delights? Admittedly, gentle reader, a good and virtuous spy—the kind you know from your books—would have been careful not to yield to the temptations of the flesh, or would at least have acted with circumspection to make sure that, while lying in his siren's arms, he was not stabbed by a counter-spy lurking behind the heavy curtains. No such mean thought entered my mind. Maud need only lay her round, blushing little head against my chest, as though she had found there her first haven of peace in a wicked world, and immediately there awoke in me those paternal instincts which, unfortunately, are not always followed by strictly fatherly behavior. There is, sad to relate, no more secure protection a man can give a woman than his arms, and whenever he casts about for a shelter for the asylum-seeking woman in his arms his eye will instinctively fall on the haven-providing bed.

Maud did all she could not to let me forget, even for a moment, how much she needed my protection. But though I have just mentioned my protective arms, I was only speaking metaphorically: in fact, once I had carried the feather-light girl into the bedroom I hardly needed them again. From that moment onward it was enough that I was there—as the roof beneath which the flustered peasant wenches shelter from the rain, as the rock under which the animals of the forest seek protection, as the tree up which they scuttle when threatened by the barking dogs. Whatever pleasantries the girl showed me seemed to be performed for her own benefit—just as though I were personified Nature, assuaging the thirsty, the freezing, and the hungry, spending itself only in order to renew itself. That Maud did not easily content herself was by no means out of character, for anybody who admires Nature and is close to it also wants to savor its blessings to the full. It was to Maud's credit, not against it, that throughout this natural hour she did not blush once.

Yet I was not such a frivolous spy as I might appear from this account. While the bed is not the natural habitat of a man—who as a rule resorts to this well-sprung piece of furniture only for the sake of pleasant exhaustion or necessary rest—most women feel at home nowhere as in bed. There, they not only like to sleep and make love, but also to eat, drink, read good books, consult their mirrors, and, finally, make conversation. I have found most women in the prone position exceedingly loquacious, not to say garrulous, and Maud Leoni, *recte* Grete Prochaska, proved no exception. Physical love—and this is another point—to a man does not necessarily mean an exchange of confidences; yet I have known few women who did not immediately derive from physical intimacy a claim to more-than-physical intimacy. I was not therefore surprised when, in the course of the night, Maud felt that she had to confide to me a great deal more than she would ever have done in other circumstances.

What she told me was most flattering, for it put me in the always highly enviable position of a confidant. A woman, she pointed out, did not live by material things alone. Desirable as a pretty apartment no doubt was, a woman's heart also wanted a shelter for itself. It would therefore hardly surprise me, she continued, and it certainly must not offend me, to learn that she had a man friend. At the last words she blushed—most becomingly, as her embarrassment, like a little pink cloud in a clear sky, spread from her face over her breasts and down to her navel. Her friend was a rich Englishman, she said, but that need not worry me since luckily he came up to New York every other Sunday, his residence being in the Federal capital. She could have kept quiet about the relationship, and, as it were, concealed the man from me, she concluded, but that was not her way—least of all with a dear fellow-countryman.

Feigning jealousy—or, more correctly, lending exaggerated expression to my awakening jealousy—I demanded to know more about my rival. And although Maud assured me that the thing between him and her was "something entirely different" and not an affair of the heart, I insisted on making the stranger's acquaintance, at least from her description, since, as I put it, "it is more difficult to fight a shadow than a living person."

"All right, then," said Maud, pouting her lips in slight irritation, "he is comparatively young, he has a mustache, and he doesn't look as if he were rich, but he is in fact so rich the money spills out of his ears. He also drinks like a fish. He is half comical and half repulsive, and besides he is a pervert."

"A pervert? In what way?" I demanded.

She sat up, crossed her legs, and gave me a frank look.

"If he came in now," she said, "—by the way, he's got a key to this apartment—he wouldn't make a scene. In fact, he would probably be pleased."

"Well," I remarked innocently, "there are such people . . ."

"You are a pig," said Maud with conviction. "I didn't mean it like that."

However, I was not to find out that night how she did mean it. As if seeking protection from some monster, Maud again fled to the shelter of my breast, and had I not known better I might well have thought that her repulsive, rich man friend and his unnatural propensities had been invented merely to unleash a thunderstorm from which she might then flee into my sheltering arms.

A week passed and I had made no progress whatever—from a secret-service point of view. I saw Maud every day; I visited the Golden Girl without discovering anything suspicious; I met her after her performance; I even bought a spare razor; but I did nothing to earn the confidence of my employers. Naturally they were beginning to get a little impatient, as I was told pretty plainly by my contact, the second-hand-car dealer Joe Brown, an extremely boorish fellow, whom I had once gone to see, for the sake of order, with a preliminary report, and who had examined my expense account in the most insolent manner, very nearly calling me a crook because of a doubtful item of barely thirty dollars.

At last, on a Sunday, exactly a week after my first visit to Maud's apartment, things began to move.

With tears and unsolicited assurance Maud had asked me, her true love, to release her for the weekend. The "man from Washington," as she called him, had arrived in New York. I therefore dined in solitary state at Longchamps, in spite of its name a genuine American restaurant, which served clean American food and made no Continental pretensions. Shortly after ten, feeling in need of sleep, I went to bed.

At two o'clock I was awakened by the ringing of the telephone. Still half asleep, I thought that Maud would probably want to assure me of her undying affection, being acquainted with the way in which a bad conscience leads to a sincere deepening of feminine sentiments. But for once this was not a case of sentimental confessions. She must see me about something, Maud said, and she must see me at once; she needed my urgent and immediate advice. This did not sound at all as if her helplessness were, as usual, a put-on challenge designed to evoke affectionate protectiveness. Without awaiting my consent she named a little place that kept open all night, on Broadway, not far from my hotel. She would meet me there in about twenty minutes. As I hastily put on my clothes my eyes fell on the revolver which I had been given in Washington, but I must confess that in the hurry I again forgot about it—a thing I was to do a few more times in the course of my career.

Exactly twenty minutes later I entered a cafeteria at the intersection of 40th Street. At this hour the only people in it were, apart from Maud, a coffee-counter man in a white jacket and a black postman.

Maud was sitting at one of the small tables, evidently she had not let the door out of her sight. She was wearing her mink coat, but I suspected that underneath she wore only a light nightgown. I disapproved of the mink because of the late hour and the dubious joint, and of her flimsy garment underneath because of the chilly, almost wintry, drizzle outside.

"I think," said Maud, after a hasty grateful opening, "I have done something very silly, and maybe I've got to do something straight away to get it back from him before he leaves New York."

I asked her to express herself more clearly.

Well, she explained, the "man from Washington" had arrived punctually as usual. He had accompanied her on a little shopping tour in the afternoon; he had had his scotch-and-soda at her place—or, more correctly, four of them; they had then gone to a show; they had dined at Sardi's; and towards eleven they had

eventually gone to her apartment. There her visitor had downed
three more scotch-and-sodas which, considering he had had one or
two cocktails at the restaurant, was more than his usual ration.
After that, however, he had not acted "as usual" but had produced
a paper and asked her to sign it. There had been four or five
sheets typed in English, and naturally she had wanted to read what
she had been asked to sign. The man had acted strangely from the
start, but now he began to act even stranger. He had snatched up
the papers, almost tearing them from her hands, and all she had
been able to take in amid the excitement and rush was the fact
that the name Sobrin occurred in them repeatedly. For an hour—
yes, she was sure it must have been that long—the man had then
wrestled with her; no, not in the physical but in the figurative
sense. He had first asked her not to deny him this "little favor,"
which was a pure formality and a personal matter. When she had
refused he had begun to threaten her. He would withdraw his
support from her and get her "into frightful trouble." In the end
he had begged her on his knees—"I'd never seen a man on his
knees before"—not to refuse him this first and only request.

"And did you sign?" I asked, when Maud at last made a pause
to take a sip of the steaming coffee.

Without looking at me she nodded into her cup.

"Do you suppose he intends to blackmail you?" I asked with
feigned innocence. "Could it have been something like an I.O.U.?"

"No, no," she said firmly. "It's about Sobrin."

"And who the devil is Sobrin?"

Of course I knew who Sobrin was, but it took quite a while
before I could get any details out of Maud. After all, I was in the
position of Maud's true love and confidant, and she was most anxious at this moment to convince me that, apart from the rich
man friend to whom she had confessed, she did not have a second
benefactor. Before I was even told that Sobrin was a Russian, presumably a Soviet diplomat, Maud assured me that he had a wife
and four children, that he had never tried to approach her, and
that, moreover, she believed he was impotent. I was a little surprised that Maud should find it necessary to tell me all this, since
after so short a time I would not presume to lay exclusive claims

to her, but her protestations convinced me that she was maintaining intimate relations also with Lieutenant-Colonel Sobrin. For, alas, it is the practice of women to pacify their lovers with the assurance that their rivals are either impotent or homosexuals.

"I never thought anything of going out with Sobrin now and again," she eventually came to the point. "I was so bored before you came, Georgie. Of course the Russians are all a bit odd, and I never quite understood how a Communist could have so much money—but then diplomats are diplomats, and everything just goes down on the expense account."

"The expense account?" I said, and Maud did not see why I should linger on this point for so long. "And how do you explain the whole business?"

She ran her fingers through her unkempt blonde curls, which were a little damp and therefore even more enchanting. "I've told you, the Englishman is a pervert. Now I'm beginning to see daylight. I once mentioned Sobrin to him. Maybe I wanted to make him jealous—it was quite at the beginning and I still rather liked him then. I offered to break with Sobrin, but he wouldn't have it; on the contrary, he said he quite understood and he wanted me to go on seeing Sobrin. It wouldn't worry him, he said; it wouldn't worry him at all. Surely you must admit that this is perverted?"

I admitted it. "And," I continued, "did he want to know anything about Sobrin?"

She shook her head. "No. I've just been trying to remember. Because now, suddenly, everything looks suspicious . . . but no, he merely asked if I was still seeing Sobrin."

"And Sobrin?" I inquired. "Did he know about the man from Washington—what's his name, by the way?"

"McKay," said Maud. "Vernon McKay. Of course Sobrin knew about him. Why on earth should I keep it secret from him? I'm telling you there's nothing between me and Sobrin . . ." and again she burst into reassuring accounts of the Russian's ideal domestic life.

I seized Maud's hand across the little aluminum table.

"Baby," I said—it sounds cheap, but I called her Baby—"I'll try to help you. I've got an idea—it may be crazy, but perhaps it isn't so crazy. I am going to ask you a very odd question, and you've got to answer me truthfully or else I can't help you. Tell me, do you think your friend Sobrin is a pervert as well?"

"You mean, does he . . . ?"

"I mean, did he too seem anxious that you should stick to McKay?"

"Well, he didn't want to carry the sole responsibility," Maud replied with a blush.

"Good," I said, without thinking it necessary to enlighten Maud as to what I thought good about it. "You have, of course, been terribly silly to sign the paper, a real silly goose as we'd say back home—but that can't be helped now. You've signed it and that's that. Your friend McKay's name is probably not McKay at all, any more than your Russian's name is Sobrin—so there would be no point in tracking him down, and, besides, he wouldn't dream of handing the document back to you. The less dust you stir up the better, because your diplomat and your millionaire are obviously engaged in the same dirty business."

Maud stared at me, wide-eyed. I would have staked my entire career as a spy that her horror was not acted.

"You really think that they're both spies, Georgie?" she stammered.

Then she began to cry and seemed more in need of protection than ever. However, it was four in the morning and my paternal instincts were too sleepy for me to have seriously considered taking Maud home and comforting her. I did what I could to calm and reassure her; I promised to come and see her in the afternoon and, having given the problem my mature consideration, would advise her then in her predicament. I took her across a totally dead Broadway, whose suddenly arrested neon advertisements gave it the air of a Christmas-tree on Twelfth Night, put her in a taxi, and strolled through the drizzle to my hotel.

I found no sleep and spent also the next morning deep in thought.

Although it is the normal practice, and probably even the duty, of agents to mix up numbers, so that eventually two and two make any conceivable sum, including the most complicated logarithms, but on no account four, I set out to examine calmly all possibilities and, after eliminating one eventuality after another, arrived at the conclusion that two and two did add up to four. Equipped with this knowledge I called on Maud the following afternoon.

The icy October rain had not ceased for a moment and all free taxis seemed to have suddenly vanished from the face of the earth. I was soaked to the skin when I arrived at 72nd Street, so that I appreciated Maud's housewifely solicitude more than ever. Only when she had satisfied herself that I was most comfortably settled did she allow me to say what I had come to say. But then she huddled at my feet and listened attentively while I reported to her the results of my speculations.

"Baby," I began. "I've given much thought to the business as a whole and to your predicament in particular. In the war I was concerned for a time—though only casually and not in a very exalted position—with the kind of thing that is now troubling your pretty little head and causing you, not unnaturally, some anxiety. There's no point in our beating about the bush or in refusing to face up to facts. Listen to me, and I'll tell you what the whole thing is about. Last night you mentioned something about an expense account and, without knowing it, you thereby handed me the key to the whole mystery. Your two friends—no, don't interrupt me: it doesn't matter what has or hasn't happened between you and the Russian—your two friends are both working for Intelligence or, as the more popular expression goes, the secret service. Whether they hold an important or insignificant post in their organizations I cannot tell—but, within the limitations of their trade, they seem to be perfectly decent fellows, the man from Washington, as you call him, working for British Intelligence and the Russian for the Soviet. Now you're staring, Baby, and you think your eyes have really been opened—but don't you believe it. Not by a long shot. I can guess what you're thinking now, you think they wanted to rope you in for their dirty work, to turn you into a spy, another Mata Hari, a Fräulein Doktor. That's true in one way, but not in another—you'll see it all in a minute. When the two met you, independently of each other, they had no evil intention. Why should they? You have no important connections and you're no more cut out for spying than I am for

tight-rope walking. Their professional interest in you, if I may call
it that, began only when each discovered that you knew the other.
In short, at first they were interested simply in you, just as I am,
as one of the most ravishing creatures that ever walked the New
York pavement." I accompanied these words with a gentle caress of her hair, and continued, "Well, they weren't so lucky as I
am—but then, they didn't come from Vienna and, if I am to believe you, they also lacked my irresistible charm. On the other
hand, Baby, you weren't doing so well just then—you told me so
yourself. But an entertainer from the Golden Girl—and that is the
advantage of such joints for girls like yourself, since otherwise
you'd do something more interesting—as I am saying, an entertainer from the Golden Girl, an international attraction, and especially if she was as sweet as you, Baby, was entitled to be demanding. The two gentlemen therefore began to rush into heavy
expenses, each of them wanted to outdo his yet unknown rival. A
cocktail dress was followed by an evening gown; but in an evening gown a delicate little creature like you would freeze to death
unless she wore a mink coat over it; but no sensible woman
would travel by subway in a mink coat—well, you know how it
is, Baby . . ."

Baby dropped her eyes, but I was not put off by this coy ad-
mission. I went on:

"You're quite right, diplomats, as you call them, can put a lot
of things down on the expense account, but these expenses are subsequently examined—very carefully, often even pettily, down to
such sums as twenty or thirty dollars—you can take it from me.
Diplomats must also justify their journeys, and your two friends
no doubt found New York a very powerful, and probably rather
too frequent, attraction. Then, suddenly, each of them learns of
the identity of the other, and that, to them, is a real godsend. They
simply put you on their expense account, Baby. Your Briton reports to his superior that he has discovered a woman who has connections with the Russians—intimate relations, one might also say
—and your Russian puts in for an Order of Lenin straight away,
on account, as it were, because he has found a girl who is, if you'll
forgive the harsh word, the mistress of a British Intelligence man.

Now, all of a sudden, the trips to New York are fully justified; the expenses are barely examined; and the mink coat is quite in order—no matter whether you've had it from the Briton or the Russian. Do you follow me?"

Maud nodded contritely, confirming that I was on the right track. I lit a cigarette, pulled her over to me on to the settee, and said:

"And now I'm going to tell you something, Baby, that'll perhaps scare you—but your Georgie is right here and there's no cause for panic. The Mata Hari story began in just the same way. There was a German Military Attaché in Madrid, who couldn't afford the 'Red Dancer,' and so he reported to Berlin that he'd discovered a master spy—only he omitted to inform her of it, but that's by the way. I don't know much about these things, but one thing is certain: most of the famous women spies never spied out anything in their lives. The same is true of famous men spies, but that's beside the point. The most important thing about espionage, Baby, is the expense account. Unfortunately, now and again, some high officials get a bit impatient with their pleasure-seeking subordinates and demand results; they want proof that their money hasn't been poured down the drain. That's what I think is behind your experience of yesterday. Your friend McKay, I imagine, has been instructed to supply some information at long last, some written report from his able woman agent. Once or twice, I suppose, he must have concocted something, probably something trivial, and without your signature; then perhaps his people in Washington got a bit suspicious and wanted to learn more. That, Baby, is what led to the scene yesterday, and that's why Sobrin's name figured in your friend's report. I may be wrong, of course, but I'd be willing to stake my head that your Russian friend, that idyllic family man, will shortly approach you with a similar request, since his fairy-tales are no doubt also getting a bit hot for him. Thus your name will get into the files of the British and the Soviet secret services; they'll give you a cover name, such as 'Golden Girl' or something equally original; and then some day the ones will steal the secret files of the others and decode them, and if war broke out they'd shoot you at dawn, on this side or the other," I concluded, "and you'd fall forward to the ground, with never an idea what you'd done to deserve to be lying there with a bullet in your sweet curly head."

Maud shivered, as if she were not lying in my caressing arms but as though the bullets of the firing squad were already singing past her.

"I shall never see them again!" she exclaimed.

"Steady now, steady," I said. "Nothing would be more wrong. If you stopped giving them your favors, if you were to decline their attentions, or if you were to ask questions or make vague accusations, they'd know at once that you'd seen through their intentions and through their sombre game. And they'd set their dogs on you to tear you to pieces. You've got to act carefully, slowly, circumspectly, gradually——"

"But they'll shoot me at dawn," Maud interrupted.

"That's what I am here to prevent," I said, drawing her into my protective arms. "I hope my business will keep me in America for some little time, and even when I've left I can get some reliable friend or other to help you for my sake. From time to time you'll simply write down what you've heard from the two of them, what they have said to you, what they have told you to do, and what questions they have asked you. I shall pass on these reports—that, of course, is too grand a word for them, they need to be no more than a few jottings—to the American police. If anything happens, if you should get into trouble, you can always state on oath, and what's more prove, that you'd kept up with the two of them merely in order to serve the country whose hospitality you'd been enjoying. Besides," I added, after a little reflection, "I can't have you being dependent on those two fellows in the long run—there's got to be an end some time. No, please, don't contradict, Baby! So long as I'm here you shall have enough money from me to make sure you're independent of the two. I can't buy you a mink coat or furnish a new apartment for you, but I shall. be taking an important business trip in the next few days anyway, and if I can clinch the deal—as I have every confidence I shall—I promise you won't have anything to worry about. My firm, too, is quite generous about expenses. After all,

Baby, we're compatriots and must help each other in a strange country."

Maud began to cry. She did not cry the way I had seen her cry before. She was sobbing, and her tears ran over my suit and down my shirt front. I do not know whether she cried from a sense of relief after her dire tribulations, or from gratitude, or because she knew that I would try to comfort her—but I rather suspect the last reason since, after a few tearful minutes, she rose abruptly, walked swiftly over to the gramophone, and put on a Viennese tune which we used to call "our song."

The gramophone was an automatic record-changer, a British or a Russian gift, and one could listen to it from the bedroom without having to incommode oneself by going to the living-room every time a record came to an end.

But this brings me to the final episode in the story of Grete Prochaska, alias Maud Leoni—and this episode is of such awkward character that to record it one would need the pen of a Boccaccio, a Balzac, or a Casanova. How can I—without making the reader turn away in disgust, accuse me of vulgarity, and forbid this book not only to his children and his children's children, but even to himself for all time to come—how can I describe those intimate matters without which, on the other hand, the history of my first assignment in New York would lack its point? Very well, I shall probably have to risk the plunge into the icy waters of indiscretion—or perhaps I should say, the sizzling hot waters—and the more swiftly it is done, and with the fewest possible words, the sooner may I hope not to have unduly offended the reader's sense of delicacy.

Our hours of love-making which followed the above dialogue, or more correctly monologue, differed from our earlier amorous encounters as impassioned oratory differs from polite conversation. The excitement of the past few hours, my sleepless night, Maud's overbrimming gratitude for her rescue from the brink of disaster, my vain self-congratulation—all these had made us forget (or perhaps regard as a profanation of our perfect union) those precautions which we normally practiced in our more playful encounters. When at last we rose from the bed—we had of course forgotten about dinner and the time had come for Maud to go to her job—and when the girl inquired how long I proposed to be out of town, and I replied that it might be two or even three weeks, she asked, not by way of prompting but rather as if giving expression to a mutual anxiety, what would happen if in the meantime there were to be some consequence of our senseless, or rather sensual, madness.

"I shall of course call you," I said, in a flush of chivalry. "We'll speak to each other often enough, and we'll write. . . ."

"Good," she said, reassured, gracefully stretching out one of her slender legs and testing the firm tautness of the stockings she had just put on. "If I say to you 'Red has arrived' you'll know that everything's all right."

I turned away and this time, I swear it, it was my turn to blush.

The telegram to Vernon MacMahon—I had completely forgotten about it in the recent excitement. And now a capricious fate had answered that question, too, on the edge of a bed.

"Don't worry, Baby," I said.

I certainly did not worry. I knew that Washington would be satisfied with me.

18

ფფფფფფფფფფფ

General Greehahn's Archives

AN AGENT can have no greater piece of good fortune than to be a fully informed witness when his secret service is made to look foolish.

When I handed my report to Mr. Brown, my contact—needless to say with the recommendation that Maud Leoni, alias Grete Prochaska, be placed on the payroll of U.S. Intelligence, so that in future she should supply information about both her British and her Russian friends, but in fact with the secret intention of having my future diversions financed by Intelligence—when I handed in my half-factual and half-ironical report I was afraid that Washington might feel embarrassed over its foolish exposure and might work its discomfiture out on me.

Nothing of the sort happened—and for good reasons. To be accepted as a full member of the organization, which has more secrets of its own than it knows about anybody else, one has got to prove his readiness to remain a member even though he does not think much of the organization; in other words, he must pass a test in spinelessness—and this, personally, I did not find at all difficult. One may become a highly successful agent without ever discovering a secret other than the internal secrets of one's own secret service—in much the same way as the accountant of a dishonest firm is allowed to retire on his pension so long as he tacitly records his employers' false tax returns. My anxieties were therefore needless. With a mixture of annoyance and respect, Mr. Brown informed me that Washington wished to see me.

The assignment I was given there—and this time not by a colonel in disguise but by a gentleman in a far more exalted position—proved to me that I had made much headway in a short time.

Before describing this assignment—one of the most important, and, in its unforeseen consequences, unfortunately also one of the most dangerous missions in my entire career—I shall have to say a few words about my frame of mind at that time.

I had decided, drifting passively at first, but later with full deliberation, to make the secret service my career. Yet nothing could be further from my mind than to become one of the "Intelligence proletarians" of whom Mr. Smith had spoken with such justified contempt.

Heinrich Heine, whose works I enjoyed reading, even at the time when the *Lorelei* had been attributed to an "unknown author," describes in one of his books a visit he paid to the Louvre in Paris. There he caught sight of an Englishwoman, recognizable as an elderly spinster even by the velvet ribbon round her scraggy neck, lost in rapturous admiration in front of a nude statue of Hermes. On his way out of the museum, more than an hour later, the poet found the gaunt lady still gazing at the naked man in marble with concupiscent fascination. In reply to the poet's impertinent inquiry whether she was not beginning to feel a little ashamed of her curiosity, the Englishwoman eyed him through her lorgnette and declared: "Sir, in the face of these dimensions there is no such thing as smut." This seemingly frivolous but, in fact, very profound episode gave me much food for thought, chiefly because it confirmed me in the belief that morality is above all a matter of quantity. In other words, decent behavior in small doses lacks all value, whereas indecency, provided it is on a sufficient scale, is certainly deserving of respect. I have never joined in the philistine complaint that small thieves are hanged while the big ones go scot-free. It serves them right if they swing. Why did they not steal more?

This philosophy I now proposed to put into practice—and indeed it was high time. True, ever since the Countess in Baden had honored me with her trust I had been living quite comfortably—especially if one considers the lean time everybody was having just then—but I had, after all, inherited some of my mother's sense of economy. I wanted not only to have a good time, but also to acquire some more solid possessions. The Devil is a respectable person, respected even by God—but not the little devils who, like grimy and ill-paid stokers, shovel the coal under the brass cauldrons. I felt that the time had come for me to act, not as an exploited servant of the Devil, but as a devilish employer in my own right.

For several days after my arrival in Washington I had to familiarize myself with the person of a certain Wilhelm Engljähringer, an Austrian by birth, who had played a subordinate but, it seemed, notorious part in German Intelligence during the Second World War. After the Russian occupation of Vienna he had been either taken to Siberia or—nobody was quite certain which —done away with, presumably because of his close connections with the Gestapo. In the character of Colonel (retired) Wilhelm Engljähringer I was now ostensibly interned, in a house in Washington's "residential center." The house was already occupied by the German Lieutenant-General Helmuth Edler von Greehahn, whom the Americans had brought to the States from a P.O.W. camp, partly for the purpose of interrogating him more thoroughly, but chiefly because they intended to entrust this experienced man with the creation of a Western espionage center in Germany. I was to spend the next four or five weeks in the General's company, gain his confidence—that was the idea behind my masquerading as a professional officer, a pro-German, and an enthusiastic National Socialist —and to test his reliability, his beliefs, and his intentions, though not his oft-proved professional ability.

The General received me with friendly reserve. He looked like a shaven fish—an impression that was heightened by his uniform, which had been stripped of all decorations and badges of rank. I remember how, during the war, the Italian partisans used to taunt us with a poster which they would stick, with remarkable perseverance and under cover of night, on the walls of the officers' quarters. It showed a German officer, or rather, a most malicious caricature of a German officer, looking like a carp that had been stripped of its scales. In his prominent right eye he wore a monocle, and the right corner of his fish's mouth was grotesquely distorted, as though he were afraid his eye-glass would otherwise drop out. Below this truly uncomplimentary, and no doubt also unrealistic, portrait, on the partisan poster were only the words *Il Nemico,* meaning 'The Enemy.' It can hardly be assumed that the Italians had met Lieutenant-General Helmut Edler von Greehahn, the German Intelligence Chief on the Eastern Front, but if ever there was a man who could have served as the model for "The Enemy" then, without a doubt, it was my fellow-lodger in Washington.

I soon discovered that this was no accident. The General possessed a rare quality which, I must confess, commanded my respect: he did not want to seem different from what he was. His favorite quotation was the dictum of Accius, the pre-Christian and un-Christian author, handed down to us identically by Cicero and Seneca: *Oderint, dum metuant.* He too would rather be feared than loved, and nothing would flatter him more than to be instantly recognized as *Il Nemico.* Once, when we had come to know each other better, I asked him why he wore a monocle—a habit which was neither attractive nor fashionable. He surprised me with the frank reply: "Certainly not because I am short-sighted; as you see, my dear Engljähringer, it's made of plain glass. I wore my monocle out of opposition, even under Hitler, and I'm wearing it out of opposition now. Not so much to annoy people, which would be a matter of indifference to me, but in order to facilitate our relationships. The less they deceive themselves about having to take me as they find me the better for all of us."

Even his brief account of the General—who was as thin as a rake, at least six feet tall and barely more than forty-five—will make it clear that the American secret service had made a mistake in dispatching me to the Washington house of their luxury-internee in the guise of an ardent National Socialist. The General, as I soon found out, was no Nazi. The only loyalty I could discover in him was toward the Greehahn secret service, to which he would refer, not in the past tense, nor in the future, but as if speaking of a firm whose operations were temporarily suspended. I soon readjusted myself accordingly, and since he appeared to know very little of my—that is, Engljähringer's—past history, there was nothing to stop our relationship from becoming most cordial.

As the General was to play an important part in my future career I shall have to say a few more words about his character, his weaknesses, and his accomplishments.

He was, to put it mildly, a complex personality. Side by side with his extensive military and historical knowledge he maintained an almost coquettish liaison with literature, which was reflected chiefly in his habit, in the manner of the semi-erudite, of introducing quotations into his conversation, on every suitable as well as every unsuitable occasion.

As our acquaintanceship deepened the General confided to me his real secret: he wrote poetry. Now and again he would produce from his bedroom a little copy-book in black covers, into which he had written his poems in a tidy hand—"The job I had convincing those idiots that this wasn't a secret code!"—and, moved almost to tears, would read me his verses.

The General's other weakness was that he drank, as the popular saying is, "like a fish." But I feel sure that fishes cannot possibly drink anything like General von Greehahn, or else all streams and rivers, and perhaps even the seas, would have long gone dry. It was nothing to him to empty three bottles of Veuve Cliquot by himself in the course of a cozy evening's conversation

—and even though at the end of it he was as sober as his boots it nevertheless seemed to me an improper habit for an espionage general.

The General's tender lyrical leanings combined with his boundless thirst, his knife-edge intelligence combined with an almost feminine capriciousness, so confused me that I was in no way prepared for the fateful conversation which took place one wild December evening.

Our spacious house, tastefully—if a little sparsely—furnished, stood at the end of a cul-de-sac off a quiet street. That day had seen the winter's first snowfall, but the snow had not settled on the ground and had merely turned the garden outside the tall bay windows of our big sitting-room into a morass. The wind was howling round the house—"as in a Brontë novel," said the General—and the bare trees were creaking, as if their branches were about to snap. The General had been standing by the window for some time, watching the two sentries who, muffled to the eyes, were stamping up and down the garden, as if on duty on the Russian front. When he turned to face me there was a broad, unhealthy smile on the General's narrow white features, and like everything about the General this grin, too, came as a surprise.

"The idiots," he said. "The damned idiots! Here we are in an over-heated room, drinking Veuve Cliquot"—he poured himself another glass—"and smoking Coronas, and outside our jailers are getting their toes frostbitten. Why the devil should we take it into our heads to run away—even if they didn't lock our doors every night? Can you tell me that, Engljähringer?"

"It really is too silly, Herr General," I said, reaching for the cigar box.

He drained his glass. "Don't look at me so disapprovingly, Engljähringer." I had not looked at him at all: he was still standing with his back to me. "I know what you're thinking," he continued. "But you're thinking wrong. You're thinking: How can a man in his position drink like a fish? I will tell you because I like you, and because, maybe, I have a few plans involving you. If one of my agents drinks heavily I have him shortened by a head." He spoke of "his" agents as though he were still sitting in his H.Q. at Smolensk. "An agent mustn't drink because he might know something which he could betray. I can't betray anything, Engljähringer, because I don't know anything. So long as I remain sober enough to conceal my ignorance—and I'd remain that all right if I emptied all the cellars of Rheims."

For four weeks I had avoided asking the General any questions. I felt that the moment had now come to reap the fruits of the trust I had nurtured.

"But you're being questioned all day long, Herr General," I said. "I should be much surprised if for once those fellows were to give us a rest tonight. On the other hand, the privileged treatment that's given you—and, incidentally, also to my humble self——"

"I know, I know," he interrupted. "After all, I didn't offer myself to the Americans without knowing my value. I knew they'd handle me like a piece of delicate china. Armies come and go, but the secret services endure. Which, if you come to think of it, is no more than logical. 'The dead do not rise again,' as it says in *Don Carlos.* You can lock up the general in command of an Army or an Army Group, and you can hang him; his organization is shattered at the moment of defeat, and nothing is risked by putting him up against the wall or pillorying him as a vile dog. But my troops—if you want to call them that—have not died for Führer and Fatherland; I can pull them out of my hat tomorrow if you like. My armies are intact, Engljähringer." He had turned to face me and was now scrutinizing me with a thoroughness I had not seen him practice before. "Besides, the Americans think they can strike a political bargain with me."

"How do you mean, Herr General?"

He sat down facing me, in a comfortable arm-chair, and stretched out his long, slim legs.

"Haven't you noticed, Engljähringer, that treason always starts in Intelligence? Canaris is now becoming a popular example, on both sides, either as a hero or as a traitor—but in any case a legendary figure. But you go and read up your Ferrero and see whether the Intelligence service of ancient Rome ever acted differently. This game has been going on for centuries. Provided an Intelligence service is working only moderately well it must know that a war is lost long before the rest of the army does, and its leaders act the way the other generals would also act, if only they realized the pointlessness of their patriotism in good time."

"But you, Herr General . . ." I said.

"No, I didn't go over to the enemy," he said, "because I should have had to go over to the Russians."

"There you are, Herr General," I declared, with pretended admiration. "First you accuse yourself, at least by implication, of spinelessness, and yet you declined——"

He stopped me with a gesture. "Don't talk nonsense, Engljähringer! I am an expert on Soviet affairs—probably the best for miles around. To offer to the Russians what I know about them would be like carrying owls to Athens."

"May I point out a contradiction, Herr General?" I retorted. "Or, at least, what looks like a contradiction to me? A moment ago you described yourself as the greatest expert on Soviet affairs —and I feel sure that was no idle boast—yet a little while earlier you claimed that you knew nothing at all. May I take it that in the first case you were pleased to joke?"

"I feel less like joking tonight than I have done for a long time," replied Greehahn. "Today is more critical for me than you think."

He stood up and began to walk about the room, performing almost geometrically precise figures-of-eight on the sitting-room floor. Every time he completed the smaller circle he stopped to look at me. I had the alarming impression that I was not the General's fellow-lodger in the well-guarded house, but that I was his prisoner, and in his power. The thought that the shivering soldiers were patrolling the garden was suddenly very pleasant.

"I want to talk to you frankly, Engljähringer," said the General. "Not so much from choice as from necessity. To start with, you may rest assured that we are not being overheard. I removed that ludicrous microphone gadget from behind the fake Velásquez an hour ago—only an hour ago, since otherwise those blockheads might have had enough time to install another behind the fake Ruisdael. Secondly," he continued, resuming his circuit of the floor, "I am of course aware that your name isn't Engljähringer, even though—permit me to congratulate you—you've made an excellent study of his person. My dear colleagues of the American

Intelligence have overlooked nothing, except the small detail that
in 1939, when I was still commanding a division in Poland, Engljähringer served under me for a few months. Your real identity,
Engljähringer—I'll continue to call you that for the sake of simplicity—is of course not known to me in the circumstances, but you
would seem to be a Viennese who is fed up with being inadequately fed. I presume that you have some experience in Intelligence work, though evidently not as much as you pretend. These
remarks were indispensable by way of introduction and I have no
intention of reverting to them again." He stopped by the table
on which the champagne stood in an ice bucket. "Another glass,
Engljähringer? No? Very well." He filled up his own glass and
sat down.

"I presume you are pursuing an aim with your sudden frankness, Herr General?" I said.

"You've taken the words out of my mouth. 'One must view
one's aim as long and from as many sides until one has come to
like it,' Klopstock says somewhere." He smiled, but his eyes did not
share in the smile. "I have viewed you as long and from as many
sides until I have come to like you. I believe we might come to a
satisfactory arrangement, Engljähringer."

"Wouldn't you like to drop the name, Herr General?" I asked.
"As far as I know, Engljähringer is dead."

"That could be a portent," he said, but without giving the
threat the least emphasis. "Let's stick to your pseudonym. But to
come back to your question: no, there is no contradiction between
my knowledge and my ignorance." He interrupted himself again,
as was his manner when he was about to utter some dictum.
"Do you know what learning means? Learning, my dear fellow,
is not encyclopaedic knowledge—for nobody has that. Learning
is simply the knowledge of where to look things up. The Americans
are quite correct in thinking that, in a matter of weeks, I can set
up the best Intelligence organization in the world. But they are
wrong in supposing that I carry the organization in my breast
pocket."

"You would have to 'look things up,' " I interjected, to prove
my quick understanding.

"Quite right. I've got to get hold of my hidden archives. They contain the names of all my agents in the East, of all my contacts, of all Eastern traitors, of all persons considered unreliable by the East, of all saboteurs and informers, and whatever else the West might want to know. In my head there is nothing except the location of the archives and the way of getting to them."

I was watching him closely. He was speaking rapidly, almost as if he were reading a manuscript that had long been completed, checked, and proof-read for publication. Yet I had the impression that for once he had drunk a little too much, even for his exceptional head.

"You will understand," he continued, "that I have no intention of surrendering my knowledge. American Intelligence would be quite incapable of doing anything with it, and at best would grant me a pension or magnanimously forgive me those war crimes which I never committed anyway. On the other hand, the gentlemen won't dream of setting me free until I've convinced them of my value by some tangible results."

"That looks like a pretty hopeless dilemma," I said, my heart pounding fast. I was beginning to see what Greehahn was getting at.

"As you say," he surprised me by admitting. "Even if they released me I couldn't move a step without being watched—quite apart from the fact that the archives are not even accessible to me personally."

"I seem to have come to you as a messenger from Heaven, Herr General," I said calmly.

"For the time being, merely as a messenger from U.S. Intelligence," replied the General. "But let us assume, Engljähringer, that I trusted you. It would be a venture, of course, but I have always liked Ulrich von Hutten's motto 'I have ventured with eyes open.' If I ventured to confide in you I should indeed be doing so with eyes open. I presume the Americans are paying you a fixed salary; perhaps they have also promised you some little contingency-fee if you pull the job off. Moreover, you are a foreigner, which always means a lower pay-scale in our profession, even if you did not come from a small, defeated country." He poured himself another glass and drained it at one gulp. "You intended to watch me, but of course I have watched you. This is my proposition:

one hundred thousand dollars if you obtain the archives and deposit
them at a place to be named by me. Don't look at me as if I were
raving! Even in captivity I am still more powerful than those
blockheads at liberty. The moment I convince the Americans of the
existence of my organization they are going to put a sum of
twenty-five million dollars annually at my disposal. Surely, the U.S.
treasury is an adequate guarantee to you, Engljähringer?"

I found it difficult to hide my emotion.

The sound of large sums of money has always made my
head spin, and now, again, the figures acted on me like an aphrodisiac.

"I don't think you are raving at all, Herr General," I said.
"What does surprise me is your trustfulness—I might almost say
your naïve trustfulness. True, you are in a dilemma. But supposing
I set out with your instructions, tracked down your archives and
everything that's connected with them, and then sold the whole
treasure to the Americans for, say, two hundred thousand dollars?"

"There's no danger of that," replied the General. "First of
all, the victors pay badly. Victory means a right to cheap prices
—otherwise there'd be no point in it. Secondly, I believe you're
clever enough to make inquiries about me. In which case you'd
be discouraged from double-crossing me. I told you Engljähringer's
death could be a portent. The real Engljähringer, I mean—for the
moment."

"I think, Herr General, I'm interested in your proposition," I
said.

I considered how far I could go. But then I told myself that
espionage was really a very pleasant occupation and one where
the risks were greatly overrated by an uninformed public. Even
supposing that behind the Ruisdael, or in the crystal chandelier,
or under my chair, or in some other absurd place, another half-
dozen secret microphones had been installed, which the General
had not discovered—although I hardly thought he would be
guilty of such negligence—even the most loyal agent of the
Americans could not have acted differently, in my position, from
the way I was acting. So long as U.S. Intelligence did not instal a
microphone in my heart, they could not tell whether I was ac-

cepting the German's offers with personal gain in mind or merely in order to deceive him.

"If I might have a glass of champagne now," I said, rising to my feet.

He poured it out for me.

Holding the glass in my hand, I paced the room for a few moments. At last I halted at the window. The snow was now coming down in big, soothing flakes.

The General broke the silence. "I can guess what you are thinking," he said.

I regarded him questioningly, but said nothing. My opposition to the man who had just offered me one hundred thousand dollars—a fortune in any country and in any currency—grew with every minute that passed. Within me arose a vague plan to accept the General's proposition, but at the same time to face him across the board as a calculating player, rather than become one of the inert pawns on his chessboard.

"You're wondering what my plans really are," said the General.

He had more or less guessed my thoughts, but I did not care to admit it.

"A hundred thousand dollars is a lot of money," I said. "As the number of zeros grows, so one's interest in the motive diminishes."

He got up, drained his glass and stood next to me by the window. He removed the monocle from his eye. He was holding it carefully between two fingers, but I observed that he could barely control the trembling of his hand. In his watery fish's eyes a fire was burning—and this mixture of water and fire, or rather, the realization that these two elements could coexist with one another, terrified me. I knew that we were leaving the shores of corruption, so dear and familiar to me, and heading, under full sail, out into the—to me—unknown seas of fanaticism.

I was not mistaken. The views which General Helmuth Edler von Greehahn unfolded to me that night were monstrous, and were made even more so by their blend of reality and unreality, just as the ravings of a lunatic become truly frightening whenever flashes of sound logic break through his phantasmagorias, idées fixes, and diseased obsessions.

The war, said the General, had come to its conclusion by a mistake, and with a wrong grouping of victors; the present armistice was lasting too long and was threatening to turn into a wretched peace. What had come to be known as the cold war was a dangerous state of affairs—not because it might turn into a real war but, on the contrary, because there was a risk that the fronts might freeze up properly and become consolidated. Agreement between the victorious Powers would mean not only the defeat of Germany —a real defeat now, a defeat for decades and centuries to come, and perhaps for ever—but it would also mean the end of the white race, whose only superiority over the "inferior" races was nowadays in the military field. Only by the extermination or total subjection of these races, and of course of all the white traitors who had espoused their cause, could Western civilization be saved. He, General von Greehahn, had offered his services to the Americans, not because he loved them or respected them, and least of all because he expected any personal advantage from them, but because he had reason to believe that, not having been directly affected by the Second World War, and hence by that fatal sentimentality which spelled the end of our world, they could be most easily persuaded into new warlike ventures. Moreover, the Americans were a young nation and had not yet developed that condescending attitude of knowing everything, which marked the Russians or the Germans, not to mention the British and the French. They were therefore still susceptible to being "corseted," to having their spines stiffened, and to having their dormant instincts of self-defense aroused. "Napoleon," he concluded, "was right: *'Il faut sauver les peuples malgré eux.'* "

I did not engage in controversy with that, to my mind, pathological political philosophy; however, I asked the General if he seriously thought a secret service, no matter how powerful, could intervene decisively, or even with a marked degree of influence, in the course of history.

He laughed. He laughed so loud that I thought the soldiers outside were bound to hear him. Then he fell silent abruptly, walked back to his arm-chair, poured himself another glass, took a sip, and sat down. Apparently quite sober again, he resumed, in the manner of a university professor or a lecturing Chief of Staff.

THE DEVIL'S AGENT   (189)

"I am not talking of secret services as they have been in the
past. What happened in the past? Listen to me carefully, and I'll
give you a few examples. A Government wishes to appoint an industrialist as its ambassador. It instructs the secret service to make
discreet inquiries. The secret service makes its inquiries conscientiously and supplies its findings. If the result is unfavorable—that
is, of an incriminating character—the plan to appoint the man is
dropped. In other words, the secret service—with very few excep-
tions—can choose the diplomatic personnel according to its own
preferences. But does it do so? No, it doesn't. It doesn't dream of
placing its own people in all key positions. Let me proceed. An international conference is being prepared. The secret service is instructed to discover the mood in the opponent's camp. That is a
matter of supreme importance, since human beings—and this in-
cludes statesmen—are so made that they attack whenever they
believe themselves to be under attack. In other words, if a hostile
atmosphere is reported from the other side a hostile atmosphere is automatically created on one's own side. What an opportunity for a secret service—and in more ways than one! If it
reports a hostile mood, and a hostile mood is, in consequence,
created, the negative outcome of the conference will merely confirm the information supplied by the secret service, and the au-
thors of the atmosphere in which a negative outcome was inevitable will earn the reputation of prophets. But do the secret
services exploit their opportunity? No, they don't. They find out the
wishes of their governments and collect information designed to
support them—instead of reporting what they consider correct for
the attainment of their own ends. You follow me, Engljähringer?
Say a country intends to send its troops into another country, or
merely into foreign territory. The secret service is instructed to find
out if the country to be attacked will defend itself, if it will call
on its allies, and if those allies will in fact come to its aid. If Intelligence reports a firm resolve to resist, readiness to help on the
part of the country's allies, and fully operative defense measures,
the attack will in all probability not take place. In other words,
Intelligence can decide over war and peace—yet in fact it fails
to do so, or at least it does so not in pursuance of an independent
political concept, but on the basis of some ridiculous so-called

factual evidence. I could continue these speculations indefinitely, Engljähringer—but I'll give you just one more example! It is the duty of the secret service to explore the enemy's progress in military science and technology; it is charged with the thief's task of stealing the results of the enemy's scientific research. What in times of peace is called international scientific exchange is nowadays done by the secret services which, as a result, by dint of theft, bribery, blackmail, and all sorts of other useful methods, bring about an equilibrium of forces which is conducive only to peace. It is further the duty of the secret services to establish reliably the enemy's superiority or backwardness in scientific research and industrial production. In the atomic age aggressive intentions will be governed chiefly by the enemy's destructive potential, or rather by the secret service's estimate of that potential. Are you beginning to understand, Engljähringer?"

"I am beginning to understand, Herr General," I said.

But he had not finished. He was not free from the usual prison-camp psychosis, even though, unlike most other generals, he had spent the best part of his two years' internment under the most pleasant conditions. He had been silent too long, or dissembled his true thoughts behind deceptive words. His need to speak his mind was now erupting irresistibly.

"What I am dreaming about, Engljähringer," he continued, "what I see in my very concrete and wakeful dreams, is the liberation of the secret-service slaves. First: our people in all posts; next: deliberate influence upon all conferences, negotiations, and treaties as the groundwork for war; lastly: action at the right moment! The slaves are always able to cast off their chains provided they realize their power. I, and I alone, am aware of the power that is given into our hands." He jumped up, fitted his monocle in his eye, and began to pace up and down excitedly. "But don't think I'm forgetting my country. Never! I shall never permit Germans to fight against Germans—and I am the only one in a position to prevent it. The secret service—*my* secret service—is a moral institution. How do you suppose the injustice of this pestilential armistice can be corrected—corrected, that is, for the time being? By keeping alive the contacts between the two Germanies—as if there would be two Germanies! And who, even allowing he wanted to, is able to keep these contacts alive? The Americans? The Russians? Some future West-German Government? It makes me laugh!" He again laughed noisily. "The contacts must be underground, secret—in other words, through our line of country. My project is logical—it's the only logical project. The Soviets will send my men to the West to do their spying for them; the Americans will send my men to the East to collect information—and involuntarily, both sides will see to it that the contact is not broken. Thus my secret service will become the only mediator between Germans and Germans, the unbroken column amid the clash of conflict." He stopped in front of me, pulling himself up. "But one day, when a unified Germany is on the march again, Engljähringer, they're going to raise a memorial to me—but on the pedestal there won't be my statue but, cast in bronze, the Unknown Agent."

I saw that he had exhausted himself. His features grew suddenly limp, the flush disappeared from his face, and his eyes again floated in water.

"We will have to discuss this in greater detail tomorrow," I said.

I looked out of the window. The sentries were standing to attention. They were being relieved.

The General nodded agreement. He freed himself from his trance and said, "I'd better put that microphone right, or else it'll be noticed . . ."

He moved away from the window, put a chair up to the wall, and handed the Velásquez copy down for me to hold while he got to work expertly on the loose pieces of wiring. Still on the chair, he turned to me: "Sit down, Engljähringer. I want to read you a few beautiful poems. We need some relaxation. Besides, why not give those blockheads the pleasure of finding their listening-gadget working again? . . ."

PART FIVE

19

The World's Profoundest Magic

EXACTLY A FORTNIGHT after my critical conversation with General Helmuth Edler von Greehahn I arrived in Vienna.

I had submitted to the secret services in Washington a carefully worded report of forty closely written pages which was to buttress the plans that had meanwhile matured in me. I praised the General's ability and knowledge and emphasized his loyalty towards the West but, at the same time, I made a number of reservations. As for the General's reluctance to reveal his entire knowledge to American Intelligence, I put forward two possible explanations: firstly, he was not sure of his own future employment; secondly, he guessed that the Americans would not be able to manage without him, so that he ran no risk by being unco-operative for the moment. It would be necessary, I said in my report, to convince the General of the friendly intentions of the American secret service while making it clear to him at the same time that they were not absolutely dependent on him. How was this to be achieved? During my six weeks' extremely close association with the General, I explained, I had succeeded in gaining some valuable knowledge about the personnel at his disposal and about his hidden, but by no means exhausted, sources of information. I would be prepared, in certain circumstances, to verify the General's statements on the spot. If my guess turned out to be right, and the General did indeed still control a considerable organization, then this would be doubly useful. First of all, Intelligence would have the assurance of employing the right man in the right job; and secondly, it could use its greater knowledge as a bargaining point in dealing with the General. If, on the other hand, the General should

be found to have deceived me, then my investigations would fore-
stall a disastrously mistaken decision. I added that, provided his
information proved correct, I would recommend the General's immediate transfer to Germany to enable him to prepare for the setting up of the Greehahn Organization.

I shall have opportunity to show how this report was in line
with my intentions; all that need be said at this moment is that
my account was received in the most gracious manner and that I
was given the welcome instructions to return to Vienna. There,
furnished with good advice and a not inconsiderable sum of dollars, I was to await further orders.

The reader may feel surprised at the impatience with which I
engineered my return to Vienna. My acquaintance with Maud
Leoni, alias Grete Prochaska, the fruits of which I had again
enjoyed after my return from Washington, thanks to the unwitting generosity of U.S. Intelligence, may have given him the
impression that I had forgotten Nora Güldendag, or that I was a
frivolous character given to using the sacred concept of love
lightly. I may assure him that neither was the case.

I was in love with Nora. I had been in love with her since our
first meeting, but only now did I realize my feelings. All my life
I had been distrustful of others—not viciously distrustful but decidedly skeptical—and I had shown the same distrust or skepticism
in dealing with myself. I did not credit myself with the ability to
love, and was anxious to explain away, by all kinds of rational
argument, whatever looked as though it might be love. What was
love? I searched in vain for a definition. Adjectives came to my
mind—helpless adjectives such as *spiritual, platonic, physical, unselfish,* and *selfish;* inexperienced as I was in the emotion of love,
I did not realize that love began where the adjectives gave out.
My nightly dreams of Nora were sultry, and my daytime thoughts
of her were serenely transfigured. Only slowly did it dawn on me
that this seeming contradiction was in fact confirmation. In my dis-
belief of my own emotions I subjected myself to psychological
questioning—in other words, I mobilized the enemies of emotion.
I searched for explanations and therefore found them: my yearn-
ing for something pure, or my subconscious reaching out for a
lifebelt in the torrent that was threatening to carry me away.

But gradually I ceased to question myself as to the motives of my love and as to the nature of that irresistible force which drew me towards Nora. Intensity replaced time and space; the need to be with her was love without adjectives and love with all adjectives —physical, and spiritual, and emotional: love entire.

But there was something else. Nora had come into my life just as I had been trying to find myself. Until those hours in Budapest I had lived from hand to mouth, rarely, if ever, feeling the need to look into myself. I do not know to this day whether Nora caused me to make this inspection of myself, or whether she had been bound to come because I was seeking a mirror in which I could recognize my likeness. I believed I had to protect Nora from myself, but in fact I was avoiding the glass in which, if I yielded to love, I would, inevitably, sooner or later perceive my own grimace. Love meant defencelessness against the mirror: the urge that was driving me towards Nora was greater than my fear of being brought up face to face with my reflection. I began to discover myself, but I paid the price of discovery: I had to share that which I had discovered. In the past I had not known myself, but I had called myself my own; now I was coming to know myself, but I had become only half of myself. I made plans, I acted, and I reacted—but I was conscious at the same time of my incompleteness. Another being bore half my ego in herself, and my decisions remained indecisive so long as I was not reunited with that part of me which I had lent out.

The nearer I got to Nora the more clearly I came to see myself. Had I seen myself earlier, before meeting Nora, I should have smashed the merciless mirror; to-day, if I were to meet Nora again, I might perhaps attempt to change the person watching himself in the mirror. But at that time it was neither the one nor the other. I no longer had the strength to smash the mirror, and I had not yet the strength to change the image. I gave up neither Nora nor my own plans. Looking down from the plane, as it approached Vienna, I seemed to be watching two trains heading towards each other at full speed, both on the same set of rails. It was a nigthmare rather than a vision, for while I saw the inevitable disaster approaching, I knew also that I was sitting in each of the trains—spectator and victim at the same time.

There was no doubt about it: I had sold myself to the Devil—to the infernal regime controlled by devils. There was no consolation in the knowledge that the Devil had bad servants as well as good ones, unwilling tools as well as willing ones, unbelieving helpers as well as believing ones. Certainly I was determined to betray the Devil's Republic; but to work against evil was not remotely the same as to work for good. My belief that bad service was no service was the crux of my delusion up to that moment. But anyone challenging the Devil is as pitiful a creature as Goethe's Prometheus who, in vain, curses the deity, his very curses acknowledging the deity's existence. I wanted to be not better than the Devil but more devilish. That was what Nora could not understand: to the pure the attempt to outwit the Devil is as incomprehensible as readiness to serve him. The nearer I got to Nora the more hopeless seemed my prospects of holding on to my love and yet realizing my plans.

I put up at Vienna's most elegant hotel, the only one among the big hotels in the city center that had not been requisitioned by one of the four Powers. I did so not only because I had again become accustomed to luxury, but also because I did not wish —at least not for the time being—to resume contact with the Soviet secret service, which was only too well acquainted by my former address. I booked a suite, consisting of bedroom and sitting-room, at the Ambassador in the Bauernmarkt—only a few yards away from Meissl and Schadn's restaurant, where my father had spent his life as head waiter—and sent word to a black marketeer of my acquaintance that if he cared to meet me he might profitably buy—that is, profitably for both of us—a few hundred dollars.

Then I rang the number of Countess Tydings, at whose flat Nora—as I had learned from her brief but cordial letter which had been waiting for me in New York—was still staying.

"George! It's good to hear your voice again," she said, and at every word my hard-boiled heart beat louder.

"I'm happy to find you still in Vienna, Nora," I said, trying hard to cover up my emotion. "When I say that I must see you at once I really mean at once—certainly this very day." And thinking that a confession would come more easily if I did not have to face her at the same time, I added: "I've missed you—but you probably gathered that much from my foolish letters."

She laughed, a little embarrassedly but not forbiddingly.

"I missed you too," she said quickly. "How about this evening? My friend is in Stockholm. There isn't a thing in the house, but you've probably eaten enough for a whole year. Would you like to come after dinner, for a glass of wine, about nine o'clock?"

I gladly accepted.

It was midday then. I ought to have reported my arrival to Mr. Smith straight away, but I decided to do nothing of the sort —not before my meeting with Nora. That afternoon, every minute of which was filled with the most perfect pleasure, the pleasure of anticipation, I began to waver for the first time. I played a silly, superstitious game with myself. If Nora yields to me tonight, I said to myself, I shall tender my formal resignation to Mr. Smith in the morning and start a new life. But immediately I felt ashamed of my bargain—not only because I knew that, like a child promising the Almighty, under certain conditions, never to steal a sweet again, I should inevitably cheat my bargaining-partner in the end, but also because I had made Nora, even in thought, the object of my haggling.

Now that I was certain of seeing her again in a few hours I had no objection to preparing myself suitably for the occasion. On my bed I spread out the presents I had brought her from America—they were neither too modest nor too importunate: a black-leather handbag, a scarf, half a dozen nylons, and two pounds of coffee—and considered the order in which I ought to hand them over. At Fossatti's, a florist's next door to the American-requisitioned Bristol Hotel, I chose the finest blooms with loving care, lingering rather more than was necessary. I then took a stroll down the Ringstrasse, which seemed more familiar to me than it had been for many years, because its new shabbiness was almost entirely hidden under a luxuriously white cover of fresh snow. At a café, where no coffee was served, I read one of the emaciated local papers. I met my black-marketeer friend, who gratefully converted my two hundred dollars into a fortune. I took a light meal and returned to my hotel. The last half-hour was longer than all the eight hours that preceded it. At half-past eight exactly I set out to look for a taxi.

Nora opened the door to me herself. I noted with pleasure, though instantly reproaching myself for my thoughts, that we were alone.

Nora was more beautiful than I remembered her. She was no longer wearing one of those nun-like dresses I had seen her in before, but an afternoon dress of pale gray silk, which did not entirely conceal her figure. The dress left her long neck and a hint of her shoulders bare; neither did it entirely hide her breasts which, for a woman of her height, were perhaps a little too small, too girlish, but whose outlines nevertheless filled me with an indescribable excitement. Her light-brown hair was, as always, brushed back and gathered in a small knot; as always, her regular face radiated an astringent freshness, but this time the coolness of her features seemed to contrast with the warmth of her skin, and the restraint of her movements with the—however unwitting—provocation of her figure. Acoustic memories are even more inadequate than optical ones, and thus it was that her voice now stirred me with redoubled intensity, that voice which had first enthralled me, the soft dark voice that would always say "Yes," even if her lips were to utter a thousand No's.

The first few minutes passed in the giving and receiving of the presents. "You are overwhelming me, George," she said, but she did not in the least seemed overwhelmed, any more than a child is overwhelmed with a present, and her pleasure at my gifts was quite enchanting. She tied the silk scarf round her neck, probably without suspecting how piquant the colorful cloth appeared on her bare neck and light *décolleté;* she hung the handbag over her arm and thus marched up and down the room, earnestly consulting me whether it suited her better to let the bag swing in that way or to carry it, in a more sportive manner, tucked under her arm. Naturally she insisted on opening the tempting can of American coffee, and although a bottle of Gumpoldskirchner was all ready on the coffee table, she allowed me to accompany her to the kitchen, where she made some deliciously smelling coffee in the best Viennese manner.

Apart from danger, can there be a more cunning matchmaker than distance, a subtler go-between than longing, or a more eloquent advocate than silence? No doubt Nora had conducted many a silent conversation with me during the past few months, just as I had with her; no doubt she had, like me, regretted our wasted hours and lost opportunities; no doubt she had, like me, resolved not to prolong the stimulating game of refusal, hesitation, and promise. The lost time, it seemed to me, had won her for me.

But while I was happy to observe a change in Nora's attitude, a more ready relaxation and untensing, I knew her too well, in spite of our short acquaintance, not to be a little surprised and anxious over the change in her. Something must have occurred during my absence, something very fundamental, to allow the dry wine, that was her character, to turn into that heavy sweetness, which is not ordinarily achieved by wines after such short storage. The answer to my speculation came sooner than I had expected and too soon for my liking.

After we had drunk our coffee, as I was drawing the cork from the bottle of Gumpoldskirchner, I felt that tact demanded that I should make a cautious inquiry as to the state of her researches into her husband's fate.

Nora's face clouded over. "We have found a lead," she said, "or, at any rate, we've got some information, the reliability of which is beyond question."

I put on that hypocritical air of sympathy for which, in circumstances like these, there is no substitute.

"George," she said, "what I'm about to tell you is for your ears alone. Apart from my friend, Countess Tydings, who pulled every string she could in Stockholm in order to get me this information, nobody knows what I am going to tell you, and, if it depends on me, nobody shall ever know."

Evidently this was not going to be, as I had expected, an authentic report about Gunnar Güldendag's tragic end. With an interested but far less embarrassed mien I leaned a little closer.

She fell silent, as though regretting her decision to entrust herself to me, or as if unable to utter the confession.

At last she said, almost in a whisper, "Gunnar was an agent." And rapidly she continued, as if trying to get away from that difficult sentence. "He was working for M.I.5—the British secret service. Can you imagine that?"

I was glad Nora was not looking at me. I said, "An agent? Since when?"

"Probably all the time. No, don't misunderstand me, what Gunnar did in Hungary, the help he gave to those in distress, risking his own life time and again—that he undoubtedly did of his own volition. I've no proof of that, but I believe it. But that he was able to do it—the food which was sent to us, the false passports he could obtain, the escape routes he knew—all that was possible only because the British Intelligence service shielded him. Even in two previous appointments, so they say in Stockholm, he had worked for the British secret service. The moment I had this clue my eyes were suddenly opened. His private journeys to London; the visits of strange Englishmen; the radio-room at the Legation, to which he alone had access—all these and a lot of other things are now coming back to me. I could never understand why he, a sworn enemy of the Nazis, should follow the Russian advance on Budapest with such anxiety. I could understand even less why the Russians, as was generally believed, should have arrested and deported him when he had always worked for the Allied cause exclusively. Now I understand why the Allies did not help me in my search, and why the Swedish Foreign Office denied me its assistance." She covered her beautiful narrow face with her fine strong hands. Then, as if making up her mind, after a hard struggle, to be completely frank with me, she continued: "Now I also know that he lied to me. You see, we always lived beyond our means—or rather, beyond the means of a Counsellor to the Royal Legation. He spoke of some money we had come into, a legacy left him by the sister of his long-dead father, and now"—she looked at me—"Countess Tydings has established that there's never been such an aunt. We lived at the expense of the British secret service."

I stood up and began to pace up and down the room. I was hoping that in this way Nora would not be able to watch my face so closely.

"Well," I said, "supposing all that is so—aren't you, perhaps, over-estimating the significance of these revelations? You say 'an agent,' and you utter the word as if you were speaking of a criminal. I understand your disillusionment, for nothing is more disillusioning than the discovery that one has been deceived. You thought your husband had no secret from you and now you find he had a big secret. But once you've got over the personal side of it —there's nothing all that contemptible in what he did. Think of Lawrence of Arabia and all the many other agents who have gone down into history as heroes——"

"He was a Swede," she interrupted me, "not an Englishman."

"I understand. But Sweden was neutral in the war. It preserved a neutrality which, if you'll forgive my saying so, many of us did not understand. Only the other day I looked at a book—I forget the name of the author—entitled *Only the Stars Are Neutral*. Only the stars, argues the author, were entitled to remain neutral in that great crusade. Besides, your own feelings weren't neutral—yours least of all. You may think it strange, Nora, that I should talk like this after taking part in the war on, as it were, the wrong side—admittedly without much enthusiasm, but also without rebelling. There are countless ways of not remaining neutral, of sabotaging a hated neutrality, and Gunnar Güldendag chose one of them—not, perhaps, the most ethical one in the accepted sense, but still a very inconvenient, risky, and dangerous one. I doubt if you, Nora, would have refused him your approval or even your help if he had come to you and confided in you. He did not do so—but can you condemn him without hearing him, without learning his motives?"

What confusion had I got myself into? Here I was, frantically pacing up and down the old-fashioned living-room of the patrician flat, which looked out on to the elegant, quiet Bellaria—pacing up and down the big, high room, with its baroque stucco ceiling and its multitude of delightful and pointless little *objets de vertu!* Here I was, parading up and down in front of the woman I loved, making an impassioned and hypocritical plea for the man who was my rival! But was my speech really hypocritical? Was it not rather a plea in my own defence, in defence of a man who was on the payroll, not of one, but of several foreign secret services, and who was nevertheless acting the respectable citizen who knew these dastardly things by hearsay only?

"You don't understand, George, you can't understand," she said, moving up into the corner of the settee, as if inviting me to sit down beside her. She was speaking even more softly than before. "I have never spoken to anybody about Gunnar—neither to you nor to anyone else . . ."

I sat down beside her. I could feel that a second secret was in the air.

She continued, almost as if talking to herself: "I don't know if I ever loved him, after that possibly happy first year. After that it was respect, esteem, maybe even admiration—but not love. I am a ridiculously old-fashioned woman, George. I must be able to look up to a man in order to love him—and while I can look up to him, then perhaps I don't need love. To another woman this disillusionment might not mean so much, because more might be left to her—but what's left to me if I can't respect Gunnar any longer?"

The Devil was in me as I objected.

"But why shouldn't you respect him, merely because he———?"

"I know too much about agents," she interrupted me. "My father was a diplomat. I grew up in that *milieu*. The Lawrences of Arabia are a rotten legend; idealistic spies are a fairy-tale. Nearly all spies work for both sides. They work for the sake of the money, and wherever they start from they end up in the mire." She caught hold of my hand. "Didn't you see today's papers? The Russians have kidnaped a girl who was working as a secretary in an American office. Just look round Vienna, your beautiful, friendly, charming Vienna!"

I should have liked to have interrupted her, but there was too much on her mind.

"I've done a lot of thinking these past few months," she said, "and I can assure you that I am not exculpating myself entirely. Is a woman entirely innocent if her husband turns to drink or to gambling? Why does a man become a spy? Gunnar had an excellent position, a brilliant future, and plenty of opportunity for active protest against his country's neutrality. There must have been something akin to despair in him—did I cause it or did I thoughtlessly overlook it? In either case, I am guilty."

"And your search?" I asked. "Does it confirm the original suspicions?"

"Everything seems to show," she replied, "that he is in Soviet hands. In their hands and yet at liberty . . . and you know what that means. A member of a Swedish child-welfare organization claims to have seen him in East Berlin a few weeks ago. My friend has read the confidential report in Stockholm, but she could not find out the name of the lady. I have even considered having myself included in some mission going to Eastern Germany, but of course they won't consider my request. They'd think I too was trying to escape—that's what things have come to, George."

"So you are pursuing your inquiries," I said.

"I want to be certain," she said.

I reached for my glass and drained it. I needed courage.

"There's no need for you to go to East Berlin, Nora," I said firmly. "I have a very influential friend in Berlin, who is in charge of certain inquiries for the Americans. Not an agent," I added with a false smile, "but a man who traces missing persons for purely humane reasons. I shall shortly have to go to West Berlin on business anyway, and the first thing I'll do there will be to get in touch with him."

Nora shook her head. "No," she said, "on no account! Don't you remember Budapest? Once before you got into serious trouble through no fault of yours, and I couldn't bear the thought that you had for my sake . . ."

"Not for your sake, Nora," I said. "For my own sake."

I was holding both her hands and looking into her eyes.

I could feel a good temptation hovering over me—good temptations, in fact, are no less frequent than evil ones. For a moment I believed myself capable of saying: Nora, I too have been an agent, a much more despicable and a much more dangerous one than Gunnar Güldendag. I deceived you in Budapest, during our escape, later in Vienna, and later in my letters—and I came here to deceive you anew.

But even while still toying in my mind with these words, I knew why honesty had come to me like an unfamiliar bird that flies against a closed window and at once turns and soars up toward the open sky. Nora's eyes told me that she was ready to receive me instead of the accused, who could not defend himself, to receive his counsel for the defense, who ought, by rights, to be in the dock; instead of a cheat to receive another cheat; instead of a missing man to receive another missing man. Afterwards, it would be too late. The fatal temptation of falsehood had given birth to the redeeming temptation of truth, but it had strangled its child in the cradle.

I said nothing. I felt the pressure of Nora's hands as, with the few words, "For my own sake," I confessed my love to her. I released her hands. I took her in my arms.

How am I to describe the next few hours, when everything in me rebels against the revelation of that which belongs to Nora and me alone? And yet it must be done, because the strange, zigzag course of my subsequent life would be incomprehensible without the consummation of that night—as would also the fact that today, in my villa on the Bisamberg, I am committing these recollections to paper.

I had desired Nora, but I had not suspected the extent to which she returned my love. Now, it was as if the cold season was suddenly succeeded by summer, without the gentle, budding, modest transition of spring. There was nothing of the awkward embarrassment of a first encounter, when lovers are aware only of each other and are apt to falter themselves; when they eschew the pleasure they strive for and conceal that which is their pride. Just as our conversation that evening had been the continuation of long, silent, remote conversations, so our bodies now continued a dialogue that they had been conducting with each other from the first day of their maturity and, who knows, in some previous existence. On the peaks of that night I felt that there must be such a thing as reincarnation. Nora and George must have long before belonged to each other, and though their souls had migrated into different times, regions, and bodies, they nevertheless recognized one another immediately and were instantaneously aware of the fulfillment of their search. The happiness of that night I owed to Nora alone, for I was inhibited by my shameless deceit, my cheap conquest, and, possibly, her betrayal. I could not quite banish the picture of her lost husband, and I felt like a thief rather than a guest. Yet the matter-of-fact way in which Nora received me freed me from the constraint and the considerations of a stranger in a strange house. I could not be a thief where I was expected. I was familiar with unchastity, while chastity embarrassed me— but Nora was neither chaste nor unchaste. She taught me that chaste love is not love, any more than unchaste love is love. Physical love, too, had no adjectives. In the past, at the moment of lust, I had always had to destroy the half-finished pictures I had formed of women and create new ones, but Nora completed her own picture. In the closest proximity she was equally free from hypocrisy as she had been at a distance. During the vain and pernicious rivalry of the first hours of love, hypocritical women are fond of turning each hour of love into the round of a love-bout, and to lean back against the ropes while their man is being counted out; but Nora, knowing that love triumphs only in drawn contests, disdained victory over hasty love and, hastening herself, she succumbed as I succumbed.

Never before had I felt so clearly the overwhelming phenom-enon of the union of man and woman, the bridge that is built in a matter of minutes, in defiance of time, across the gulf of not-knowing. Nora extended her bare arm to the small bedside lamp with its parchment shade; a small circle of light appeared outlined on the tall white ceiling—and the face over which I bent told me more in that first illuminated second than it had done throughout the months of our acquaintance. The idea of it was almost super-human: that in an hour, between the switching off and the switch-ing on of a lamp, everything that stands between two people, all the strangeness and distrust and hypocrisy and misunderstanding, should be wiped out; that two strangers should be able to sub-merge into darkness and emerge from it familiar, kindred, without secret.

"Why are you looking at me with such perplexity?" asked Nora.

"I'm just looking at you," I said. "I never dared look at you before."

"And what do you see?"

"The world's profoundest magic."

She laughed. "Liar. You're perplexed because I am not ashamed. I can't be ashamed of happiness."

She got up and ran across the room, towards a small door which I had not noticed before.

Just as in daytime her walk had something touchingly awkward about it, as if being so tall worried her, she was now also running, barefoot, as if more ashamed of her height than her nakedness.

She was wearing a bathrobe when she returned. She went into the living-room and brought me a glass of wine. How much devotion can there be in a trifling ministration, I thought to myself while I sipped the tart new wine as if it were the most precious champagne.

"Did you say you would have to leave again?" she asked, sitting down on the edge of the bed.

"Yes," I said. "But I hope I shan't be away long. I'm off to Berlin for four or five days."

"I never asked about America," she said.

"Some other time," I said. "Selling wine isn't a very exciting job."

"Why aren't you staying at your old flat?" she asked.

"It's been let in the meantime," I lied. "The housing shortage . . ."

"But isn't the Ambassador very expensive?" she asked.

For the first time I thought I heard something like distrust in her voice, but I ascribed my sense of uneasiness to my bad conscience.

"Do we have to discuss prices on an occasion like this?" I laughed and drew her closer to me.

It was three o'clock when I left the house. The sky was one big cloud, but the white city was plunged in a ghostly light.

Snow was falling in big heavy flakes. They were descending so slowly, as if they were tied to fine invisible threads, like the Christmas decorations in shop windows. I should not have been surprised if the heavenly window-dresser had pulled them up again, suddenly. But he let them float down gently on to the ground, on to the roofs and the trees and the park railings and the monuments: thus the black streets became white, the dirty houses clean, and the ancient monuments as new. I was, as usual, not wearing a hat and the snow was settling on my hair. I thought how pleasant it would be if the snow could work its transformation on me also.

For a moment I hesitated whether to cross the Volksgarten, which lay ahead of me with its tall pointed railings, reminiscent of the lances of noble knights in armor, but I recalled that I was in a Vienna that had been changed into darkest Chicago, and that a stroll through the deserted Volksgarten would not be advisable. Then I remembered that I too belonged to that new Vienna, and that only the past hours had made me forget it. I still felt the warmth of Nora's proximity and did not wish to linger on the unpleasant thought.

I decided to walk along the Ringstrasse, past the dark mass of the twin museums, whose mighty domes seemed, under their cover of snow, like a pair of huge police helmets: a frozen guard of honor by the tomb of past glory. Between the two museums rose the monument of the Empress Maria Theresa, who was sitting majestically in her stone arm-chair, in a white garment, and looking down sadly on her four knights who had frozen in their movements, as if realizing that in this city there was no longer any point in going anywhere.

I stopped and turned. Perhaps, I thought, I could still see the house on the Bellaria, with a light in an upper window, where a woman was thinking of the hours that had just passed. I wanted to cling to that lighted window—but of course I had moved too far away from Nora's house to be able to see it. I turned up my coat collar and quickly continued on my way, ashamed of my romantic thoughts.

At that moment a car pulled up beside me. It had come alongside noiselessly in the snow, or else I had been too engrossed in my thoughts to notice its approach. But instinctively I stepped back the moment a deep voice called out: "Taxi, sir?"

They were only two words, but I realized at once that this was no Austrian voice addressing me. Kidnapers, I thought. There was no other word in my brain. My muscles tensed. I thrust my hand into my coat pocket as if I kept a weapon there to defend myself with. I knew that there was no point in shouting for help, nobody would hear me except the stone Empress, the bare trees, and the lifeless tram rails.

I tried to get my back to the railings of the Volksgarten. I thought: General Greehahn, Nora, Gunnar Güldendag, the Countess in Baden, the black-marketeer, again Nora, and again Greehahn.

"Drive on or I'll shoot," I said.

But even if I had carried a weapon I should have had no time to implement my threat. Several men—I am unable to say how many there were—jumped out of the ancient vehicle. While I defended myself against two of them a third one hit me as hard as he could over the back of my head. He must have used a heavy object.

That was the last thing I knew.

20

The Knitting Pacifist

WHEN I CAME TO I was lying fully dressed on a sofa in a small but pleasantly furnished room. It was evening. A ticking pendulum clock which hung over the sofa showed seven. In one corner stood a tall lamp with a rose-colored silk shade. The shade reminded me of a similar monstrosity which, the result of many evenings' conscientious sewing by my mother, had disfigured our living-room in the most cozy fashion. Memories of the past always had a reassuring effect on me—so much so that I believed the familiar objects of my childhood could protect me against the hardships of the present. Nothing very terrible, I was saying to myself, could happen in a strange house which held such a familiar object.

My head did not hurt as much as I would have expected from the size of the bump on the back of it, but in my brain there was a suspicious dog uttering growling sounds. But I remembered quite clearly the circumstances of my abduction, and the more I thought about them the stranger my new surroundings seemed. My imagination had not entirely escaped the effect of detective stories and spy thrillers, and I should have been less surprised to find myself awakening in a dank cellar, gagged and trussed up, than in this room filled with plush furniture, vases, little ornaments, miniatures and other pleasant knick-knacks, and, moreover, with complete freedom of movement.

But this was not the end of my surprises. Raising myself on my elbow, I discovered that my winter coat had been tidily hung over the back of a chair, and when I examined the contents of my wallet I found that it had not been ransacked. With bitter irony I recalled the countless exercises we had at our spy school in Maryland and regretted that I had not been taught the correct behavior in the event of a comfortable kidnaping.

I got up to test the condition of my limbs. Then, though not hopeful of success, I tried to open the plain, brown wooden door. It yielded at once to my pressure.

I found myself in the dimly lit hall of what seemed to be a middle-class detached house. One of the first things I noticed was a tall, massive cupboard on which several jars of pickled gherkins and bottled fruit—no doubt the products of housewifely virtue—were neatly arranged in three rows. On my right was a door, which was half ajar, and since I was more interested in discovering the secret of my abduction than in getting shot while trying to escape, I politely knocked at the door.

A deep female voice said, "Come in!" and I stepped into a spacious room whose old-fashioned appearance accorded perfectly with my first impressions of my cozy prison. This room, very much a living-room and furnished in the style of the early part of the century, had a certain rustic character which was emphasized chiefly by a heavy Tyrolean cupboard and a white-tiled stove.

By the well-stocked stove sat an old lady, knitting, while in another corner a pretty little girl of about six was earnestly rocking a somewhat battered doll. At the old lady's feet lay a cat, warming itself in front of the stove—a perfectly ordinary cat, which added the finishing touch to this picture of domestic bliss. The old lady wore a dress of indeterminate color and similar felt slippers. She was about sixty-five, but of active appearance. A pair of round steel-rimmed spectacles had slipped down to the tip of her small, slightly reddish nose. She was rapidly plying a pair of long knitting needles. At a cursory glance the old woman in her dignified pose of rest was reminiscent of Whistler's famous painting of his mother—but only at a cursory glance. The small dark eyes behind the spectacles were of a penetrating, almost uncanny, sharpness; from her small mouth radiated little hard wrinkles like the rays of the sun in a child's drawing; and her mousy-gray hair was cut so short that I was reminded of the suffragettes early in the century, who had also seemed anxious to deny their femininity.

"So you've woken up, Herr Droste," said the old woman, just as if she were the landlady of a boarding-house, archly chiding a lodger for appearing late at breakfast. "Won't you sit down?"

The little girl left her doll lying in the corner and planted herself in front of me with undisguised curiosity, her arms behind her back. "Say good evening to the uncle," the old lady commanded her, casually looking up from her work. "And then you run upstairs like a good girl and stay with Kathi. You know it's time for you to go up."

The well-behaved child extended her little white hand and performed a salutation that was part girlish bob but still had something of a boyish bow about it. Her bright blue eyes looked at me encouragingly as she said: "Are you staying here, Uncle?"

I had to smile. "I don't know yet, child. What's your name?"

"My name's Paula—and I have no time at all."

"She never has any time," the old lady commented, and again called on Paula to take her leave. After some childish hesitation the girl obeyed.

I sat down in a comfortable chair facing the old lady. My hostess glanced up only to hold out in front of her the half-finished sleeve of a jumper, so as to judge it for length.

"As you have rightly observed, madam," I began after a brief silence, "I have woken up. Which does not, however, mean that I am quite sure that I have stopped dreaming. May I, with all due respect, inquire for what purpose I have been brought here and what awaits me in your hospitable home?"

"You must be hungry," said the old lady. She rose, carefully put down her knitting on her chair, and made for the door. "Please, keep an eye on Kuki," she said. "She is rather fond of getting entangled in my wool."

The old lady returned with a tray on which a plate of scrambled eggs, two slices of salami, brown bread and butter, as well as half a bottle of milk, were appetizingly arranged. And as my stomach was making the same growling noises as my head I immediately began to eat.

My hostess resumed her work. She did not say a word. The curtains over the two little windows were drawn and I regretted that, out of shyness or caution, I had not lifted them while the old woman was out of the room.

"Madam," I said at last, "would it surprise you if I now inquired the nearest railway station?"

"You will have to be patient a little longer, Herr Droste," the old woman replied, still in a friendly tone.

"How much longer?"

"That's not for me to decide."

Silence fell again. Again the cuckoo clock sang out, again the cat woke, again the old woman cleared her throat. I fished in my pockets for cigarettes and found them in my evidently untouched silver cigarette case.

"There are some matches over there," said the old woman.

I lit my cigarette. My head began to clear and my situation seemed no longer entirely mysterious. Whoever my kidnapers were, they were evidently determined to let me stew in my own juice until, worn down by waiting, anxiety, and uncertainty, I was prepared to tell them whatever they wanted to hear from me. It was not a bad method for that matter. I thought of Nora. Sixteen hours had elapsed since I left her. What would she be thinking? How should I be able to explain my absence to her? Had she, in this sombre Vienna, done the obvious thing and notified the police? What would they think of the wife of a missing Swedish diplomat if she now reported a strange much-travelled Viennese businessman as missing too?

"Madam," I broke the silence. "I am making no secret of the fact that I am in a hurry to return to where your thugs snatched me from. Boredom is an excellent method of making taciturn people loquacious—but I can assure you that I won't be any more loquacious in a fortnight's time than I am already. So why not start the questioning now?"

"My thugs?" retorted my hostess. "Whatever gives you that idea?"

"You must forgive me, madam," I said with a slight bow, "if I say that you fit perfectly into the picture that I had always formed of the secret services. Intelligence people, on your side as well as on the other, are invariably romantics. They are all out to surprise their victim. The setting of this house and yourself are surprising. I confess to being utterly amazed. Now can we get down to business?"

I thought I could see the old woman pausing for a moment in her knitting.

"If it makes you happy, Herr Droste," she said, "I'm willing to listen."

"Wouldn't it be more to the point if you asked me your questions?" I said.

The old lady, as I had noticed before, had a most irritating habit of conducting a dialogue in such a way as to disregard her interlocutor's remarks.

"I am an old woman," she said, "and have seen two generations of young men. My eldest son was killed in the first war and my youngest in the second war. Can you think of a more poignant symbolism? Do you never think, Herr Droste, of how your actions help to bring on a new war?"

The last thing I had expected was an abstract ethical question such as this.

"I am not aware . . ." I said falteringly.

The old lady glanced at the stove. "If you'd be kind enough to put a few more logs on the fire, Herr Droste," she said. "That stove is due for an overhaul; it just eats firewood."

I did as I was bidden.

"Well then, if you insist on talking about your plans . . ." suggested my hostess.

"My dear madam," I said. "Your invitation reminds me of the story of the over-keen reporter who pushes his head out of the window of a skyscraper to call out to the suicide, who is hurtling down past him: 'And what, sir, are your plans for the future?' "

"You've misunderstood me," said the old lady. "I wasn't thinking of your immediate plans. That, perhaps"—she chuckled softly —"would be asking too much. I am talking about your plans subsequent upon your return from Washington, the plans you are about to carry into effect."

The masculine terminology of the old lady, her skilled way of conducting the conversation, no longer surprised me. It was obvious that the part she really played was considerably more important than the supporting one of the knitting landlady.

"Ask your questions. I will answer to the best of my knowledge," I said.

"If the Americans get hold of the Greehahn archives," she said, "we'll be yet another step nearer to war—the third in our time."

There seemed to be little point in feigning ignorance.

"Aren't you overrating Greehahn's importance?" I asked.

She regarded me with her small, alert eyes, as if commending me for not evading the topic that interested her.

"It's like the oriental fable of the wicked sorcerer and his miraculous pills," she replied, obstinately sticking to the grandmotherly note. "Do you know it?"

"I don't think so," I said, astonished at this latest turn in the conversation. "But I am eager to hear it."

The old woman put down her knitting in her lap and took off her cheap glasses.

"Once upon a time," she began, in the manner of a bedside fairy-tale, "there was a wicked sorcerer. This is, more or less, how the story begins. I forget why he was angry with the world and all human beings—it is a long time since I read the story. But that doesn't matter. Anyway, this sorcerer travels from court to court, from one king to another, from one caliph to another, offering, selling, or giving away his miraculous pills. 'If you take these pills,' he tells each ruler in turn, 'six of them, one each day when the moon begins to wax again, you will become so powerful that no other ruler can resist you. When the moon waxes for the sixth time and you have taken your sixth pill, then you can conquer your neighbor's land, and your neighbor's neighbor's, and so forth until you are ruler over all the lands of the earth.' Naturally, the vain rulers took the pills after every new moon, and no sooner had they swallowed their sixth pill than they went to war, each of them certain of victory. There was war on all frontiers and in all kingdoms, and boundless misery came upon mankind—just as the wicked sorcerer had intended." She replaced her glasses and began to ply her knitting needles again. "I cannot recall how the story ends, Herr Droste," she said. "My memory is beginning to let me down. But there is one thing that left a lasting impression on me, and that is why I told you the story. Do you know what the pills contained? They were little balls of wax—nothing else. The wicked sorcerer, however, was as clever as your General Greehahn, whose archives are equally valueless as the sorcerer's pills. But once you give people a sense of power, my dear Herr Droste, you may rest assured that they will abuse it."

The cuckoo announced the full hour. The fairy-tale was over.

"If I have correctly understood your parable, madam," I said, "you want to prevent the Americans from swallowing the Greehahn pill, lest a further illusion of their own strength should induce them to commit warlike actions. How well I can see your point! Yet the parallel doesn't seem to apply altogether . . ."

The old woman was smiling. When she smiled the tiny wrinkles around her mouth scattered in all directions, like frightened chickens in a poultry run; they came to rest at various places in her face; as she turned serious again they returned concentrically to her small mouth and settled down, brooding, in their old places.

"You have an acute mind, Herr Droste," she said. "You were going to say that the sorcerer offered his pills to all rulers and kings, and that this very circumstance caused war."

"That is precisely what I was going to say," I said. "What point would there be, therefore, in the Americans' opponents' gaining possession of the Greehahn archives?"

"We have progressed since the days of the sorcerer, Herr Droste," she replied. "One of the achievements of mankind is the cold war. It is like a refrigerator in which peace can be preserved indefinitely. In the cold war the Powers learn about each other what they would otherwise have learned only in a war—that is,

too late. If we"—for the first time she used the significant little
word "we"—"if we hold the key to the Greehahn Organization,
then the worthlessness of the pill is ensured in good time. It would
be worthless to us, but at the same time it would be worthless to
the other side. You can do a great service to the cause of peace, Herr
Droste!"

"You are overestimating my knowledge."

"Indeed not."

"My mission came to an end with my Washington visit."

"You are wasting time," she retorted in the same motherly
voice. "Don't you want to return to Vienna as a free man?"

I had to admit that I did.

"If one works for peace, Herr Droste," she said, "one cannot
afford to be choosy in one's methods. I should be very sorry to have
to hand you over to the people who brought you here. They are,
as you quite rightly remarked, brutal fellows."

"General Greehahn has not confided to me anything beyond
the existence of the archives," I said.

"You are stubborn, Herr Droste," she chided me. "I shan't be
able to protect you, you know—especially as you've deceived us
once before, in Budapest. The brutal fellows are only waiting to
settle accounts with you."

"Who would profit by that?" I replied. "Supposing I knew
where Greehahn's archives are kept; supposing, even, I were to
reveal the secret. My disappearance would tell the Americans that
the Greehahn archives have fallen into your hands. A new organization would be set up—an organization about which you would
have no information at all."

"Is this a proposition, Herr Droste?"

"Under certain conditions," I said.

"What conditions?"

I decided to stop dissembling. The fact that I was no hero and
that I took my hostess' warnings quite seriously was not the main
consideration: now that I had a rough idea which way the conversation was heading I was again seized with the familiar temptation of tricking the secret services.

"General Greehahn," I said, "has promised me a certain sum
of money for obtaining his archives."

"What sum?"

"One hundred thousand dollars."

The crow's feet around the old woman's mouth again made themselves independent.

"Your life must be worth as much to you as a hundred thousand dollars," she said.

"How do you mean?"

"Greehahn pays in dollars. We pay in freedom."

"Greehahn doesn't pay unless he gets something," I said. "I am a capitalist, madam. To me affluence is an integral part of freedom."

There was a knock at the door. A woman, of whom I saw nothing except a brightly colored head-scarf, opened the door a little.

"Paula is awake again," she said.

"I'm coming up," said my hostess, rising. "Will you excuse me, Herr Droste? I must see to the child."

I was again left alone with the cuckoo and the cat.

Although I assumed that the old lady had merely withdrawn at this suitable moment to consult with her accomplices, I no longer doubted that she was in a position to take independent decisions.

What a rotten comedy, I thought. The Soviet secret service could easily have sent a negotiator to my hotel with an urbane offer that I should supply a copy of the lists of agents, listening posts, letter-boxes, representatives, contact-men and whatever else there was in the Greehahn archives. It was, of course, clear to me that the Eastern Intelligence was not interested in the exclusive possession of the archives, since information about the future Greehahn Organization would be valuable only if the organization was in fact set up. But no, an urbane conversation in a hotel would never do for a secret service. At least a dozen people must have been involved, directly or indirectly, in my abduction. They all had to live and to justify the budgets of their superiors. The old lady, too, might have identified herself straight away as the Intelligence chief of, at least, this sector—but in that case she would have had to conduct our conversation on business lines, and the entire previous kidnaping would have been unnecessary. Yet she had to act the part of the dear old pacifist grandmother—knitting, stroking her cat, maintaining an entire ostensible household —just to prove to her superiors that she was capable of the most original wizardry. That was all very well, I thought, but I did not like the performance to be staged at my expense! No doubt a sum of money had been made available for Operation Droste— maybe a considerable sum—and instead of sharing this sum with me the dear old grandmother and her associates had chosen the unspeakably mean method of magnanimously granting me my life while keeping the money for themselves.

It was an annoying thought for a greedy man like myself, but it was mitigated by the consideration that in future I need worry no more about the rules of conduct than the secret services did. A crisis of conscience? Nothing of the sort. While I was sitting in the well-heated room in no-man's-land, the purring cat by my feet, awaiting the return of the old lady from, allegedly, little Paula's bedroom, I realized at last, with complete clarity, that the secret services had no more in common with the ideologies of their employers than the mercenary troops of the Middle Ages had with the policies of their masters. The struggle was no longer for secrets, but merely for secret services. The real secrets could be found in the newspapers any day, or at least between the lines of the newspapers. All that was needed for their discovery was a few intelligent readers, speculating scholars, shrewd diplomats, or analysts with hunches—but certainly not brutal or adventurous agents. The secret services no longer had any connection with reality. Viewed at close quarters, they existed merely to outwit one another, to cheat one another, and to disrupt one another—a sporting contest over which an excited public (who had to foot the bill) was apt to forget that the secret services discovered not really what was happening, but only what the other secret service said was happening.

My hostess had returned to the room. She did not sit down this time. Nor did she think it necessary to knit. I had succeeded in cutting short the lengthy procedure she had envisaged.

"Well," she said, "is your offer still open, Herr Droste?"

"I do not remember having made an offer."

She ignored my objection. "Let me sum up," she said. "We are not out for exclusive possession. You will lead our agents to Gen-

eral von Greehahn's archives—naturally with all the precautions
necessary for your own protection. The contents of the archives
will be copied. The originals will be returned to you for passing
on to General Greehahn. Is that agreed?"

"Supposing it were," I replied, rising from my chair, "what
guarantee have I that you will return me to Vienna unscathed,
and what guarantee have you for the reliability of my word?"

"If we did not return you unscathed, Herr Droste," my hostess replied, "you would not be able to perform your mission and
our contract would go by default anyway. You will have noticed
that we know everything; hence, we also know that you have first
to find the archives."

Her words impressed me less than she supposed. Of course
there were Soviet agents in the Washington secret service, and of
course they were informed of my assignment. Though only scantily
acquainted with the intentions of the enemy's Government, secret
services were invariably fully informed of the intentions of their
opposing secret service. That I had inaccurately informed the Americans and that, moreover, I was operating on my own account,
these know-alls of course did not know.

The old woman did not notice anything.

"I shall have to ask you," she continued, "to take a few perfectly harmless sleeping pills. We do not wish you to make your
return trip in a conscious state."

"I hope they aren't the pills of the wicked sorcerer," I replied
with a smile.

I was no longer afraid of the old lady. On the contrary, she
was beginning to strike me as slightly ridiculous.

She did not smile. "Our guarantee, Herr Droste," she went on,
"is your considerable *joie de vivre*. Though we attach no particular
importance to your death at this moment, we should, of course,
have no interest in prolonging your stay in this world if you were
to betray us. You are, as you said, a capitalist and hence, no doubt,
anxious to get hold of, and enjoy, General Greehahn's one hundred
thousand dollars."

"Very well, madam," I said. "In the circumstances there is nothing left to me but to wish you a good night."

My hostess walked over to the tall, deep cupboard, that massive piece of Tyrolean furniture I had admired upon first entering the room. But I had greatly underrated the multifarious magic of my Eastern espionage-granny by thinking she was merely going to get the promised sleeping pills from it. As she opened the double doors, deliberately letting them swing wide open, I was looking at a magical box of tricks which would have made every boy's heart beat loud with excitement. There were radio receivers and transmitters, several telephones, valves and coils, small and big microphones, loudspeaker assemblies, small lamps, levers, and tools. Two flat plastic reels were softly revolving: presumably our conversation throughout the evening had been recorded on tape.

The old lady was watching me out of the corner of her eye, as if expecting some sign of applause; but, as none was stipulated in my contract, I declined to oblige her. She then threw a little white porcelain switch and immediately a deep microphone hum came from the cupboard.

"Are you there?" asked my hostess, bending closer over a microphone.

"We are here," replied a deep male voice.

"He'll be asleep in ten minutes. Get ready," the old woman commanded into the microphone.

"Ready in ten minutes," came the male echo.

The old lady flicked the switch back. She seemed to realize that the performance would have to end without applause from the victim and grumpily picked up a tin, which had been lying under some bits of wire, from the bottom drawer of the cupboard.

"Got to keep the pills here," she said, relapsing into the bogus tone of our original conversation. "Nothing is safe with Paula." She shook three yellow pills into my palm. "You can calmly take them without water."

For a moment I looked at the minute pills.

"Much simpler than those brutal methods," I said, pointing to my head. I put the pills in my mouth. "Good night, madam."

"Good night," said my hostess, as unpleasantly as an underpaid boarding-house keeper.

I settled down comfortably in the easy chair by the stove.

21

〰〰〰〰〰〰〰

Assignment in Berlin

THE HOUSE could not have been very far from Vienna, for it was still dark when I woke up on a bench in the Volksgarten. I was shivering, and I rose at once to get my circulation going. How true to type, I thought, they had brought me back to almost the exact spot from where they had kidnaped me about thirty hours earlier. I might think it had all been a dream. But that, of course, would be neither in their interest nor in mine.

I was still a little dazed, but returned to my hotel as quickly as I could. To the night porter I explained that I had been the victim of an assault with robbery. The little man in the box regarded me as indifferently as if I had told him I had stayed up too long drinking at some nightclub. He handed me my key without even suggesting that the police ought to be informed. Clearly the Viennese had lost their traditional respect for authority.

When I had had a bath I thought the time had come to ring up Nora.

"George," she said, in a voice that was filled at the same time with alarm and relief. "For Heaven's sake, what's happened to you?"

"I was careless enough," I replied, "to walk home through the Volksgarten. I was attacked. I have a bump on my head and I've lost my wallet," I continued in a jocular tone, "but their wasn't a lot in either of them, so there's no cause for alarm."

"But that was the night before last," she said. "Where were you all that time?"

I had thought out my answer beforehand.

"They must have confused me with somebody," I said. "Perhaps with some political figure. They knocked me out and abducted me in a taxi. That's all I remember. When they discovered their mistake they left me in a ditch by the road in Nussdorf."

"And where are you now?"

"At the hotel. I've had a bath and am feeling fine again."

"Have you informed the police?"

"The porter advised me not to," I lied. "The wallet's gone, anyway, and the people might take their revenge if I did anything. I don't want to get into more trouble by doing something rash."

"Perhaps you're right," she said. She sighed. "I had just about worked myself up to the point . . ."

"Surely you haven't reported my disappearance to the police?"

"I ought not to have waited so long . . ."

"Not at all," I reassured her, relieved. "In your position! Everybody would have immediately jumped to the craziest conclusions."

I promised to see her in the afternoon and rang off.

In the morning I paid my overdue visit to Mr. Smith. He had a new office in the Mariahilferstrasse, a modern place, which looked more like an American travel agency than an espionage center. His white hair seemed even whiter and his rimless glasses even sharper. He looked tired and old.

He received me cordially and with some warmth, like a teacher meeting a favorite pupil for the first time, after many years, when he has duly made his expected brilliant career. My anxieties that Mr. Smith might have been informed of the exact time of my arrival, and might have begun to miss me, proved unfounded. On the other hand, he was minutely informed about my assignment in connection with General von Greehahn.

"I am to arrange for your trip to Berlin and to speed it up as much as possible," he said. "Can you fly tomorrow?"

I said I could.

"Washington," he said, "has come to the conclusion that you had best be allowed to operate independently. Presumably your suspicion that the archives are in the Soviet Zone, somewhere near Berlin, still holds good? Do you think you have enough clues to track them down in the Soviet Zone?"

I feigned surprise. "I may be a model pupil, Mr. Smith, as you once kindly put it, and I also feel honored by Washington's confidence, but the thought of venturing once more into the lion's den does not appeal to me greatly. I did not promise to produce the Greehahn archives. I merely said in my final report—and I don't think I am misquoting—that I would undertake to form an opinion, on the spot, of General von Greehahn's reliability and the potential value of his organization."

"And how did you imagine yourself doing that, Herr Droste?" asked Mr. Smith.

"I assumed," I continued innocently, "that American Intelligence would put at my disposal in Berlin, if not its organization, then at least a few trained agents."

Mr. Smith laughed. "You haven't quite reached that stage, my dear model pupil. Even officers must prove themselves in the field for some time before they are given a desk." More seriously he added, "Nobody expects you to take the Greehahn archives on your back and carry them over to the West. You just establish their whereabouts and leave the rest to us. Of course I shall put you in touch with our Berlin branch, which will give you what help it can. I am, moreover, authorized to settle another matter, which is no doubt close to your heart."

"When you refer to my heart, Mr. Smith," I retorted, "you are probably thinking of my wallet."

"The same old honesty!" laughed Mr. Smith. "I am authorized to hand over to you an advance of five hundred dollars and to promise you a further one thousand in the event of your being successful. At the same time, I hope you are not going to retire on these payments."

I found it difficult not to act out of character. General von Greehahn had promised me one hundred thousand dollars, the Soviets had at least promised me my life—and now, the wealthy Americans were about to fob me off with a mere gratuity. But I could not reveal to Mr. Smith the extent to which my appetite had meanwhile grown on what it fed.

"Fifteen hundred dollars will scarcely be enough for that comfortable retirement that I am longing for," I said, "but I appreciate the opportunity offered me by your fellow-countrymen, alongside with the opportunity of breaking my neck. That is why

I should like to make you a counter-proposition which you may find of some interest."

"I'm listening," said Mr. Smith.

"If General von Greehahn's claims are correct," I said, "his organization will undoubtedly be of enormous value to the West. At the same time, it might be wise to make sure that Greehahn's head doesn't swell too much. Supposing I succeeded in getting even a fraction of the archives out of the Eastern Zone, then Washington's hand would be strengthened in dealing with Greehahn. He would then be in the position of a company chairman who does not personally hold all the shares. For this far more favorable set of circumstances I would suggest an additional contingency fee."

Mr. Smith regarded me quizzically through his two monocles.

"First you don't want to enter the Eastern Zone," he said, "and then you undertake to smuggle the archives out of the Zone."

"Not personally," I said. "That's just why there will be overhead expenses."

"How much?" asked Mr. Smith.

"Ten thousand," I said.

"You're a veritable Shylock," declared Mr. Smith. "But I don't want to say 'no' and I can't say 'yes.' I will let you know our answer before you take off tomorrow. At least there's no danger of your becoming one of the 'Intelligence proletarians.'"

"I have taken your words to heart, Mr. Smith," I said.

I had lunch at a small restaurant and set out for Nora's.

When I think back to that afternoon and that night—for Nora, anxious for my safety, did not let me go until the sun rose behind the green domes of the twin museums—it seems to me that my fate was finally decided then.

If it were not for the fact that I am committing these recollections to paper under pressure of time and with increasing haste, so that my son Johnny can read them one day and derive from them that slight measure of instruction which one human being is at best capable of transmitting to another, I might adduce a good many excuses for the ignominious outcome of my wrangle with my conscience.

My temptation was great. My plan, which had begun to take

shape in the lonely villa in Washington, had taken on clearer out-lines in the house of unknown location, and had finally crystallized in Mr. Smith's airy office, was now clear. If I succeeded in gain-ing possession of the Greehahn archives it was my intention—the exact details would have to be left to a benign fate—to divide the discovered files in such a way that General von Greehahn (most closely acquainted with the volume of the documents) re-ceived the lion's share, while the Russians and Americans would likewise get a fair deal. I did not for a moment propose to supply the entire material to each of my three employers, by way of making copies, for in that case my deception would, sooner or later, be discovered. Provided the archives still existed—and that, of course, was the premise of my entire scheme—they must have been preserved by a miracle, and none of my three clients would be surprised to learn from me that the remainder had been lost through bombing, fire, enemy action, neglect, or ill fortune. There was therefore the by-no-means improbable prospect of obtaining one hundred thousand dollars from the liberal General, ten thou-sand dollars from the stingy Americans, and indulgence from the otherwise vindictive Russians. One hundred and ten thousand dol-lars, an appreciable sum of money at the best of times, was then an almost astronomical fortune. To gain possession of such a sum at one single stroke represented a temptation which, no doubt, many a stronger character would have found impossible to resist. To this must be added the fact that the very complete-ness of the immorality of my scheme convinced me of its justifica-tion. If the world were inhabited by thieves exclusively the ques-tion of whether theft was still theft would have to be re-examined. I, for my part, felt convinced of being in the employment of three thieves: why, then, should I not join them as a fourth, an even cleverer, thief? Thieves? No, they were worse than that. They were out, or so it seemed to me, to turn down the lamps of the world, or perhaps douse its light altogether, so as to practice their thievish tricks the more undisturbed in the resulting darkness. A dishonest servant of the Devil, I believed, was almost an honest servant of the Lord.

Nora, after I had settled myself, began to talk about the future. Can there be anything more delightful than walking with a loved person along imaginary paths, building dream houses, and lending to a brief, ephemeral happiness the aspect of permanence? My good temptation urged me to start on the future at once: to stay with Nora; to settle with her in the country; to invest her savings, as she suggested, in a small vineyard; to live for each other, and to turn our backs on the confused post-war and unsavory prewar world. We did a lot in those hours of what lovers, as a rule, do only after a longer acquaintance: she read me one or two of her favorite poems; she sang, with a small but pleasant voice, while I laboriously accompanied her on the piano; we conducted a serious political conversation which abruptly ended in kisses and embraces; we rose from our couch and ran out into the street, spending an hour roaming among the old houses of the inner city; we bought some food and together prepared a simple yet delicious supper; we wasted our time as if we really owned it. In fact, we crammed a lifetime into less than twenty-four hours. It was as if she wanted to prove to me, by way of generous examples, that there was another way of life than mine, and as if I tried to pack my forfeited future into the few hours of the present.

And yet, my troubles emerged again and again from the sea of my happiness, like some big predatory fish. In the manner of lovers we indulged in detailed portrayals of each other's characters, taking it as a proud token of our love that we knew one another so thoroughly without really knowing one another. It was then that I became particularly aware of my deception. Whereas Nora with delighted surprise agreed with my picture of herself, I knew only too well that the man she was describing did not exist.

There was a great tranquillity and also great haste in these hours, for there was a striking contrast in the way we treated time: she, the serious-minded person, treated it frivolously, in the belief that our future really lay before us; I, frivolous by nature, doled it out parsimoniously, because I distrusted the future. Of course I tried to convince myself that our castles in the air, like those of Ibsen's Master Builder, had "firm foundations." I swore to myself that after my return from Berlin I would not accept any further assignments, and that I would put a final end to a brief but highly successful career as an agent. During our leavetaking my fatal entanglement was once more borne in on me. Nora, though distressed at our parting, nevertheless accepted it as a matter of course, whereas I felt like a departing soldier who conceals from his wife that he is going into action.

Shortly before my take-off, Mr. Smith sent word to me that my conditions had been accepted by the highest quarters.

I arrived at Berlin's Tempelhof airport. Mr. Smith had given me the address of a small hotel, but I preferred to forget it. I did not necessarily trust the American Intelligence's trust in me and considered it wiser to obliterate my traces for a while. General von Greehahn had recommended the Pension Schmidtkamp near the Kurfürstendamm, and there I took a room under the name of Richard Lehmann.

Still following the General's minutely worked out plan, I went to Dahlem twenty-four hours after my arrival, where Dr. Hermann Rebendonck had his surgery in one of the few villas not requisitioned by the Americans.

In the crowded waiting-room, where a pretty receptionist immaculately dressed in white had asked me to take a seat, I was scrutinized with surprise and interest by everybody present. They were all ladies, for Dr. Rebendonck was a gynaecologist and obstetrician, and the only men ever likely to visit his surgery were expectant fathers. I am using the word "ladies" advisedly, because "women" would not be an adequate description. Two of the ladies were identifiable by their long, well-groomed hair, their cosmeticized skin, their fur coats, and, above all, by their new shoes —for the social position of anyone in the land could be judged at that time from a worm's eye view—as Americans; a fact that rather astonished me, since they were officially forbidden to consult German doctors.

I was kept waiting for a full hour. An actress was the last to leave the surgery. The receptionist asked me to go in.

I found myself in a room which was furnished half as a doctor's consulting room and half as the office of a big musical impresario. By the wall stood a glass-fronted case with instruments and medicines; in the center stood a gynaecological chair; by the doctor's desk stood a divan covered with American cloth. But on all four walls, in discreet narrow black frames, hung the portraits of film stars, actresses, singers, and musical-comedy *prima donni,* most of them with the handwritten dedications of grateful patients.

The Robinson Crusoe of this luxurious island rose from behind his small white desk and approached me with a smile. He was a slight man in a surgical overall buttoned up to his chin, which gave him an even frailer appearance. Although he was of extremely small build his figure was excellently proportioned, so that the general impression was definitely pleasing. Two deep lines dominated his pale face, but, strangely enough, these did not start by the side of his nose but immediately below his eyes, running past nose and mouth and abruptly ending immediately above his chin. A feverish gleam, of the kind that is often found with people whose passions lead to excess and obsession, emanated from his deep-set eyes. His movements were soft and almost feminine, but by no means of the femininity of the homosexual; on the contrary, they had the femininity which often characterizes the ladies' man, who owes his success with the opposite sex to his very kinship and familiarity with the female element.

My feeling of uneasiness, which had gripped me even more firmly in the insular waiting-room than in the ruined city, was growing as Dr. Rebendonck sat down again and got ready to take down in writing the purpose of my visit.

"I am not a patient, Herr Doktor," I said, as I sat down facing him. "I have something confidential to tell you, but I would first like to make sure that we shall not be disturbed."

"You may speak confidently," said the doctor.

I quoted softly:

> *"Roses, tulips, and carnations*
> *Flowers have their day*
> *Steel and iron perish*
> *Yet our love will stay."*

Instead of regarding me as a lunatic after this unsolicited recital of album verses, Dr. Rebendonck only looked up briefly from his blank index card.

"All millers love to wander
To wander,"

I proceeded.

"Have you finished?" asked the doctor.

"Yes."

"Can you answer a question?"

"I hope so."

"Does the word 'hunting' suggest a poem to you?"

I smiled.

"The sun on the hill-tops
The mists fill the vale
A-hunting we'll go
Through forest and dale."

I had carefully memorized the lines: the General had warned me to be ready for the doctor's counter-question. I knew that the outcome of my mission depended on the correct answer to Dr. Rebendonck's question, but even so I could not quite suppress my native sense of the ridiculous. I asked myself if I had not, in fact, become an actor in a world which had turned a childish game of Red Indians into bloody reality.

"How is the General?" asked Dr. Rebendonck.

"As well as may be expected," I replied. "He is being detained in Washington, but—provided my mission is successful—he may shortly return to Germany."

"And what is your mission, Herr Lehmann?"

"You will have guessed that from the verses, Herr Doktor," I retorted. "I am to discuss with you possibilities of getting the archives over to the West."

"In order to surrender them to the Americans?"

"No, to him personally."

"So you know where the archives are?"

"Naturally."

He was eyeing me distrustfully. "Did you see the General face to face?"

I affirmed.

"You are an Austrian, Herr Lehmann?" asked the doctor.

"Why do you ask?"

Dr. Rebendonck rested his elbows on the desk top and inter-linked his slender white fingers.

"Isn't it a little strange that an Austrian should have been able to meet the General? It would be less surprising in an American agent."

I was getting impatient. "Herr Doktor," I said, "I am not here to answer your questions. If I were in the pay of the Americans, and if they, as you seem to suspect, had tricked the General into revealing his secret, I should have ways and means of getting the archives out of Potsdam. I have come to you because the General trusts you."

The doctor rose and walked up and down the room a few times. He stopped by the gynaecological chair.

"Are you acting out of political conviction, Herr Lehmann?" he asked.

"I work for money," I said.

"Has the General any money?"

"He is going to have money."

"Are you authorized to discuss financial matters?"

For the first time I was perplexed.

"The General said nothing about that," I replied quite honestly. "He assumes that you are acting out of conviction."

"Nearly two years have passed, Herr Lehmann, since I last saw the General," Dr. Rebendonck said wistfully. "Our supreme conviction then was final victory. You have no idea what a disastrous effect defeat has on a man's convictions."

The telephone rang. The doctor went to his desk and lifted the receiver. He was evidently talking to a woman, for his melodious voice, his most attractive feature, turned to an ingratiating cooing. He gave the caller some advice, which I took in with only half an ear, did not then put down the receiver, but instead arranged a rendezvous with her for the coming evening. I had an opportunity meanwhile of adjusting myself to the new situation.

"I understand you entirely, Herr Doktor," I said. "Disillusioned idealists are the most ruthless materialists. However, your views on final victory appear to differ from those of the General. The General believes he has lost a battle, not the war. If I were in your position I should reinsure myself accordingly."

"Very sound advice," said Dr. Rebendonck. "One's got to swim with the current. But which way is the current flowing?"

"In Greehahn's direction," I said with conviction.

The specialist walked thoughtfully up and down. He stopped in front of the photograph of some beauty and appeared to be scrutinizing it closely. "Very well," he said at last. "I am ready to answer your questions."

"I am to ask you," I said with a sigh of relief, "whether Herr Fuchs is still in his post?"

"A week ago he undoubtedly was," replied Dr. Rebendonck.

"Do you know of any way of getting the archives across the Sector boundary?"

"That is a question of money."

"Assuming the necessary sum could be found," I said.

Dr. Rebendonck sat down behind his desk.

"Once a week," he said, "an exchange of coffins takes place between the Eastern and Western Sectors. People who have died in the Western Sector are, for some reason or other, to be buried in the Eastern Sector or in the Soviet Zone. Workers residing in the Western Sector die in the Eastern Sector and have to be transported back to the West. Thus the dead," he continued, with what seemed to me macabre delight, "slip through the Iron Curtain. If Fuchs can make sure the coffins are not examined on the Eastern side I can see to it that they are allowed to pass without inspection on the Western side. Do you follow?"

"It would be a case," I said, "of accommodating the contents of the archives in a number of coffins."

"In a very few coffins, needless to say," replied the doctor. "A sudden mass death would arouse attention. I suggest, therefore, that you get in touch with Fuchs—how you do that I must leave to your ingenuity." He looked at me searchingly, as if to see whether the General had revealed to me the road to Fuchs. "Let me know what day you will be ready. The exchange, provided there are corpses, takes place every Wednesday at 10 P.M."

I got up.

"I am glad," I said, "that the General did not deceive himself about you, Dr. Rebendonck."

The physician also rose, but without acknowledging my compliment. He did not look at me any longer. His glances swept over his gallery of beautiful women.

"It would of course be advisable to make timely preparations for the transport on the Western side. How big is the sum at your disposal, Herr Lehmann?"

The question was not unwelcome to me. If there was any ground in common between me and that successful gynaecologist and strange friend of the General's it was the solid ground of money.

"Three hundred dollars," I said.

"In notes?"

"Yes."

"Unfortunately I am not in a position to advance the sum out of my own pocket," said Dr. Rebendonck. "We have become poor in Germany," he added with a little sigh.

"That won't be necessary, Herr Doktor," I said in a confidential tone.

I counted out six fifty-dollar bills and laid them on Dr. Rebendonck's desk. They were six of the ten fifty-dollar bills which the American Smith had paid me as an advance for my endeavors. I believed that my investment would pay.

22

Coffins from Potsdam

IN SETTING OUT to describe the events which followed my visit to Dr. Rebendonck, and which ultimately put me in possession of that fortune which I have managed to preserve by wise husbandry, and to increase by cautious speculation, I am fully conscious of the disbelieving and possibly irritated shaking of heads which my account must provoke, from even the most willing of my readers. That is why, at the risk of halting the flow of the action—an offense of which I have already been guilty a few times—I must make a few fundamental observations, illustrating them wherever possible by examples from real life.

The secret services of all nations are directed or influenced by personalities which are marked by a criminal, a perverted, a criminal-pathological, or, in any case, an exceedingly vulgar imagination. In the course of nearly ten years' employment in the secret services I have discovered more than one reason for this regrettable though perfectly understandable phenomenon.

Perversity is invariably the result of impotence. A sexologist could no doubt demonstrate that the various perversions in sexual life all stem from impotent men or women who, incapable of normal love and consummation, have invented those erotic peculiarities for the purpose of their own difficult satisfaction. Similarly, a "normal satisfaction" is impossible in the life of the secret services, because those who direct them lack this capacity. Supposing the intentions of the Soviet rulers were to be examined. This would require not only a thorough study of the domestic, international, and economic situation of the Soviet Union, a detailed knowledge of the existing system and its leading exponents, but also a far more profound investigation of the history of Russia and the Slav nations generally, of the history of Eastern civilization, of Marxist doctrine and socialist theory, and of other no less complex spheres. Anybody possessing even a fraction of this solid knowledge would not need to sell himself to the secret services. A secret service, on the other hand, composed as it is of mentally impotent characters, chooses those "perversions" which promise an ostensible satisfaction. Thus, in our example, the valet of a Soviet leader would be "encircled," as the technical term goes; when he has been won over he mixes some knock-out drops into his master's vodka; he then abstracts a document from his master's safe —though not without appropriate breath-taking complications. This document is then copied in invisible ink—for invisible ink serves as a mental aphrodisiac—and is next smuggled out of the country in the most adventurous and fantasy-stirring manner. And at the end of all this it will yield the same information that, if only one had a normal political potency, one might have deduced without the slightest difficulty from any public pronouncement by the doped ruler.

An impotent person suffers from his disability: but not only because he is incapable of satisfying his desires. Impotence, like any other human weakness, becomes a social problem. The impotent man is in a continuous state of bitter rivalry with the normal, potent world around him. Similarly, the secret services are in competition with the scholars, diplomats, statesmen, and military leaders whose capabilities, since they are in the public eye, must reach the customarily required standard. The impotent secret service, which lacks these capabilities, must compensate itself by way of proving other, "abnormal," skills. In the course of my work I obtained incontrovertible evidence of an espionage school in Eastern Germany which specialized in the training of sexual "supermen" and "superwomen." Future women spies, for instance, were here—by means of sexual intercourse, repeated up to thirty times a day, by means of films showing the most monstrous perversions, and by many other hideous practices, which decency forbids me to relate—deliberately deprived not only of their ability to attain orgasm but also of all taste for physical love, so that they could be employed for the seduction of enemy spies or other persons in the opponent's camp without running the risk of becoming "victims" of love themselves. In the entire history of espionage not a single instance is known of a secret of any importance being betrayed during love-making. There was, therefore, not a hope of any of these artificially produced "superwomen" performing any useful work. The purpose of the training, or rather its monstrous purposelessness, consisted merely in creating a group of persons distinguished by a peculiarity not found in other, normal, human beings, so that the secret service, incapable of intellectual competition, should be able to score a point with this regiment of cripples.

But the worst perversion of the secret services—and how could there be a worse one?—is that of human sacrifice. We attach the label of despicability to an organization, a person, or an enterprise that speculates on what are known as "base instincts." Hence we are fond of expressing our disapproval of the proprietors of gambling dens, yellow-press journalists, and brothel-keepers. Yet over our righteous indignation we are apt to forget that to speculate with human instincts is despicable in itself. The moral emphasis is on "speculation," not on "baseness." Indeed, it seems to me that speculation on what are known as "good instinct" is more despicable than speculation with base instincts, just as it is more contemptible to betray somebody's trust than to deceive a suspicious person. In this sense, the most dastardly of all human institutions is the army, for it speculates (without even a semblance of reserve) on a man's courage—that is, on a good instinct—but immediately perverts it into the lowest of instincts: the instinct of murder. Immediately after the army comes the secret service, and in one respect it even exceeds the army in vileness: in that it drives its victims into an utterly pointless death. This aspect, too, can be explained by the impotence of the secret service. The secret service—by no means a necessary evil, as some people are ready to believe, but an entirely unnecessary one—shares with the impotent male an urge to boast, to exaggerate, to tell tall stories—all the embarrassing exhibition of virility which almost invariably follows the loss of potency. But while the impotent individual who shoots lions, starts a fight with a stronger man, or otherwise "sublimates" his disability in the shape of various "manly" actions, at least stakes only his own skin, the secret service sublimates its impotence by exhibiting the virility of its agents. To statesmen, members of parliament, taxpayers, military men—in short, to all those from whom it draws or expects financial allocations—the secret service is forever proving its "courage," a courage that is exceptional and totally different from all other kinds of courage. During my time in the Far East I have watched Chinese Nationalist agents smuggling newspapers from the Chinese mainland out to Formosa, in ramshackle fishing boats, under cover of night, and in the face of a thousand perils. How many of them lost their lives in this wretched enterprise I do not know. But I do know for a fact that the same papers—the papers which these agents so daringly smuggled across the sea—were on sale at all newspaper kiosks in Tokyo on the same day. In the perverse game of the secret services the human losses on one's own side are not subtracted from those on the other side, but, on the contrary, are boastfully added, so that the service which is most reckless with the human lives entrusted to it also considers itself the best.

I believe that the events which occurred in Berlin, and which I am about to relate, will seem more credible and also more comprehensible in the light of the foregoing reflections.

I hope the reader will believe me if I say that it was no accident that the Greehahn archives were hidden in the Potsdam morgue. I could easily list a dozen other places where the General's men could have concealed those irreplaceable secret-service files at the time of Germany's collapse with about the same chance of survival. But their imagination simply moved on that grisly macabre level. No doubt Herr Josef Fuchs, the cemetery administrator in whose care the archives had been placed, was a reliable person from Greehahn's point of view—yet I fear that at that time Greehahn could have found many other equally reliable keepers of his secrets.

My journey to Potsdam, though involving certain risks, was by no means as difficult an undertaking as it might seem. I took the U-Bahn, the Berlin Underground, into the Eastern Sector, and from there took a local train to the classical birthplace of Prussian militarism. The trip was short and—since checks were performed there only rarely—uneventful.

The director of the morgue, who was also the administrator of the Potsdam cemetery, occupied a comfortable detached house on the outskirts of the town. The Russians had not requisitioned it, either because they respected things and people connected with death, or perhaps, on the contrary, because they were impressed by vigorous life: for Herr Fuchs had seven children ranging from four to seventeen, and, moreover, his wife was very much pregnant. This fertile man, as is not infrequently the case with the fathers of big families, appeared to be somewhat shrivelled—almost as if his numerous family were feeding upon his substance. He was quite small and seemed to consist of nothing but skin and bones. His hooked nose, springing sharply from his narrow face, gave him the air of a starved bird—an impression that was heightened by his black frock-coat, his gray pin-stripe trousers, and his flying coat tails. At first I thought Herr Fuchs was about to attend a funeral, but I presently learned that he always wore his formal threadbare suit just as he was in the habit, whatever the subject under discussion, of expressing himself in round and unctuous phrases, as though permanently engaged in a funeral oration.

While three or four of the children—all of them of their father's birdlike appearance—were gambolling around us, I handed the cemetery director half a postage stamp with Adolf Hitler's portrait on it, and with the General's handwritten initials on its yellowed back. This highly symbolical token of introduction had been entrusted to me in Washington by General von Greehahn. I made no secret to Herr Fuchs of the purpose and urgency of my mission—a circumstance that impressed him as much as my connection with Dr. Rebendonck which, admittedly, I succeeded in representing in a rather more intimate light than accorded with the strict truth.

Shortly after three, when Herr Fuchs had evidently satisfied himself as to my genuineness, we set out for the morgue.

It was a long walk, and it made me feel decidedly uneasy.

Potsdam, as I soon discovered, was a Soviet garrison town, and at every step we met Russian officers and other ranks. The Russians, with a tremendous capacity for assimilating their surroundings to themselves, had within a short time transformed the residence of the Kings of Prussia into a Russian provincial town. Their rustic horse-drawn carts fumbled through the fine old streets, on them sat privates in off-white fatigue uniforms, in the relaxed attitude of Russian peasants, carelessly holding the reins, almost as if they were asleep on the box. They looked like the farm carts that used to come into the town from the neighboring villages on market-day. Among the wreckage of the Garrison Church, whose stones looked like children's upset building blocks, sat more soldiers, enjoying the mild weather and levering their broad thumbs against the rind of their chunks of streaky bacon, as they cut it into slices to eat with their black army bread. Although the soldiers took no notice of the civilian population—indeed they seemed to ignore their existence—I had the impression that the inhabitants of Potsdam were walking about rather more intimidated and frightened than the Germans of East Berlin. This impression was probably due to the fact that among the people I saw there were many who displayed an old-world behavior: the widows of senior civil servants, retired officers of the Kaiser's army, gentlemen and spinsters of obscure but none the less proud nobility, who spent their lives among dusty pieces of porcelain, types as old-fashioned as the ornate private houses, palaces, and residences in the imitation-French style, who could not understand why the vulgar yesterday of the Third Reich had been succeeded, not by the day before yesterday, but by an even more vulgar today.

The morgue was near the cemetery, in a building that had been preserved as if by a miracle—a building, moreover, in a challengingly modern style, almost like an office block, so that the fanciful thought struck me that in Potsdam only the dead were keeping abreast of the times. Herr Fuchs, still hopping in front of me like a small black bird, led me down to the cellar and along several cold passages and past inhospitable rooms till he halted in front of a heavy steel door. For a while he manipulated the handles, just as if he were opening a safe deposit of some immensely wealthy bank—and indeed the door was so heavy that I had to lend him a hand in opening it.

A breath of icy air hit me as we stepped through and I felt as if I had entered a giant refrigerator. We were now in the morgue.

"Poor attendance," said Herr Fuchs.

This rather odd remark referred to the fact that at the moment there were only two corpses in the big vaulted room. Most of the huge cube-shaped ice blocks, which were lined up with Prussian orderliness like the ranks of recruits, were not "engaged." Only on my left, entirely hiding the ice block beneath his broad body, lay a colossus of a naked man: a truck driver, as Herr Fuchs explained to me, who had crushed his truck into a Russian military vehicle and so met his death. Over to the right I discerned a little heap of a tiny old woman, for whom the ice block was far too massive: the aged woman was stretched out on it as if, for the first time, she had found real comfort. If I thought that in this dim cellar, lit only by a bare bulb whose filaments were plainly visible, there was an odor of corpses, this must have been my imagination, for there was no lack of hygienic precautions—but nevertheless there was a stale smell in the air, like a refrigerator that had not been cleared out and aired for a long time.

Herr Fuchs produced an impressive key from his jacket pocket

—for some reason it reminded me of the well-guarded larder key of my good mother—and unlocked a wooden door, which was almost entirely hidden behind some ice blocks. We descended two steps. The morgue director explained that during the war, when there was no cause for complaint of "poor attendance," this room, or rather cubby-hole, had served as a kind of "cloakroom," a depository for the clothes, coats, and other possessions of unidentified corpses.

Herr Fuchs had left the door to the morgue open—for there was no light in the little room—and in the gloom I now noticed a number of packing cases, some of them small and others the height of a man, marked *Winter Relief.* Evidently they had once served the transport of *Winter Relief* articles. Not all the crates, explained Herr Fuchs, contained the papers entrusted to him by the General; some still contained the clothes and chattels of air-raid victims. "Regulations say," he declared, "that they must be kept for five years; and regulations are regulations. Certainly they will not be disregarded while I have anything to say here."

I commended the good man on his civil servant's correctness and the solicitude with which he had guarded both the belongings of the dead and the secrets of the General. He was evidently flattered by my words, which made him even more trustful. With a wink of one of his small, bloodshot eyes, he informed me that those cases on which the *W* in *Winter Relief* had a red-pencil bar through the middle, so that the lettering read *inter Relief,* represented the worldly goods of the very much alive General von Greehahn.

I must add here that, unlike the good-looking gynaecologist, Herr Fuchs really was an idealist—as we are fond of designating those people who work for certain causes without material rewards. He did not even think it necessary to inquire whether I was acting out of conviction myself—a circumstance generally accepted as an excuse for even the meanest actions—but naturally regarded me as a fellow-believer, and spoke of the past with such tearful emotion as though he stood by the graveside of a beloved person.

The moment I recognized Herr Fuchs for an idealist I began to dispose of his time ruthlessly. Time, as is well known, is money— and a man who does not care for money has therefore no need to be stingy about his time. I informed Herr Fuchs that I had to open the Greehahn crates and examine their contents before deciding what part of the archives to take with me. Herr Fuchs declared his agreement and an hour later, after he had procured the necessary tools, we got down to the job. Now, at last, the cemetery director took off his formal jacket, and it would be unfair to deny him my unstinting praise for the hard physical labor of hammering, pulling out nails, and ripping out boards which, ever averse to physical work, I largely left to him. We worked practically throughout the night, by the light of candles, and through most of the following day. Herr Fuchs, in a most praiseworthy manner, had brought some food along from his home, neatly wrapped in greaseproof paper, and we took our meals seated cozily on a little bench between two ice blocks in the morgue. Twice our activities were interrupted—by the removal of the truck driver and the old woman —and once Herr Fuchs thought it wise to give me an hour's leave of absence, as a young woman suicide, and an obese ex-brewer, who had died of a stroke in the street, were expected in. Otherwise our labors proceeded undisturbed. The Greehahn papers fortunately turned out to be tidily labelled, and after a brief inspection I divided the entire archives into four boxes, in such a way that each group of documents—such as lists of agents, addresses of "letter-boxes," saboteurs, informers, rendezvous, details of illegal routes, maps, code-books, etc.—was split up. At seven o'clock in the evening of the second day I returned to Berlin.

I was not surprised to find a man waiting for me at the Pension Schmidtkamp who identified himself as a representative of the Soviet secret service—that is, as an emissary of my aged lady friend. The man spoke with a Slav accent and looked like a former dancer of the Don Cossack Choir who had since run to fat. I thanked my good instinct for not having put up at the pension suggested to me by Mr. Smith: no doubt Soviet Intelligence knew that Mr. Smith was in the habit of accommodating his agents there, and my Don Cossack had now lost forty-eight hours before tracking me down at the Pension Schmidtkamp. After all, no matter how surly and reproachful he was, my Don Cossack could hardly blame me for not following the American instructions; he even had to swallow his annoyance that, for lack of contact with the East, I had been compelled to act independently. I told him how very sorry I was that he was too late to take a personal part in the original discovery of the Greehahn archives: although I do not think he believed me, he nevertheless had to put a brave face on it—either because he was afraid of his superiors' anger at his slow discovery of my hiding place, or simply because he had no instructions as to what to do in the present circumstances. I assumed that my mustachioed visitor with the foreign accent would presently make a report to his superiors, and so I told him frankly that the archives were at Potsdam. Where precisely they were hidden I should only learn from my contact on Thursday—this was Tuesday evening. We therefore arranged to meet on Thursday morning, and with many good wishes I saw the martial agent to the door.

I was, of course, aware that from that moment onward I had to expect to be "shadowed"—as the ugly term is—by the Soviet secret service. Instead of waiting, therefore, till my Cossack had made his way back to East Berlin and set certain new measures afoot, I left my dingy pension barely an hour after his departure, with my light luggage, and took a room in my real name at a better hotel near the Bahnhof Zoo. If questioned by Soviet Intelligence about my change of address I could quite plausibly explain that American Intelligence had spotted me at the Pension Schmidtkamp. I next rang up Dr. Rebendonck and arranged to meet him later that night: he told me then that, luckily, an exchange of coffins at the Sector boundary had been fixed for Wednesday. I could easily get Herr Fuchs to make out the necessary papers for the "transportation of bodies," he thought, after all, that was how the archives had been brought to Potsdam in the first place.

The following morning I got up early; so early, in fact—against my ordinary practice—that the streets of Berlin were still almost deserted and it was not too difficult for me to make sure whether I was being "shadowed" or not.

When I think back to that eventful Wednesday I see myself as a somnambulist walking over the roof-tops with the sleepwalker's assurance—but safe from falling only so long as no voice challenges him.

Did I, during those most turbulent twenty-four hours of my life, really display exceptional courage or uncommon sang-froid? I am almost inclined to think so. And yet, none of the usual definitions of courage applied to me. Some people believe that courage springs from a lack of imagination: only a person incapable of visualizing the danger is not afraid. But lack of imagination was never one of my failings, and in the present adventure I was quite well aware of the dangers threatening me and my enterprise. Others maintain that courage is the moral ability to take the necessary course, even if one is afraid to do so—in the way that Napoleon wanted to present the palm of heroism to every soldier who marched into battle with shaking knees but with firm determination. Yet I was by no means convinced of the moral necessity of my action: hence the courage I displayed (if you will call it courage) cannot have been of that kind. Others still believe that courage is not a quality at all but a condition: certain people, they argue, have a way of getting themselves into situations in which, if they wish to escape unscathed, they simply have no alternative to courageous behavior. Though I much prefer this skeptical interpretation, I do not necessarily share it. I have never regarded courage as a moral disposition, but as a rational skill. Experienced people, no matter what their other qualities are, are invariably regarded as courageous—simply because it is exceedingly foolish to be cowardly. Everybody knows that the wicked dogs bite only those who are afraid of them—and much the same applies to wicked people. If I am told that a person "cannot help" being afraid of dogs, or of people, then I must reply that it is perfectly easy to deceive both dogs and people, simply by acting as if one were not afraid of them. And this gets me to my own definition of courage. We are all of us, more or less, afraid—but by hiding our fear we acquire that good habit—for it is a habit and not a virtue, a quality, or a condition—that is commonly labelled courage. Courage, in fact, is the ability to deceive the dogs.

That Wednesday—I still take some pride in the thought—I did everything in my power to deceive the dogs.

I was wearing my oldest suit, no tie, and a proletarian cap which I had bought in Berlin. As soon as I got to Potsdam I went to the little cemetery director, with whom I had discussed the technicalities of the transport the night before. That conscientious man had procured three coffins—which, of course, had not been difficult, in view of his job. I should add to his credit, however, that they were second-hand coffins, that he gave me a detailed account in writing of the expenses incurred in their acquisition, and that, at the price he paid for them, they seemed to me a real bargain. With the help of two gravediggers, who had worked for the cemetery director for many years and of whose loyalty he had no doubt, the coffins were taken to the morgue. There, actively assisted by the director, I accommodated the contents of three prepared boxes in the three coffins. About a quarter of the papers I left behind, on the pretext that a transport of more than three coffins would attract attention and that Dr. Rebendonck had advised me against such foolhardiness.

No doubt the gentle reader will already have grasped the nature of the plan which I was about to put into effect.

I had deliberately ordered three coffins. Two of them were intended—or rather their contents were—for General von Greehahn, while the third was my tribute to the American secret service. This in itself testifies that, as an honest broker, I was distributing the goods in at least the approximate ration of the payments promised to me. As I have said, the three coffins were to be taken to the Sector boundary at 10 P.M., within the framework of the regular exchange. Once this was accomplished, I intended—since in the West I could more or less act at liberty—to have two of my "dead" respectfully buried in a certain West Berlin cemetery. The third coffin was to be similarly interred in another cemetery. I would then supply to General von Greehahn the names of the two "dead" beneath whose modest gravestones "his" two coffins reposed; Mr. Smith, on the other hand, would receive the name and place of burial of "his body." There was no reason why Greehahn should ever discover that I had filled not two but three coffins with the contents of his archives, just as the Americans would no doubt content themselves with the buried treasure in "their" grave. Even if Greehahn were ever to learn from Fuchs that I had stowed the papers away in three coffins, I could always claim that, under pressure of circumstances, I had been forced to carry out a redisposition in East Berlin. The risk that the Americans might get on to the cemetery director's tracks seemed to me too slight to be even considered. But what about my third employer, the Soviet secret service? They were not to go empty-handed either, if my plan worked out all right. At my rendezvous with the mustachioed Don Cossack I would declare truthfully that I had discovered the Greehahn archives in the Potsdam morgue. Since Potsdam was in the Soviet Zone the Russians would find no difficulty in surrounding the morgue and seizing the packing cases which I had left behind there for this very purpose. Whether Herr Fuchs would be held responsible must depend on circumstances, but I hoped my friend would be able to protest credibly that he had had no knowledge of the contents of his "cloakroom." Besides, to be perfectly frank, I could not be bothered how he got himself out of his difficulty. One thing was certain: Herr Fuchs would keep quiet about the contents of the three other coffins and the removal of the material—firstly, because, as I have mentioned, he was a trustworthy idealist and would not wish to help the Soviets, but chiefly because his knowledge would reveal him as an accomplice, not merely of myself but of General Edler von Greehahn, who occupied a high place on the Soviet black-list. These were my immediate plans. The more remote ones will have to be discussed presently.

The lids of the three coffins were nailed down, and at four o'clock in the afternoon—the customary time for the transfer of bodies from the morgue to the cemetery—Herr Fuchs had the coffins taken away. This gave us an opportunity to convince ourselves that neither in weight nor in handling did my coffins differ in any way from less valuable ones. I myself replaced the material intended for the Russians in some *Winter Relief* crates so that, when they were discovered, they should look exactly as I had found them. At the cemetery office Herr Fuchs made out the death certificates and travel papers for three persons who had been resident in the West but had died in the East—to wit, Messrs. Emil Meyer and Heinrich Gerber, and a Frau Sofie Andermatt. My self-respect compels me to mention—though I do not wish this to be taken as an embellishment of my character—that while I gratefully accepted the death certificates and transportation forms from my little friend I did not allow him to put his name to them. Instead, I forged his signature on the documents, though of course with his consent, so that in the event of discovery he could always claim that the forms must have been stolen from his office and his signature forged by some Enemy of the People. Herr Fuchs was appreciative of my solicitude for his safety and our farewells were made in an atmosphere of brief but cordial comradeship. For the sake of completeness I ought to mention that the little man in the dark jacket, when I said good-by to him in his office, stood up behind his desk, shot out his right arm in the Nazi salute, and delighted in giving me a dramatic, though of course softly uttered, "Heil Hitler!"

It was shortly after six o'clock when I climbed into the cab of the cemetery administration's truck, which was to take the coffins to East Berlin, and settled down beside the driver. The man knew nothing of the contents of the coffins he was carrying and regarded me as an employee of the Berlin Graves Administration. Not being able to count on him as an accomplice would not have mattered so much, since he was taking his truck only as far as the East Berlin cemetery administration, where the coffins were to be transferred to another truck which, as Herr Fuchs had established by telephone, was already waiting there with two other coffins, so that the whole lot could be taken to the Sector boundary together. What worried me more was that Dr. Rebendonck had overrated the connections and influence of Greehahn's contact in Potsdam, to wit our friend Fuchs. The coffins might be examined, and perhaps even opened, on the Eastern side of the Sector boundary. That was the stake on which I had to gamble.

Rain was beginning to fall as we left Potsdam—a fact which I took as a good omen. As an experienced traveller I knew that frontier guards go about their examination more quickly in bad weather. I was keeping quiet: although I had picked up quite a few Prussian expressions during the war I was afraid of attracting attention by my Austrian pronunciation.

"Are the coffins being taken right through to their destination today?" inquired the driver.

He was an unshaven man of about fifty. I had expected him to be surly and taciturn, but now he seemed not averse to a little chat.

"Certainly," I said.

"Three corpses," he remarked. "Never been more than one in the past."

I could offer no explanation for the phenomenon of three deaths at Potsdam.

"What did you do before?" he asked.

"How do you mean?"

"Well, you didn't always escort corpses?" he said.

"No, no," I laughed. "I used to be a clerk in a brewery." The brewer in the morgue had suggested the idea to me.

"I used to be in the entertainment business too," he said.

Politeness demanded that I should ask for further details.

"I used to have a merry-go-round," he said. "Before the war I actually owned three. Two for grown-ups and one for children. All gone, of course. Bombed to smithereens. Wife's gone too. Caught it while she was working. She ran the merry-go-round while I was in Russia."

Behind us, under the tarpaulin, the coffins collided with each other. As if he had guessed my thoughts he said:

"Ought to have fastened them down."

The fine rain trickled monotonously down the windscreen.

"It isn't far now," I said.

I was hoping he would confirm it. I needed some encouragement because I felt everything had gone too smoothly so far and my share of lucky breaks was getting exhausted. It also occurred to me that it might be a good idea to pray, but then it seemed to me questionable whether the Almighty, even if he heard me, would show much sympathy for my prayers. I thought of Nora and wondered what she would say if she could see me like this: in the Soviet Zone, by the side of a driver who used to own a merry-go-round, aboard a truck with coffins which held no corpses.

"We've got to be there by nine," said the driver. "Or else they won't take the coffins. Once they left my coffin sitting there for a whole week."

He got out a cigarette and offered me half of it. If only he knew, I thought, that those three coffins were worth one hundred and ten thousand dollars and a human life. I accepted the half-cigarette and gave him a light.

At nine o'clock sharp we entered the city. Another ten minutes passed before we reached the Graves Administration.

The black hearse with the two coffins was still standing in the yard. A uniformed official ordered our three coffins to be loaded on to the waiting vehicle. The two uniformed drivers were cursing: they claimed that the Potsdam coffins were unusually heavy. The official seemed surprised that anybody from Potsdam wished to accompany the coffins across the Sector boundary, but made no difficulties. I tried to say as little as possible. After saying good-by to the merry-go-round owner I got in next to the new driver.

The rain had stopped, and since fear begets superstition I regarded this as an ill omen. We drove through the ruined streets of nocturnal East Berlin. A few houses were still standing among the ruins, but they, too, seemed deserted. The driver, a dark young man, was whistling a popular ditty. My nerves were so taut I was quite incapable of further fear. Only once did I reflect whether the adventure was really worth while. It occurred to me that only a year had elapsed since I accepted my schoolfriend's invitation to Baden. Now thoroughly despondent I was wishing I had never accepted it.

The driver stopped whistling.

"Better get your papers ready," he said. "They don't like being kept waiting."

This did not sound too promising. I extracted my papers from my wallet.

At the same moment the figure of a policeman rose up before me. He was standing in the middle of the road. There was something ominous about his appearance.

"What's up?" I asked softly.

"Sector boundary," said the man beside me.

"Oh, I see," I said, almost relieved.

Now I could see that the policeman was standing beside an illuminated guard-house, in front of a lowered barrier.

The vehicle stopped. Out of the guard-house came two Russian soldiers. I remained in my seat and passed my papers to the policeman. He took them and disappeared inside the guard-house while the Russians were nosing around our vehicle.

The policeman returned.

"I can't let you through," he said to the driver. "The truck from the other side hasn't come yet."

"Shall I wait?" the driver asked indifferently.

"If it doesn't take too long," said the policeman.

He explained the situation to the two Russians. One of them, a boy of no more than eighteen, with a medal gleaming on his chest began to show rather a lot of interest in the coffins. He tapped them as if to test the wood.

"Has this ever happened before?" I asked the driver.

"What?"

"That there's no truck from the other side."

At once I regretted my loquacity, for I had made up my mind not to speak much; my question, moreover, betrayed my inexperience. I had the impression that the policeman was watching me closely.

There was no movement on the other side. I asked myself whether Dr. Rebendonck's organization had slipped up, or whether the little doctor had simply kept my dollars for himself.

Suddenly I heard the policeman's voice: "He wants to open this one."

He was referring to the young Russian who had evidently got bored with waiting and now wished to examine one of the coffins.

I remained in my seat. I did not want to see which coffin they were opening.

The driver got out of his seat and went to the back. At the same moment the headlights of a truck appeared in front. It pulled up opposite us, on the American side of the Sector boundary.

"Here he is!" I called out to them at the back.

In the glare of the headlights I saw that one of the coffins had been lifted down from our hearse—but I was still uncertain which it was.

"He's insisting," said the German policeman, pointing to the Russian.

I could hear hammering, the groan of tearing wood, and curses.

When I turned again the coffin was standing in a pool of light on the ground outside the guard-house. The Russian lifted the lid.

I was gazing into the white face of a woman. I don't believe a human face, living or dead, had ever seemed so eloquent to me.

The coffin was laboriously fastened down again. The driver climbed back into his seat. The policeman lifted the barrier. The hastily reloaded coffin swung from one side of the truck to the other. Slowly the hearse rolled into West Berlin.

PART SIX

23
ᘛᘛᘛᘛᘛᘛᘛᘛᘛᘛᘛᘛᘛ

Halcyon

AFTER MY RETURN from Berlin to Vienna it really seemed as if I could make true the promise I had made myself and wind up my short but successful career in the Devil's service.

Mr. Smith received me with a degree of cordiality from which I felt entitled to deduce the unreserved satisfaction of our joint employers in Washington. Heads of departments, personnel managers, secretaries, and all the other middlemen of power, are like lenses magnifying the mood of their superiors: one need only look through them to know what is going on behind the closed doors of the boss' inner office.

"You're a genius, Droste," said Mr. Smith, welcoming me for the first time at his private house in Döbling. "I've known it from the start. We have opened the coffin of the good Sofie Andermatt—however did you think of that pretty name?—and had a look at the material. No, of course we don't think it represents the whole of the Greehahn archives—but then, the General would have hardly been so incautious as to deposit the entire archives in one spot. But, even so, it's valuable material, and what's even more valuable is the knowledge that Greehahn is the right man for us."

I was surprised to find him continuing our conversation even when an exceedingly handsome young man in a white jacket, looking more like a bright student than a butler, brought in our very American but—for all that—quite eatable dinner. However, Mr. Smith waited till we were alone before informing me that General von Greehahn was on his way to Munich.

"We have very high expectations of the Greehahn Organization," he said, "and I shouldn't be surprised if Washington decided to attach you to it."

"Fortunately that won't be possible," I objected, "since the General believes that I am Colonel Engljähringer."

"Why fortunately?"

I smiled. "You are forgetting, Mr. Smith, that I have no doubts of the probity of American Intelligence, and am therefore firmly counting on the ten thousand dollars which you have promised me."

"Quite so," said Mr. Smith, "although Washington intends to pay over the sum in twelve monthly installments. You will understand that we do not wish to throw ten thousand dollars on the black market in one fell swoop. But the fact that we are keeping our side of the bargain doesn't mean that we want to see you reclining on your laurels, my dear Droste. By all means, take a well-earned rest for a while—in any case, your assignments will now become less frequent but at the same time more important: after what you've done, no one would dream of risking your neck lightheartedly or for the sake of a small gain."

"You're too kind," I said with a slight bow.

Mr. Smith ignored my ironical interruption.

"What we are suffering from is mediocrity," he continued. "It's easy for the theatrical people: they don't put on a show until they have found the right cast. But we've got to play every night, and often we've got to stage the most important plays with the most wretched actors. Getting agents is a rotten business, you know. In any other business, if you want to enroll a new staff, you've got their references to go by, their previous experience, or at least your own judgment. But you can't get any professional references about an agent. And as for moral qualifications—the fact that a candidate was a rogue in the past may give him an opening into a most brilliant career. As I say, it's a rotten business. . . ."

With these words he switched over to renewed compliments about my own person and my achievements.

It seemed a favorable opportunity for me to broach the subject that was closest to my heart. At great length, and with ample justification, I put it to Mr. Smith that I was in urgent need of rest and hoped to retire to the country for a while.

"At the same time," I went on, "my plans depend on you—and not only in a professional sense. The private individual Droste also wishes to place himself in your hands."

We had moved into the sitting-room. I was sipping an ancient heavy Armagnac, while Mr. Smith was slowly and pleasurably draining several glasses of green Chartreuse. I waited till the young servant, who was courteous and efficient but a little too importunate for my liking, had left the room before I took my host into my confidence.

Mr. Smith was familiar with Nora Güldendag's name from my Budapest report, and I did not find it difficult to come to the request I had long wanted to make. I made no secret to him of my feelings for Nora and, as if speaking to an old friend, I described to him my shadow-fight with the missing Legation Counsellor. The Swedish and British secret services, I said, and possibly also the American secret service, were bound to be better informed about Gunnar Güldendag's fate than his wife. I did not want to discover any secrets: all I was interested in was the question of whether the missing diplomat was still alive. Mr. Smith showed sympathy for my position, and when I left his home at an advanced hour I took with me his promise that he would do all in his power to get me the information I wanted.

While I was anxiously awaiting the reply of my immediate superior, I learned with considerable relief that General von Greehahn, far from seeing through my double or treble game, was also highly satisfied with my achievement.

I had, so to speak, staked everything by informing the General through Dr. Rebendonck that his archives had arrived at a West Berlin cemetery—for at that time I had not only not received a single dollar from him but, on the contrary, had invested some of my own money. If Greehahn had not been a man of honor he would have had no difficulty in robbing me of the fruits of my honest work. The General, however, was one of those people who will bury enough dynamite to blow the whole world to pieces without batting an eyelid, but who will conscientiously and unfailingly honor a bill on the day it falls due. Greehahn did not yet possess one hundred thousand dollars to dispose of, but he promptly paid me five thousand dollars through a courier, and he promised me the balance within a matter of weeks. The courier was a former senior official of the Nazi Secret Police, a man of bureaucratic appearance and corresponding habits. I had to sign for the receipt of the money on a special printed form, which he carefully folded in four, not without handing me a neat slip to show that he had received my receipt. Greehahn's courier dispelled my last anxieties. He informed me that the coffins which had reposed in Berlin, under crosses inscribed Heinrich Gerber and Emil Meyer, had already arrived in Munich and had found pleasure with the "Herr Präsident." The President was Greehahn, whose new organization had been entered in the trade register as the Bavarian Oil Processing Corporation, a limited liability company. As soon as "the American oil well" began to gush—as my visitor wittily expressed himself—I could expect a further consignment from the General.

I need hardly say that my third clients, the Soviets, caused me the worst headache—firstly, because I had not yet heard from them, and secondly, because I was not unacquainted with the rough and ready methods they were fond of using for the punishment of disloyal agents. On that memorable Thursday, after arriving in West Berlin with my coffins, I had disclosed to my surly Don Cossack the secret of the Potsdam morgue, and no doubt the Russians must have impounded the remaining packing-cases straight away. I do not know to this day whether the contents of the files, maps, and photographs really satisfied them, but I can state, at the risk of anticipating, that a considerable time passed before I heard any more from my Eastern employers. True, a few months later I learned with genuine regret that Herr Josef Fuchs, administrator of the Potsdam cemetery, had lost his life in an accident. Now and again I would see him in my nightmares, but I do not believe that his premature death had anything to do with my mission, or else I should have suffered by now all those unpleasant things at which the Soviet Intelligence granny had hinted in such an unmistakable manner.

My second interview with Mr. Smith took place a fortnight af-

ter my first visit—again in the private setting of his tastefully furnished villa. I was particularly grateful that Mr. Smith had invited me, for he was indisposed: an acute conjunctivitis, not dangerous but very stubborn, prevented him from leaving his house.

We are all inverted prophets, capable of presenting past events
in such a way as if, at the time they occurred, we had foreseen
their consequences. I do not wish to gain the reputation of that
kind of soothsayer, but I should not be telling the truth if I did
not record that on that spring day the atmosphere in Mr. Smith's
house struck me as decidedly strange and filled me with fore-
boding.

The living-room, into which I was shown by a corpulent cook
—the youthful butler with the smooth dark hair seemed to be ab-
sent—was almost in darkness. But it was not the darkness that
made it difficult for me to recognize my discoverer and friend. He
was sitting in a deep arm-chair, without that characteristic pair of
spectacles on his nose which I had mentally christened his two
monocles. Deep wrinkles had appeared around his mouth; his head
was resting against the back of his chair; a damp white cloth had
been tied over his eyes, and his well-shaped fingers were nervously
drumming on the arms of his chair. At the same time he spoke
so benignly and wisely, as people do only when fate has handled
them roughly, and when they suddenly feel that they ought to
practice, in a compressed form and possibly too late, all the good-
ness and wisdom they omitted to show over the past years and
decades.

"I made inquiries about Gunnar Güldendag," Mr. Smith said,
wasting no time in coming to the point, "which was more difficult
than you would believe. From the British, who were naturally
more secretive vis-à-vis the secret service of a friendly Power than
they'd be towards an enemy agent, we couldn't get anything at
all. The Swedes, too, were most reluctant to give anything away.
Well, in the end I pulled a few private strings and I am able to set
your mind at rest. Swedish Intelligence are firmly convinced that
your invisible rival was deported to Siberia and has met his death
there. Naturally, Swedish Intelligence doesn't want to give any
guarantee, and the Royal Government has so far refused to issue
a death certificate—but no serious observer believes that Güldendag

will return. The Russians have hinted to the Swedes that the Legation Counsellor was killed in a gasoline-dump explosion. Gas-dump explosions, allow me to tell you, are a well-tried means of letting awkward persons disappear in such a way that there isn't even an awkward corpse to account for. I mentioned to my friends the rumor that the Legation Counsellor had been seen in East Berlin, and the fact that they had heard the rumor seems to me to support the reliability of the rest of their information. The lady who claimed to have seen him in Berlin is well known as a bit of a fool, with a bent for adventurous fancies and self-advertisement. When she was questioned by Swedish Intelligence she got herself all tied up in contradictions. Thus the misfortune of one," Mr. Smith ended sententiously, "becomes the good fortune of another, for on this earth, my dear Droste, there is a lack of space, just as in an overcrowded parking lot, where one motorist can't pull in until another has pulled out. Frau Güldendag is now undoubtedly a widow, and though we may occasionally find it more difficult to deceive the dead than the living, you have, nevertheless, both done your duty. Hence there is nothing left for me but to wish you the best of luck for your future."

He sat up in his chair but did not take off the bandage from his eyes, so that I could not rid myself of the embarrassing feeling of conversing with a blind man. He modestly disclaimed my thanks and even seemed reluctant to accept my sincere wishes for his speedy recovery.

"There are advantages in being blind for a while," he said with a gentle smile, which for once escaped refutation by his steel-hard eyes. "Yes, indeed, there are advantages." He motioned to the French window leading out into the garden. "I had not listened to birdsong for years, Droste, and I had never noticed the smell of lilac until the very last moment, when spring, as is its bad habit, was on the way out, even before one had noticed its arrival. We speak with pity, and sometimes even with disdain, of people who live in the past, although we really ought to be sorry for those who live in the future. A person living in the past does not inevitably miss the present moment: it's not the serene past but the turbulent future that's the enemy of the present."

"I am amazed to hear you talking like this, Mr. Smith," I said.

"Am I wrong in thinking that your momentary physical condition is making you feel unduly depressed?"

"Depressed? Not in the least," he replied. "I have been thinking a lot these past few days, and I have arrived at surprising conclusions. Perhaps you are too young to understand," he added, with that paternal condescension which men of sixty are fond of showing for those of forty, "but it seems to me that hope impairs our happiness just as much as fear does. The word 'hopeless' has a sad ring, while 'free from desire' sounds serene—and yet the two are essentially the same. It is no more paradoxical, my dear Droste, to be hopelessly happy than to be happy through freedom from desire, for both signify contentment with one's present condition, or at least that peaceful resignation which we may call contentment. A fearful preoccupation, as much as a hopeful preoccupation, with the future impairs the intensity of the present moment—which alone should be what matters." He laughed—an uneasy, blind laugh. "Parsimonious people, for instance—among whom, fortunately, we need not count you—deny themselves certain pleasures so that they should not go short in the future; in other words, they abstain today because they fear tomorrow's poverty, or because they have hopes of tomorrow's plenty. You can see how closely fear and hope are related; you can probably also see how absurd, on closer examination, all preoccupation with the future is. If today you find me devoid of hope," he concluded, suddenly serious again, "you also find me devoid of desire. But I would not have you think me depressed."

For a while Mr. Smith kept up his philosophical monologue, but he did not convince me of his serene frame of mind. I left the darkened house in Döbling in what was almost perplexity, and today it seems to me that I had a premonition that afternoon that this was my last meeting between my mentor and myself. It is not just a phrase that certain people are said to bear the mark of death upon them: they are like goods in shops, bearing the label "sold," and which, though they can still be viewed for a while, already belong to someone else.

A few days after my visit there appeared on the local page of the Viennese papers a brief notice to the effect that an American by the name of Francis K. Smith, representative of a New York typewriter firm, had died of an overdose of sleeping tablets at his villa in Döbling. Although it was evidently a case of accidental death the military authorities had, nevertheless, taken charge of the body. More than a year passed before I learned any details about my friend's death—but I never believed the version of the fatal accident, even for a moment.

Mr. Smith's death tipped the scales of my decision to retire from the secret services. On the one hand I was seriously persuading myself that American Intelligence had now definitely lost touch with me, but on the other hand I could not quite suppress the uneasiness which the prolonged silence of the Soviet secret service was causing me. At the beginning of May I moved with Nora to the Wolfgangsee, in the American Zone of Austria, not far from the charming baroque city of Salzburg, which at that time held the unofficial position of Austria's second capital.

If I now present the story of the next eighteen months in a condensed and almost hasty manner, I am doing so not because it is less deserving of full treatment than the rest of my account. Indeed, I should very much prefer to linger over the description of this happiest period of my life, which began in the summer of 1948 and came to an abrupt end in the spring of 1950. But time presses and I have only a few months left for the completion of my memoirs—and it is the story of my secret-service work, not of my private life, that the reader is rightly demanding to learn.

During this happy period I often remembered Mr. Smith and his remarks about the present, the past, and the future; for throughout these months Nora and I never gave a thought to anything else but to welcoming each day as it rose behind the Schafberg, and to giving it a grateful send-off as it declined behind the hills of St. Gilgen.

Gently, and with all the tact I could muster, I had intimated to Nora what I had learned about the end of her husband. She received the news collectedly, or rather, without any hypocritical show of tragedy, though of course with the shock which finality invariably produces.

We stayed at a farmhouse near St. Wolfgang, with a family consisting of father, mother, and four sons, who cheerfully put the entire upper floor of the spacious house at our disposal. The large stone building, with its tall, steep roof, its massive walls, its small windows, its cool stone floors, its warm cowsheds, and its colorful, seventeenth-century Salzburg, peasant furniture, stood on a hill, facing south across the lake.

In front of the mountains were the lake, the fields, the woods, the farmsteads, and a few private houses. That was why the mountains were far enough away to seem not like warders watching prisoners, but like guardians protecting our liberty. We grew so close to nature that the seasons to us showed not a quaternity but a multiplicity: within a single spring the pale green of the meadows would change to the delicate yellow of the primroses; the delicate yellow was succeeded by the pale blue of forget-me-nots, and this in turn by the fiery hue of rose campions; no sooner had the campions faded than the wild purple orchids sprang up along the edges of the forests; the same meadows were white on the next morning with newly opened daisies, and among them the mauve harebells were already ringing in the summer. Within the span of a single spring the periods of trees and shrubs and bushes likewise succeeded one another in an ever changing pattern: at first the landscape was dominated by the white-and-pink blossom of the fruit trees; then the box, the lilac, and the elder advertised themselves by their fragrance; next the horse-chestnuts lit their red-and-white candles; and, finally, syringa prevailed over lilac, and box, and chestnut. Summer and autumn and winter were here as many-faceted as spring, each season a multiplicity in itself—when the black earth yielded its fruits and the crimson poppy was bright among the corn; when the autumnal trees showed that they were individuals, only seemingly of the same kind or color; when the mists pushed between the hills, as though wanting to cover the chilly earth with a soft feather bed before it went to sleep; when the lake froze over and the water turned to solid ground, and when the solid ground burst open again to turn into water.

The village, though still scarred by the war, hospitably received the two strangers who were prepared to share its joy and grief. I discovered that the countryside was not only more peaceful than the big city, but also more stimulating. Whereas the many people in the big city lived far from each other, the few who lived here were all close. The birth of a child; the death of a dog; a horse who had broken a leg and had to be put down; a commercial traveller who had got a local girl pregnant and had vanished into thin air; a woman who had run away from her husband and had come back, with a lot of new clothes, but humble; a peasant who had bought back a patch of woodland which his father had drunk away—all these were genuine and personal sensations with which the cold collective sensations of the city could not compete.

Just as nature receives hardly anything and yet gives everything; just as earth, trees, shrubs, mountains, lakes, and streams renew themselves out of their own substance; just as everything grows from itself and from within—thus Nora and I also grew from ourselves and from within. Whether our surroundings reminded us of ourselves, or whether we noticed our surroundings because we had found one another, I am unable to say. Likewise, I do not know how great in all this was the measure of resignation, of fear and escape, and even (I must admit it) revulsion of the world—to what extent, in fact, I was enjoying not so much that which was around me, as that which I did not have to see. But there is no need to determine this question, since maturity and resignation are twin sisters, just as maturity and happiness are—from which it follows that happiness and resignation are more akin than a superficial observer might assume.

Everything that I felt was genuine—only my life was not. There was just one year, the past year, of which I could not, or dared not, speak to Nora frankly. But just as a story becomes untruthful when its conclusion has been faked, so one single lie made my entire past life untruthful, and, at times, even unreal. Whole weeks might pass in blissful self-deception, but one word was enough to break the spell. In the manner of lovers, Nora would return to our first meeting, gaily examining on what day, at what hour, and at what minute the spark had flashed from her to me and from me to her—and we were back at once in the Budapest convent and right in the middle of my lie. Nora knew a lot of people and I knew even more—but we had few acquaintances in common and hence reverted to those few again and again—to Mother Martha and the gruff Count, to Countess Tydings and the peasant leader Vass —and the moment they came up we were back again in that one year that I did not want to mention.

More difficult than the past was the present. We had gone to St. Wolfgang because a cousin of Nora's, who was married to an Austrian Baron Czernatowski, was living at Sotbl on the Wolfgangsee and was anxious to help Nora acquire a small but profitable farm property. When we had first come to know each other I had given Nora an approximately truthful picture of my financial position: how was I now to explain to her that, almost over night, I had become very much wealthier than she was, and that I was now in a position to buy the estate out of my own pocket, or at least make a very substantial contribution. Once a month I had to go to Vienna to collect the monthly installment of my reward from American Intelligence, at an address which Mr. Smith had providently given me: on these occasions I also had to put through various deals with my black-market friends. And when I then returned to our farmhouse I had to string lie upon lie for days to come. For the first time in my life I lied badly, like a man who is certain of being found out eventually and hopes that having lied clumsily will then be accepted as an excuse. We were in the habit of collecting our letters at the village post office, making this trip the pretext for a lengthy walk—and for a long time I approached the post office with an ever new feeling of anxiety. I had to lie again when the long-awaited and very carefully phrased letter from General von Greehahn arrived—or rather, from the Bavarian Oil Processing Corporation—and when I left post-haste for Munich to take possession of the balance of my dollar fortune.

Greedy though I was, and remained, the promptness with which both Greehahn and the Americans were rewarding me for my services filled me with misgivings. I found it hard to believe that both should simply consider themselves bound by an unwritten contract and should meticulously keep their promises and arrangements; it seemed to me that their payments were not so much in settlement of past transactions as on account of future ones. What would I do, I kept asking myself, if they were to approach me with new demands? I was reminded of those ever recurring trivial plots of the silent-film period, when a criminal decides to go straight, takes a good wife, begets a lot of healthy children, and peacefully, under a new name, plies his trade of locksmith or village grocer until one day, to the pianist's furious strumming of

Schubert, his one-time accomplice appears behind the bushes—a coarse, broad-shouldered, and unshaven fellow—and encourages the reformed character to crack another safe with him. Many a time, in the nearby provincial town of Bad Ischl—where life, even after the Second World War, was still very traditional and imperial —sitting at a marble-topped table in a pastry shop, or returning from a brief shopping tour in Salzburg, or facing each other by the window, reading, and gazing out into a monotonously rainy landscape, I really believed that I saw those figures approaching: the messengers of the Americans, or the Russians, or the Germans— the same coarse, broad-shouldered, and unshaven fellows. These thoughts did not oppress me all the time, but they cropped up often enough. I could gauge my anxiety by the superstitious comforts that I invented for myself. I would tell myself, for instance, that no messenger could get through while there were snowdrifts across the road, or that I would be safe on Wednesdays—my lucky day.

Why—I have since often asked myself—did I not confide in the woman I loved? I have a lot of explanations, but none explains my perseverance. If Nora had loved me merely physically, or merely intellectually; if she had loved me from passion alone, or merely from a need for love—who knows, everything might have turned out differently. But that was not the way of Nora's love. It was a mature love, composed of passion and respect, of the harmony of our bodies, but also of serious admiration. Hence, unlike Dorian Gray, who kills the painter Basil Hallward before destroying the portrait of himself, I feared that by destroying my picture I should also destroy the artist. Whether I lied out of love, or whether I did not love Nora sufficiently—to this day I do not know the answer to this question.

And yet, what I said about the happiest time of my life is quite true. What distinguishes righteous and unrighteous people is not good deeds as against bad ones, not a calm conscience as against a disturbed one—since we are all of us committing good deeds and bad ones and have a calm conscience sometimes and a disturbed one at others—but the fact that the ones are unable to live at peace with a disturbed conscience, while the others settle down with it quite comfortably. My conscience was never silent, but I managed to live quite well with my bad conscience. Like most bad men I had strong nerves, and I often lulled the anxiety within me into sweet slumber for weeks and months.

Thus came the second spring of our happiness. The date was May 3, 1950. It had been raining ceaselessly for two days—that fine Salzburg "thread rain," which fell intensively and almost invisibly, and settled over the lake, like a hundred gossamer-thin veil curtains on an operatic stage. From the chimneys of the farmhouses rose comfortable columns of smoke; above the roofs they encountered the descending clouds. The mountain landscape had changed into that of a plain: beyond the water were fields and woods, but the mountains behind them had vanished. It was as if the guardians of our safety had silently withdrawn.

In the afternoon the rain suddenly stopped. The deep-green fields seemed to draw new breath: everywhere fresh flowers had sprung from the moist ground. The wet gravel crunched under our feet as we walked along the lake front to the post office, where our letters—if there were any—had been lying unclaimed for the past forty-eight hours.

The rustic post office, which smelled of wood and rain, was empty. Only the little gray-haired postmaster sat behind the counter, under his lamp. He glanced up as we entered in cheerful conversation.

"Herr Droste," he said, "a gentleman inquired after your address a few minutes ago." And, with a shrewd smile behind his glasses, he added: "A strange gentleman in our St. Wolfgang at this time of year."

"A strange gentleman?" I repeated, with my heart in my mouth.

"Yes, a Japanese or a Chinese—I can't be sure which," said the postmaster.

24

Summons from the Devil

WHEN WE LEFT the post office the gentleman who had inquired about me was standing in front of the grocer's shop opposite. I recognized him instantly. He was Dr. Lu Wang, my Chinese colleague from the spy school in Maryland.

I greeted him with all the cordiality I could muster and introduced him to Nora.

"Mr. Lu Wang, a business friend from America," I said.

Lu Wang caught the drift at once.

"I was in Salzburg," he said, "and was told that you were now living here. I did not want to miss the opportunity of seeing you, especially as I have intended for some weeks to discuss a business matter with you—an urgent and, as I believe, not inconsiderable business matter."

He was speaking English, without a foreign accent, and apologized to Nora for his inability to converse in German. Nora answered him in her fluent English and, hospitable as always, asked Lu Wang to give us the pleasure of staying with us.

"Like a proper tourist I have booked a room at the White Horse Inn," the Chinese said with a smile. "Perhaps you, madam, and Herr Droste, would care to come over tonight——"

"Perhaps we ought to get our business settled first," I interrupted, "and you'll give us the pleasure of your company at lunch tomorrow."

"Excellent," agreed Lu Wang. "May I then expect you to dinner about eight o'clock, Herr Droste?"

On the way home I told Nora about my acquaintance with Lu Wang—or rather, I embroidered his person and our first meeting with much fiction. He was the son of Chinese parents, I lied, but had been born in the States and was now one of the biggest importers of foreign wines there. He probably did not know that I had retired from business, but that was no reason why I should not have a chat with the pleasant and highly respected man.

I had a feeling that for the first time Nora was watching me distrustfully. I did not know whether the impression was due to my bad conscience, or whether the strange man outside the St. Wolfgang post office had really aroused her suspicions; or whether she was simply afraid that his tempting offers might entice me back into the hustle and bustle of the city. At any rate, I was aware of lying clumsily that afternoon. I was utterly out of practice and lied with that excessive caution which is as detrimental to really smooth lying as excessively cautious movement is to sport. When I left the house in the evening to go down into the village I thought that her farewells were chillier than they normally were when we parted for a few hours, and that there was in them a touch of reproach.

As I crossed the main square, as I passed the famous village church which contains Michael Pacher's masterpiece, the late-Gothic altar representing the Coronation of the Virgin—as I walked along the musical-comedy façade of the Post Hotel and through the low gateway below the church, I was suddenly and grotesquely reminded of the chorus of the song which had started out from this little village and circled the globe:

> "At the White Horse Inn on the Wolfgangsee
> There's happiness waiting for you."

No one, I thought, would be waiting for me at the quiet hotel, which was slowly getting ready for the coming holiday season, except Dr. Lu Wang, who would be waiting for me in the glassed-in dining terrace. Yet it seemed more than doubtful that he would bring me happiness; indeed it was more likely that he had come to destroy it.

Dr. Lu Wang had chosen a corner table overlooking the lake.

Although he was not tall, he was taller than the customary European notion of a Chinese—which is based on the fact that in Europe one usually encounters only the intellectual Southern Chinese, whereas Lu Wang came from the North, with its broad-shouldered, more robust, and less well-mannered type. He had a friendly and almost benign, though by no means always smiling, face. There was nothing about his eyes of that sly cunning which Europeans are so fond of attributing to the yellow race simply because the eyes of white men, whenever they hold an expression of cunning, take on the slit appearance of the Chinese. On the contrary, his small nut-brown eyes reflected an open mind; they were observant rather than servile. I had noticed even in Maryland that Dr. Lu Wang must be very short-sighted, for while he talked he was for ever taking his heavy horn-rimmed glasses off his nose and polishing them eagerly, almost as if the dust or steam on them were responsible for his defective vision. I need hardly say that the yellow-skinned man in his well-cut tweed travelling clothes indeed, as the postmaster had remarked, looked strange in this half-rural and half musical-comedy setting.

"How delightful to see you again, Herr Droste," said the doctor, without finding it necessary to explain how he came to address me by my real name when he had only met a Mr. Lehmann at the spy school.

"I, too, am really delighted," I said, and the words were not as hypocritical as they might seem. I had always preferred Lu Wang to my other colleagues.

When Lu Wang had said a few complimentary words about the beauty of the scenery and the charm of my companion in the afternoon, and when, like schoolfriends meeting after a long interval, we had exchanged a few amusing reminiscences about classmates and teachers, he came to the point of his visit without further beating about the bush.

"I have come from Washington," he said, "even if by a somewhat roundabout route. Washington believes, not unnaturally, that your valuable gifts have been lying fallow long enough. You are required to report to Washington, by the quickest way and in my company, in order to receive new instructions."

"Before commenting on this news," I replied, suppressing a groan, "may I inquire, Dr. Wang, why you have been chosen as the bearer of this surprising and not altogether joyful message?"

"Of course," Dr. Wang said obligingly. "It was not done, I assure you, because I was thought to fit particularly well into these charming surroundings. The point is that I am in a position to introduce you to certain details of your urgent mission while we are still *en route*."

He uttered the words "while we are still *en route*," as if there could be no doubt of my readiness to follow him to America at once.

"You are, in other words, authorized to initiate me into this mission?" I said.

He nodded. "I shall have to go back a good deal to enable you to understand the situation. You know that ever since the Potsdam Conference Korea has been divided into an American and a Soviet Zone—or rather, was divided for exactly two years. North of the thirty-eighth parallel—a very arbitrary and imaginary boundary line, as you will agree—the Russians were established until May 1948, and to the South the Americans. But when the Americans withdrew last June, in order to establish Korea's independence within the meaning of the Potsdam Agreement, the Soviets for their part left a very considerable military force behind in the Northern part of the country. Their satellites duly set up a Korean People's Democratic Republic, with Pyongyang as its capital—a kind of rival capital, since the ancient capital of Seoul is situated in the South. You follow?"

"Absolutely," I said, a little intrigued, since I could not imagine how my mission could be connected with these Far Eastern events.

"The Americans, as well as the United Nations," continued Lu Wang, "cabled all sorts of protests into the world against the perpetuation of this partition of Korea—but you know as well as I do that Solomonic judgments have little prospect of success in contemporary politics since the contending mothers prefer to see their children cut in two rather than submit to reasonable arbitration. In the end, the world got used to the idea of two Koreas, just as it has got used to two Germanys, and you yourself probably did not display overmuch sympathy whenever you heard or read about the divided country during the past year. But now," he concluded, "the Eastern rulers have decided, to our certain knowledge, to reunite Korea in their own way—in other words, to invade South Korea by force of arms and conquer it."

"Wouldn't this mean war with America?" I objected.

"It undoubtedly would," said Dr. Wang.

"And do the North Koreans know this—or rather, their wire-pullers in Moscow and Peking?" I asked.

"Your question, Herr Droste, is very pertinent," said the Chinese approvingly. "And it leads me to one of the most intricate, and also one of the most embarrassing, episodes in the history of the secret services. A few months ago," he continued, lowering his voice even further, "there was a secret session of the U.S. Cabinet. Only members of the Administration were present; even the minute clerks were excluded; it was an 'only-for-the-ear' meeting and the discussions and decisions were intended for the ears of Government members only. At this top-secret conference the American spheres of influence in the Far East were defined. This term, as you know, describes those geographical and strategic areas which the Americans, though they do not in fact own them, are determined to defend. You will no doubt be surprised to hear that after several hours' discussion it was decided to exclude Korea—in other words, to give up Korea in the event of an armed conflict. This did not mean that the U.S.A. would have denied its sympathies to a South Korea defending itself against aggression from the North—but sympathies are not much use against tanks and bombers."

"I presume that the U.S. Government had good reasons for withdrawing from active guardianship," I said.

Dr. Wang polished his glasses.

"We'll leave that point open," he said, and I could feel how deeply he was distressed by this sacrifice of members of his race. "At any rate, the decision of the U.S. Cabinet was known, within a matter of hours of the conclusion of the meeting, to the Red Chinese secret service in Washington and, presumably, also to the secret service of the Soviet Union."

"How is that possible? You said yourself . . ."

"How it was possible, Herr Droste," said Dr. Wang, "is outside my ken and I very much doubt whether there is a person in Washington who could answer your question. Anyway, U.S. Counter-Intelligence, though of course unaware at first of the Cabinet decision, was on its toes for once and reported a few days ago that Peking was excellently well informed about the American surrender of South Korea in the event of a Communist attack. But this is not the end of the story. About a fortnight ago another secret meeting of the Government took place, under the chairmanship of the President. Although the Cabinet was not at that time aware that its earlier decision had leaked out, that first decision was reversed."

"Let me get this straight, Dr. Wang," I said. "At its second meeting the Cabinet decided to defend South Korea after all, in the event of aggression from the North?"

"Just so. South Korea was once more included in the defensive perimeter of the United States. I am not acquainted with the mysterious ways of high politics, Herr Droste, and cannot therefore offer any satisfactory explanation why Korea, after first being dropped, was suddenly recognized again as an American sphere of influence. But then it is hardly our business to ponder the ways of high politics."

I do not know if Dr. Wang noticed the little jerk I gave at his words "our business." He tasted the light Austrian wine with an expert's concentration and continued.

"I am gradually coming to your mission. A few days ago the Government received an extremely unwelcome report from our Intelligence. To put it in a nutshell: the Red Chinese espionage organization in Washington, which had been so excellently informed about the first Cabinet meeting, had learned nothing about the second one. This time the secret of the Government's decision was kept."

"You say: an unwelcome report, Dr. Wang? Why should you call the failure of the enemy's espionage unwelcome?"

"You must put yourself in the position of the Chinese Communists for a moment," declared my visitor. "Powerful though they are, confident as they are of Russian support, and favorable as the strategic position in Korea may seem to them, they still have no desire to provoke a military conflict with the United States. Underestimation of an unprepared America proved the downfall of your fellow-countryman from Braunau—and my fellow-countrymen believe in the ancient saying that, while the cleverest man may fall into ever new errors, only a fool commits the same error twice. In short, Peking would definitely not condone an attack of their North Korean allies across the thirty-eighth parallel if such an attack meant almost certain war with America. As a result of the successful *coup* of Red Chinese Intelligence in Washington, Peking is now informed about the first meeting of the U.S. Cabinet; but since the same Intelligence fell down on the second occasion, nothing is known of the outcome of the other meeting. In other words, Peking, and hence also Moscow, is convinced that America is prepared to surrender South Korea. And it is on this, now erroneous, premise that the plans are based for the attack which will undoubtedly come this very summer."

I recalled my highly confidential conversation with General von Greehahn at the Washington villa. Perhaps he had not overrated the significance of the secret services after all; perhaps he had not misjudged the diabolical possibilities which a secret service could provide in the hands of unscrupulous politicians.

"Would it be possible, Dr. Wang," I said, "that on the first occasion Red Chinese Intelligence did not work any miracles either and that, instead, someone deliberately allowed the secret of the first Government meeting to leak out in order to encourage the Chinese Communists to launch an attack?"

He shrugged his shoulders. "It is not for us to speculate," he said, "and you would probably do better not to concern yourself with this problem." His soft voice, which seemed incapable of loud sounds, held no threat even now; on the contrary, I thought I could hear in it a note of resignation. "Anyway," he resumed after a short while, "the fact is that America is not prepared for a war in the Far East and does not want war—at least, not at this moment."

"What is preventing the United States," I asked, "from letting the East know in good time that it will not remain passive in the face of an attack on South Korea?"

"A communication of this sort, through diplomatic channels for instance," the Chinese replied, "would be hellishly like an ultimatum. For another thing, the concept of a 'sphere of influence' is itself entirely unofficial; strictly speaking, it is illegal to designate countries one does not own as defense zones. And, finally, such sabre-rattling by the U.S.A. would not be taken seriously in Peking or Moscow, since they believe themselves to be reliably informed about the outcome of the Cabinet meeting. Every day diplomacy yields more ground to the secret service, and spies nowadays are the real ambassadors."

I pushed the plate with my crisp golden *Wiener Schnitzel* away from me. I had lost my appetite.

"Will you please come to my mission, Dr. Wang?" I said.

"Very well. It is, as you will see, a paradoxical mission. Our Intelligence has to make up for the failure of the enemy's Intelligence, a failure which might well lead to disaster. Measures have to be taken, and taken as quickly as possible, to ensure that the North Koreans, or—more correctly—the Chinese Communists, learn the truth—the truth being that the United States is determined upon defensive intervention. Just as they were informed of the first Cabinet decision through illegal channels, so they must again be informed of the second one through their secret service, in which alone they will place credence." He cut up his Schnitzel into such minute pieces that it almost looked like a Chinese dish. "You are to take a confidential message to the President of the Republic of South Korea, informing him of America's change of mind—that is, of her readiness to intervene in the event of aggression. Needless to say, the message is not really intended for the South Koreans— because a message of this kind might easily tempt them into reckless and rash action. Things will be so arranged that you, complete with your message, shall fall into North Korean hands."

I put my knife and fork down so abruptly that they clattered noisily against my plate.

"Wait a minute, Dr. Wang," I said, "this is getting beyond a joke. Even the Japanese used only volunteers for their suicide-missions in the last war, even they did not send regular troops into certain death in cold blood. I don't think I have ever shown myself tired of life . . ."

"There can be no question of a suicide-mission," Dr. Wang replied calmly. "Your aircraft is going to make a forced landing north of the thirty-eighth parallel. North Korean Intelligence will unobtrusively inspect your luggage, examine and photograph the coded papers they will find, and after a few hours, or at most a few days, they will release you again. The North Koreans have no interest whatever in provoking a diplomatic conflict with the United States."

"I happen to be an Austrian citizen," I pointed out.

"You will of course travel on an American diplomatic passport," said Dr. Wang.

"I will not travel at all," I replied. "Why, I ask you, did they have to pick on me? My expert knowledge, such as it is, is surely confined to European affairs, and my modest successes were all scored over here or in America. I don't even know whether Korea has a population of five or fifty million."

"South Korea has a population of about twenty-one million and North Korea of about nine million," said Dr. Wang, with slightly sarcastic precision. "The fate of thirty million human beings depends on the success of your mission, Herr Droste."

"That doesn't tempt me in the least," I said. "Napoleon's grandiloquent phrase, while sending his soldiers forward to death, that the world was watching them from the summits of the pyramids, has always been exceedingly distasteful to me. The service has so far avoided appealing to my idealism, and I really wish it wouldn't start doing so now. An appeal to my vanity would similarly be of little use, Dr. Wang. The thought that the lives of thirty million Koreans, and possibly also a few million Americans and Chinese, depend on a secret courier does not flatter me, but horrifies me. I regard the secret services, if you really want to know, as a lot of miserable quacks, and the tragi-comedy of errors which you have just convincingly related to me only confirms me in my opinion. I believe that it is the duty of statesmen and diplomats, possibly also of military leaders, to warn the Communists in good time; but the adventurous quackery for which you have cast me runs counter to my best convictions."

The Chinese allowed me to finish without interruption.

"I don't recognize the model pupil from Maryland," he said, when I had finished.

"If I were General von Greehahn," I said, deliberately introducing the name, "I should be quoting to you from Schiller's *Don Carlos*: 'I am not the same he that parted from thee at Alcalá.' All sorts of things have happened, Dr. Wang, since we parted from each other in Maryland—or more correctly, since I, in true secret-service manner, dissolved myself into thin air. I should be greatly obliged if you would inform Washington that neither van-

ity nor idealism, nor even money, will induce me to convey coded
letters from continent to continent, to addressees who are not intended to get them; or to make forced landings on foreign soil for
no technical reason; or to make good what others have bungled; or
generally to take part in that revolting farce which is called counter-espionage, Intelligence, or secret-service work."

As I spoke these words I was thinking of Nora. A great serenity
came over me at the thought that she would be happy to hear me
speak in this way; it occurred to me only incidentally that I should
first have to disclose to her the secret of my past misdemeanors to
allow her to share in the rejoicings over my conversion. But I also
felt for the first time that for the sake of the proud triumph of my
conversion I would at last be able to penetrate through that barrier of lies and to confess to her what was now definitely a matter
of the past. There was another thought that gave me pleasurable
excitement: my confidence in myself had suddenly returned. For
nearly two years I had distrusted myself; I had doubted that I should
be able to resist. And behold, now that the moment had come I
had shown myself armed against temptation. Everybody, I thought
—though not so clearly as I am now making out—everybody was
for ever seeking a judge to whose verdict he could submit; most
people did not find him, either above, or within, or without. But
I had found my judge: in our home, up on the hill, my judge was
waiting for me, and I would be able to face her unashamed.

Dr. Wang had been scrutinizing me through his thick glasses.
He now thoughtfully drained his glass. Thoughtfully he
said:

"I understand you well, Herr Droste; I understand you exceedingly well." He looked at me. "It is not difficult to see that you
have found your peace here—perhaps, even, some wise happiness
by the side of the beautiful Frau Güldendag."

"You know . . . ?" I interrupted him in some alarm.

He shrugged his shoulders. "I wasn't sent here, Herr Droste, to
your pleasant retreat, without being equipped with the weapons to
disturb it. If I were myself free from greed, vanity, or idealism, as
you have fittingly named the three evils, I shouldn't have accepted
this awkward mission. But even if I were free from any or all of
these evils I should still realize that the same applies to my present

mission as to your future one: if I had not undertaken it someone else would. But someone else would have shown no sympathy for you or your difficulty, and he would have delivered himself unfeelingly of what I am trying to put to you with friendly understanding." His voice had a warm ring, and his small slanting eyes held a warm look as he continued. "How well I know the position in which you are finding yourself, Herr Droste. You have not revealed anything of your past to the woman you love—nothing of the school in Maryland, nothing of Maud Leoni, nothing of General von Greehahn, nothing of your adventure in Berlin. And because you were happy, and because you were allowed a long time, you were hoping more and more confidently that your illusion would become reality. Now reality occasionally turns out to be an illusion; but never the other way round, Herr Droste. If you stop to think for a moment you will realize at once that Intelligence could compel you without further ado to submit once more to its instructions. My opinion of the secret services is not much higher than yours, but I realize one thing: even if as a rule they know little about their opponents, they invariably know all that's worth knowing about their own agents. It goes against the grain, Herr Droste, to act the Inquisitor and to describe to you, in the manner of cheap plays, all the torments you would be subjected to in the event of your persistent refusal. I have esteemed you ever since I made your acquaintance in Maryland, and I should feel embarrassed to have to tell a man of your intelligence things that can be no secret from him. I was instructed, if necessary, to threaten you with exposure before the woman you love; even a report to the Austrian authorities would be seriously considered; I even know some people who would not shrink from drawing Frau Güldendag into your affairs, or hatch even worse plots against you. I sincerely ask you, do not let me go on like this: my mission, though less dangerous than yours, is no less distasteful to me than yours is to you. We are both of us agents of the Devil, my dear Herr Droste; so don't let's for the Devil's sake operate against each other. We all of us have our vulnerable spots: love may be yours; something else may prove to be mine; a fatal passion for a handsome boy was the downfall of Mr. Smith, your mentor. Instead of regarding me as your enemy, regard me as your friend. Though I can't do anything to help you in this matter I will at least do everything in my power to sweeten the bitter pill."

I did not doubt his sincerity. For a moment I forgot my own problems. What, I speculated, had driven this man into the arms of the secret service? How had he become a captive whose task it was now to whip a fellow captive into slave's work? Then I caught myself reflecting what I would say to Nora, how I should justify my departure to her. My resistance had been genuine, but it had been of short duration.

"How long would my mission take?" I asked.

"As far as can be humanly calculated, no longer than four weeks," said Dr. Wang, visibly relieved.

"And afterwards?"

"I am authorized to promise you another protracted period of rest."

I laughed. "So long as the rest isn't eternal," I said. "It is no accident that a foreigner is to be entrusted with this mission. Alien birth reduces even further the slight value attached to human life."

"As a rule that is so," said Dr. Wang, "but I hardly think it applies in your case. You are so valuable that you are almost regarded as an American."

"I am flattered," I said.

He accompanied me through the narrow passage, past the porter's box, to the entrance outside which the inn sign—a prancing white horse in stone—stood out against the night sky.

A moment later I was walking alone across the deserted main square, where only the window of a local dress-shop and the light-blue shield of the gendarmerie station above the door of the elegant little baroque mansion were illuminated. Through the arched doorway of a darkened pastry-shop gleamed a baroque statue of the Virgin. The sky had cleared and was full of stars.

The cheap old film, I thought. The cheap old film with the accomplice popping up behind the bushes. Did this kind of thing happen in real life? Yes, this kind of thing happened in real life. I said good-by to the village, with its fairy-tale houses, its peaceful gables, its niches with the statues of saints, its silent streets, and its sleeping people. I said good-by to Nora.

25

Dr. Wang and the Crutches of Kuang Chun

I NOT ONLY LIED to Nora, but Dr. Lu Wang became my accomplice. I had thought up an involved story, the way liars do, believing that complicated lies are less transparent than simple ones. Dr. Lu Wang had sought me out, I explained to Nora, because he urgently needed my help and testimony in a law suit. During my business trip to America, I continued, I had negotiated extensive consignments of Austrian wine from the firm of Schlögelhammer and Co. to Wang's company, and the firm I had then represented had guaranteed the correct and punctual delivery. A few months ago, however, when the consignments arrived after no end of difficulties and bureaucratic obstacles, the wine had been in hopeless condition. The original contract had been signed by me, but my Viennese firm was now taking the line that I had not been authorized to conclude contracts independently. Dr. Wang had gone to Vienna to sort out the matter and, if possible, to reach a settlement out of court; but the crooked firm had stuck to its point of view. The case was now going to be heard before a New York court, I concluded, and I owed it both to a fair business partner and to my own good name to appear in person before the American tribunal. The Chinese businessman would not only defray the costs of my trip and all my expenses, but he might even be inclined to convert my useless Austrian schillings into dollars at a favorable rate of exchange—whereby the purchase of our farm property, which had been dragging on for nearly two years, would at last become a realistic possibility.

I was able to furnish this implausible story with a lot of plausible detail as I had once been involved, though in a very minor capacity, in a similar law suit. I must also admit that I deliberately played upon Nora's ever alert sense of justice. My friend, who quickly succeeded in gaining her sympathies, supported my fabric of lies most skillfully, and I left Nora with the conviction that her confidence remained unshaken.

This did not make my departure any easier. Only now did I realize how little need I had felt for people and their company while I had been with her.

As the distance grew I began to miss Nora, but it was—why deny it?—a peculiar sense of loss. In her absence I was seized by a strange feeling of lightness. Hard though the parting had been, with every hour that passed I was more and more enjoying my freedom from conscience. In the two years of our solitude together I had seriously persuaded myself that I was in fact the person she saw in me; that not only my previous life but also my previous character had been a mistake; that on the brink of forty I had at last become myself. But now, *en route* for a new adventure, I felt as though I was only just returning to my true self; as if the two happy years which lay behind me had been experienced by another person. Oddly enough, I was ashamed less of the dubious actions I was about to commit than of the hypocrisy I had practiced during my virtuous period; my past conversion suddenly struck me as humiliating, and my return to my worse ego was like liberation. Was I the one George Droste or the other? The George Droste who had stayed behind at the house on the hill by the lake was the one I liked better; but the George Droste who was putting an ever greater distance between himself and that house was the one who was more like me. My longing for Nora was a longing for an ego which only existed in her presence; but since this ego had detached itself from me and stayed behind, I was travelling light.

In Vienna, where I spent forty-eight hours with Dr. Wang, I called on a notary I knew and deposited with him a will, under which I bequeathed my entire, now no longer inconsiderable, fortune to Nora. Simultaneously I deposited a letter, to be opened at the same time as my will, in which I confessed to her everything that I had concealed from her since the first days of our acquaintance. The will and the letter were not good deeds; rather—though I did not quite realize it then—they were the ransom I paid to my conscience for my freedom. It was therefore not surprising that, when a bargain occurred on the house market, I acted swiftly. I found time to visit my uncle, the innkeeper Joachim Welser of Korneuburg, and to discuss with him the purchase of a house on the Bisamberg near Vienna—the same where I am now writing these lines—and to arrange at least the preliminaries. It seemed to me that it would be an excellent investment of my capital, since the house was situated in the Soviet sector of the city and the owner was anxious to dispose of it at almost any price. But why should I buy it if I was so certain of returning to Nora as, on the fringes of my conscious mind, I felt sure I was? The U.S. Consulate General provided me with a visitor's visa valid for six months, and on June 10, a four-engined bomber of the U.S. Air Force took us aboard.

Our flight was not accomplished without a protracted stop, which was to convince me afresh that fate favors the unrighteous: its immediate result was a highly instructive conversation with Dr. Wang, and its more indirect result, which will have to be mentioned later, was that it probably saved my life.

When we made an intermediate landing in Newfoundland in the early dawn of June 11, we were informed that one of the engines had been developing a defect during the last few hours and had altogether cut out for a few minutes. There could be no question of repairing it at Gander, and until such time as a new engine could be flown out to Newfoundland from America, probably something like twelve hours, we should have to stop on the inhospitable island.

Inside the overheated but far from cozy cafeteria, it seemed the suitable moment to ask Dr. Wang—needless to say, with appropriate tact—how a man who did not seem at all cut out for this kind of work had got involved in the secret service.

"I might tell you that my motives were idealism and patriotism," he said, "but this would be as incorrect as the contrary. Or I could tell you that, like yourself, I have since regretted having voluntarily entered captivity—but that, too, would be no more than a half-truth. The motives which first drove me into the arms of Intelligence are as different from those which induce me to persevere there as night is from day—and yet they are more alike than I had thought for a long time. Between my enrollment and the present day lies a long and laborious mental process. I was brought up in the ideas of Lao Tse—my father taught philosophy at Harbin University—and it took me a long time to shake off my passivity and to accept the law of action. Even so, I can use only the weapons which I myself have forged, but surely"—here he interrupted himself—"the philosophy which underlies my actions can be of little interest to you."

"On the contrary," I said. "Since my own actions have always been based on the simple principle of the higher bidder I am most curious to learn what conclusions a moral person in the service of the Devil has arrived at."

Dr. Wang polished his glasses with almost impatient thoroughness and regarded me sadly with his short-sighted eyes.

"I don't know," he said, "why you should suppose that a thinking person is necessarily a moral one. But let me tell you a parable." Slowly he sipped his coffee. "In a Chinese village, a long time ago, there lived an old beggar, Kuang Chung by name. Everyone in the village knew him. As he passed by people would throw alms to him; the children would tease him; he would be asked to weddings and funerals. The rich men suffered him because his poverty reminded them of their wealth, and the poor men suffered him because he was even poorer than they. But one thing the villagers could not understand: Kuang Chung, though enjoying the full use of his legs, and generally of sound constitution, always walked with the aid of two crutches, which he had laboriously carved for himself. At first it was thought that he was hobbling about on his crutches in order to arouse more sympathy as a cripple. But one day it so happened that a wealthy citizen, probably the richest man in the village, fell down and broke a leg. He immediately sent for Kuang Chung and promised him a high reward for his crutches. The beggar, not usually averse to easy money, refused to accept payment for his services: free of charge, he lent the rich man one of his crutches—but only one. He could not, he explained, do without the other in any circumstances. Another time, when Kuang Chung was again in possession of both his crutches, he happened, while roaming the countryside, to spend the night at a remote tavern. That very evening a madman broke into the house—today we would call him a lunatic or a maniac running amuck—and threatened the landlord, the landlord's family and the guests with a long sharp knife. The desperate landlord picked up one of Kuang Chung's crutches and felled the raving intruder. On a third occasion it happened that the child of a peasant, a pretty little boy and the darling of his parents, while bathing in a stream, lost his footing on the slippery ground and, unable to swim, was about to drown. Kuang Chung, engaged as usual in doing nothing, had watched from the bank. He rose quickly and hopped along the stream—as I said, the beggar could run perfectly well although he acted the cripple— and held out one of his crutches to the boy, who was furiously struggling with the current. The boy caught hold of it, and Kuang Chung pulled him up on to the bank, dripping with water. Henceforward Kuang Chung's crutches became a legend and nobody ever asked again whether he really needed them."

"It's a good story," I said, when the doctor paused for a moment. "I presume that it has a moral, though I'm afraid it escapes me."

"Kuang Chung proved that none of us can manage without crutches," said Dr. Wang. "He needed them to arouse pity; the rich man needed them because he broke his leg; the landlord needed them to disarm a lunatic; and but for the crutches, the boy would have lost his life. What distinguished the beggar from the rest of the villagers was his realization that his crutches were a necessity. To me, Kuang Chung's wisdom is the beginning and the end of all wisdom—though, admittedly, a kind of wisdom that is being increasingly forgotten. In the past there existed in the world certain moral institutions which could be compared to Kuang Chung's crutches; with their aid mankind was able to hobble a little way forward."

"Could you name such an institution?" I asked skeptically.

"The institution of marriage, for instance," said Dr. Wang. "Which of us does not look with envy at the matrimonial and domestic life of our fathers! Now our fathers did not fundamentally differ from ourselves: to them, as to us, as the years went by, the matrimonial bed became a place of rest rather than love. Parents found children tiresome, just as they do today, and children their parents. I don't know of any threat to marriage, or to the family, which was not known at the time, or which has only lately been discovered."

"Then you must admit," I interrupted Dr. Wang, "that the marriages of our parents and grandparents were no happier than ours, but merely more durable. I think I can guess what you are getting at. Respect for the institution of matrimony kept the family together. True enough—but were our fathers and grandfathers not worse off than we in this enforced relationship?"

"That's just where you are wrong," replied the Chinese, almost as if my objection confirmed his point. "It is generally accepted that love does not last for ever; but who says that dislike lasts for ever? A normal marriage is a continuous chain of alternating sympathies and antipathies. I could also liken it to an accordion whose ends are for ever drawing nearer to each other and then again away from each other. It is due to the peculiar and disastrous impatience of our age that we should be in such a hurry to draw our conclusions from a negative phase, instead of waiting for it to give way again to a positive one. Emerson coined the phrase of a 'philosophy of cycles'; he maintained that every end is a beginning, that a new morning is born at every noontide, and that a new depth opens up below every depth. If you keep an old suit long enough, Herr Droste, you may rest assured that it will become fashionable again; the things of yesterday become obsolete, but those of the day before yesterday are bound to return."

I had to smile. "If I believed in your theory I would have to assume that the true revolutionary is in fact ultra-conservative, since in the eternal cycle of events the morrow would belong to the day before yesterday. Applied to your philosophy of marriage, one would simply have to hold out through the unhappy periods; with the aid of the crutches of the institution of marriage one would have to hobble along until one of the phases of pleasant coexistence returns."

"Something of the kind is in fact what I do mean," said Dr. Wang. "Modern philosophy preaches that we should let ourselves be left behind on the road of life. I don't agree with this, any more than I agree with the idealistic philosophy which attempts to change the cycle of life. I believe the cycle ought not to be disturbed."

I raised my hand. "You have ventured forward too far, Dr. Wang," I said, "and you will now have to answer my questions to the bitter end. Your philosophy, if you will forgive my saying so, seems to contain a good deal of hypocrisy."

"How do you mean?" Dr. Wang asked, not in the least offended.

"Let us stick to the example of marriage," I said. "What about the man who submits to the institution without believing in it? Is it not hypocrisy to keep up a marriage which has long broken up?"

"What is hypocrisy?" countered Dr. Wang. "It is, I think you will agree, the pretending of non-existent feelings. But what presumption to declare categorically what feelings are in a man's chest and what are not! Is it not a fact that, in the final analysis, we have within us the whole range of feelings—only some are dormant at greater depth than others? They are buried within us, just as the seed is buried in the soil, as the roots are in the soil, and the nourishment and the minerals, and the springs. But are the diviners, in their search for water, oil, or gold, all hypocrites simply because what they want to unearth is hidden from sight?"

"If I understand you correctly, Dr. Wang," I objected, "you are denying the existence of hypocrisy altogether. If all feelings are ever present then there can be no pretending non-existent ones."

"I not only deny the existence of hypocrisy," said Dr. Wang, now warming to his subject, "but I go even further. It is only hypocrisy—if we still want to use the term—that makes human relations possible and bearable. Painful though it is to have to admit it, we are born without a single good instinct. Children are thieves, liars, egoists, murderers, ethically unreliable, and sexual perverts. You've got to admit that the only characteristic that all types of criminals have in common is their infantility, their arrested development in that hideous infantile stage. Luckily, however, most people learn to dissemble at a tender age: in other words, they conceal their thievish, mendacious, and murderous instincts with much fine discipline and at the same time, pretend to have better, originally not present, instincts. They feign pity, friendship, helpfulness, and love—all of them feelings which begin to exist only through their practice. But this is the point, Herr Droste—they begin to exist! The adult who no longer breaks the cat's neck is not a hypocrite, even though originally he would have liked to have done so; a re-grouping of feelings has taken place and, through a pretense of love for animals, real love for animals has in fact sprung up. The murderous instinct, though continuing to exist, has been relegated to the lowest levels of the soul. I concede that these banished instincts continue to exist, but by means of persistent hypocrisy they can be prevented from erupting. The German poet Jean Paul remarks that 'Nothing is more dangerous than to pretend to be in love: a minute later it comes true.' I would say: 'Nothing is more salutary than to pretend to be in love: in the end the love becomes real.' "

I settled down in my chair. There was a great temptation, here at this Newfoundland airfield, in the overheated waiting-room of an army hut, *en route* to America, and also *en route* to the Far East with a secret mission, to learn a little more of the Chinese agent's philosophy.

"Is your institutionalism," I asked challengingly, "—for that is what I would like to call your theories—applicable also to spheres less personal than marriage?"

"You will find," replied Dr. Wang, "that it applies even more convincingly to other spheres, such as politics. If, for instance, the Americans justly pride themselves that, though no less susceptible than other nations, they have never yet succumbed to the temptations of dictatorship from the Right or from the Left, then this is due not to their maturity, or their morality, or even their intelligence—for we know that they do not possess these qualities in any greater measure than other nations. Neither is the insular existence an explanation; firstly, because there is no such thing as insular existence nowadays, and secondly, because other States on the American continent are riddled with dictatorship. The truth is that in 1787 a number of wise men met at Philadelphia to draft the Constitution of the United States—a Constitution which has not become obsolete for the simple reason that it was at least a hundred years ahead of its time. That Constitution represented anything but the views of a politically immature nation of pioneers when it was proclaimed: but the American nation gradually grew into its Constitution. The fathers of the States, in other words, gave their people the crutches they needed, and ever since, when other nations began to waver, the American people have quickly snatched up their crutches again. What is called tradition is in fact a set of durable institutions; and institutions are the crutches which enable us to walk though we are all born lame."

"Your views, at first sight, seem to me eminently conservative, Dr. Wang," I objected.

The Chinese smiled. "Quite the contrary! I am talking about motion on crutches, not immobility. Immobility results from the illusion that we can move without crutches."

I was about to make a reply, but just then our lunch was served and our conversation got stuck for a while. The telephone rang shrilly in the big room. The captain of our aircraft got up and a moment later returned with the good news that we should probably be able to take off before dark and reach New York by midnight. Outside, a weak shaft of sunlight had stolen through the gray blanket of cloud and was reflected from the silver fuselage of our bomber.

My Chinese friend divided the steak, which had been served thick, bloody, and raw in the American manner, into minute little cubes.

He was a mystery to me. The man who had appeared to remind me of my sombre duties had been different from the person I had met at the spy school in Maryland, and the philosopher in the wooden hut at Gander was again different from the man who had snatched me out of my happy dream-world but a few days previously.

Over our coffee I resumed the thread.

"You deny being conservative, Dr. Wang," I said, "and yet your theories run counter to all modern discoveries."

For the first time the Chinese smiled in the sly manner attributed to Orientals.

"You are probably referring to modern psychology," he said, "that pseudo-science which is more dangerous than the atom bomb, though invented for the same purpose—mankind's self-destruction."

"Just a moment!" I interrupted. "You can't get away as easily as that. I don't profess to be familiar with Chinese philosophy, but at least I know that it, too, was at its center the search for the Tao, for truth. No matter what the effects of modern psychology may be, it is at least likewise concerned with the discovery of the truth.'

"No matter what the effects of modern psychology may be—that is what you said, my friend," retorted the Chinese. "But what, I ask you, gives us the right to commit any action without considering its effects? That truth is something in itself an erroneous idea, for what use can it be to anybody if it harms mankind as a whole and each human being individually? Indeed, modern psychology, practical, handy, and impressive as an atom bomb, is no less murderous than that bomb. It lays bare the primal human instincts which civilization and religion have tried for the past thousand years to cover up. May I quote to you, so far as I am able from memory, a few lines from the book of Lao Tse?" He leaned back, closed his eyes behind his thick lenses, and said:

> "In the repressing of great hatred
>   a little hatred will certainly be left;
>   how can that be considered satisfactory?
> The wise man therefore holds the left tally-stick
>   and does not ascribe the blame to his opponent.
> The virtuous man will repress all blame,
>   the unrighteous will nail it down.
> But the Way of Heaven is impartial:
>   it is always on the side of good."

He chuckled softly. "Six hundred years before Christ, Lao Tse here gives his answer to Freud and his disciples. Twice in these lines repression is praised—that repression upon which modern psychology has declared war. Do you believe Lao Tse thought hatred and blame would disappear through repression? Indeed not; he frankly admits that they remain. They remain, but they have no effect—the effect which you think is irrelevant but which, in fact, is the one thing that matters. If modern psychology were a science one could not deny it the right to search for truth—but it is not a science but a religion. As such it contradicts all existing religions, which, much as they may differ from one another, are all unanimous in their demand for repression."

"In their demand for purification," I protested. "Religion demands that we should purge our hearts of hatred, not that we should keep it repressed in the nethermost recesses of our hearts. And religion is not merely concerned with effects. It demands not only pure actions but also pure thoughts—which is why one would probably meet the most surprising people in Heaven."

"Quite so," said Dr. Wang. "Religion makes the highest demands so that the least of them should be fulfilled. But that is just what I am trying to do with my modest philosophy, to which you have given the impressive name of 'institutionialism.' Why, do you suppose, is religion—and none has escaped the charge—invariably accused of hypocrisy? Because it demands that purification should be accomplished by the only possible way—that of repression. Religion, chronologically speaking, puts prayer before faith: the believer prays that the Almighty should grant him faith. Is a man who prays without faith therefore a hypocrite? No; he is the very opposite. He is a man who tries to attain faith by way of the institution. Starting from birth, which is an unthinking action, action naturally always precedes thought. Because we do not commit murder, even though all our primal instincts tend towards murder, we cease to want to commit murder. Just as parts of our anatomy, which are no longer required, become atrophied in the course of generations, so our homicidal instincts wither away, through lack of application, in the course of a human life. Purity of thought is born only out of purity of action. Religion with its prohibitions and commandments, is the greatest of human institutions, and hence the best crutch for a humanity born crippled. Modern philosophy and its kindred sciences, which are all of them anti-religious, cannot possibly be striving for truth, proceeding as they do from the lie of human adequacy, of man's ability to move without crutches. I have nothing against their denial of the deity—to me they are anti-religious because they proclaim man's divinity. Even to the richest man in the village Kuang Chung did not lend both his crutches: his wisdom was the realization of his own inadequacy. Now mankind, admittedly, is wise enough to believe in the lowest and the highest of institutions—the police and the deity— but since neither the arm of the law nor hell-fire are ever present in our mind we need a number of other institutions, a little less remote than the one and a little less close than the other. In other words, the sphere of the police is too small and that of the deity too big."

"Considering the practical nature of your theory, Dr. Wang,"

I said, "I hope you won't mind if I ask you, as an eager disciple, to throw some light upon your practical application of it."

"I don't quite understand," said Dr. Wang, and I could see that he really did not get my meaning.

"You referred earlier, when I asked you about your motives, to the law of action which you had come to believe in," I said. "Does this law compel you to serve an institution which you have recognized as despicable?"

"Remember my example about marriage," replied Dr. Wang. "Who would benefit if I left Intelligence? I propose to pursue my aims within the framework of the institution."

"In spite of your protestations, Dr. Wang, you have confirmed my suspicion that you are in fact a moralist, though of a somewhat unusual kind," I said. "I am not a moralist. When I serve the Devil I do so from a certain logic. Your logic strikes me as more dubious than mine."

"You ought to have paid more heed to my first parable," said Dr. Wang, with a gentle touch of reproof in his voice. "Didn't I say that Kuang Chung's crutches served the most varied purposes, and that one of them was to fell the raving madman? I also mentioned that I was not spending my time, like the beggar in the Chinese legend, sitting idly on the banks of streams. Good thoughts are of no avail against the institutions of the Devil."

"If I understand you correctly," I said, utterly perplexed, "you did not, after all, haul me back from my voluntary exile for the reasons that you professed?"

"No," said Dr. Wang, and there was no gentleness in his voice now. "I came because I wanted an ally."

For the time being I had to content myself with this answer.

An hour later we left Newfoundland. It was a sultry, rainy summer night when we touched down in New York.

26

♊♊♊♊♊♊♊♊♊♊♊

Report to Bomber Yellow

I HAVE SAID that the twelve hours' delay caused by our engine trouble in Newfoundland probably saved my life: I shall presently elucidate this statement.

Although we landed in New York during the night of June 11-12, I did not leave America until the morning of June 24, when at long last I set out on my exceedingly delicate mission with the patent aim of serving the cause of peace.

For twelve days the secret services in Washington, whither we had proceeded straight away, were unable to reach agreement about my mission. I myself spent most of my ample leisure at the Mayflower Hotel, a very comfortable if not exactly exciting place, but Dr. Wang, who appeared to be entirely at home in Washington, kept me fully informed about the details of the lively quarrel that was being fought out over my body.

In point of fact, the most complete difference of opinion existed not only about my important mission but also about my unimportant person. Military Intelligence argued that I "belonged" to them, since it had been for them that Mr. Smith had originally enrolled me, and that I had since successfully accomplished the Greehahn assignment. That was all very well, retorted the political branch of the secret service, but the events in Korea were—for the time being at least—of a political character. Central Intelligence agents had discovered the Chinese knowledge of the first Cabinet decision and their ignorance of the second: it was a contemptible trick on the part of Military Intelligence to try to rob Central Intelligence of the fruits of their labor at this stage. Presently, as if this were not enough, the Federal Bureau of Investigation entered the field: they had been charged with investigating the domestic problem of how the information about the first Cabinet meeting had got into the hands of Communist agents in Washington. With this investigation, the F.B.I. now argued, my mission was closely connected. Besides, the F.B.I. altogether objected to the choice of a foreigner whom they themselves had not screened.

The Government eventually adjudicated the quarrel at a secret meeting by making me over to Military Intelligence, and there would have been no further obstacle to my departure if only Intelligence could have made up its mind about the nature of my mission. The first question to be settled was whether, within the framework of Intelligence, I came under Espionage or Counter-Espionage. For forty-eight hours, I was told, this question was argued at sometimes rather turbulent conferences. The Espionage Branch took the view that my mission had nothing to do with the enemy's espionage activities and hence with Counter-Espionage; on the contrary, Espionage was now compelled to make up for the serious blunders committed by Counter-Espionage. Quite wrong, protested Counter-Espionage: if they had not discovered the Communists were in possession of secret information about the intentions of the U.S. Government the question of my mission would never have arisen. No sooner had the two branches more or less agreed to share what glory my future actions would bring than one of the sabotage branches of Intelligence promptly intervened. My mission, they argued, must be regarded—psychologically, if not physically—as a misleading of the enemy; and such deception came unquestionably under the Deception Branch. And now we were back again in the vicious circle as the Branch for the Deception of the Enemy had never heard the name of George Droste and most vigorously opposed the selection of an unknown person for such a vital task. After a further twenty-four hours the conflict was submitted to the supreme Chief of Intelligence for a personal ruling. He decided that my mission was not, in the strict sense, a case of deception of the enemy, and Dr. Wang at last told me to stand by for my departure.

However, a further forty-eight hours elapsed before my take-off.

While the different services had been fighting over my person and my mission like a pack of hungry dogs over a bone, nobody had thought of drafting the fictitious letter to the South Korean

President—or rather, no one had wanted to draft it since no department was inclined, by penning this subtle document, to give a leg up to some other department that might grab the kudos of the mission for itself. Finally, Intelligence drafted the letter and made out for me a Courier Passport in the name of William S. Mill, First Secretary to the United States Embassy. At this point the State Department lodged an objection. A false passport, just as a proper passport, could only be issued by the State Department or with its consent, they maintained. The State Department, however, relied in these matters entirely on the F.B.I. and had therefore no intention of issuing me with a Courier Passport without F.B.I. clearance. It was obvious that the Federal Bureau of Investigation, seeing its prize getting away, had complained to the State Department about Intelligence. A further Government meeting was necessary before I got my passport. I might mention in passing that the whole conflict threatened to flare up again during the night preceding my departure, since nobody could agree on who was to supply the aircraft. Air Force Intelligence declared that they did not propose to gamble a machine on an escapade which had not the slightest connection with Air Force Intelligence proper. Two hours before our scheduled time of take-off the Defense Secretary was dragged from his bed, and only after he had given his "personal O.K."—as the informal service slang put it—for the Air Force to supply the machine did we leave Washington at ten o'clock in the morning.

With the haste of those who have wasted too much time we now made such short landings at Los Angeles and in Hawaii that all I saw of the city and the Pacific coast was a few oil derricks and film studios, whereas in Hawaii I did not even get a glimpse of the charming hula-hula girls. At 6 A.M. on June 25, we took off from Honolulu for Korea.

The crew of our aircraft consisted of the captain, the co-pilot, a radio operator, and a navigator. They were all regular Air Force personnel, but I gathered from a few hints that they were accustomed, from time to time, to carry out special assignments for Intelligence. Apart from the captain none of them seemed older than thirty.

As soon as the naval base of Pearl Harbor had slipped behind us and the Pacific Ocean was spread out underneath, the co-pilot took over the controls and the captain sat down beside me.

He was a tall, loose-limbed man of a little over thirty, with good-natured pale-blue eyes, a small snub nose, and a face covered with thousands of freckles—just like those dead-end kids of the American films who at one time enjoyed such popularity inside and outside America.

He lowered himself into the soft seat, stretched out his long legs, and pushed his soft service cap with the American eagle down on to his nose by brushing his palm up over the back of his head —almost with the gesture of a drunk—and letting the cap slip over his eyes.

"You ought to get a few hours' sleep too," he said. "Stock up in advance. We'll do our 'forced landing' late at night, and after that the North Koreans won't let us go till they've squeezed us dry like lemons."

"I'm quite fresh," I said. "I'm afraid I wouldn't drop off for some time."

The captain wriggled in his seat with the elastic suppleness of a man who is used to turning any chair into a bed.

"Scared?" he asked.

"Middling-scared," I said. "And you?"

"I don't mind this so-called forced landing," he said. "I can rely on my crate. It's the interrogation I'm not looking forward to. Those goddam yellowskins are suspicious."

"Did you volunteer for this, Captain?"

"The name's Jim," he said. "Sure I volunteered. Got to do something to relieve this goddam boredom."

"And the others?"

"They'll have their reasons. I never ask questions. The radio operator is the only one I've known for any time. Bob's got a wooden leg. They wouldn't let him fly unless it was something special. He'll do anything so they'll let him fly."

"And why so bored, Jim?" I asked, attempting a jocular tone. "Aren't there any pretty girls in Washington?"

The captain was still sprawling in his seat, his cap over his eyes.

"The pretty girls all want to get married," he said. "Once an airman gets married he's dead. Worries that someone's worrying about him—if you get me, Bill."

"Are all the crew bachelors?"

"They only take unmarried men. It's a goddam woman's world. We can break our necks all right—so long as we don't leave any widows. Well, I must get some sleep. Good night, Bill."

He turned his back on me. A few minutes later his regular deep breathing told me that he was fast asleep.

The captain had said good night, but in fact it was morning and bright daylight. I judged that we were flying rather high, but there were no clouds below us. Along the horizon the light blue of the sky abruptly changed into the deep blue of the ocean. The sun shone on the large, curved engine-housings on my left, and in their silvery surface the entire aircraft was clearly reflected. It was as if on the wings of our machine we were carrying large convex mirrors. Visibility was so good that looking down I could make out the white foam on the waves. A steamer was moving peacefully and majestically from the west towards Honolulu.

Tonight, I thought, Jim won't be able to say good night to me. Where would I spend the night, I wondered. Suddenly the full humiliation of military service was borne in on me: a serving man forfeited even that most elementary right of choosing where to rest his head.

The four young men in the plane suspected nothing of the details of my mission. They only knew what they had to say after the forced landing: that they were carrying a courier from Washington, that they had lost their direction, and that they had made a forced landing north of the thirty-eighth parallel. I, on the other hand, did not know at what point in North Korea the forced landing was planned and with what dangers it was fraught. The only certain thing was that we were all of us actors in a comedy whose author was unknown to us, whose scene of action we only suspected, in whose production we had taken no part, and of which each of us only knew his own lines, without having any idea of the other parts. It was also certain that tonight we should be prisoners in some Korean locality: suspect, to say the least, and under interrogation.

With a sudden shock I realized that in this ghostly comedy I was playing a part which I had not at all undertaken to play. When selling myself to the secret services, had I not decided to pursue only my own advantage, to avoid the risks of this dubious profession, and to deceive my employers whenever possible? Well, I had not fared too badly so far. True, my excursion to Potsdam had been accompanied by certain dangers, but they had not been dangers imposed on me by the secret service: I had operated on my own account and on my own conscience. But how had I got myself into this aircraft?

My glance fell on the slender, elegant briefcase on the seat beside me. Yes, they had thoroughly prepared me for my journey. They had replaced my Viennese suits by American ready-mades; they had replaced my monogrammed silk shirts by shirts obtainable on Washington's Massachusetts Avenue; and they had my new initials embossed on my diplomatic briefcase. They had only overlooked the small detail that their courier's English, though fluent, had a slight Viennese accent, and that my speech was bound to arouse the suspicion of any interpreting officer with some linguistic experience, and certainly that of an interpreter. Panic seized me. Ought I not to shake the sleeping pilot by my side, to persuade him to turn back, and, if I succeeded, face the men in Washington and inform them that they had miscast the lead of their comedy?

I quickly dropped the idea again. The pilot had instructions to force-land with me in North Korea and he could not alter his course. He was my prisoner in that, whether he liked it or not, he had to take me to my destination; but equally I was his prisoner. I picked up the magazines and illustrated periodicals I had purchased at Hawaii and tried to engross myself in them. I do not think I shall be accused of disgraceful cowardice if I admit that neither the divorce scandal of a Hollywood film star, nor the optimistic article "Cancer gave me peace of mind," nor yet the memoirs of the music teacher of the two British princesses, nor even the serious essay "Why we Americans are not as popular as we deserve to be" fully engaged my attention. The divorce-seeking lady, the contented sufferer from cancer, Their Britannic Royal Highnesses, and the unpopular Americans all seemed unreal and yet, at the same time, enviable up to a point: they were free and not entirely bereft of their power of decision. What was real was our flying prison and the prison it would land us in.

The navigator woke the captain, who was instantly fully awake. He gave me a disapproving look because I had not slept, and went forward into the cockpit while the navigator took his turn in the seat beside me.

"Bad weather coming, thank God," he said.

He was a boy of about twenty-six, a little too broad around the hips, with a milky face, still immature, thick, childish lips, and brown, nut-sized eyes which peered curiously out at the world.

"Thank God?" I asked.

The lieutenant loosened his tie, undid his collar button, and let the tie dangle freely. "Otherwise not even the stupidest Korean would believe we'd lost our way," he said.

"Presumably bad weather had been forecast, Lieutenant?" I asked, like one who wants to have confirmed the knowledge of those who hold his life in their hands.

"Sure," said the navigator. "But weather forecasts are shit. Pure luck they guessed right this time. By the way, my name's Stephen."

"What time do we land?" I asked, anxious to keep the conversation going.

"If all goes well, at about eleven o'clock—Korean time."

"Aren't you going to sleep?"

"I'm a bad sleeper," said Stephen. "That is, when I'm scared stiff."

"You scared stiff?"

"Aren't you, Bill?"

"Of course," I said, almost apologetically, because for a moment I had given the impression of being unafraid. "But then, I'm not a volunteer."

"Neither am I," replied the lieutenant, fiddling with his tie.

"I thought you were all volunteers."

"Aw, shit! There's no such thing as a volunteer. It's like this: some major from Intelligence comes along and says: 'Which of you guys is in on this? It's a secret, delicate mission. Sure, anyone with cold feet can stay behind. Well then, those who haven't got cold feet, step forward!' Well, would you like to have cold feet in public? You step forward. All the other guys step forward. Twenty out of twenty, on an average. Why? Because none of them has the guts to admit to cold feet. And suddenly twenty airmen, who a moment before were standing peacefully along the wall, have turned into twenty volunteers, simply because they took one step forward. Then the major walks along the rank and picks the one who looks the stupidest. His eagle eye alights on me—and a hero is born!" He gave me a friendly slap on my back. "Come on, we're going to make some coffee and chew a few sandwiches. I can't offer any whisky, we are flying dry."

We got up and went forward. Stephen switched on the electric coffee machine. He thrust two ham sandwiches, hygienically packed in cellophane, into my hand. It struck me as odd that, having sent us out on this kind of mission, they should be so concerned about the cleanliness of our food.

I remember clearly that I had eaten my first sandwich without appetite and had just freed the second from its transparent wrapping when the radio operator, who was sitting with headphones on at a little steel table by our side, suddenly started to wave both his arms.

"Code message coming through. Keep quiet!" he shouted, although he could not hear us anyway.

We fell silent. The captain left his seat at the controls and joined us.

"Won't be anything much," he said softly, shrugging his shoulders. I was not sure whether he was trying to calm any incipient fear in us or discourage any premature hope.

I put my sandwich down on the table.

The radio operator said: "Roger!" and took his headphones off.

"Decode at once!" ordered the captain, and bent over the operator, who had produced a thin little book and was busy decoding the message he had written down. He was now writing the signal down in clear, on the paper in front of him, so that the captain could read it.

Jim straightened up and looked at us. He said:

"Well, fellers, the fun's over. We're changing course and we're landing at Seoul."

We had no time to discuss the message or even to let its meaning sink in, for the instrument was again signalling that it wanted to be heard.

"There's more coming," said Stephen.

The navigator and I stood motionless by the softly purring coffee machine while Jim was again bending over the radio operator. A minute later the same performance was re-enacted: the operator took down the signal, confirmed receipt, and decoded the message. Only this time the captain turned to me.

"This one's for you," he said. "Bomber to Bill." Bomber was Intelligence's call-sign for our particular mission. "Burn letter. Report to Bomber Yellow." Bomber Yellow was the arranged codename for the Chief of U.S. Intelligence in South Korea.

"Are you sure the message comes from Washington?" I asked.

Bob, the one-legged radio operator—a pasty boy with an exceedingly keen face which suffering had refined and aged before its time—nodded.

"From Washington via Honolulu," he said. "Unquestionably."

"What's going on?" the co-pilot called out towards the back. He had noticed our commotion.

"No forced landing," the captain roared to him. "Regular landing at Seoul."

The radio operator stood up. He poured himself some coffee. Although he had taken only two steps I could see that he dragged his left leg. I wondered whether he was feigning indifference or whether he was really the only one among us who was unmoved by the message.

"Can you explain this?" I asked Jim.

"Any goddam explanation is O.K. by me," said the captain. "Or is anyone here particularly anxious to force-land among the goddam Communists?"

It sounded like a challenge—as if he wanted to say: I'm not a hero, but if anyone here insists on being a hero I'm quite ready to push his face in. "Anyway, you are all invited to a glass of whisky."

From his own flying bag he produced a bottle of whisky and opened it with loving—and, it seemed to me, excessive—care, as though trying to hide his emotion behind a humdrum operation.

I looked into the faces of the men whom "almighty Time and eternal Destiny" had made my companions in this vast empty aircraft, which was now, as though bumping along a rough country lane, beginning to climb higher and higher in order to avoid a gathering thunderstorm. From the three young faces—the shrewd boyish face of the captain, the innocent mother's-darling face of the navigator, and the prematurely aged face of the radio operator—the tension had vanished. The captain made no secret of his delighted pleasure; the navigator was gazing out of the window as though trying to spot among the gathering clouds the power he wanted to thank for his deliverance; the operator was pointlessly cursing the coffee, as if to show that the message meant nothing to him.

Around us black clouds were piling up into a menacing skyscape. It was only five o'clock in the afternoon, but we were suddenly thrust into night—just as if from bright sunlight one had suddenly been cast into a deep, dark cellar. Eddies of fog were swirling around the now blind mirrors of the engine-housings. The engines were grating—the way an animal grates its teeth when it has dug them into flesh that is too tough. It sounded as if the engines could not bite their way through the clouds. A few minutes before I should have paid little attention to the thunderstorm—but it is human nature to fear new dangers as old ones recede.

"Only a small drop all round," said the captain, half filling four water tumblers with whisky. The elements did not seem to scare him now that he had escaped the danger from human beings. "To our survival!"

He was raising his glass in a toast when the radio again emitted impatient noises. Our hands holding our glasses slowly dropped: no doubt we were all superstitiously thinking that we had spoken too soon. The operator sat down to his instrument. We stood around him, glasses in hand, trying to read his impassive face. A flash of lightning, brilliant like a white flag rending the black night, flickered past us. The aircraft lurched.

"Not in code," said Bob, pressing both hands against his headphones.

"He's not taking it down," Stephen whispered to me.

"Probably listening to dance music," said the captain.

"He probably can't hear anything," I said.

I hated the thunderstorm which interfered with reception. I hated the minutes which were reluctant to pass.

The operator took off his headphones. He said:

"Now we know. This morning North Korean forces crossed the thirty-eighth parallel in a southerly direction over a broad front. South Korea is in a state of war with North Korea. The North Koreans are advancing in the direction of the capital." He looked at the captain. "A total black-out is in operation at Seoul. Got to make a blind landing. Detailed instructions to follow. You're to take the southern course."

"Here's luck!" said Jim.

It was not quite clear what his remark referred to, for he raised his glass to his lips.

I am unable to say today what my first thought was—whether it was that I had arrived too late and that the war between nine million North Koreans and twenty-one million South Koreans was already in full swing, or whether I merely thought that I could now calmly burn my letter since no forced landing would be made on dangerous territory. Today, thinking back to that hour, there arise in me visions of distracted fleeing women; of lost children on bomb-wrecked railway stations; of gaunt bearded old men wading through rivers; of weeping peasants among gutted farmsteads; of pitiful refugee convoys with pitiful belongings; of the bodies of soldiers washed up on swampy banks—but I know that these are visions which came to me and left their imprint on me only subsequently. Then, in the storm-cradled aircraft, I was mercifully saved by my feeble power of imagination and all I thought of was my salvation and the failure of my mission.

The others' imaginations were even more merciful, even more feeble than mine. The captain returned to the controls, apparently concerned now only with the thunderstorm around our machine, indifferent to the thunderstorm that was engulfing an entire country in the Far East. Stephen, the navigator, picked up his dividers. Bob, the radio operator, sat down again to his instrument.

I returned to the cabin and groped my way to my seat. Only from the nose of the aircraft did a weak light seep into the fuselage. My briefcase with the initials of the non-existent courier

William S. Mill was on my seat. I opened the zipper and took out
the letter with its big, solemn, red seals. I could have opened the
envelope and read the letter, but my curiosity had evaporated.
With the envelope in my hand I made my way forward again to
the navigator.

"Got a match, Stephen?" I asked.

He handed me his lighter.

I set fire to the letter. On the little steel table stood a large
aluminum ashtray. In it, the letter which was to have prevented
the war in Korea turned into ashes. A puff of wind from the
ventilator over the cabin door blew a little ash on to the map
spread out in front of Stephen.

He said: "Shit!" and brushed the ash off.

At 10:20 Far Eastern Time we made what is technically
known as a blind landing on the blacked-out airfield of Seoul, the
capital. The American major who met us informed us that their
first assault had carried the attackers thirty miles across the thirty-
eighth parallel.

27

∿∿∿∿∿∿∿∿∿∿∿

Evacuation of a Frogman

THE UGLY FACE of war was drawing nearer to Seoul.

At seven o'clock on the morning after my arrival an army
jeep called to take me to American Intelligence headquarters. By
then the whole city knew that the North Koreans were marching on
Seoul in an unchecked advance.

Through the narrow but tidy streets with their curious houses
—curious because European buildings were topped with pagoda-
like undulating roofs—surged a crowd many thousands strong.

I had seen panic in the war, but here I witnessed it for the
first time in its oriental form. It was a silent and patient panic, almost a polite panic, for the fleeing people were not pressing, or

pushing each other aside, or forcing their way through. The exodus from the city resembled an unending funeral cortège, and instinctively I looked about for the coffin which was surely being borne somewhere, a long way off, at the head of the procession. Moreover, as at an Eastern funeral, the mourners seemed to be burying not only their dear departed but also his entire belongings; it was as if these people were carrying on their backs not their own chattels but someone else's property.

This quiet panic did not reassure me at all: it intensified my own anxiety. Our European impatience, I thought, our rebellious fear opens the flood-gates for our nervous tension; but these people's resignation must crash in tidal waves against the dam of their nerves—and the fact that the dam did not yield only made the phenomenon more alarming.

What worried me even more was the circumstance that the exodus from Seoul seemed to be lacking all order or system. While one half of the population was setting out on a journey into the unknown, the other half appeared to be taking no notice whatever of the war which was rapidly approaching the capital. Merchants, who had either opened their shops very early or had not closed them at all over night, were standing in front of them, astonished and no doubt delighted to see the blinds down on their rivals' establishments. I could not understand what they were calling out to the refugees, but I gathered that they were hurriedly offering the emigrants—who were staggering along with their wretched bedding, a few days' food, and some touching family picture—the treasures of their shops at unrepeatable bargain prices. The children, with their round faces, their slanting eyes, and their pitch-black hair—the young of the yellow race always seem to me much more yellow than their elders—these children, who seemed to be scurrying about the streets in exceptionally large numbers, had suffered no hardships as yet and were unaware of what was happening. They would break away from their fleeing parents and join in the games of other children who were staying behind. Scrapped U.S. military vehicles, trucks, and jeeps of decrepit appearance were rattling over the uneven cobblestones, loaded with Korean soldiers. Yet I derived no sense of security from these defenders of Seoul: in their uniforms with high stiff collars, with their puttees, and with their old-fashioned rifles cradled in their arms, they reminded me too much of the pictures from the Russo-Japanese war of 1904. They looked like resurrected fighters, destined for a second death rather than renewed battle. Outside some houses stood trucks on to which soldiers were loading furniture and human beings—bearded men and ailing women—and whenever the stream of refugees flowed past one of these trucks some of the people stopped and begged to be allowed to climb on. During a flight soldiers, old men, and invalids are objects of envy.

The lobby of the big hotel where my jeep dropped me was like a warehouse in process of liquidation. It was a vast expanse, furnished with the full pomp of the turn of the century, in imitation of European style and yet entirely Eastern, and even a little eerie as the sunlight filtered in through a colossal dome of violently green glass which spanned the entire lobby. Picking their way over the red-plush furniture, half-naked, sweating men were carrying packing cases, tables, chests, a refrigerator, and a painting in a gilt frame toward the hotel doorway. Little yellow men in morning coats, presumably managers or receptionists who had not yet found the time to doff their professional attire, were scurrying and stumbling among boxes, books, and crockery, their coat-tails flying, in turn haranguing the half-naked workers to make even greater haste and reassuring the guests—Koreans, Europeans, and Americans—that there was no cause for alarm. A truly grotesque touch was provided by a wide Regency bed which stood, apparently forgotten, in the middle of the ornately gilt lobby. On the bare mattress, however, sat a very blonde American woman of uncertain age, frantically gripping with each hand a lilac-and-pink striped hatbox, and a minute hat supporting a veritable orchard perched upon her curls. There she sat, staring fixedly in front of her, clearly resolved not to budge until she was evacuated complete with her hatboxes. Inside the hotel, even in the shady lobby, the heat was just as unbearable as it had been outside. It welled forward to meet you, as if from an open boiler door. The very walls seemed to sweat, and the old-fashioned fans under the ceiling pointlessly sent the hot air gyrating in circles.

A very different picture presented itself to me on the fifth floor when I entered the suite of rooms which served as the headquarters of American Intelligence. Here, too, some packing was going on and a strong smell of smoke suggested that considerable quantities of paper had been burned—but there was nothing to be seen here of the confused haste in the city and in the rest of the hotel. Evacuation was proceeding smoothly according to plan—undoubtedly a plan that had been rehearsed countless times. In these rooms, which were fitted with the most up-to-date air-conditioning plant, young men were at work in those neat American shirts which have pressed creases even on the sleeves: calmly they were packing or burning papers and documents. Telephones and radios were functioning, and so was the ticking teletype. A few pretty, well-groomed secretaries sat at their desks—now bereft of their typewriters—nonchalantly engaged in various cosmetic pursuits. It was obvious that the fifth floor of the Grand Hotel in Seoul housed a Great Power which would not allow itself to be impressed by a little war.

A friendly young American immediately took me to the chief's office.

All that was left in the big, tall room with its over-abundant white stucco ornaments was a desk and—lined up by the door—a few neat packing crates. On one wall hung a huge map of Korea. The air-conditioning unit in the closed balcony window was purring softly: the superfluous fans had been switched off and were now sticking to the ceiling like gigantic dead flies.

The man whose code name was Bomber Yellow had been looking out of the window. He now turned and came to meet me.

Though undoubtedly American by birth, Kenneth Breen, as is frequently the case with people who have lived a long time in the East, had become assimilated to his environment in his appearance also. True, he was tall, slim, and completely bald—but not only was his skin more yellow than white, but his pale lips also disappeared in his flat features, and his eyes, though not, of course, slanting, were small and slit-like, and overpowered by heavy lashless lids. Looking at him I was reminded—may the reader forgive me—of a discolored tongue: the soft, granular skin of cheesy consistency was not necessarily part of his face, but seemed like an alien, unhealthy layer spread over the Intelligence Chief's proper skin.

"I can't offer you a seat, Mr. Droste," said Breen, with an oriental smile after a brief introduction, "unless you would like to make yourself comfortable on the desk."

He seated himself on the edge of the desk and I followed suit.

"First of all, I should like to inform you about the situation," continued Breen. "The President has ordered the Seventh Fleet to put to sea and protect South Korean waters. Naturally, this means war with North Korea. Units of the Seventh Fleet will also evacuate all U.S. citizens, possibly even today, to Japan to start with. The invading North Korean army is expected to reach Seoul the day after tomorrow. The resistance which the South Koreans are able to offer isn't worth talking about."

"Has the attack come as a surprise, Mr. Breen?" I asked.

My interlocutor thrust his hands—surprisingly small hands for a man of his height—into the pockets of his navy-blue double-breasted suit.

"Of course it hasn't come as a surprise to us here in Seoul," he said calmly. "But as you know, we come directly under Washington. For that reason the gentlemen in Tokyo have been systematically sabotaging our reports by idiotic contradictory ones. But time is getting short, Mr. Droste, and we want to talk about you. Much as I regret that your mission—about which, by the way, I am not informed—has been overtaken by events, I must say that your presence here is most welcome." He pointed to a telegram which was lying on the desk behind him. "In view of this extraordinary situation we are most seriously under-staffed here. I am delighted that Washington has decided to put you at my disposal."

I was given no chance to point out—as I should have liked to have done—that I was anything but delighted to find myself treated as a piece of merchandise that was put at the disposal of this person or that. Before I could say anything the familiar note of the air-raid warning cut into our conversation. We both went to the tall window. Below us the main street of Seoul was like an antheap. People were scurrying towards the doors of the buildings; vehicles and handcarts were left unattended; newsstands and street-vendors' stalls were knocked over.

"Nonsense," Breen said scornfully. "The North Koreans aren't going to bomb Seoul today. They want to take the city undamaged." He returned towards the room as if assured that any impending bombing could not concern him. "Please listen carefully to what I've got to say to you," he remarked. "The accurate observance of my directives is extremely important, both to us and to your own safety."

He stepped up to the map which was hanging on the wall, and reluctantly I followed him.

"Five days ago," he said, pointing to the map, "the Russian cruiser *Novgorod* dropped anchor off the port of Karyo. Karyo, as you can see, is on the East coast of Korea, at roughly the same latitude as Seoul, but right on the other side of the peninsula. As the North Koreans are pressing along the railway line from Gensan to Seoul, that is from North-east towards South-west, they will probably by-pass Karyo. They'll certainly not take the port till after they have taken Seoul. That much I want you to understand before I come to your mission proper." He turned away from the map, towards me, but avoided looking me in the face. "Four days prior to the North Korean attack—that is, five days ago—the *Novgorod* called at the port with the consent of the Government. On the day before I had sent off a team of seven divers, popularly known as frogmen, to Karyo. They had instructions to dive in the neighborhood of the cruiser and to make certain investigations. All seven have disappeared without trace."

Outside the sirens had fallen silent, but the monotonous hum of the air-conditioner was now blending with the engine throbs of low-flying aircraft.

The strangeness of the story did not fail in its effect. Though I had no desire to be involved in the activities of U.S. Intelligence in Korea I could not suppress a question as to the objectives of the missing underwater agents.

"Our Navy," explained Mr. Breen, pacing up and down the room but still studiously avoiding my eye, "is interested in certain recent Soviet developments. During their last naval exercises Soviet warships had live torpedoes fired at them without suffering the slightest damage. We conclude that the new Soviet naval units have a special type of armor which is unknown to us. Likewise, we don't know anything about the construction of their rudder, which clearly gives them greater maneuverability. Thus the newest Soviet warships are able to perform the most complicated maneuvers without pilots or the customary steering aids. I might further add that we are interested in the size and shape of their latest propellers—the Russian cruisers go faster with two propellers than ours do with four—but even that would give you only an approximate idea of how vital the mission of my agents was. You are not a naval expert, Mr. Droste," he added, a little peevishly, "and there's no point, therefore, in my wasting your time with detailed elucidations of the problems my agents were supposed to solve. The fact is that the *Novgorod* is one of the most modern Soviet cruisers and that I could not let this unique opportunity slip by unused." He uttered the last sentence like a man who justifies himself to himself, so that he should subsequently be able to justify himself before others. "Besides, your mission has nothing to do with the *Novgorod*—or only very little—and anyway the ship has long left port. You are to find out what happened to my seven men."

We had been walking up and down the room together. We now halted by the desk.

"Your proposal, to put it mildly, comes as a bit of a surprise," I said, seating myself again on the edge of the desk. "I came to Korea with a very definite political mission and had instructions to return to America as soon as it was accomplished."

"No," the Chief sharply interrupted me. "Those weren't your instructions. You had explicit instructions to report to Bomber Yellow when your mission was finished. And you have done so."

"I believe that I am totally unsuited for this surprising assignment," I said firmly.

"That is a matter of opinion," said Breen without raising his voice. "And since my opinion is the one that counts I must ask you to desist from pointless discussion." He paused for a moment to listen to the All Clear. "My office is today being evacuated to Fusan," he continued. "Needless to say, at this juncture we are evacuating only the personnel indispensable to us. I don't suppose, Mr. Droste, that you would wish to become unfaithful to Intelligence at this moment."

"I have no doubt," I said, "that all American citizens will be evacuated from the zone of hostilities in good time."

"You are an Austrian, Herr Droste," said my interlocutor with a smile.

"If I understand you correctly," I retorted, still not prepared to admit defeat, "I am not to be evacuated in any event. You wish me to go to Karyo."

"That's no more than a detour, Mr. Droste. You'll have twenty-four hours at the most, in Karyo, to look around for my men. After that the port will fall to the enemy. That's just why the assignment is so urgent. My representative in Karyo is going to take you along to Fusan in his jeep and then there should be no further obstacle to your return to Washington."

"Unless, of course, you should still find yourself short of staff," I interposed.

"Quite so," said Breen, lighting a cigarette.

I, too, took a cigarette from my case. I realized that it would be pointless to offer any further resistance.

"And what makes you think, Mr. Breen," I said, "that your seven frogmen are not at the bottom of the sea? Although I have not even a nodding acquaintance with the world below the surface of the sea or any other water, subaqueous excursions seem to me to be not entirely without risks. I hope you don't expect me to turn myself into a frogman in order to search for your agents among the fishes, the corals, and the seahorses. Why shouldn't your diving spies simply have perished in the deep? Personally, I have always thought it most remarkable that a diver should ever show his head again above the surface."

Mr. Breen did not prove receptive to my sense of humor.

"Of my seven men, whose names and descriptions you shall have in a moment," he said, "only five were instructed to go below water. The other two, though themselves divers, were—as is customary—to maintain contact with the frogmen either from ashore or from a boat. But they have disappeared too, just as the divers. But here's the most vital detail. One of the frogmen, Lieutenant-Commander Walter S. Hees, has been seen in a pothouse in Karyo harbor."

"Why didn't your branch in Karyo take any steps?" I interrupted Breen.

"My branch in Karyo consists of a single officer, Captain Cook, and an N.C.O. If the frogmen team are hiding—as I assume they must be—then they are hiding principally from Captain Cook, to whom they were supposed to have reported after the completion of their mission in Karyo. You see now, Mr. Droste, why I have to send you to Karyo."

"Do you consider it possible that your men should have gone over to the other side?"

"Out of the question," replied Breen, "if only for the reason that they disappeared four days prior to the invasion. Anything else you'd like to know?"

There was nothing else I wanted to know. An hour later, after an assistant of Mr. Breen's had supplied me with some useful information and photographs of the seven men, I was on my way from the Western to the Eastern coast of this unfamiliar country.

The journey by jeep was difficult, but it was not nearly so dangerous as I had feared. Our jeep, driven by a young American sergeant in civilian clothes, moved over bottomless roads—but the population around us was still unsuspecting. Panic had not yet seized the country south of Seoul; besides, we were driving in a straight line from West to East, whereas the war, as Bomber Yellow had correctly foreseen, was moving from North to South. The June sun was beating down on the miserable mud huts, whose irregular straw-thatched roofs echoed the undulating contour of the mountains and hills on the skyline. The terraced fields on both sides of the derelict road seemed like crumbling amphitheatres from antiquity. The peasants were moving around among their houses and fields, going about their daily round with impassive heavy gait. Again I was depressed by the people's unsuspecting innocence or their resignation: even if they knew that tanks, guns, and armies would churn up their land tomorrow, they would still till their soil with the same dull application today.

The journey had been depressing but not alarming—but the port of Karyo presented an entirely different picture. We arrived there long after nightfall, after negotiating a steeply climbing track up the Diamond Mountains and plunging just as precipitately down on the other side. Although my driver had repeatedly been to Karyo he had some difficulty in finding his way about the little blacked-out town, whose better-informed inhabitants had largely left. The only policeman we encountered regarded us as if we were ghosts, and our horn signals echoed weirdly among the empty streets. It was nearly eleven o'clock before we found the house where Captain Cook lived.

The Intelligence captain was a pleasant young man with good manners, and an open, intelligent face. He clearly came of good family—a fact that was confirmed by his cultured college English. He received us cordially, almost like old friends, treated us with generous hospitality, and in concise terms, without unnecessary verbal flourishes, gave me all the information I required.

"Since you left Seoul," he said, "the situation here, if I may put it this way, has become both simpler and more complicated. You don't have to look for Mr. Hees any more." In the Navy all officers below the rank of Commander were given the civilian designation of Mister. "I found him today. He is lying in a room at the Golden Anchor, a harbor tavern, totally drunk. He has threatened to shoot anybody who gets near him. If my sergeant, or I, or anybody known by him to be connected with Intelligence, were to attempt to break into his room he would undoubtedly let fly blindly. Perhaps you'll have more luck—though I doubt it."

He walked over to a Japanese display cabinet, which might at one time have held some delicate pieces of porcelain but which at this moment contained nothing but a revolver.

"I hope you know how to handle this shooting iron," he said, handing me the weapon. "Unfortunately, none of us can afford to sleep tonight. We've got to leave Karyo tomorrow morning. By six o'clock at the latest I must know whether Mr. Hees is prepared to come along with us voluntarily."

"What will you do if he refuses?" I asked.

"On no account must I let him fall into Communist hands," said the captain. "If he won't listen to reason I shall try to load him on to a vehicle by force. If, as I fear, I don't succeed in doing this—we just haven't got enough people—I shall shoot him."

He spoke with the regretful matter-of-factness of a veterinary surgeon, unless the dog recovers from its distemper by the morning it will have to be put to sleep.

"I shall do my best," I said. "Take me to the Golden Anchor."

The Golden Anchor, a narrow two-story wooden building

which looked ready for demolition, was situated hard by the harbor. The captain shone his flashlight through the glass door of the blacked-out tavern and knocked on it with the handle of his torch, but it was a long time before the landlord could be roused. Captain Cook talked to him rather excitedly in a language I did not understand, and eventually gave him several banknotes. Only then did the landlord agree to show me to the room of the American, the only occupied room in the establishment.

"I'll be waiting in the jeep just round the corner," said the captain.

The Korean guided me through the darkened tap-room into the interior of the house, which was likewise in darkness. He took my hand and brought it up against his suspenders, which were dangling loose from the rear buttons of his trousers. I understood. Holding on to his suspenders I followed the landlord up a narrow wooden staircase which groaned pitifully at every step.

We reached a narrow passage which smelled unpleasantly and penetratingly of saffron. The little man stopped outside the only door below which showed a faint, flickering light, evidently from a candle. Hastily he pointed at the door, and just as hastily he pushed his way past me. The creaking stairs told me that he had made his retreat. I was alone.

I still believe that only my ever lively sense of the ridiculous saved my life at that—as the most hardened reader must admit —exceedingly delicate moment.

I had thrust my right hand into my jacket pocket: it was resting there on the weapon which Captain Cook had so kindly put at my disposal. For an instant I seriously considered bursting at the point of the gun into the room of the missing and now recovered frogman. Luckily, however, I am one of those people who, though vain enough to consult their mirror with undue frequency, are not quite so vain as to be blind to what they see there. Before my mind's mirror I saw myself bursting into the commander's room, brandishing my revolver, and the vision struck me as rather ridiculous. If people really burst into other people's rooms at gunpoint quite as often as happens in novels, plays, films, and other figments of imagination the world would be a shooting gallery —whereas in actual fact most people grow to a ripe old age with-

out ever having touched a revolver. Besides, I had sworn to myself that I should never, in any situation and under any circumstances, behave like an agent—that is, like a man acting his
part—and since my fear of appearing ridiculous was stronger
than my fear for my life I decided on a course of action that
would scarcely have occurred to a well-trained alumnus of one
of the cops-and-robbers schools of Intelligence. I turned the door-
handle. It yielded. Without another thought for my gun I entered the commander's room. The man I was looking for was lying
on the bed, snoring; he was in shirt-sleeves, but otherwise fully
dressed.

Soundlessly I closed the door behind me. In the weak light
of an almost gutted candle I took in the bed, the rough table with
a candle, a whisky bottle and a dirty glass, as well as the dilapidated bedside cabinet and the shabby wash-stand. Instead of
thinking useful thoughts, I speculated—for so unpredictable is
the human brain—about the curious and possibly symbolical circumstance that such a weak light should cast such colossal shadows.
The shadow of the bedside cabinet stood on the wall like a gigantic
black column. On the bedside cabinet I noticed an army pistol.

As cautiously as I could I tiptoed over to the bed, let the
frogman's weapon slip into my left jacket-pocket, returned to
the table, and sat down on the one chair. Only then did I wake the
man on the bed by means of a friendly clearing of my throat.

Lieutenant-Commander Walter S. Hees opened his eyes. He
was instantly awake. Sitting up, he automatically reached for his
pistol: discovering that it was gone he leapt up and came for me
menacingly.

The frogman was about ten years younger than I—about
thirty-one or thirty-two. As I watched him in the flickering light
of the candle I felt no desire to get involved in a fight with him.
He was no taller than I, but his broad shoulders and narrow hips,
his enormous hands, and his whole athletic build revealed a
physical strength against which I could not match myself. If I
did not regard my situation as desperate the reason was not so
much my two weapons—which anyway I could not have brought
into play quickly enough in case of need—as the man's face which,
in spite of its momentary devastation, filled me with a certain

calm. The commander had not yet slept off his intoxication, as testified by his bloodshot eyes which still seemed to be floating in alcohol—but these same eyes reflected a high degree of intelligence and genuine, though temporarily confused, benignity. The pale oblong face, with its hollow cheeks, with its finely-drawn though rather large nose, its young, well-shaped, and not at all weak chin, held not a trace of brutality. The man who was coming for me was a desperate man, but one who was more dangerous to himself than to others.

"Mr. Hees," I said, without getting up, "I have not come as an enemy and I only removed your pistol from the bedside cabinet because I was afraid you might fire before you had a chance of hearing my, I believe eminently reasonable, proposal. Now that you are again in full possession of your senses, permit me to return your weapon to you."

I handed the young naval officer his pistol without being aware of doing anything particularly courageous. On the contrary, I was motivated by the thought that if I did not behave like a professional agent Lieutenant-Commander Hees might be perplexed by my actions—and this perplexity I intended to turn to good use.

The commander put his weapon in his hand, making sure I had not unloaded it, but did not point it at me.

"Who are you?" he said.

"My name is George Droste," I introduced myself, rising with a slight bow. "Austrian by birth and nationality, but in the service of U.S. Intelligence which has charged me with the task of tracking down you and your colleagues, Mr. Hees, and, if you are so disposed, assisting you with your evacuation. Luckily Karyo has not yet fallen into the hands of the advancing North Koreans, but the enemy is expected at any moment. . . ."

Hees flopped on to the chair from which I had just got up. He picked up the whisky bottle, which was only a quarter full, hesitated for an instant whether he should pour the amber liquor into the dirty tumbler, finally put the bottle to his lips and took a deep swig. He looked at me. In his watery-blue eyes was more mockery than hostility, more scorn than hatred, more sorrow than anger.

"So you want to evacuate us," he said. "You want to evacuate the lot of us. All seven of us. Bobby and Tom and Francis and Stewart. Stewart as well, eh?"

"Stewart as well, naturally," I said.

"And Mike?"

"Mike, too."

"And Bobby?"

"Of course."

"You want to evacuate them all?"

"I'm telling you, Mr. Hees."

The commander leaned forward. He planted his elbows firmly on his knees, as if to ensure the stability of his body against any impending concussion. Then, as if all his preparations had been for this purpose, he began to laugh. His laughter was like a sick fit. It shook his bowed body, it possessed him like a fiend and shook him from within. At last he wiped the tears from his eyes and said:

"They are evacuated already, Mr. Droste. They've all been evacuated." In the manner of a drunk, who tries to stress, bring home, and explain every one of his difficult ideas, Hees kept repeating that his partners had long been evacuated. "A big ship has evacuated them . . ." With his hand he described the motion of a ship rolling on the waves. "Down below the water the big ship evacuated them—do you get that, Mr. Droste?"

Although the truth began to dawn upon me I said: "No, I don't quite understand, Mr. Hees."

"Of course not, of course not," said Hees.

For a while he sat staring ahead of him. Just as though he were sitting on the shore, staring into the deep water. The unscrubbed floor was the sea and Commander Hees was sitting by its edge. I was waiting patiently, in silence, for I could see that he would presently want to unburden himself. That was the moment I wanted to be ready for. Abruptly he threw his head up, regarded me, and asked: "Do you want to hear what happened?"

I nodded.

He gritted his teeth.

"You'll have to hear it whether you want to or not," he said.

"I'm listening," I said.

He began:

"They went in—Bobby, Tom, Stewart . . ." he pulled himself up, as if even remembering their names was now an unspeakable effort. With a resigned gesture he gave up the struggle with his clouded memory. "Only Ensign Mike Kovalsky and I stayed behind in the boat," he continued. "You see, we'd tossed up who was to stay behind. Heads or tails. So we were to stay behind in the boat—Mike and I. Ensign Kovalsky was the youngest of us. He was twenty-four. Always after the girls. He was engaged to some Korean girl. Back home, in New York, he was also engaged. And in Tokyo. He got engaged all over the place. Mike had his headphones on. I had mine on too; I was working the set. Suddenly Mike looks at me. I can't see him, but I can feel it. I look at Mike. There's something wrong with the set. I check the set. We both check the set. The set's all right, but there's no signal coming in. I try to send a signal out, but I don't get a reply. Everything's totally silent down below. I'm hammering on my signal key, but there's no answer. A few lights came on aboard the *Novgorod*. There are lights in her portholes. They stare at us like eyes, only bigger. We are all alone on the water, in the night. The portholes are watching us."

The commander broke off. He looked at me with wide eyes, as though trying to imitate the circular portholes. There was a little madness in his round blue eyes.

"We row a little distance away from the *Novgorod*," he resumed his narrative. "Still no signal. Mike says: 'I'm going down. There's something wrong there.' I tell him: 'You're crazy.' He says: 'Crazy or not—I'm going down.' 'You'll do what I tell you,' I say to him. 'I'm a lieutenant-commander and you're just an ensign.' 'Nuts to your rank,' he says; 'I'm going down to have a look.' So I says: 'O.K., we'll toss for it: heads or tails.' 'I'm younger than you,' he says. 'So what?' I say. I try to find a coin. I can't find one. I got no money on me at all." Suddenly he looked straight at me. "I didn't have a single coin on me, do you understand? Not a dime, not a nickel, not a quarter."

He lingered so long on the point that he had had no money on him that I feared my nerves would not stand the strain of this seemingly trivial detail. Four or five times he repeated that he did not have a cent in his pocket. Unobtrusively I glanced at my wrist-watch. The time was three-fifteen, and I knew that Captain Cook would not wait in his jeep for ever. Some time, perhaps at dawn, Captain Cook would resort to force. Some time, before six o'clock, he would finish off the sick dog rather than leave him behind.

"Mike finds a big fifty-cent piece," the commander resumed his story. "I choose heads, he chooses tails. We toss the coin up. It drops on the floor of the boat. We can't see it. We feel the surface. It's tails. Mike pockets the coin again. He gets ready. Meantime I'm trying to resume contact with the others. Not a thing. 'You'll signal me at once,' I say. 'Sure,' says Mike, and puts on his helmet. I help him into the water. A few seconds later he sends the first signal. A shiver runs down my spine. So it wasn't the set, I say to myself. What's happened to the others? Bobby and Stewart and Francis. Francis was one of them." Again the commander's thoughts were straying from his narrative. "He came from Oklahoma. Used to be a cowboy. Can you beat that, George —a cowboy and then a frogman!" He laughed. "Cowboy and frogman—don't you think this is funny?" He stopped short and picked up the bottle. "Mike sends one more signal. He says: 'I can't see anything. They must be quite close to the *Novgorod*. Am approaching the *Novgorod* myself.' That was the last I heard from Mike. I sit in the boat, hammering at the sending key. I'm so mad I could smash the set. I shake it like a naughty child. I start ripping out the wiring. I hate the set. Did you ever hate an instrument, George? And then I decided to have a look for myself. Of course, it was crazy, but I had to find out. Don't look at me like this—I'm not a hero, I was just curious. Or else I lost my nerve—I just don't know. I row back to the shore, tie up the boat, check my oxygen cylinder, and put on my helmet. I go down not far from the *Novgorod*. I don't need my flashlight. There is a light coming from the *Novgorod* below the water line. Have you ever seen light below water, George? If you've got any kids you must take them below water at night. Below water there are submerged fairy-tale castles. Castles with many lighted windows. They're inhabited by fishes. And by dead bodies. All round the castles are gardens. In the gardens lie the dead bodies: they have star fishes on their chests, like orders. Divers get specially beauti-

ful star fishes. With very big eyes. I swim towards the fairy-tale
castle. At first I can't see anything out of the ordinary. I only see
that the hull plates are gleaming on the outside. A bright, metal-
lic, golden gleam. I am now rounding her stern. That's when I
catch sight of them, George."

He buried his face in his hands. His whole frame was shaken
by sobs, just as it had been shaken by laughter a few minutes
earlier. Never before and never since have I seen a man cry like
this. It was as if electric shocks were passing through his double-
bent body. He was not crying from inside; it was as though some
invisible being were present in the room, tugging at his body
with superhumanly powerful arms.

Then he got up without looking at me, reeled towards the
primitive wash-stand, bent over it and vomited into the basin. He
looked as if he wanted to vomit his soul out. A stale, acrid smell
pervaded the room. The candle had almost burned down, and I
had difficulty in seeing the man's face as he turned towards me
once more. He was still crying, but he cried without tears—not
even with his eyes, but just with a grimacing half-open mouth. He
wiped his lips with his shirt-cuff, came closer, and stopped in front
of me. His voice sounded completely sober as he said: "They
were sticking to the hull of the ship. Do you know what that
means?"

I looked at him uncomprehendingly.

"A magnet had attracted them. A new invention. Every one of
our men had metal parts on his person—Stewart and Bobby and
Tom. A little piece of metal was enough. Or a fifty-cent piece—
do you understand? And the magnet just attracted them. Pulled
them right through the water!"

With all ten fingers he illustrated the attractive force of the
magnet. He stood before me with wide-open eyes, gesticulating,
as if he wanted to attract me to himself. He looked like a con-
juror producing a rabbit from a hat. Now that he had relieved
himself and was more sober than before his eyes struck me as
even madder and eerier.

"The magnet pulled them through the water," he repeated.
"Pulled them as if they were on a string. And then the magnet
flung them against the metal hull-plates. With full force. Smack!

went the bodies. Smack! went the heads. They cracked up against the hull. Just stuck there. Have you ever seen flies on a fly-paper, George? Back home, down South, we had plenty of flies. Our black cook always had some fly-papers dangling from the ceiling. Yellow strips. Sometimes there'd be hundreds of flies on a strip of paper spread with honey. There isn't room for human beings on a strip of fly-paper. But there's plenty of room for them on the hull of a ship." He was talking rapidly, hastily. "I didn't recognize them all. They had their diving suits on, but that wasn't why. Their helmets were crushed. Smack! gone were the helmets. They were sticking there like flies—not neatly, next to one another, but all over the place: one with his head up, the other with his legs up, the third as though power-diving. Francis, I think, was lying right across, his feet in Mike's smashed skull. Why I didn't go smack against the hull, why I didn't stick to the fly-paper, I just don't know. At least, I don't know for certain. Maybe I had no metal on me, or maybe I hadn't swum close enough to the cruiser. But the most likely answer is that they'd just switched off the magnetism. Stupid chance." He laughed. "Just as I am turning to swim back—I was beating it, George, as fast as I could under the water—the bodies suddenly detach themselves from the hull, all together. It looks to me as if they are following me—the corpses of my companions. Stewart and Bobby and little Lawrence —for he was one of the party too—little Lawrence with his prominent ears. I run away under the water and the corpses are chasing me. Only, of course, they aren't chasing me: they can't swim, just as flies can't fly once they've stuck to the fly-paper. They are dead, the flies. They can be scraped off the fly-paper and chucked away. They can chuck us away now, George—Stewart and Bobby and Mike and me. . . ."

I could not utter a word. At last I laid my hands on the commander's shoulders.

"Walter," I said, "you've got to pull yourself together. What's done is done and can't be undone. I understand you. I also understand why you didn't go back. But now the time has come for you to go back. Intelligence will make allowances for your condition. They haven't got a thing on you. You did all you could do. Look at the window: it's getting light. In a few hours the enemy will be in Karyo. You need rest and treatment. I'll take you to Fusan by jeep. From there you'll be evacuated to Tokyo and sent back home."

The candle had gone out. I turned and thrust open the crumbling, dilapidated shutters. The gray dawn was filtering through the window. When I looked again into the ashen face of the commander I felt ashamed of the banality of my words. He was staring at me, for the first time in a hostile manner, and said:

"So you want to evacuate me? Why didn't you evacuate Bobby and Mike while there was time? No need to evacuate me. I know what the game is." With his big hands he roughly gripped my lapels. "Do you know why we were sent here? Don't look so stupid: you don't know at all. You're only a fly yourself. You can't know. We were sent here for no reason at all—do you understand? Surely that swine in Seoul did not seriously believe a few swimming spies could find out anything about propeller construction, or rudder design, or the nature of the armor plating, or their acoustic detectors." He was clearly quite sober now. Soberly he continued, without letting go of me: "He knew quite well that at best we'd swim round the ship a few times, surface again, and then fabricate some phoney report. That's what he was out for. Unless he was out for something else!" He screwed up his eyes and tightened his grip on me. "Unless he was out for something else!" he repeated, threateningly. It was obvious he was voicing an idea which had been occupying him for some days. "Perhaps he didn't want to know anything about propellers, or maneuverability, or thickness of armor. Because even he knows that you can't find out about those things from outside. But perhaps he had heard about the magnetic device. He could test that magnetic device from outside all right: he could test that with a few swimming spies. If five out of seven didn't return he could make his report. Magnetic device tested. New magnetic device found to function. Five agents —smack—crushed against the hull. Two agents returned to base to report. Splendid average; excellent result; promotion certain; *Novgorod* departed complete with flies." He pushed me away from him. "No, he's getting no report from me. No need to evacuate me."

Quickly he stepped up to the table. The pistol which I had returned to him at the beginning of our conversation was still lying on it.

I too instinctively felt for the revolver in my pocket.

"No need to evacuate me," repeated Hees. "I can evacuate myself."

But instead of picking up his pistol he seized the whisky bottle. With one long gulp he emptied it.

"Do be reasonable, Commander Hees!" I said, attempting a tone of command.

I went at him.

Quick as lightning he turned, snatched the pistol up from the table and levelled it at me. Then he moved his weapon slowly, almost like a man at target practice bringing his pistol down in a quarter-circle from his shoulder into firing position. Only he described the quadrant upward, from the level position. Unhurriedly, almost solemnly, he put the muzzle against his temple.

Before I could free myself from my frozen stupor, before I could leap at him, he had fired.

He crumpled up. His head struck the edge of the table. The falling body swept the table with it. With the table, the candlestick and the bottle crashed to the floor.

I stepped to the window, flung it wide open, and shouted for Captain Cook.

The first rays of the rising sun fell on the square harbor of Karyo, where only a few miserable fishing craft were riding at anchor. From afar came the dull crump of gunfire.

My mission in Korea was finished.

Second Interlude

BY NOVEMBER 5, 1955, George Droste's memoirs had reached the point to which the reader has now followed them.

The day was Saturday. Droste had slept till ten o'clock—a luxury he permitted himself every Saturday. Over breakfast he booked a call to Geneva to speak to his foster-son Johnny.

As a rule Johnny would talk at length about his life, his progress at school, and even about the most trifling events—certain in the knowledge that Droste would be interested in anything concerning him—but this time the boy spoke of practically nothing else but the impending Christmas holidays.

At eleven o'clock Droste ordered a taxi which took him, as every Saturday, to his bank near the Schottentor. In spite of a snobbish dislike of briefcases, he carried a little-used black case, whose contents—the week's instalment of his memoirs—he deposited in the bank's vault.

It was the first Saturday of the month and Droste took a local train out to Korneuburg, a pleasant little town, even in this unpleasant early-winter weather, where his uncle Joachim Welser still kept his inn.

A cozy afternoon passed, sweetened by excellent coffee and a home-made Guglhupf cake, followed by an evening over a good glass of wine in the wood-panelled saloon, where the leading citizens of the small town dropped in for a little political gossip. Droste was on the point of leaving for the station when his uncle called him to the telephone.

"You're wanted by police headquarters in Vienna," said old man Welser. "Whatever have you been up to, Georgie?" he added teasingly.

An uncomfortable feeling came over Droste. A clear conscience had never been a cushion for his weary head and he disliked the sound of the word "police." He had left word in the morning, as was his habit, as to where he could be reached— but Marie, his housekeeper, had likewise gone to town shortly after him, and apart from her, nobody knew the Korneuburg telephone number.

Droste picked up the receiver and immediately a voice at the other end introduced itself as Superintendent Dr. Hrovacka. To Droste's astonishment the Superintendent proceeded to address him familiarly in the second person singular—but the mystery was soon cleared up when he asked:

"Don't you remember me? We were at school together. . . ."

"But of course," Droste hurriedly declared, as a vague memory rose up in him of a lanky boy with unruly fair hair.

"You know, Droste," said the Superintendent, addressing Droste by his surname, "it's a damned funny coincidence—me being on duty today. You see, they've just brought a man in——" He interrupted himself. "Do you happen to know a man called Quatthelm?"

"Don't think so," replied Droste, instinctively adopting the nasal drawl affected by the higher grades of the bureaucracy of his native city.

"As a matter of fact," said the Superintendent, "I should be most obliged if you could drop in here—the Rossauerlände H.Q., Room 100C. Fact is, there's been a burglary at your place this evening . . . no, please, no cause for alarm . . . nothing's been taken. We clamped down on the fellow straight away —man called Quatthelm. Only it's a bit odd . . . so if you're sure you don't mind . . ."

"Not in the least, Hrovacka; quite the contrary," said Droste. "Exceedingly kind of you . . . really most amusing that you, of all people . . . very well then, I'll be with you in about an hour."

The November rain hung over the city like a grimy curtain when Droste arrived in Vienna. He took it as an ill omen that, in spite of the late hour, both the telephone boxes he had wanted to use were engaged. At last, after a protracted and impatient wait, he got through to his home.

An unfriendly male voice answered.

"This is Droste," said the caller. "I'd like to speak to my housekeeper."

"This is Detective Inspector Wallach," replied the strange voice. "I am sorry, Herr Droste, I cannot put you through to your housekeeper at this moment."

"May I ask what this means?"

"I cannot give you any information over the telephone."

Droste rang off.

He had difficulty in finding a taxi, and it was long past mid-night when the vehicle pulled up outside the ugly, fortress-like building on the Danube embankment.

The long, badly-lit corridors smelled of police—to wit, of wet clothes, ink, and urine. A uniformed policeman announced Droste to Superintendent Dr. Hrovacka.

The man who rose from behind his old-fashioned desk on the fringes of the pool of light bore little resemblance to Hrovacka the classmate, whose Christian name Droste was vainly trying to recall. He was a gaunt man with a bad-tempered nose, thin lips, and short ice-gray hair. He wore a correct but rather threadbare suit, and Droste felt somewhat embarrassed, not only because he did not remember Hrovacka nearly so well as Hrovacka remembered him. As always when he met a schoolfriend, Droste had a bad conscience because he had done better for himself than they.

Droste's sense of *malaise* and guilt was only heightened by the Superintendent's pronounced, and almost exaggerated, courtesy.

Dr. Hrovacka offered his visitor a comfortable arm-chair and a cigarette before sitting down again behind his desk. But even when he knew Droste to be comfortably settled he displayed no eagerness to come to the point. Instead, he began to reminisce about their years at school and to recall, with an astonishingly accurate memory, the various masters and their, almost invariably funny, mannerisms.

From their boyhood memories the Superintendent proceeded to the story of his own life, and Droste suspected that this was done with a view to drawing out the visitor in turn about his career.

"Well, then, to put you in possession of the facts," the Superintendent suddenly announced, after much delay but somewhat abruptly, "last night, at twenty-one hours, a certain Theodor Quatthelm attempted to break into your house. Or rather, he succeeded in breaking into your house by way of the kitchen door. He did so by means of a skeleton key. How he gained possession of this key remains to be investigated. Is your housekeeper reliable?"

"I'll vouch for her absolutely," said Droste.

"That's my impression too," said the Superintendent. "Nevertheless, the man was accurately acquainted with the topography."

From a dog-eared folder he produced the photograph of a man of about forty-five.

Droste examined the picture carefully. He had expected to recognize Quatthelm, even though he might have known him by another name; now to his relief he found that the face in the photograph, which looked like a white Negro, was that of a stranger.

"Never seen him before," he said with conviction.

"Now then," Dr. Hrovacka continued. "The man went straight from the kitchen into your study, where he first of all subjected your desk drawer to a thorough examination. Can you think what he should have been looking for there?"

Droste began to see what the Superintendent was getting at.

"I don't usually keep any money in the house," he said evasively.

"Being accurately acquainted with the topography," the schoolfellow behind the desk continued, "being, as I say, accurately acquainted with the topography, he next proceeded to have a go at the safe in your bookcase. He was unlucky, and soon gave up his attempt at opening your safe by peaceful means. He thereupon produced from his bag an electric drill and other professional safe-cracker's implements. But so that your pretty safe should come to no harm," the Superintendent smiled, "we interrupted him at his work in good time and, if you'll forgive the expression, nabbed him. Your housekeeper, by the way, happened to come in just as we were taking him away."

"How very odd," said Droste. "Did the man tell you all these details?"

"Not exactly," replied the Superintendent. "In fact, quite the contrary. He's a very obstinate fellow, our German friend."

He uttered the last two words with deliberate emphasis. He was scarcely trying to conceal his suspicion as he watched his visitor closely.

"So he is a German, is he?" said Droste, without betraying his alarm.

The Superintendent made no reply. He pushed the lamp with its oblong green shade a little way aside, as if to see Droste better.

"Tell me, Droste, did you ever have anything to do with the Greehahn Organization?" he asked.

"You mean that new German espionage organization that's

being written about as much nowadays as if it were a new brand of cigarette?" returned Droste.

"The same."

"What an idea!" observed Droste.

"You see, Herr Quatthelm belongs to the Greehahn Organization," the Superintendent explained. "Naturally, we're again unable to compete with our German friends . . . we're short of the necessary cash . . . but all the same, we'd been tipped off about the visit of this Greehahn agent. We've been trailing him for the past three weeks." He leaned back and elaborately lit a cigarette. "Strictly speaking, it's not the business of the police —but one's got to help where one can. You've only got to look at the foreign papers to see Vienna invariably referred to as the 'city of the Third Man.' All due to the Occupation, I'll grant you that—but surely this rot's got to stop some time. After all, we have the Opera and the Burgtheater and St. Stephen's Cathedral and our picture galleries—I really think we can do quite well without the dubious fame of being the meeting-place of international spies. Don't you agree?"

"Absolutely, Hrovacka, absolutely," said Droste. "By the way, I've been racking my brains: didn't you sit in the third row on the right, immediately behind von Bosswell?"

"Bravo!" said the Superintendent. "Right behind Bosswell. Only it was the fourth row. I was going to say: have you any idea what interest the Greehahn people could have in your safe?"

"Possibly, yes," said Droste. "They might conceivably be interested in me, even if only from a historical point of view."

"How do you mean?"

"During the war I was privileged to serve in Intelligence," Droste said calmly. "Naturally I made a few notes which I intend to use when I write my wartime reminiscences. The German magazines are exceedingly keen on this sort of thing just now, and since I've retired from business a few thousand marks wouldn't come at all amiss. Maybe the Greehahn people got wind of it. By the way, if you'd like to inspect my safe . . . ?"

"Most obliging, Droste, most obliging," the Superintendent said jovially. "You're really doing me a great favor. I should have hated issuing a search warrant . . ."

"Not at all necessary, I assure you," laughed Droste. "I've no secrets—and my house is entirely at your disposal, Hrovacka. As for those reminiscences of mine, I'm afraid I haven't got down to putting pen to paper yet, but if they ever see the light of day I shall not fail to send you an inscribed copy."

"Very kind of you," the Superintendent said approvingly. "Very kind of you, Droste. Just to be on the safe side I've kept two of my officers at your place. So perhaps, if you would allow them . . ."

"With pleasure," said Droste. Suddenly he remembered that the Superintendent's name was Hubert. Hubert Hrovacka, pupil of the class VIIIA. Used to sit in the fourth row on the right, immediately behind that goliath Bosswell. In fact, the two had been friends—Hrovacka and Bosswell—and both had been particularly good at algebra. "With pleasure," repeated Droste. "Is there anything else I can do for you?"

The Superintendent got up from his chair.

"Let us know at once, please, if you notice anything at all suspicious," he said, and his request sounded almost sincere. "This Quatthelm, you should know, was carrying a weapon in spite of the ban. I shouldn't want you to have any further trouble. Needless to say, I am always at your disposal."

Droste rose to go. The Superintendent saw him to the door.

"By the way," he said, as he shook hands with Droste, "do you remember the thin Baron Staub?"

"Yes, of course," said Droste.

"Unpleasant business," said Dr. Hrovacka. "Vanished immediately after the liberation, together with his sister, a certain

Countess Cosimano. The Russians probably took him along. Strange, the things that happen to one's class-mates. . . ."

"Very strange indeed," said Droste. "I hope we'll see a little more of each other, Hrovacka."

"So do I, Droste; so do I," said the Superintendent.

PART SEVEN

28

Good-by to Nora

IN SETTING OUT to recount my last meeting with Nora I feel full of hesitation and serious inhibitions. It is over five years now since I have seen her, and only rarely does a piece of news about her reach me in a roundabout way. And yet I do not know whether I am able to judge fairly the day on which we parted. Gunnar Güldendag, who that day rose from the dead and returned to life, is now dead. Dead for a second time. And among my papers, which some inquisitive agent recently tried to steal, there is a newspaper photograph of Nora following his coffin: an upright woman in a black dress, full of tragic dignity. How often have I not studied this picture, held it close to my eyes, examined it—I must confess it—under the magnifying glass. But how was I to learn from a gray picture on a crumpled newspaper page what I was unable to discover that summer day after my return from Korea? Why had Nora left me? Was it fair of her to leave me? Did she no longer love me or was her stubborn loyalty turning into new love? Could she expunge the memory of our years together, or did she carry them in her as I do? The blurred picture offered no answer. But I had better report how it all came about.

No more than four weeks had passed since I had said good-by to my home on the Wolfgangsee and ventured forth into grim adventure. Now I was sitting in a small, shabby compartment of the narrow-gauge local train from Salzburg to Bad Ischl, engrossed in strange reflections, which seemed to be out of tune, and indeed almost at odds, with my character and my past life.

I had since been in three continents, and their diversity had struck me more than ever in view of the condensed time-scale of my chase. What did they know of the world, I thought, those humanitarian fools who talked of "one world" instead of rejoicing in its multi-faceted variety! They did not resemble one another: the Koreans saving their carved Buddhas from the deluge; the Russians who worshiped other, rather more changeable, deities; the Americans for whom the future had already begun, and my fellow Austrians for whom the past had never ended. They did not resemble one another. But why should they not be able to coexist, like the apple-trees, the pear-trees, and the cherry-trees? Why? Because, while there are as many strange crosses in Nature as there are among human beings, the trees merely fertilize but never rape one another. No apple-tree ever wants to turn a cherry into an apple-tree; no pear-tree is ever so "idealistic" as to expect a cherry to bear pears. That is why Nature lives while Man dies. Crusades are launched only by human beings, because forcible cross-fertilization must inevitably fail—and it fails doubly after a crusade.

I gazed out into the familiar, rain-drenched, moistly green landscape through which the antique toy train was puffing at a comfortable pace. Were not my Austrian compatriots right when they escaped from the future to their consolidated positions of the past? *"Le seul avenir est notre objet,"* Pascal had said with conviction. And perhaps in Pascal's seventeenth century the future had indeed been the only aim. Returning from a war-torn Korea, where the future had started already, I suddenly realized what was the most significant feature of our generation: that it had to fear the future instead of gladly hailing it. Around the laboratories where the future was being brewed up circled the bird of death; at the heart of the new ideas gnawed the worm of self-destruction. Progress meant return to the stone age; frivolous disregard of the future was wise foresight; planning for the future was foolish speculation; death was the only escape from mass extinction and pregnancy was a cruel gamble with a doomed life. Who was bold enough to change the world? Mankind was Don Quixote, tilting at windmills it had itself erected. If there was any salvation, it could only be in orderly retreat. Only thus might a disorderly retreat—the inescapable consequence of any further advance—be still averted.

The sun cleft a narrow path through the low mist over the lake. I thought of Lieutenant-Commander Walter S. Hees. We had sat his body upright on the back seat of the jeep. All the way to Fusan he had sat there next to me. My actions seemed to be receiving a belated foundation, rather like a house built from the roof downward. How had those fared who had faithfully served the Powers of this earth, who had tried to bring on the future? Suddenly my deception seemed justified: deception seemed the only answer to the presumption of the rulers. What else could one do but deceive the deceivers by delaying the fulfilment of their wishes? Was it not a fact that I had acted from avarice, fear, and selfishness, but that I could not have acted differently if I had been prompted by understanding, mature judgment, and moral considerations? A confusing sense of gratification came over me—confusing because I had taken the wrong road and arrived at the right end. Or was the right end altogether only attainable by wrong roads? Did one, in order to do good, have to intend evil? Was deception damnable in itself, or did it cease to be damnable if the deceived were damnable? Fate was kind to the sinners whom it granted absolution; it was kind also to the sinners whom it punished— but what about the conscience of the sinner whose sinful actions had yielded beneficial results?

About thirty-six hours ago I had cabled Nora from New York, asking her to send me a wire to Munich, where my plane was taking me. But when I had called at the Munich hotel to collect the telegram there had been no message for me. I had rung the post office at St. Wolfgang—since we had no telephone in the house— but before I could get through I had to leave for the station. The fear that my double life would one day be discovered had never entirely left me during the past two years—but during the last four weeks my fear had largely vanished, together with my over-estimation of the importance of my own life. Now my fear had returned: it seemed to be galloping alongside the train.

From the little railway station on the south side of the lake I crossed by the post boat. Throughout the trip I remained on deck so as to spot Nora at the landing stage as soon as possible. After many hours of anxiety I heaved a sigh of relief when I made out her tall, slim figure in the familiar maroon dirndl dress.

However, the welcome delusion that my misgivings had been needless was of very short duration. The moment I faced the pale and almost sickly-thin woman I knew that something had happened. The smile with which she greeted me was only a clumsy attempt at imitating a smile from the past. And when I was about to order my cases to be put in a taxi she asked me, without further explanation, to deposit them by the landing stage. She wanted to talk to me—not at the house, but at a nearby café.

Did I just say that I knew something had happened? I could swear that I knew more than that. The moment we threaded our way between cheerful summer guests, green-aproned hotel porters, and children playing over at the little café in the Seeplatz I knew exactly what had happened. I knew that Gunnar Güldendag had come back.

Nora had returned from Vienna only that morning. A telegram from Stockholm, accepted at first with incredulity, but confirmed presently by a telegram from Gunnar Güldendag himself, from Vienna, had told her what was still unknown to the press and was due to be suppressed for another twenty-four hours. Abruptly, without any diplomatic preliminaries, the Soviet Government had admitted what for the past five years it had hushed up, and indeed vigorously denied—that Legation Counsellor Gunnar Güldendag had fallen into Russian hands during the siege of Budapest, that he had been taken to the Soviet Union, sentenced to twenty-five years' imprisonment on a charge of espionage, and detained until quite recently in a prison camp near the Persian frontier. It was not yet entirely clear why the Soviet Union had, at this very moment, decided not only to vouchsafe this belated information, but also to release the prisoner, but it was thought—explained Nora—that in view of the war in Korea the Soviets were anxious to win the sympathy of the neutral nations. Besides, the release and subsequent deportation of the diplomat had not been performed without a certain sarcasm on the part of the Russians: they had reported Gunnar Güldendag's resurrection not to the Swedish but to the British Ambassador, justifying this deviation from diplomatic usage on the grounds that the Legation Counsellor had been a member not of the Swedish but the British secret service.

All the time she spoke—in a frighteningly businesslike tone, as if reading out an official communiqué; without even once pausing to examine the consequences which her revelations would have for the two of us—Nora was steadily watching me. And just as steadily grew my confusion, because in her businesslike tone there was a touch of suspicion that I had known all this all the time, or that at least I had known Gunnar Güldendag to be still alive. But since Nora was incapable of hypocrisy she paused for a moment at the end of her account, looked at me even more searchingly than before, and said: "You knew that he was alive!"

The monstrous nature of the accusation took my breath away. Stammering and blushing—not because Nora was telling the truth or anything like the truth, but because I felt ashamed at this shameless defamation I began confusedly to protest. But after the very first words Nora cut me short.

"Why," she asked, "should I believe that you were really convinced of Gunnar's death when every sentence you have spoken to me over the past two years has been a lie, when your entire relationship to me has been a lie?"

I did not have to ask what she meant. She concealed nothing of what she knew, and she knew a lot. She did not look at me while she was speaking; she dropped her eyes, as if wishing to spare me a silent confession. She knew that I was a spy, she said—a spy for the Americans, the Russians, and the Germans. She mentioned three coffins and a morgue in Potsdam. And she knew that I had been to America not for some commercial law suit but because of the Korean war. When I asked how and from whom she had found out—denial seemed to me pointless and humiliating—she answered without hesitation. Since Gunnar Güldendag had been employed by the British, and they had been informed about his fate, they had of course been watching the wife of the missing man. That was how they had come to notice me and to follow my tracks. "They were probably annoyed with you," Nora concluded bitterly, "because you didn't offer yourself to them as well."

"And now?" I said. I did not know what else to say.

"I shall go back to Gunnar," she said firmly.

I demanded an explanation. I believed I was entitled to an explanation. I did not gloss over what I had done, and denied only my knowledge of Gunnar Güldendag's detention in a Soviet camp. But I challenged Nora's right to condemn me, and the right of the resurrected man to accuse me. All that I had ever said to Nora had been one big lie, I declared, picking up her accusation. One big lie—but only one. I had kept from her nothing except my connection with the secret services: in every personal word and in everything affecting the two of us I had been sincere. I even went a step further. What sort of feelings, I asked, had a woman, whose love sprang from pedantic morality, who loved not a man of flesh and blood, a human being with all its contradictions, but an animated, ethical principle, which collapsed when its moral foundations were found to be false? I reminded her that at the time when she revealed to me Gunnar Güldendag's secret at the flat on the Bellaria, I had acted as his advocate. Even when another man had been involved, even a dead rival, I had been unwilling to see her become unfaithful to him out of moral indignation—for any other reason, in fact, than extinct love. I demanded to know in what way the British spy Güldendag differed from me, or whether she was trying to tell me that his lies had been more pardonable than mine. Or were lies exonerated under some statutory terms of limitation, in the way that undiscovered crimes were? I spoke like both counsel for the defense and counsel for the prosecution—imploring and threatening, clutching at the merest straw, and never stopping to ask myself what would happen if Nora were to forgive me, and how we could possibly continue after what had passed.

She let me finish without interruption.

"I am not returning to Gunnar because his eyes were any better than yours," she said. As gently as ever she put her hand on top of mine. "Not even because he acted from other and better motives than you—although I realize today that he did. I don't love Gunnar; I love you, George. I don't love him, but I can try to live with him. I love you, but to live with you would be quite hopeless. Tomorrow it will be in all the papers that Gunnar was a spy—and even if many people refuse to believe it, the information will be worthless to those who do. Gunnar is no longer a prisoner of the secret services. He has escaped from them in the only way in which a man can escape from their captivity: by dying for them. But you, George, are alive and a prisoner. To live with you would be to acknowledge a law which I will never acknowledge—not even for the sake of my love. No, George, don't interrupt me. A murderer, a burglar, or a thief can promise to reform, and a woman who loves him may believe his promise. I know that at this moment you would like to make a final break with your past. Don't think that I am doubting your love for me, or that I don't realize how much our white house and the hills and woods and valleys mean to you—and the dreams which we have dreamed together. But now, I also know why you used to wake up at night bathed in perspiration, groping for my hand: you knew that even your dreams were lies. You can't start a new life, George, the way a murderer or a thief can. All the world demands and supports the reformation of murderers and thieves —but the world which gave you your assignment demands imperatively that the spy should remain a spy. But that isn't all. I believed myself Gunnar's widow; I now find myself his wife. He needs me and you don't. Gunnar is a broken old man. He walks with a stick and his face is like the wall of a prison cell into which a prisoner has scratched the passing years with a tin spoon."

Only at the mention of Gunnar Güldendag had she released my hand.

I now clasped her hand.

I cannot remember exactly what I said to her, but I know that there was no accusation in my voice. I implored her to stay with me. I suggested that we should escape together, to South America or to Africa—but even before my romantic plans took shape they collapsed under Nora's glance. I adjured her by the best days and the best nights of our years together, not shrinking from the cheapest sentimentality and, indeed, wallowing in it till my own eyes were filled with tears. Nora's hand fluttered in mine like an injured bird, but she did not falter.

"He needs you and I don't?" I asked. "Do you know me so little, Nora? Have you really no idea what kind of person I was when I first met you? And the kind of person I shall be again if you leave me? There are many who are doomed though at liberty, and others who are saved though behind prison walls. I am still a prisoner, but with you I am saved already. Are you going to leave me now?"

She withdrew her hand from me, for the second time.

"It's impossible, George," she said. "It's impossible for me to believe you. You have lied too skillfully, with too much enjoyment and practice. In the same voice that you are using now you used to speak about your trips to Vienna and about our plans. I should have to ask myself at every word how far truth went and where deception began. Perhaps I could have gone on living with a lie, for I love you very much—but we can't live with an unmasked lie. I don't want to be brave, George, but I've got to be. I promise you I shan't be happy." Her voice failed. Then she began: "And besides . . ." but she did not finish.

It took all my powers of persuasion to make her tell me what she had been going to say. I insisted, because I sensed that it was something important, something which she had so far kept from me, but something that wanted telling. At last she admitted that she was acting not only under the hateful pressure of her conscience, not only under the painful impulse of resignation, but also for my sake. She did not say—or even hint—that Gunnar Güldendag had made her return to him the condition of his silence, but I gathered that she could not have stayed with me even if she had found it in her to forgive me.

"Tomorrow," she said, "the world will be looking towards Stockholm, where Gunnar has gone today under an escort from his own Government. People will expect to see me with him. If I am not found at his side tomorrow they will ferret about and they will find me here with you, George. And then you would be under the full blaze of the spotlights. . . ."

"And in the light I cannot endure." I finished the sentence for her.

We stayed at the little café for another hour. Around us was the hustle and bustle of the peak season. Laughter and jokes were exchanged between tables; a crying child demanded a cake; rowing boats made fast outside; tourists stopped and peered through the café windows. I do not remember what we talked about. I only know that I spoke without a break—words without sense and purpose, no doubt, or with the sole purpose of putting off the moment of our parting. While I was still sitting next to Nora and holding her hand behind the little marble-topped table our life together was already beginning to seem a thing of the past. The longer I managed to drag out the present moment, the longer, I thought, would the memory survive. But perhaps I was waiting for a miracle. A miracle which could happen only so long as we had not parted. My speech ran in circles; my sentences were without stops; my eyes were seeking help, and I did not know what I was waiting for.

It had got dark outside. Across the lake, on the southern bank, the little steamer station was lit up. Like a shining pearl dropping out of a string of pearls the steamer detached itself from the far shore. With a loud splash of her paddle-wheels the *Kaiserin Elisabeth* was approaching the minute harbor of St. Wolfgang.

"My boat," I said.

Nora nodded.

We walked across to the landing stage.

"When are you leaving?" I asked.

"First thing in the morning."

"I'll send my address to the people here," I said. "Because of my things."

"Yes," she said. "Everything will be seen to for us. I shan't dare return here." And after a little pause. "Don't try to see me, George. Will you promise?"

"I don't want to lie any more," I said. "I just don't know."

"I know you'll be generous," she said.

Generous. I don't know why this word should have gripped me with such irresistible force. I took her in my arms. Our lips did not let go of each other.

The tinkling of a little bell announced the ship's arrival.

Nora once more stroked my hair; then she freed herself from my embrace.

Quickly I walked down to the baggage shed and had my cases put aboard.

When I returned Nora had gone.

And as I am putting these lines down I have before me her

photographs: a childhood picture; a snap taken behind our house; two pictures at a picnic; a passport photo; the newspaper cutting of Gunnar Güldendag's funeral.

Shall I still be generous once this book is finished . . . ?

29

The Hospitable Widow, the Professor, and 173 Prostitutes

THAT MEN who have been ruined by alcohol, or rather, by its excessive consumption, still seek in it consolation and oblivion may be paradoxical, but nobody would claim that it was at all unusual or incredible. No less paradoxical, and yet perfectly understandable, was the fact that after my parting with Nora I immediately hurled myself into the very activity through which I had lost her. I say understandable, not only because my last inhibitions had vanished, but because I called out to Fate, resentfully: You could have shielded me, but you failed to do so—and now, anything that happens will be your fault!

If Gunnar Güldendag had not come back from the dead to rob me of the only person around whom my weak will could twine, like a young plant round a stake, I should have put my good resolution into effect in spite of all obstacles. Or if I had known Johnny at the time Nora left me, I might have started on this book then. But things were so arranged by Time that, after Nora's departure, I had no other anchor left than the secret services and that I was looking in vain for a haven until, on my second visit to Korea, I met Richard Grant, Johnny's father.

I realize that the reader will regard my account of events between 1950 and 1953 as frivolous: for what I did during those years was indeed a relapse into my worst period, made even worse by the circumstance that I no longer needed the proceeds of my imposture and espionage. But then, I never claimed that a man could change fundamentally in his forties. In fact, my relapse may well have been nothing else but a natural reversion to my proper self. The pain which I felt after Nora's departure—and which has not gone even today, but on the contrary wells up ever afresh with elemental force—was tempered, I must confess it, with a certain sense of relief. Although people improve now and again, they are not invariably happy over their improvement. And what may therefore strike the reader of the next few pages as frivolousness was, to a large extent, bitterness. Looking at myself in the mirror I could say with bitter joy: a revolting face, but my own.

By discharging my mission in Korea I had earned from my American employers a certain period of grace, a kind of spy's holiday, and could have rested on my laurels for some time. The greater was the joy in Vienna when, to everybody's surprise, I reported there for new orders. The man who had succeeded to the post of my late mentor may have felt instinctively that for the first time in my career I was ready to tackle my new assignments with a kind of unselfish ambition, that I was no longer out to make the most money in the shortest possible time, but that I was willing to put zeal and hard work into my effort.

The new American Intelligence chief in Vienna was a delightful man. I got on with him splendidly from the first day of our acquaintance, largely because he displayed a cynicism beside which my own cynicism was the purest idealism. He insisted on having his cynicism recognized as a general philosophy, and, what is more, as a moral philosophy, on the grounds that mankind consisted of cynics on the one hand and of hypocrites on the other. "The cynic," he said to me once, "boasts of opinions which others conceal but, nevertheless, hold." He was a pleasant person to work with because he made no secret of his views and would frequently give me such instructions as: "Stay away as long as possible, or else Washington might get the idea that your assignment was easy," or "Better describe the situation a little more elaborately— otherwise even a layman might grasp it," or "How are we to get Congress to O.K. our expenditure if your own expense account is so modest?"

Don Luckner, as my new boss was called, was a man of dusky, almost Latin-American appearance. He had small piercing eyes, whose pupils had a way of hiding; a small moustache challengingly twirled upward at the ends; and a rather unusual hairstyle, in that his parting started over his right eye and thence described a perfect three-quarter circle around his head, ending up over the other eye. It thus seemed to carve out a slice of his scalp, not unlike the lid of an inkwell or of a German pipe-bowl. He was a short man and believed that sticking out his chest boastfully and pulling his shoulders back would make him seem taller. Altogether he wore a rather arrogant expression, as if to say: "I could take your wife away from you any day"—a circumstance which made him unpopular with most men but did not worry me.

The first task that Don Luckner gave me was not at all to my liking.

At about that time Zürich, whose foreign currency and stock exchanges have long enjoyed a high international reputation, had also become the center of a "news exchange," a regular news market where the agents of East and West exchanged their information. There was, of course, nothing to be spied out in the friendly little petty-bourgeois city of Zürich—except, perhaps, the truly admirable and enviable secrets of the Swiss cheese and chocolate manufacturers. The reason why this lake-side town had become an espionage center was simply that neutral Switzerland could be entered without great difficulty, not only by British, Americans, Frenchmen, and other Western nationals, but also by East European business representatives, or those pretending to be just that. Western agents found it comparatively easy to meet their Eastern opposite numbers here, and vice versa. They could place their orders here and clinch their deals in complete comfort. I am using these commercial terms deliberately, and am presently going to explain why.

The term "news exchange," which I have just used, is to be taken quite literally, even though the curious tourist might search his Baedeker in vain for its premises. When I arrived in Zürich the news exchange was established in the hospitable house of a certain Frau Übekleber, in one of those solid villas on the Dolderberg which is well known for its rack railway, its golf course, and its well-run hotels. I shall discuss the hospitable and good-natured lady in a moment; all I need to say now is that two or three times a week Eastern and Western agents, their identity openly declared, used to meet in her living-room over a cup of coffee and there discuss their business deals in the most correct and harmonious manner. The layman may think that there is a certain logic in those spy stories in which hostile agents are for ever trying to outwit, outsmart, and outstrip one another in the most subtle way, whereas an honest exchange of information, such as took place in Frau Übekleber's living-room, is utterly pointless and senseless. That would indeed be the case if the agents represented their Governments—which, of course, could keep each other informed in far simpler ways if they really wanted to. But the agents do not represent their Governments: they merely represent their services. Say, for example, the Soviet secret service is instructed by its Government to obtain a detailed illustration of the first N.A.T.O. rifle manufactured in Belgium, as for some reason or other the Soviet General Staff is urgently interested in this weapon. The Chief of Soviet Intelligence thereupon passes the instruction on to one of his Swiss agents, say a Herr Güggeli; at the same time he tells Herr Güggeli to be sure to inquire politely what the Belgian agent, who is going to supply the picture of the N.A.T.O. rifle, would wish to have in return. In Frau Übekleber's drawing-room the Belgian agent accepts the order; a few days later he informs his Soviet colleague that the Belgians would be grateful for a map of Soviet air bases around the Rumanian oilfields. No doubt the reader has by now tumbled to the crux of the matter. The Chief of Soviet Intelligence is interested in one thing only: to earn the pleasure of his General Staff by the quickest possible delivery of the desired N.A.T.O. weapon. And in fact the Chief of Staff is absolutely delighted when, often within a matter of days, the "ordered" illustration is put on his desk. Naturally, he does not suspect that the Soviet secret service has handed over in return a map of Soviet airfields around Ploesti. Similarly, the Belgian General Staff has no idea how its secret service has managed to pull off that sensational *coup* of lifting the Rumanian map. And even if it were to turn out one day that the Russians are informed about the N.A.T.O. rifle no one would dream of connecting the two facts. In short, the secret services are the only business enterprises which enter only their takings but not their expenses; consequently, no matter how stupidly or criminally they run their affairs, they are bound to finish up with a favorable balance sheet. A news exchange is therefore a perfectly logical and—for the secret services, if not for the nations—a highly profitable institution.

What worried the American secret service at the time was the stubborn neutrality of Frau Übekleber. Frau Johanna Übekleber, to whom I was introduced, though not of course by accident, at an American Embassy reception in Berne, was a corpulent lady at the change of life, buxom, with an overbrimming crown of hair above an unlined forehead—a woman bound to arouse in any man the most comfortable filial feelings. Frau Johanna Übekleber was about fifty, and had been a widow for the past twenty years. She came of a well-to-do family, though not exactly rich; she was childless and of such impeccable reputation that even the small-town gossip had never as much as touched her. But whereas the hosts or hostesses of espionage exchanges, both paid and unpaid, usually belong to one side or the other, or even operate their establishments at their direct behest, Frau Übekleber was an enthusiastic and absolutely disinterested amateur hostess, who simply delighted in the thriving espionage business around her as other women do in cookery recipes, lovers, fashion journals, or visits to the movies. Her husband, who had lost his life in a tragic accident, had once been a member of the extremely active Swiss Intelligence—and upon closer acquaintance with the widow I came to the conclusion that one of her chief motives in putting her spacious house, with its fine view of the fair city of Zürich, at the disposal of the news exchange was a sense of loyalty to her late husband. In this loyalty for her dear departed, whom the Lord had taken unto Him after a short marriage two decades ago, Frau Johanna went to what seemed to me rather excessive lengths also in other respects: the house was a veritable museum of photographs, paintings, pipes, tobacco barrels, and various articles of daily use connected with the late lamented Johannes Übekleber, so that the Russian, British, American, and Hungarian spies, who had the freedom of the place, were reminded of the gentleman at every step.

My mission was not by any means to participate in the activities in Frau Johanna's living-room—I was too important a person by then to be given such a menial task—but to gain the neutral widow firmly for the West. Seen against the general background of the parlor game played by the secret services the idea—no matter who its author was in U.S. Intelligence—did not lack a certain originality. True enough, the Americans had always in the past been able to find out what their Soviet business contacts were interested in—but now they also wanted to know what happened, say, between a French purchaser and a Hungarian vendor, or between a British vendor and a Yugoslav purchaser. Moreover, as is usual in the secret services, the Americans did not entirely trust their own people and would therefore have liked to be able to keep an eye on them and to see them and hear them in action. In short, I was to persuade the widow Johanna to arrange for microphones and recording gear to be installed in her house, and for those mirrors to be built in through which a man can look from the back, as through a plain windowpane, while from the front they look like ordinary mirrors.

I might almost save myself the trouble of relating how I discharged my mission—for my purpose in recounting this Zürich episode was to illustrate the institution of the news exchange, rather than boast of my modest successes. I have subsequently had occasion to study similar news exchanges in a Lisbon café, in the airport restaurant at Casablanca, and in an elegant ladies' fashion salon in Rome—yet the conclusion of my little Zürich adventure seems to me to be amusing enough to merit at least a brief outline.

I took a suite at the luxurious Grand Hotel Dolder, which was only a few minutes' walk away from Frau Johanna's villa. A few days after I had made the lady's acquaintance at the Berne Embassy and engaged her in the most polite conversation there, I paid a courtesy call on her and invited her to lunch in the ostentatious dining-room of my hotel, with its grand view of the golf course. Although I was determined to reveal myself sooner or later to the good lady as an emissary of the Americans—for only professional spies regard their fellow-beings as stupid enough to agree to the installation of secret microphones without a declaration of their real business—I described myself for the moment as a journalist and author of travel books. Both these occupations, I allowed it to be understood, I practiced principally for pleasure, since a not inconsiderable annuity enabled me to lead a carefree existence. It did not take me long to discover that Frau Johanna was greatly in need of love, for her devoted widowhood had been quite unduly protracted; besides, she was for ever in contact with men, many of whom were attractive, but all of whom were apt to confuse her maternal appearance with an early resignation. Nothing could be further from me than to commit such an error. If I were to write a handbook of conquest—and perhaps I am not entirely unqualified for the job—I should put down as the first rule that, in order to achieve success with women, as well as with men, it is imperative to praise them for the very virtues which they possess the least. Instead of, as other agents did, getting myself invited for Frau Johanna's excellent pancakes—which, admittedly, were of surpassing excellence—and instead of resting my care-worn head in her maternal lap, I eschewed both the culinary delights of her table and her wise and well-meaning counsel. Instead, I took her out to Zürich's restaurants, bars and nightclubs, which she had never been to before, I complimented her on the exquisite taste of her petty-bourgeois clothes, and if I laid my head in her lap it was not in the mood of a weary penitent.

Need I say that after barely a fortnight's acquaintance I could reveal my identity to Frau Johanna without danger, and put to her the plan of American Intelligence.

Without danger, certainly—but not without any immediate success. The Swiss do not take their neutrality lightly: they imbibe it with their mother's milk and, still impartial, they are lowered into their graves. The agents of East and West, Johanna maintained, were perfectly welcome to fight out their prettiest duels in her living-room—but she herself had no intention of joining the one side or the other. Wearing a long diaphanous negligee of charmingly old-fashioned cut and combing her long light-brown hair in front of her bedroom mirror—there was even a pair of black curling tongs, complete with collapsible spirit burner, on her very feminine dressing table—she told me that my employers' proposal was not all that original. As a matter of fact, the Soviet secret service had approached her with exactly the same plan a few months before. Frau Johanna's disclosure seemed to favor my purpose and I immediately rose to the occasion. Neutrality, I remarked, was susceptible to more than one interpretation: either in the sense that one did not supply arms to any belligerent country, or in the sense that one supplied arms in fair shares to both sides. Why not, I suggested to Johanna, take up that Russian offer and allow both the Soviet and the American secret services to listen in to all conversations passing between agents at her house on the Dolderberg? Johanna, surprised at my generosity, stopped combing her tresses and turned to face me, who was stretched out in the most informal position: did I really believe, she asked, that such an arrangement would represent a neutral solution? Absolutely, I declared; moreover, there would be other advantages in my plan: "Frequently, Johanna, you don't know yourself what goes on in your living-room. Whereas like this we would be able"—I included myself—"to keep an occasional eye on your guests and make sure they aren't plotting anything against your own country." This argument eventually convinced Johanna. She glanced up at the oval oil painting of her late husband, Johannes Übekleber, evidently to make sure of his approval, and having received the dear departed's silent consent she declared herself willing to fall in with my scheme.

Merely for the sake of completeness I might add that on the same day I got American Intelligence, or rather, its branch in Zürich, to pay me a nice round sum in Swiss francs as a fee for Frau Johanna Übekleber—since it was, after all, none of their business that my neutral lady friend was acting out of passion and for no reward. And as for the American taxpayer, the little contribution he was making towards my new house and a few personal needs cannot have burdened him unduly. I returned to Vienna in that carefree frame of mind that springs from a clear conscience: by enabling both Russians and Americans to supervise the Zürich news exchange I believed myself to have done a real service to the praiseworthy principle of Swiss neutrality.

My next mission of any importance—or more correctly, the next one that was sufficiently different to merit inclusion in this account—I performed on behalf of the Russians, who had got in touch with me again on the occasion of a private visit to Paris. I do not know to what extent they were informed of my work for the Americans, but I hardly think that they can have been entirely ignorant of the prominent position I had been holding in U.S. Intelligence. This is not to say that it is a matter of complete indifference to the secret services whether they are dealing with a reliable exclusive agent or with a double spy—but agents above a certain standard are about as rare as really outstanding representatives of any other profession. A car manufacturer, for instance, would rather make an exclusive contract with an outstanding constructor and thus own him body and soul; but if he cannot get him on those terms he will content himself, *faute de mieux,* with a short-term arrangement and accept the fact that one day his man may drift over to some other firm. This sort of agreement, needless to say, presupposes that the motor manufacturers between whose firms the brilliant man oscillates should be convinced of his moral qualities; they must feel confident that he is not going to betray their production secrets. Just as the industrialists must be sufficiently sure of their specialists' morality, the espionage firms must be sure of their immorality. In my case, for instance, they knew that I was not actuated by any patriotic or ideological motives, and that I would therefore work just as conscientiously for the fine firm as for the other. At the same time they realized that I would not risk my good reputation and my career by betraying their trust.

Before dealing with the case of Professor Spencer Sheridan, the British atomic scientist, I should like to point out in my favor that I had declined several previous offers by the Soviet secret service. During the past few decades the secret services have, most regrettably, been going to the dogs. In what are, quite rightly, called the good old days the tasks of the secret services were usually confined to discovering the opponent's intentions, plans, and position, while preventing him at the same time from peering into one's own cooking pots. The game of the secret services then was as different from their work today as a Florentine rapier duel is from an American boxing match. To throw enemy agents on to the rails from moving trains; to penetrate into

Embassies at the point of a gun; to kidnap diplomats and scientists and carry them off, gagged, across the frontiers; to blow up dangerous opponents by means of infernal machines—these were tasks which even the secret services of the Austro-Hungarian Monarchy or the British Empire, both of them renowned for their ruthlessness, would have indignantly refused. Secret service and secret police used to be two utterly different things: the spy was a scout, not a murderer; the agent was a detective, but not a terrorist. During the past few decades, however, the division between secret service and secret police has tended to become blurred, and I was not therefore surprised when Soviet Intelligence in Paris proposed that I should take part in all sorts of violent actions. I was not surprised, but I firmly refused—on the grounds that, while not disputing the part which murderers, burglars, and thieves had to play in our society, I had myself been born a swordsman, not a wrestler.

Just then—in the spring of 1952—a congress of atomic scientists was held in Paris. It was scheduled to last four weeks and one of the participants was to be Professor Sheridan. The Soviet secret service, I was told, had conclusive evidence that this scientist, a man of about fifty, had an illicit fondness for his own sex and, more particularly, showed that affection toward young men which had proved the downfall of Socrates before him. The Eastern secret service had hatched the diabolical plan of luring the atom scientist, in whose knowledge of secret formulas and new theories they were particularly interested, into a trap from which they would release him only on condition that he was prepared to undertake the leap, or rather the flight, across the border posts. It is a sad fact that the secrets of the third and last world war—that scientific war directed at mankind in its entirety and ultimately designed to disintegrate our planet into those very atoms from which the new science derives its name—it is, as I say, a sad fact that these secrets are no longer found on paper but only in the brains of a few geniuses. It is therefore no longer sufficient to capture one document or another: the brains themselves must be caught and carried off.

The scheme for blackmail—for any other name would be a euphemism—was intended to operate like this. Together with a youth of eighteen, whom the secret service had placed at my disposal in the role of my son, I was to put up at the same hotel as the scientist. I was to engineer an encounter between Jean—that was the beautiful boy's name—and the professor; I was to make it possible, unobtrusively, for the scientist to become friendly with Jean, to meet him in secret and to seduce him. I was then to catch Sheridan and Jean red-handed—if one may call it that—and to present him with irrefutable evidence of his aberrations. Eventually, as the only alternative to scandal, ruin of his career, and possibly imprisonment, I was to offer to the distinguished scientist and family man—for he was that, too—a removal to the laboratories of the Russian capital.

I took rooms for myself and Jean at the Hotel Lutetia, a middle-class hotel of excessive dimensions on the left bank of the Seine, where Professor Sheridan was also staying. I registered as Charles Duettiweiler, secondary schoolmaster from Strasbourg, and entered Jean—the secret service had supplied us with false papers—as my son.

Before relating the events which began to unroll immediately upon our arrival I had better describe the two leading characters—the professor and my putative son.

Spencer Sheridan was a man of medium height, of cheese-like skin color, a delicately built frame, and what I would call an opaque face—opaque because the gray-haired man with the rimless spectacles would never have caught anybody's attention although, on closer inspection, his features were of exceptional beauty. His eyes were large, exactly nut-shaped, and—as on Greek sculptures of young men—very widely spaced. His nose formed a rectangular triangle, almost as if drawn with a ruler; and his rather too red lips were drawn with slightly excessive precision, as if by an art student instructed to draw a Greek mouth. In spite of this, Spencer Sheridan was ugly rather than beautiful: his numerous wrinkles looked even more out of place than usual in his young man's face, and about his mouth there hovered a perpetual expression of self-pity. Only on the rarest occasions was it possible, when talking to him, to catch a glance from his ever restless and flickering eyes.

My son, the intended prey of the professor, was a beautiful

youth of quite exceptional revoltingness. Tall and of athletic build, he had the pearl-white skin of a pampered girl. He had silky black hair and very small black eyes, the sensuous mouth of a painted dockside whore and a low, almost moronic, forehead. His general appearance was belied by his broad and brutal hands, ending in short fingers whose almost square nails no amount of expert manicuring could rob of their vulgar appearance. Jean was the son of the poor widow of a civil servant from Strasbourg; he had spent several years at a reform school because of persistent theft and had then been apprenticed to a motor mechanic, where Soviet Intelligence had picked him out. I need hardly say that Jean was anything but homosexually inclined: what pocket money he received from Intelligence he promptly spent on the prostitutes on Montparnasse. He was, as he told me himself, on the look-out for a rich elderly lady who would keep him; he hated the men with whom the secret service compelled him to associate, and his main idea was to acquire enough money to buy a white Jaguar. In his intense greed for money Jean did not stop at anything: on the second day of our association I caught him attempting to relieve my wallet of a few dollar bills. Whether it was my healthy instinct or my dislike of the youth—instead of simply taking the wallet from him or giving him a fatherly talking to about the inadmissibility of his action, I simply gave him two thundering slaps on the ear. These the young man received without protest, and henceforward our relations were much easier.

It was no accident that the Soviet secret service had chosen young Jean Duettiweiler as a decoy for the British scientist. The Information of Soviet Intelligence was so impressively detailed that they were familiar not only with Sheridan's homosexual leanings but also with the particular type of his perversion: the scientist was not just one of those relatively uncomplicated homosexuals who desire a like-minded partner, but he required for his satisfaction innocent—that is, normally inclined—young men.

I button-holed the scientist in the lounge of our hotel on the evening after the inauguration of the congress, at the first public session of which he had delivered a brilliant, though to me only partially intelligible, lecture. My son, I explained, had just completed his grammar school education and intended to take up science: as other young people adored vain film stars and ridiculous adventurers he had an admiration for all scientists, and for Professor Sheridan in particular. The professor would gratify the bashful boy's most ardent wish if he would graciously say a word or two to him or perhaps even honor him with his autograph.

The transformation which the professor underwent within less than five minutes convinced me of the reliability of the Eastern secret service's information. Though the professor at first answered me in an unfriendly and almost surly tone, muttering something about humbug and nonsense, his attitude changed completely the moment Jean joined us. There was no mention of humbug or nonsense then; indeed it was almost as if the young man were bestowing a favor on the scientist by holding out his autograph album to him. Suddenly the professor showed himself interested in me also and even addressed me, somewhat exaggeratedly, as *"cher confrère"* when I told him that I taught history and geography at a boys' grammar school.

If the Sheridan affair had simply ended in the way the reader expects and, if he has nice feelings, fears—my own sense of decency would stop me from recording it here in all its, no doubt revolting, detail. But nothing of the sort is going to shock the sensitive reader, for the typical thing about my story is that, while the secret services are invariably well informed about a man's most intimate key-hole secrets, a key-hole never reveals more than a small fraction of a room.

The professor, my son Jean, and I became inseparable. It was the beginning of June—the best time of the year for Paris, even though the writers of lyrics are apt to ascribe this epithet to April, which is usually cold and wet. In the Bois de Boulogne the chestnuts had been transformed into a green ballroom lit by brilliant chandeliers; the city's natural perfume mingled with that of her pretty young women in summer dresses; fragrant wine was drunk in the evenings under the trees of the Pavilon d'Ermenonville, and at the blue hour the sky turned pink above the Arc de Triomphe. Professor Sheridan spent every minute he could spare from his congress duties in our company. He sat with us outside the café at the turbulent Rond Point in the Champs Elysées; he showed Jean the impressionists at the new pavillion of the Louvre; he hired a car for a weekend to take us round the Loire castles; and he proved an exceptional connoisseur of those Paris bistros where genial *patrons* fleece their customers in the most exquisite way.

About a week had passed when I made the remarkable discovery which was to dispense with the need to blackmail the sick man. That evening Jean had gone up to his room shortly after supper—or rather, he had pretended to go up to his room. Since he was fond of bragging I knew very well that, tired of our company, he had slipped out of the hotel to attend a strip-tease revue in the Montmartre district and subsequently to amuse himself at one of the illegal brothels. The professor and I decided to split another bottle of wine. The night was sultry. We were sitting in shirt-sleeves on the balcony of his room, above the gradually quietening Boulevard Raspail. Instead of one bottle we emptied two, and presently our conversation drifted to ideological topics.

Imagine my surprise when I discovered that Professor Sheridan was by no means satisfied with his position in London, the working conditions in his laboratory, or the scientific facilities available to him. The authorities, he said, were endowing his institution with quite inadequate funds; they were narrow-minded and totally lacking in understanding—in fact, he suspected them of deliberately sabotaging his efforts. Like many intellectuals, and specialists in particular, Sheridan seemed to wear blinkers. His horizon —I had noticed this repeatedly since making his acquaintance —was bounded by his own research, and this limitation was possibly emphasized by his pathological disposition. From an unloved wife, with whom he had contracted a marriage of convenience in his youth, he was escaping into the realm of calculations. Very soon he turned to political questions: he used the term "fascist" in the slipshod manner of intellectuals who lack intellectual tolerance; he claimed that the West was preparing for war—and he generally revealed himself as a man so thoroughly disgruntled by the unpleasantnesses of the world he lived in as to be blinded to the same unpleasantnesses in another world. In the end he openly praised the superior methods of Soviet science and repeated propaganda slogans which have long since ceased to impress less erudite but better informed men. I spoke little that evening: I confined myself to lending an attentive ear to the professor's naïve anger. But when I said good night to him long after midnight a plan, vague at first, had begun to take shape in me.

Professor Spencer Sheridan's flight from Paris via Stockholm and Helsinki to Moscow has stirred up so much dust that I need hardly go into its details. It was I who carefully engineered this flight by submitting to the professor—a week after our first intimate conversation and on the very day that the atomic conference was due to break up—a tempting offer from the Soviets, without of course disclosing that Soviet Intelligence had not originally authorized me to make such an offer but had instead equipped me with a camera designed to apprehend the distinguished scientist in a compromising situation with my dear son. In other words, the much-vaunted Soviet secret service, which was credited with the professor's miraculous abduction from Paris, knew after many years' careful observation of the nuclear physicist that he was likely to fall for a handsome boy of Jean Duettiweiler's type, but never suspected that this elaborate sexual research and scheming were quite unnecessary since Dr. Sheridan was only too ready to accept the very first air passage to Moscow that was offered him. It seems doubtful to me today whether the professor would in fact have yielded to the youth's irresistible charms to a point worth photographing, or whether he would have been such an easy man to blackmail as the secret-service brains had worked out. But I can state positively that the "abduction" of the scientist had not in any way been a triumph of the Soviet secret service, much though it was praised for it by the Soviet Government and angrily cursed by the West. For the sake of interest I may add that my "son" Jean was no doubt charged with several similar assignments during the next few years, for I read only recently in a Spanish paper that in a white Jaguar he took part in some road race near Madrid, failed to negotiate a hairpin bend with the required skill, and was recovered in an unrecognizable condition from the wreckage of his car.

Before coming to the final chapters of my account I should like to relate an episode which took place in Africa and which seems to me no less significant than my assignments in Zürich and Paris.

Towards the end of 1952 I was again summoned to Washington and entrusted there with a task which, I must admit, greatly flattered my masculine vanity. I was received by a young Air Force Intelligence general who, with many winks and much back-slapping, called me in turn a Don Juan and a Casanova—from which I gathered that my modest successes with Maud Leoni, alias Grete Prochaska, had not yet been entirely forgotten. I was rather pleased with these epithets, for, much as the two ladies' men differed from one another, it was obvious to me that I was to be employed on that most congenial sector of Intelligence work, the erotic sector.

I was proved right. The Americans, with French approval, had just set up their air bases throughout French North Africa—in Tunisia, Algeria, and Morocco—and their strategic importance could hardly be overestimated. The American strategists did not deceive themselves that, in the event of war, the Russians, sweeping from the East across their so-called satellites into Germany and France, would very soon reach the Atlantic coast. On the other hand, the Soviets were probably aware that it would hardly be possible to supply their troops over their interminably extended lines of communication as long as the West was in a position to bomb the Red Army's supply lines from bases in North Africa. Possession of the North African air bases, whose loss in the Second World War had sealed the German defeat, meant all the more to the Americans, as all General Staffs are known to be in the habit of re-fighting and re-winning past wars instead of making suitable preparations for the next. And it was in this vital North African "theater"—strategists always feel very important when they talk about "theaters"—that a certain Madame or Mademoiselle Lemaitre was giving the Americans a big headache.

Tens of thousands of American officers and enlisted men, flying personnel and ground staff, were stationed at the time at the various air bases in North Africa; Air Force engineers were moreover busy building new airfields. The Americans had been wise enough to permit their married troops to take their wives to Africa with them; appropriate numbers of service-women had likewise been posted to such places as Algiers, Philippeville, Constantine, Bône, and Bizerta to meet not so much strategic as other, equally pressing, needs—all in vain. Officers and enlisted men were increasingly falling victim to the members of what my Intelligence general termed "an immoral organization," of which the above-mentioned Denise Lemaitre was in charge. Smiling, the general assured me that he did not propose to send me to Africa in the role of a Watch Committee member; the fact was that there was no doubt that Madame or Mademoiselle Lemaitre was acting on behalf of the Russians. According to information so far collected by Intelligence Madame disposed of an army of about two hundred girls of easy virtue, who hung about the air bases, and of whom many were already living in quasi-matrimonial association with the American servicemen. In reply to my question whether Denise Lemaitre was not perhaps just a very efficient "madam," a brothel-keeper, or, at worst, a white-slave trader, the general handed me a file which disarmed even my skepticism. It contained depositions by no fewer than ninety-one officers and other ranks, testifying that sooner or later they had been questioned by the ladies of the "organization Denise" about various military secrets, such as new airfields, types of aircraft, number of machines, numbers and movements of personnel, the state of their morale, etc. My job, amusing, perhaps, but not so simple, would be to pick out, from among the thousands of prostitutes around the air bases, the girls of the Maison Denise, or, better still, capture the card index of this erotic army of the Soviet secret service. In addition, I would have to collect such evidence about its connection with the East as would at long last induce the French—"they've got such a weakness for prostitutes"—to take energetic counter-measures. With more heavy winks and backslaps the general advised me to make straight for Madame or Mademoiselle Lemaitre, since the approach by way of the lower ranks of this female espionage corps would prove too time-wasting and, even for a "great lover," too exhausting.

My memoirs would have failed in their purpose if I could still fool the reader the way Denise Lemaitre was fooling U.S. Air Force Intelligence.

Even before my aircraft landed at Algiers it was obvious to me that it could not be the Russians who were behind Madame

Lemaitre's prostitutes. No matter how greatly the Russians were interested in the U.S. air bases in North Africa, it was unthinkable that they should have succeeded in enlisting two hundred French girls—for they were French, not Arab, girls—and trained them, however superficially, for their task in such a very short time. Another point that made me suspicious was the fact that, judging by the secret file, the French authorities had arrested a few of the girls but had invariably let them off again after a thorough interrogation. Before introducing myself to Denise Lemaitre I therefore got in touch with the chief of U.S. Intelligence in Algiers, an ex-cavalry officer, and asked him to what extent the French were informed about the American bases in North Africa. Once the colonel had assured me that it was no business of the French what their allies were doing on African soil and that, in any case, one could not possibly take them into one's confidence since "what you tell those French today the Russians know tomorrow," especially as "the Deuxième Bureau is nothing but a pack of amateurs and Bolsheviks," I had not the least doubt that Madame or Mademoiselle Lemaitre had raised her seductive organization on behalf of that very Deuxième Bureau. I also realized why Washington was on the wrong track: the secret services are invariably mesmerized by their opposing secret services, whom they will credit with the most spectacular feats, while they regard the secret services of their allies, with whom they are in direct competition, as either criminal or moronic.

I need hardly have left Washington to discharge my mission —certainly a few days in North Africa would have been enough to accomplish it successfully. If I nevertheless stayed for more than five months, then this was chiefly because the reading public's idea of so-called "madams" is utterly and completely wrong.

I made Denise Lemaitre's acquaintance at a reception which I had organized in my own honor. What happened was that, through Intelligence, I had induced the U.S. Air Force to throw a cocktail party at the most elegant hotel in Algiers for Stephen Docker, Chief Construction Engineer of the U.S. Air Force, newly arrived from Washington in order to inspect airfield surveying. I was that man. An Air Force major, who was a friend of Denise's, had been authorized, or indeed tactfully encouraged, to invite her as well as some of her women friends. The rest, I thought, would work itself out.

Denise Lemaitre, the daughter of a high French colonial official and an Arab princess, bore no resemblance whatever either to the businesslike Mrs. Warren or to Maupassant's immortal brothel-keepers. On the contrary, she was a young lady of no more than thirty, of excellent education—received allegedly from the Sisters of Sacré Coeur in Paris—and of a dark beauty in which East and West were most deliciously blended. By the time I met her I had found out a few facts about her past. In the Second World War she had fought in the army of the Free French general; she had taken part in the march across the desert and had then hurried to Paris to join the Resistance in order not to miss the liberation of the capital. She was one of those busy women who lack a healthy love life, not because they cannot find a man—I cannot imagine the man who could resist Denise Lemaitre's charms —but, on the contrary, because they are so convinced of their own superiority that, showered with proposals, they finally elect a nun-like existence. I did not think it fortuitous that Denise, unable to accept an unadventurous life after the war, should have created, of all things, the Organization Denise: she despised men so much that she confined them to the brothel.

In this respect, however, the beautiful woman was unlucky with me. Politely but unambiguously I divested myself of the two friends whom she had presented to me—and since these two ladies were no doubt the finest fillies in her stable there was now nothing left to the patriotic young lady—considering the importance of my person—but to lend a helping hand herself.

But since I detest boastful men I should like to make it clear here and now that I did not learn the whole secret of the Organization Denise among Denise's pillows and cushions, but that, on the contrary, it was through my discovery of her secret that I conquered the exacting and exotic Frenchwoman.

Denise lived alone in a palatial snow-white building in the desert behind Algiers—a house that used to belong to a now de-throned chieftain. It was about an hour's drive away from the city, in a southerly direction: first, one came to a dirty Arab village, and right in the middle of this mean settlement there rose, on the desert's edge, the fairy palace of this political brothel-keeper. The very fact that Denise dared to live here, with no other male protection than that of a few Arab servants, was typical of the proud nature of this externally so feminine, but in effect extremely masculine, young lady.

Twice or three times I had accepted Denise's invitations and dined with her in company, without either of us getting any nearer to our objectives. Now, the table in her tastefully furnished dining-room was laid for two.

"Madame," I said, as we sat down to dinner by candlelight, with the desert outside the window stretching away under the fiery red glow of the setting sun—"madame, I am most deeply appreciative of your invitation but I am also distressed to observe that you are rather depressed tonight."

With a hostess's politeness Denise tried to protest. But the espionage manageress with the big black eyes, the smooth black hair parted in the middle, the lily-white skin, and the enchanting minute mole on the right side of her nose was not a good liar.

"Madame," I continued, "have I your permission to guess at the reason for your depressed mood?"

Permission was granted.

"You see, Madame," I said, "you have been irritated for some time by the fact that I have not yet risen to the bait which has been cast with so much skill and care. Believe me, Madame, it is not the fault of the hard-working young ladies who are being dangled at the end of your line in front of my nose in the role of appetizing flies or succulent worms!"

I paused and drank my beautiful hostess's health. She motioned to the Arab servant. He closed the doors through which a hot wind blew into the room. At another sign from his mistress he withdrew just as silently as hitherto he had been ministering to our needs.

"The simple fact, Madame," I continued, "is that I am fully informed about your Operation Denise. It would therefore have been unfair to swallow the flies and the little worms without also swallowing the hook. However, this is meant by way of assurance, for I have likewise no intention of putting the beautiful fisher-woman to any trouble herself."

"Will you explain yourself, Monsieur?" said Denise, her white skin turning, if possible, even paler.

In full detail and with complete frankness I unfolded to my hostess the reasons which had brought me to North Africa and the conclusions at which I had arrived.

"Nothing would be gained," I said, "if now I simply did my duty and passed on to Washington the information which I have —convincingly, I hope—laid before you. Washington would make diplomatic representations in Paris: it would describe spying on a friend and ally—for that's what it is—as a gross impropriety, and Paris would have no other choice than to close down and seal up your far-flung erotic institution, just as it has closed down similar, though politically and militarily less important, establishments back home. At the same time my mission, which I am beginning to like more and more,"—I gazed into the darkening eyes of my hostess—"would suffer an unnecessarily premature end. Besides, it would not be opportune for me—and as a shrewd colleague you'll understand my point—to enlighten the American secret service that the Soviet secret service is not everything it is cracked up to be by those of us who want to justify our expenditure and inflate our importance. On the other hand, you must understand that I cannot risk my reputation by permitting you to fool us—I mean the Americans—any longer. No, please don't say anything yet, Madame—I understand you perfectly. Your French compatriots want to know what's going on in their own territory, and your organization is therefore absolutely justified. But let me make you a proposal!" I gazed out through the tall arched windows to the sea of sand that was gradually being swallowed up by darkness. "I shall report to Washington that I have succeeded in discovering how and by whom your organization is being financed and that I am about to cut off the wicked Russians' financial pipeline. You, on the other hand, in recognition of my tactful procedure, will gradually liquidate your organization, step by step, in such a way that you withdraw a few of your charming agents from sexual circulation each day, until your business is eventually wound up. In the meantime, we two shall try to amuse ourselves as well as this desert region permits—needless to say, at the expense of a generous secret service. I shall return to Washington in triumph, as the man who has driven the Russians from the U.S. bases in North Africa, whereas you will no doubt turn to new and equally delightful assignments. Madame, you have no choice —unless, of course, you hurry up and sprinkle a little poison over this delicious lobster, but I think it impossible that you should demean yourself by resorting to such unimaginative methods."

With unparalleled grace, or rather with that typical grace of the French who know how to accept facts, Denise Lemaitre agreed to my proposal. I must repeat that I did not conquer her, as the young general supposed I would, because I was a man who broke women's hearts: indeed, until our conversation by the half-open window Denise Lemaitre had viewed me with reserve, if not with antipathy. Just as there are no seductive Mata Haris, so there are no agents who win their victories through erotic attraction. It is simply that in the espionage business, as in other fields where men and women live side by side, the awareness of defeat turns into love. This was particularly true of Denise Lemaitre, that proud woman who—I have never got rid of the suspicion—challenged a male world only to be defeated.

Denise was a charming, brilliant, and—as it now appeared—witty person. Thus, within a few nights of our professional relationship giving way to more intimate relations, she thought up a diverting game, which, though unfortunately not typical of secret-service work, nevertheless deserves being recorded here as a conclusion to this chapter.

Denise's organization—as she admitted to me and, upon my request, proved by documentary evidence—consisted of one hundred and seventy-three young ladies, partly professional prostitutes working for Intelligence and partly professional spies acting as prostitutes. The names and addresses of these volunteers, in code of course, as well as their photographs, were kept in a magnificent book bound in crimson leather. This book, and a red pencil, Denise now placed on her bedside table, informing me with a meaningful smile that it was entirely up to me how quickly the Organization Denise was wound up. Provided my amorous demonstrations were such as to convince Denise of the genuineness of my affection, one of the names on the list was crossed out and one photograph was torn into little pieces. One hundred and seventy-three photographs thus fluttered down on to the thick carpet from Denise's soft and low Oriental couch within five months and eleven days—sufficient testimony, surely, that American Intelligence did me wrong by calling me undutiful.

Thus ended my adventure in Algiers.

I wish I could entertain the reader a little longer with similar illustrations of my argument and—what matters to me more —give him useful instruction. But certain incidents which have occurred while I have been writing down these recollections urge me to make haste. It seems as if Gunnar Güldendag was not the only man to come back from the dead . . .

30

The Heel of Achilles

THE SUMMER OF 1953 saw the beginning of those events which finally decided me to leave the secret services for good, but not to keep silent about my experiences in them.

One hot August day I was rung up at my Vienna hotel by my immediate superior, Mr. Don Luckner, who asked me to see him at his house in the most elegant residential street of Hietzing. The fact that this was the first time that Mr. Luckner had invited me to his private home, as well as the exceptionally serious tone in which he had made the invitation, suggested that he wished to see me on an important, possibly a critical, matter.

Throughout dinner, at a table laid in plain bachelor style and served by a silent American, presumably an Intelligence corps private in civilian clothes, we discussed only trivial things. When we had drunk our coffee we withdrew at once to Mr. Luckner's study, an attractive though somewhat oppressive library. The house, as my host informed me, had formerly belonged to an author, who had been first arrested and subsequently deprived of his property because of National Socialist activities; clearly the former owner had read a lot of books, even though he had failed to derive any lasting benefit from them.

Mr. Luckner opened a bottle of champagne, which was all ready, poured out for both of us, and settled down behind his writing-desk. Although I noticed that he was sitting on a thick cushion in what was, in any case, a tall chair, nevertheless, behind that early-nineteenth-century piece of furniture he seemed like a child trying to look grown up at his father's desk.

The little boy with the middle-aged features and the inkwell parting in his hair twirled the ends of his mustache—not between thumb and forefinger, but rather preciously between thumb and little finger—and at last began to speak.

"Mr. Droste," he said, "I have asked you to see me on a business matter, but it is not always possible to keep a clear line between business and personal matters. You must therefore permit me to begin with a personal question. Some time ago you adopted a boy, then eleven years old, by the name of Johnny Grant. What was your purpose in doing so?"

I disliked the inquisitorial tone in which Mr. Luckner had uttered that last sentence. I disliked it very much.

"I don't know why I should answer your question," I answered, "since this is indeed a purely personal matter. At the same time I see no reason for concealing from you that I adopted him because I had greatly esteemed his father, who was a close friend of mine, and because I had got very fond of the boy. These are, admittedly, reasons whose very simplicity may strike you as suspicious —but I am not prepared to go out of my way to invent more elaborate ones, just so they should strike the Intelligence mind as more credible. It also seems to me that in order to adopt an orphan one need not necessarily have a 'purpose.' "

"You met Richard Grant in connection with your second mission to Korea?" asked Mr. Luckner, without reacting to my challenging tone.

"You are excellently informed, Mr. Luckner," I retorted acidly.

"Did you promise him to look after his son?"

Although increasingly annoyed by this interrogation I admitted this too.

"Did you know that Richard Grant would not come back?" the American inquired.

"I suspected it," I said.

"You're worrying me, my dear Droste," my boss said, shaking his head. "You're worrying me a lot. I believe," he continued in a paternal tone, "that we have always so far understood each other excellently—so I hope you'll forgive me a few frank words."

I signified my consent with a polite gesture.

"I am telling you no secret," said Don Luckner, "if I say that we have a very high regard for you—very high indeed. You have a great talent, you are an individualist, and as such you have allowed yourself—you know that better than anyone—many an escapade which would have been the downfall of anyone less gifted than you. Yet throughout your dealings with Intelligence you have shown yourself from, maybe, a capricious, an avaricious, and at times a cunning side, but only once from a sentimental one—you know what I'm alluding to. We thought that after Legation Counsellor Güldendag's surprising return you would be cured of your dangerous attack of sentimentality—for, believe me, it is dangerous—but unfortunately this does not now seem to be the case. You must admit that to adopt a boy, and what's more— the son of a man who'd been in our service, ill befits an agent and is hardly compatible with his personality, his profession, or his career."

"What you call attacks of sentimentality," I interrupted my host, "are convulsions of conscience—but I don't think they are bad for me. On the contrary. Afterwards I always feel a new man —prepared once more to do the most unscrupulous deeds."

"You don't like our profession, Mr. Droste?" Mr. Luckner asked in a tone of friendly interest.

"I detest it," I replied.

To my surprise the little man scrutinized me with a benevolent smile.

"And what are your reasons?" he asked.

"I am afraid," I replied, "that to list all my reasons would take the whole night and would needlessly bore you. Besides, they are of little importance since I have long reconciled myself to the fact that in order to act one doesn't need any convictions.

I would go even further. What distinguishes the professional from the amateur is the very fact that the amateur can act only from conviction, whereas the professional does not need conviction. As a result, the amateurs are all short-distance runners: once they've spent the breath of conviction they fall by the wayside. Only we, the professionals without conviction, have the long breath of marathon runners. Don't worry, Mr. Luckner: I am running on. My lungs don't need conviction."

"I wish you really were the cynic you are pretending to be," said Mr. Luckner. "The trouble with you, Droste, is that you are taking our profession so damned seriously. You actually believe in it, though in a negative way."

"How do you mean?" I asked.

"You believe quite seriously that the work of the secret services can affect the course of events either favorably or unfavorably. I wish I could convince you that the opposite is true: you would then be cured for ever of your convulsions of conscience. If, like me, you had spent practically all your life in the secret service, if, like me, you had studied the history of the secret services, you would realize that not a single war or even the smallest battle was ever decisively influenced by any secret service."

"We are at peace," I said. "At least we call it peace, though it might more fittingly be defined as the state between two wars."

"So you believe that the secret services contribute to the unleashing of wars," said Mr. Luckner. "I know that some distinguished people, such as our friend Greehahn, share this view —but believe me, the Greehahns are all mesmerized by their own importance. The history of the secret services is one long story of failure. Take the last war. The French had no idea of the strength of the Germans; the Germans, on the other hand, seriously believed that they could pounce on Poland without Britain or France intervening. German Intelligence after Dunkirk had no idea of the disastrous state of Britain's defenses; Soviet Intelligence refused to believe that a German attack was imminent; British Intelligence was caught unprepared by the V weapons, and U.S. Intelligence was caught unprepared by the officers' plot of July 20. The atom bomb on Hiroshima has finally buried the secret services. Just picture some new conflict breaking out somewhere in the world, say through some small country attacking another small country, or some colonial people staging a rising on an internationally important scale. Assume further that the American secret service reports that the Soviet Union does not intend to intervene, or vice versa suppose that the Soviet secret service reports that the U.S.A. intends to watch the conflict inactively. Do you really believe that in this atom-bomb age either of the two great Powers would decide upon action or refrain from planned intervention simply on the strength of such secret-service reports? We may get worried by some little war now and again; but a big war can start only if one of the Great Powers is certain that the other does not propose to intervene. But no Great Power would content itself with the 'certainty' offered it by its secret service. The risk has become too great. The one thing that is preventing an atomic war, my dear Droste, is the ignorance of Governments. And the ignorance of the secret services is most excellently conducive to that ignorance of the Governments. From which you may see that, no matter what you do, your pacifist conscience may rest unperturbed."

Mr. Luckner's attempt to pacify my conscience, though most unusual, did not reassure me at all, but on the contrary confirmed my first impression that the Intelligence chief must have summoned me to his house for some quite exceptional purpose. However, I had no intention of steering the conversation back to a concrete subject; indeed I was anxious to spin it out as long as possible. I said:

"You maintain, therefore, that the secret services are unnecessary and that one could get along just as well without them?"

"You and I," replied Mr. Luckner, "would find it difficult to get along just as well without them, seeing that they are keeping us in quite a generous manner. Otherwise I believe one could manage very well without them in time of peace; in wartime a limited number of agents and possibly a somewhat bigger number of Intelligence officers at the front should be quite sufficient. Just think for a moment. What is the purpose of a secret service? To find out the strength of the enemy? But this can be calculated without difficulty from his published official statistics. The capturing of secret weapons and other inventions? But the scientists can foresee the likely development more clearly than any spy. The discovery of the enemy's intentions? There is nothing an agent can find out that an intelligent politician could not have deduced long ago. The sabotage of enemy installations? On a big scale this has now been almost impossible for a long time. To persuade important individuals in the enemy camp to desert and change sides? Surely you don't believe that an agent can do what newspapers, books, and propaganda have been unable to achieve? To whip up rebellions and revolutions? But what a poor old-fashioned figure a secret agent is compared with the institution of radio! No, my dear Droste, you and I and our colleagues on this side of the fence and on the other don't have the slightest influence on the course of our planet's history—and it would be pointless, therefore, to let our work give us pangs of conscience."

"Listening to you, Mr. Luckner," I said, "one might think that the secret services are composed entirely of idiots. And I am not quite sure whether I prefer this impression to the one General Greehahn gave me—that they are composed of criminals."

Mr. Luckner bent over his desk. He looked more like a child than ever.

"The one doesn't exclude the other," he laughed. "Idiots or criminals—take your choice. Often, you'll find, it will depend merely on what post a man occupies in his secret service. On the other hand, to resume, it would be just as unrealistic to demand the abolition of the secret services as it is to dream of universal disarmament. This is like expecting a civil-service department to dissolve itself simply because it has become superfluous. The secret services, like the armed forces, have only one argument in favor of their necessity, but it is a powerful argument; namely, the continued existence of the secret services and the armed forces on the other side. What we've got to do is score conspicuous successes—seeming successes but conspicuous ones, the kind that will astound an ignorant public—for these alone can justify the money spent on our enemies' secret services which, in return, show their gratitude by similar spectacular successes. The secret services, my dear Droste, live not by the actual destruction of their opponents but by their opponents' apparent successes. For that reason the term 'secret service' has long become a cynical joke: the secret services all need their publicity managers. In our own interest we've got to advertise our successes, and we are therefore like film stars who wear dark glasses, not in order to hide their features, but to attract attention. The more thrills and horrors our advertisements send down the spines of a sensation-hungry though, at the same time, weak-kneed public, the better. Do you get me?"

I drained my glass of champagne.

"I not only get you, Mr. Luckner," I said, "but I shouldn't be a bit surprised if your conscience-assuaging remarks turned out to be the overture to an assignment that is particularly prone to bring on convulsions of conscience."

While I was talking I wondered whether I ought to confide my real anxieties to Mr. Luckner. My real anxieties, which had been present during our conversation like a silent third person, were centered on Johnny. Since the day when I went to Philadelphia to bring the boy the news of his father's death—his mother had lost her life, together with her second husband, in an accident a few weeks earlier—my life had again had some purpose. I had, probably unwittingly, followed Dr. Lu Wang's prescription by acting at first like a man of moral principles without being convinced of the sense of my action; later this sense had appeared of itself. I had been—as more naïve characters might put it—"rewarded," rewarded by the boy's sincere affection, rewarded by my preoccupation with an unspoiled future, rewarded by a child's gratitude. I had at last answered the question as to the purpose of my life. Why had Don Luckner opened our conversation with such detailed questions about Johnny? Wise or not—Mr. Luckner must be told that I regarded Johnny Grant as my own son.

"I want to tell you quite frankly," I said, "that your interest in my adopted son worries me a good deal more than the assignment you are about to give me. Would you mind very much telling me, first of all, the reasons for your interest—with that engaging frankness of yours?"

Mr. Luckner stood up and began to pace up and down—an action which I interpreted as a sign of genuine nervousness, since he seemed shorter standing up than sitting down. In the past he had always preferred to barricade himself behind a table.

"I only wish," he said, "I had heard about that adoption in

good time, so as to prevent it. The secret service had intended to take young Johnny Grant under its wing. You are aware"—his voice was suddenly measured and serious, as though he had never thought, let alone uttered, his cynically frank ideas of a few minutes ago—"you are aware that there are 'secret-service children' who, brought by special circumstances under State guardianship, are trained for an Intelligence career from an early age."

I jumped up.

"Never!" I shouted, realizing at the same moment that I had made a mistake in revealing my perturbation so clearly.

Don Luckner stopped in front of me, for once unconcerned by the embarrassing difference in our height.

"There you are," he said. "The adoption is a bad thing, not only because it has snatched Grant junior from right under our noses—and naturally the high-ups aren't too pleased about that—but also because you are evidently nursing very warm feelings towards him." He laid his hands on my shoulders, for which action he had to raise himself a little on tiptoe. There was no cynicism in his voice as he said: "Each one of us has a few vulnerable spots. Anybody entering the secret services, dear Droste, must carefully cover up his sore or vulnerable spots, his heel of Achilles, or whatever you wish to call it. On no account must he publicly display it. Now you, luckily furnished by nature with very few tender spots, almost in fact thick-skinned, you have now placed an arrow upon your own breast, an arrow which shows the exact spot where your heart is and where you can be most easily hit. That was an exceedingly unwise thing to do, Droste," he went on, releasing my shoulders and resuming his walk. "But don't be unduly worried. So long as I have anything to say no harm will come to your adopted son." Stopping at the far end of the room, he said: "Besides, why should you make things difficult for me, Droste? Let's come to the point!"

He sat down again behind his desk, and in a matter-of-fact and almost bureaucratic voice outlined to me the plan which finally convinced me that six years ago I had embarked upon the road of perdition.

31

Scientists of Hell

THE REASON why I did not think it necessary to explain what the assignment was which Don Luckner gave me on that August evening—or rather, which he passed on to me on orders from above—was mainly that events took such an entirely different course as to make it pointless to linger on the original instructions. And that in spite of the fact that for the first time I was working to such a precise timetable that the slightest deviation from the prescribed drill would have jeopardized the whole enterprise.

Unexpected events had considerably delayed my departure from Vienna, and it was during the first days of October that I arrived in London. Autumn had come to England early that year. Silvery wisps of fog flitted about the uncomfortable cross-Channel steamer like seagulls, and in London you could pick out the foreigners by the fact that, lacking the self-control which distinguishes the English, they were frankly shivering. I took a room under the name of Erich Matthäus at a small but respectable hotel in one of the turnings off the Strand, which lead down to the river. I had dinner at the hotel, among some youngish country gentlemen, a few families evidently in London to visit relations, and a number of permanent guests who looked like retired colonial officials. Without showing my face outside the hotel I went back up to my room and waited for eleven o'clock.

I drank a glass of Scotch—a drink which I normally dislike because of its taste of mothballs—and tried in vain to engross myself in the yachting magazine which I found on the table in my old-fashioned and old-maidish hotel room. It was not only that this nautical and forbiddingly upper-class periodical was two years old and recorded the events of a summer long since dead, nor the fact that I knew next to nothing about the handling of sleek sailing boats and dashing schooners—but my thoughts kept turning to the real Erich Matthäus, who was probably by now resting in the deep waters of the Thames. But was he really there? Throughout my crossing I had looked out for a man who would fit my picture of Erich Matthäus: admittedly a rather childish proceeding, since I neither knew what Erich Matthäus was like, nor even whether he was on the same boat as I.

I knew little or nothing about my fellow-Austrian Erich Matthäus in whose name my second passport, the false one, was made out. I cannot even say why I should have imagined that my compatriot was lying on the bottom of the Thames, for Mr. Luckner had vouchsafed no details about the manner or circumstances in which Erich Matthäus's life was to be cut off in full bloom. All I knew was that the Communist agent Erich Matthäus—a Viennese by birth, which was one of the reasons why I had been chosen to impersonate him—had been due to arrive in England at the same time as I and to be removed upon arrival. Removed in an absolutely effective and final manner, so that I could that very same evening take the part which he had been destined to play. There was no guarantee, Mr. Luckner had expressly warned me, that Erich Matthäus's mortal remains would not be discovered in the course of the night, or by morning at the latest, so that I would be well advised to bring my rendezvous, or rather his, to a conclusion by no later than one in the morning and then leave the hotel as quickly as possible. Those were the details given me by Don Luckner: the picture of Erich Matthäus's dripping body, fished out of the river and being stared at by policemen and street-walkers, had sprung up in my own brain. For all I knew, my fellow-countryman's life might have ended with a bullet from a revolver, a dropping brick, a hammer, a speeding motor-car, a dose of poison, or some other well-tried device.

But, I notice, I am making the mistake of presuming the reader to be acquainted with certain matters merely because I am myself conversant with them *ad nauseam*. I am afraid I shall have to start at the beginning after all.

The American secret service had been watching the British scientist Dr. Heinrich Azur for more than a year. I am advisedly using the term British, for the English do not like British subjects

not born in England to be described as English. The British professor Heinrich Azur had emigrated to England from his native
Austria at the time of Hitler's return to his native land and that
native land's "return" to the Reich. Very soon afterwards, Dr.
Azur was regarded in expert circles, and beyond these circles, as
one of the most important men—perhaps the most important
man—in his field, and because he had made an appreciable contribution to the advancement of nuclear physics and to the development of atomic weapons he had been granted British nationality out of turn, as a special measure, at a time when many of
his fellow-countrymen, likewise victims of the Nazi regime, were
still being ruthlessly screened and questioned on the Isle of Man
and treated as enemies of the country to which they had fled from
the common enemy. Heinrich Azur, to continue, had been maintaining contacts with the Soviets—contacts which had presumably
begun during the war but had been intensified since. They may
have been due at first to the fact that his father, an historian, held
a university appointment in the Soviet Zone of Germany; but later
no doubt there were other, political and ideological reasons, with
which U.S. Intelligence was not familiar but of which it was able,
nevertheless, to form an approximate idea, since the professor lived
in modest, almost ascetic, circumstances. According to the American
secret service, the professor had passed on to the Soviets not only
copies of his own calculations, but had also betrayed to the former
ally and present-day enemy various secret and top-secret calculations and plans worked out by the research establishment where he
was in charge of the most important department.

The American secret service could, of course, have notified the
British secret service of its observations, discoveries, and conclusions long ago, and so warned their British allies. But this would
not have been in line with secret-service usage. To begin with, the
supervision of scientists, even if engaged on work of military importance, came not under Military Intelligence, that is, M.I.5, but
under the political secret service with which U.S. Military Intelligence had nothing to do, and did not wish to have anything to do.
And to continue, U.S. Intelligence had no intention of surrendering
to the British the kudos of such a sensational revelation. On the
contrary, American Intelligence was hoping that by unmasking a

British traitor in Britain, it would conspicuously demonstrate its superiority over British Intelligence, show up the British secret service as a complete failure, and thus press home its demand that the Americans should be allowed to operate independently in the British Isles.

During the past few months Dr. Azur had met a number of agents of the Soviet secret service at a variety of rendezvous and no doubt handed them important documents. Although the Americans had not let the scientist out of their sight for a minute, they had been unable to strike because the agents had always appeared unexpectedly, as if out of the mist, and vanished almost immediately. Besides, the professor's meetings with the Eastern agents had taken place in spots decided only at the last moment. This time, however, Intelligence had found out that the next Soviet agent to meet Professor Azur would be a man named Erich Matthäus; it had also discovered the time and place of the proposed meeting, and —most important of all—that Azur was not personally acquainted with the man to whom he was to hand the fruits of his treasonable activities.

At the same time as the real Matthäus left the Continent for his brief guest-performance in London I, too, departed for England to enact the part of the Russian go-between. The objective this time was not simply the seizure of the documents. The drama of Dr. Azur was fast moving towards its effective climax. It would not be enough to catch the Soviet courier red-handed and rob him of the documents he had just taken over—a really spectacular scene was to be staged. The British, or so my American employers feared, might not trust the revelation; they might even, in order to cover up their own exposure, defend the scientist. That was why Dr. Azur was to be apprehended in the deed, in the presence of witnesses who would testify to his indisputable treason.

I mentioned that the timetable for "Operation Azur" had been worked out most minutely. I was to arrive in London at the same time as the Soviet agent; while I put up at the hotel as Erich Matthäus, the real Erich Matthäus was to be rendered harmless. Even before the Soviet secret service could learn about his disappearance and warn Dr. Azur, and even before news of the agent's sudden death appeared in the papers, my meeting with the professor was to be accomplished. As soon as the British scientist turned up at my hotel the British secret service and the Special Branch were to be informed and asked to strike at once. By one o'clock, at the latest, the Americans were scheduled to bring their British colleagues to my hotel and to have Dr. Azur arrested in my room. I was then to identify myself as an American Intelligence agent and, being in possession of the treasonable papers, give conclusive evidence against the scientist.

It was exactly seven o'clock, and I had just put down the yachting paper because the crossword puzzle in it required familiarity with all sorts of nautical expressions and I had got stuck after no more than one or two words, when the porter announced a Dr. Fennimore. Dr. Fennimore was the cover name arranged between Dr. Azur and the Communists. The night porter probably thought he was a doctor out on a late call. I asked that he be sent up.

A moment later, when the man opened the door, I was relieved to find that I disliked him at first sight—relieved because it is doubly distasteful to hand a pleasant person over to the hangman. I never could stand intellectuals, any more than so-called he-men.

Dr. Heinrich Azur was the intellectual type. He was not short, but gave the impression of being short. He walked with a stoop, almost as if he were creeping along a wall, seeking cover, or trying to hide something. His angular right shoulder was a little higher than the left; his slightly inclined head sat deep between his shoulders; and he moved forward as though he used only the right half of his thin body, dragging the left half behind, as if partly paralyzed. At the same time his movements, the gestures of his small white hands, and also his soft voice had something affected about them, an almost girlish element, as is not infrequently the case with intellectuals who, far from renouncing external vanity, display a coy and precious manner. On closer inspection, however, Dr. Azur's face proved much more attractive than the rest of his appearance: it was narrow and pale, but not without some liveliness. His mouth, though a little too small, was full-lipped and almost sensuous, and his nut-brown eyes behind the frameless lenses were alert and seemed ready enough to laugh at a well-told story.

The professor greeted me in English.

"You can talk German to me, Herr Professor," I said. "After

all, we are both natives of Vienna." I motioned him towards the arm-chair. "And to get that ludicrous formality over," I continued, "today's password is Versailles."

"Very well," said Dr. Azur, regarding me with awakening sympathy, possibly because I had said "ludicrous formality."

"Can I offer you a glass of whisky?" I asked.

The professor declined.

"So you are from Vienna, Herr Matthäus," he said. "I haven't seen Vienna for fifteen years. Do you think I would recognize the city?"

"A lot has changed, of course," I said, "but, as you know, the 'dying fairy-tale city' has been resisting death with astonishing tenacity for a long time now, and I suppose it will remain in its state of cheerful agony for a few more centuries."

"A few more centuries," Dr. Azur repeated after me, and again I had the impression that he was scrutinizing me with sympathy and surprise. He looked around the room thoughtfully and asked, "Did you have a good crossing?"

"A bit rough," I said—a description that might apply equally to a choppy sea or the turbulent air, since Mr. Luckner had failed to inform me by which means of transport the spy Erich Matthäus was going to reach the Island.

But Dr. Azur was clearly not trying to draw me. He said, "Most unusual weather."

I smiled. "The temptation is too great," I observed, "not to ask the most competent man in the world whether he believes that the unusual weather is due to certain unusual experiments?"

"I don't know, Herr Matthäus," he said. "I don't know."

He took a tin from his coat pocket. It was the kind of tin which certain English cigarette manufacturers had just reintroduced again after the war, but I noticed that it did not contain that firm's cigarettes.

"I can't offer you one of my home-rolled cigarettes," he said, with an apologetic smile.

I picked up my cigarette-case from the bedside table.

I was not particularly anxious to get down to business, for I had been instructed to keep the scientist with me till at least one o'clock in the morning and the time now was only half-past eleven.

On the other hand I had noticed as soon as Dr. Azur entered the room that he carried no briefcase nor anything else that might contain documents. I was still hoping the formulas to be surrendered might be on a piece of paper, perhaps on a few sheets torn from a notebook, in the professor's wallet or in the pocket of his light raglan. Inexperienced as I was in chemical and physical matters, I did not want to betray my ignorance by asking a question outright. As I returned to the little round table with my cigarette-case in my hand I speculated whether the time had yet come to turn the conversation from polite phrases to serious business.

I sat down by the ancient standing lamp with its cork-screw pillar and said: "Herr Professor, perhaps you would now like to pass me Number Twenty-Seven. . . ."

"As you see," said the professor, "I have not brought anything along."

"I hope I haven't misunderstood you," I replied sharply.

He shook his head. "No," he said, "you have not misunderstood me. On the contrary, I shall have to ask you to take a message to your, and my, employers." He chuckled softly as he mentioned his employers. "Number Twenty-Six was my last delivery. There won't be any more."

I had to readjust myself hurriedly, to consider rapidly how the genuine Erich Matthäus, the Soviet agent, would have reacted to this bold notice of termination. At the same time, most irritatingly, I began to wonder again whether Matthäus was still alive, or, if he was dead, whether he had been shot, stabbed, or pushed into the river.

"Are you trying to say that you have been found out, Herr Professor?" I said, jumping to my feet.

"I don't think so," Dr. Azur replied composedly. His sad brown eyes regarded me with inexplicable wistfulness.

"Have you been transferred to a different department?" I asked.

"No," he said. "All these excuses would be lies, and besides you'd soon find out. I have been neither found out nor transferred. I have handed in my notice."

"When did you do that?"

"My letter to the Institute is in the mail."

"So you have worked until today?"

"Yes."

"That means," I said, "that you could have brought the material along without difficulty."

"I have given notice so I need not bring it along any more," he said.

"You weren't entitled to do that without our consent," I retorted.

"I should like to speak to your superior," said Dr. Azur. "To our superior," he added, again with a wan smile.

I sat down. Nothing was to be gained now by acting the brutal Soviet agent. I had no instructions to hold the professor by physical violence; if I threatened violence he would simply walk out. A reasonably urbane conversation, on the other hand, might at least provide circumstantial evidence, even if not irrefutable proof.

"Our superiors are not in London, Dr. Azur. You know that as well as I do. You will have to confide in me," I said.

He regarded me quizzically.

"Maybe," he said, "I'll be lucky. Of all the couriers sent to me you seem to be the first one who is human. If you like you can carry my message."

"I'm listening," I said.

He looked around him, as if wanting to examine more closely the blotchy yellow walls, the lamp in which only one of the three bulbs was working, and the shabby brown furniture.

"I said a moment ago," he began, holding his cigarette between nicotine-stained fingers, "that I gave in my notice because I didn't want to serve your masters any longer. That wasn't true —or at least it was only half true. I don't want to serve the British either, or the Americans, or any other nation." He looked straight into my eyes. "I don't want to serve science, Herr Matthäus— that's the truth. All science is based on knowledge, on the quest for truth—and once it is based on a deliberate lie it ceases to be a science. Therefore the science to which I had dedicated my life from my youth, indeed from my childhood, is a science no longer."

"I don't understand you," I said. "What do you call science and what do you call a lie?"

"Imagine a man," he continued in a patient didactic tone, "who pretends to be working on a serum against poliomyelitis, that terrible infantile paralysis, but who is in fact trying to infect all children in the world with that disease. I can see that the very monstrousness of the idea makes you shudder—though no doubt you are a hardened man. Well, why don't you shudder at us 'atomic scientists'? We pretend to be working for the progress of mankind, but are in fact, daily and hourly, working for its destruction. Progress, Herr Matthäus, is one of those unthinkingly accepted notions which can sanctify any crime. Do you know where progress ends? Do I know? You don't have to ask yourself the question—but we ought not to take up a single test tube or build a single machine without answering that great *Whither?* There isn't a single atomic physicist in the world who doesn't know he is lying when he pretends to be working on peaceful atomic research. Peaceful atomic research is a by-product of the work of destruction, or, even worse, a public justification. Perhaps you will ask why I have not realized all this before; in fact, I shouldn't be surprised if you suspected me of having motives other than the ones I am laying before you." He chuckled softly. It was a strange chuckle, almost as if he were mocking himself. "All our understanding is mysteriously interwoven with our life. But there is no particular mystery about my sudden understanding. Some days ago I concluded a major piece of work—a few weeks after delivering my last papers to your people. I had finished my work and I began to think. Yes, it does sound absurd: first I finished my work and then I began to think. Here you have the crux of it, Herr Matthäus. The world calls us 'atomic scientists' with a respectful shiver—but we are all of us possessed men who act first and think afterwards." The rhythm of his speech was getting more lively and irregular, as though he knew that he had little time left to finish his message. "We are possessed by the fascinating power that is given into our hands," he said. "We no longer ask what is the purpose. We stare, hypnotized, into our test tubes, we measure quality by quantity, greatness by power, hope by death.

We experiment with the lives of two and a half billion human beings; we experiment with the globe itself. We have lost fear, and with fear reverence. Philosophy has smoothed our bloody path for us by delivering us from the fear which used to be the warning signal to our souls, as fever is to our bodies. But freedom from fear is a barren soil. Fearless, we have paralyzed the arm of the Creator in order to become creators ourselves. We have changed the seasons—spring, summer, autumn, and winter—we are changing the structure of the human body and of the human brain." He paused, and continued: "Do you remember the film where that great comedian acted the Great Dictator and performed a balloon dance with a globe? That Great Dictator was an innocent compared with us who, like jugglers, are balancing the globe on our finger-tips. It is untrue, like everything else we say, that we can calculate and determine the consequences. We don't know anything. Most of my learned colleagues are plagued with doubts and self-incrimination—but they have doubts only because they fear the abuse of their scientific findings. I fear the findings themselves. So much knowledge, Herr Matthäus, becomes ignorance. Such victories are certain defeat. We are no creators. We are omniscient only in the depths but not upon the heights. We are omnipotent only in destruction, not in construction. We are not awaiting punishment. We are punished already." He laughed. "Punished with ignorance. We can now calculate anything—except the consequences of our calculations. We have split the atom and forgotten our multiplication tables!" Suddenly he stared at me, as if surprised to find me sitting opposite him. "But why am I telling you all this?" he asked abruptly.

Surreptitiously I looked at my watch. The temptation to act out of character was great, almost irresistible. I had to pull myself together to say:

"I am listening to you, Professor Azur, but I still don't understand how all this affects your attitude towards us. You are an idealist—that we have never doubted, at least not until today. To stop the West from using your knowledge and your inventions, and those of your misguided colleagues, for warlike purposes—that, surely, was the reason why you have helped us twenty-six times. Has anything changed in this respect? Has the West become more peaceful, or we more bellicose? Whether you wish to cease your further activities is your own affair—is possibly your own affair —but it is our business to make sure the West, which desires atomic war, and which started the race towards atomic war, does not gain a lead on us."

"I thought you wouldn't understand," said the professor, with a resigned gesture of his delicate hand. "You don't understand," he continued, "that the intentions of Governments have ceased to matter." He paused, and asked: "Do you know how I became a traitor?"

"I have come here to receive your data," I said evasively.

He ignored my answer and leaned forward over the low smoking-table—so close I could feel his breath.

"I never loved this country," he said. "I didn't come here of my own free will. But it granted me asylum from persecution in my native country. It accepted me, but it never held me to its heart. When they released me on the Isle of Man I knew very well that they needed me. I sold my brain for a patch of ground. I didn't owe this country anything. But I trusted it. The war came to an end. And then I began to notice that my new fellow-countrymen were betraying the peace. I turned toward the Soviet Union, which alone seemed willing to avenge the shameful treatment that I and the others like me have suffered——"

"I know all that, Professor Azur," I interrupted my visitor.

My impatience was not acted. A nearby church clock had struck midnight: at any moment the door might open; at any moment they might come to arrest the professor and require me to bear witness against him.

The professor dismissed my objection.

"I became a traitor to the West," he said, "just as I should have become a traitor to the East if I had lived there and seen at close quarters how peace was being betrayed and a new war prepared."

He looked at me, and a nameless horror was suddenly mirrored in his features, as if he had only just realized the risk he was running with his challenge. His eyes widened; they seemed to grow as big as his spectacle lenses. His lips were white, making his chin suddenly look long and narrow, for there was no division between nose and chin.

"No," he said in an imploring voice, "don't misunderstand me. I have no intention of betraying the East. I have done nothing of the sort and am not planning anything of the sort. Believe me, I have come to realize that the ones don't desire peace any more than the others. But that's not it either . . ." He broke off and tried to collect his thoughts. "Do you know what I have realized, Herr Matthäus? East and West, Capitalism and Communism—all this has become meaningless. There are no warmongers any longer, and no pacifists; there is no peace and no war. Consequently, there is no sense left in espionage and no purpose in treason."

"Pull yourself together, Doctor Azur," I said. "You're talking wildly. That stuff doesn't convince anyone."

He leaned even further over the table.

"Can't you understand?" he said. "Try to understand, for God's sake! Capitalism and Communism, ideological issues, politics, pacifism, militarism—all these are words from a bygone world. We have changed the world; we changed it in our laboratories! And the world around us suspects nothing and talks in a dead language! It thinks it is throwing a chip on to the gaming table, but that chip is an atom bomb." He was speaking now even more hastily, as if aware that time was pressing. "In past wars, if you wanted to destroy the enemy, you had to drop a bomb over his territory. You won't have to do that any longer, Herr Matthäus. Tomorrow you can stay in your laboratory and blow up half the globe. One single lunatic can multiply the unleashed forces; one single suicide can take the earth with him into death. Do you understand now that yesterday's concepts have lost their meaning? They have become dwarfed. War and peace no longer depend on the will of statesmen, or generals, or nations. There will be no war, Herr Matthäus. There will be no annihilation."

He rose to his feet. His eyes did not leave me for a moment, and yet I had the impression that he did not know who I was or who I pretended to be. He stopped in front of me.

"Espionage and treason," he said, "are irrelevant, Herr Matthäus. Without us, the scientists of hell, they are all powerless— generals, politicians, and spies; East and West, Communists and Capitalists." He beat his breast. "We have unchained the forces; we are still working in order to unchain the last of them. The betrayal of secrets? I am betraying to you a secret that is a thousand times more valuable than the twenty-six documents you have received from me—and a thousand times more valuable than any that I could still hand over to you. The secret is that we have exchanged our consciences for knowledge: for every piece of knowledge we have given a piece of our conscience. The secret is that science, in its megalomania, has declared war upon our globe, that there is a traitor in every laboratory in the East and in the West, in the North and in the South—not a traitor of his own country, but a traitor of the globe itself; not a traitor of a single idea, but a traitor of all faiths that ever were. The secret is that fuses are encircling the globe like meridians and parallels, and that at the end of those fuses we, the unscrupulous men of science, are standing ready with our matches."

I too had got up. What was I to do? I did not know, I did not even surmise, what those documents, calculations, tables, drawings, and plans contained, which Professor Azur had handed over to the Soviets in the course of the past few years. I had no more than an approximate idea of the scientific standing of the professor; his past was hidden from me by a veil and I could not be sure whether his overstrained nerves had not at last given way to madness. Yet, at the same time, there came over me a certainty that this man—no matter who he had been in the past, or whom or what he had betrayed, no matter what the mainspring of his actions had been yesterday and today, whether his words sprang from crystal-clear or plague-infested sources; no matter what lay behind his words in terms of personal sufferings, unhappy love, insults, pain, affection, doubts, or impotence—that this man had to be allowed to speak out and that he had to be listened to. No secret service of this doomed world was entitled to put him behind prison walls; no tribunal had the right to surrender him to the hangman. I, the unwitting guardian of his fate, had to do something in a hurry, to save him, and to prevent him from dying the ignominious death of traitors and spies.

"Professor Azur," I said, "you have convinced me—if no one else—and I will see to it that no harm comes to you. But now, I implore you, take your coat and disappear as fast as you can. Every minute is precious."

I took his coat from the old-fashioned circular hat-stand where he had carefully hung it up less than two hours before.

Exhausted from his speech, exhausted like a man who has bled himself, the professor regarded me through his thick lenses with astonishment and—so ironical is fate—with awakening suspicion.

"Who are you?" he asked. "Aren't you Matthäus, Erich Matthäus?"

"What does it matter who I am?" I said impatiently, pressing his coat upon him.

At that moment the door burst open. I am deliberately using this trite *cliché*: it literally "burst" open, and four or five men literally "stormed" into the room. It seemed as if these trite characters were at pains to act exactly in line with cheap fiction.

One of the men, a giant in a shabby navy-blue jacket, planted himself in front of the professor.

"Are you Dr. Heinrich Azur?"

The professor had turned pale. With trembling lips he assented.

"Do you deny," asked the man, "that you came here in order to deliver certain papers to this Soviet agent?"

"That I do deny," said the professor.

The man turned to me.

"Where are the papers?" he demanded.

"He had no papers with him," I said.

The man was perplexed, but evidently thought it no longer necessary to keep up the play-acting.

"Did he admit his connection with the Soviets, Droste?" he asked.

"Yes," I said.

"Take him away," the man ordered one of his companions, who had been keeping in the background.

Two men with broad-brimmed hats took the scientist between them. One of them said in a gentle tone:

"Don't give us any trouble, Dr. Azur. We don't want to take you through the lobby in handcuffs."

They moved off. I wanted to run after them, but I stood there as if rooted to the spot. In the door Dr. Azur turned his head. There was no despair in his features, not even reproach, and only slight surprise. I even believe he was smiling a little. I believe his right shoulder jerked a bit. I believe his eyes were seeking mine. I believe so, but I do not really know. I had dropped my eyes to the ground.

32

Sources of Information

TIME IS RUNNING SHORT. The first snow has fallen—gray, wet snow, which instantly turned into small rivulets, trickling downhill between the pebbles on the Bisamberg. Outside my window, half-way up between my house and the Danube, lies a blanket of haze, like the safety net between the high wire and the ring. Shall I be able to finish this book by Christmas? I doubt it; but the essential things have been said. After Johnny's Christmas holidays I can always add a page or two, cut a passage here or there, clarify a point, alter or delete some name.

Has Dr. Lu Wang's prophecy come true? He had encouraged me to write an account of my life and my thoughts, and he had prophesied that a strange change would come over me in the writing. The bulky manuscript is still in the bank safe, for I did not dare to keep it at home; I have therefore had no opportunity to look through the handwritten sheets again. Everybody should write his autobiography—or better still, he ought to write two: the first confessing his life, to the best of his knowledge and ability, and the second recording the strange changes which came about during the writing of the first. Nobody who lays bare his life or a part of his life remains the same person at the end of his communication. Dr. Wang's "institutionalist" theory proceeds from the austere reality of our personality as part of our society: we are only what we are in our society. But if this is so, then com-

munication means change, since a communicated secret ceases to be
a secret, and since, moreover, the communicant, by making his
communication, ceases to be the receptacle of a secret and becomes, as it were, an empty vessel ready to receive some new
contents. No life story is a frank confession, except by intention.
Its execution invariably changes, if not the truth of the confession
itself, then at least the person undertaking the adventure of truth.
But as the character of the person confessing changes, so does the
life he confesses—so that in the end what he has confessed in good
faith no longer seems true to him, even though his new realization
is no more than a consequence of his earlier confessions, and the
new truth no more than a supplement to the earlier one, though
seemingly at odds with it. On the other hand, it would be a flagrant
piece of falsification if I were to rewrite the first pages of this book,
or even some pages from the middle, in the way I might have
written them after the completion of my memoirs. The years which
I have reviewed were concluded when I sat down at my desk on
that hot summer day—ruled off like a trading year, with its profit
and losses, its successes and failures. But to record facts is not the
same as to understand them. It was impossible to draw up a final
balance sheet until all assets and liabilities—to employ the commercial terms—had been neatly arranged in parallel columns. But
even while I was balancing them the events changed their character:
success revealed itself as failure, and profit as loss—so that today
I am surprised, not merely by the final result, but also by the individual items.

But I notice that I am surrendering to the mood of the dying
year. That is improper. Indeed, the dying year impels me to make
haste. I must get back to my subject.

A whole year elapsed before the trial of Dr. Heinrich Azur.
In the meantime I was kept, at a good salary, on the "waiting
list" of American Intelligence, as there was a possibility that I
might be called as a witness for the prosecution, summoned to
appear before a Magistrate or a Judge, and thus snatched out of
anonymity. I need hardly say that this would have been most
embarrassing to the secret service, since an agent who appears in
Court has his name publicized and his pictures printed in the
papers, loses his value for ever. A number of circumstances, how-

ever, made it unnecessary for me to appear at the trial—the chief of them being that the incriminating evidence against the professor was so crushing that he was easily convicted as a traitor, even without my testimony. In consideration of mitigating circumstances he was sentenced to fifteen years' imprisonment: a broken man, in whose defense I had looked in vain for that righteous zeal that had so impressed me on that autumn evening in London. Besides, my fear of having to give evidence publicly against the professor was probably groundless, since the secret services are held in superstitious awe, even by otherwise independent judges. I am certain today that the Court had received a hint from the highest quarters to dispense with the examination of the witness George Droste.

It was, of course, a piece of exceptionally good luck for me that Eastern Intelligence suspected nothing of my London mission and its fatal success—or else I should probably be no longer among the living. Their ignorance, at the same time, was not conducive to the retirement I had planned and hoped for, as I was given a number of new assignments. Yet I should like to point out here and now that I have never again performed a mission, either for the East or for the West, from which my employers could have derived even the slightest advantage. The newspapers have always been my chief source of information, as far as my employers have been concerned.

I should like to observe at this point that, as a rule, the secret services lack a staff of properly trained, politically versed, and journalistically experienced people; that is why they have to acquire in the most complicated and adventurous way the kind of information which an experienced reader of the press can deduce without difficulty. Political espionage, which at the time of writing provides a living for 80 per cent of the approximately 22,000 permanent agents of the United States and for more than 25,000 agents of the Eastern bloc, is based on the foolish idea that the political actions of Powers derive from some secret and sudden political decisions, which a spy may well be able to nose out in good time —before, in fact, they are taken. It is based on the demonstrably erroneous idea that statesmen spend their time working out cunning plans, which they then write down in code, so that all a skillful spy or an ingenious agent need do is obtain these secret documents, or else to discover those cunning plans by even more cunning counter-plans. In reality, the different States have of course certain fundamental intentions—but these are not laid down in secret documents, since they are perfectly well known to anybody reasonably acquainted with the subject. Each country is faced with a new situation every day, with which it must try to deal as best it can, and in accordance with its own interests: what it does, and how it does it, follows logically from the country's attitude in the past, its generally known aims, and the opportunities of the moment. In other words, paradoxically enough, it is not possible to discover the intention of Governments in advance, but it is perfectly possible to guess them fairly accurately at the time. Political espionage, however, lives in the superstitious belief that Governments know in advance what action they would take if this or that tactical problem were suddenly to arise, and that these plans, therefore, can be stolen from them. In actual fact, the Governments keep their knowledge and their plans to themselves, for the simple reason that they have not got any. Most political agents do a lot of irreparable damage by expending time and money, and often also unwelcome publicity, on the acquisition and transmission of information which, no matter how correct at the moment, is anything but typical. Others confuse their employers with invented or false information, designed only to further the agent's own interests; still others simply support their country's policy of the moment by supplying confirmatory evidence that will be welcome to their statesmen, without the least regard for truth. The most honest among political spies stay at home and calculate the next move of a real or imagined enemy: their "confidential" or "secret" sources are newspapers, books, and other publications which they have studied intelligently and with a certain gift for putting two and two together. The best thing an honest political agent can do—considering that the correspondents of such reputable papers as the *New York Times* or the *Neue Zürcher Zeitung* are invariably better informed than spies employed on a much narrower sector—is to study carefully a dozen of the leading European, American, and perhaps also African and Asian papers, and then to present the distilled wisdom of those publications, together with what his political instinct has led him to read between their lines, as his own information—acquired under the greatest conceivable difficulties—and to submit it to his superiors, preferably in cipher and by telegram.

To instruct a political spy to draw out a diplomat is even more ludicrous. Just as the atom bomb has buried the secret services, so modern means of transport have put an end to diplomacy. In an age when Foreign Ministers and expert advisers can fly from Washington to New Delhi, and from Moscow to Johannesburg in a few hours, the Ambassadors in India, South Africa, and elsewhere have become mere messengers: they receive and transmit notes, but cannot make any decisions for themselves, and are, as a rule, most inadequately acquainted with the intentions of their Governments. They are, in fact, no more than postmen with a special kind of passport, a gorgeous wardrobe and a C.D. plate on their cars. Their most notable privilege nowadays is to be allowed to park their cars where others are not. There is nothing frivolous in the fact that Governments today are sending more and more representative personalities to foreign countries— people who are rich, or elegant, or socially smooth. On the contrary, there is a deep significance in it. In the days of Talleyrand and, perhaps, of Paléologue, secret intentions may still have existed behind Embassies. Today representation has become an end in itself. Naturally, the secret services do not admit the ignorance of the diplomats; if they did they would be killing the goose that lays the golden egg. In the past few years I have moved a lot in Embassy and Legation circles. I have played tennis with the charming daughters of Excellencies; I have visited nightclubs in the company of gay young Legation Counsellors; and I have, even, on orders from above, conducted gallant or passionate flirtations with the private secretaries of first one Ambassador and then another. But my experience has invariably been that I could have imparted to them more secrets than there were for me to extract. Throughout the Embassies and Legations more thought is given nowadays to the seating order for dinner than to the world order; her Excellency's wardrobe is more important than his Excellency's safe; and diplomats today are better informed about the cocktail parties at other countries' Embassies than about the political parties in their own country. Newspaper readers, seeing the photograph of a Foreign Minister with an Ambassador, and speculating curiously what they were whispering about together, would be surprised to learn that it was probably some confidential account of their latest performance on the golf course; and when a beautiful woman spy buttonholes a diplomat, all she gets out of him nowadays is that he intends to spend his next leave in Capri.

To make things worse, diplomatic missions—dissatisfied with their roles of glorified post offices—have lately taken to setting themselves up as branches of the secret service. Thus, while the political importance of Embassies and Legations has shrunk to a minimum, the number of diplomats in all countries of the world has grown in inverse proportion. Each diplomatic mission nowadays has its "S-Fund"—the mysterious letter "S" standing for "secret"—and, in the same way as in the secret service proper, that Ambassador is considered the most efficient who keeps the largest number of agents. Indeed, about 50 per cent of all diplomats are nothing but agents with a diplomatic passport. This does not mean that the diplomatic secret service finds out more than the secret service proper—on the contrary, since it is more modest and more amateurish in its organization, it finds out even less— but it does mean that all diplomats today have had enough "security" training to recognize an enemy agent at once for what he is. If, therefore, you see two young diplomats in animated conversation in the corner of some ballroom, you may be certain that they are both agents in white ties and that each of them is fully aware of the functions of the other. Consequently, all they discuss is the pretty girls present, and on the following day they each submit to their Ambassador a confidential report concocted from what they have read in the papers.

My experiences in Korea—the suicide of Commander Hees and the murder of Richard Grant—my parting with Nora, my encounter in London and, finally, the conviction of Dr. Azur, had left me in a profoundly disturbed state. However, the warning might have gone unheeded but for an incident which took place in the early spring of 1955, during a period of secret-service leave —an incident I propose to relate in some detail in the next chapter, possibly the last one of the book.

The next chapter: I hesitate as I put these words down on paper. Only ten more days before Johnny arrives from Geneva. I had intended to prepare myself appropriately for his arrival. I had wanted to work out at leisure the program for our fortnight's holiday and to surrender myself fully to the joy of anticipation which is, in the final analysis, the supreme joy. We are planning a visit to the new Opera and to the rebuilt Burgtheater; we shall call together on my tailor and shirtmaker; weather permitting, I had thought of a two-day skiing trip to the Semmering, which is gradually beginning to recapture its pristine glory; and we had planned to attend a ball, so as to give Johnny a chance to meet the ever-charming young ladies of my native city. But now, glancing up from my work, my plans do not seem quite so matter-of-course and their realization by no means quite certain.

My work had driven away my fear: now it rises again from the final pages of this book. I suddenly remember Mr. Brown, the brutal man who clung to my heels in Geneva; I can see before me the slippery Albanian, whose visit had interrupted my work; and in my dreams I encounter the unknown Herr Quatthelm, who had broken into my house at a late hour, and whose photograph my suspicious school-fellow the Superintendent had pushed across his desk. I am trying to dispel my fear by reasoning: I keep telling myself that the secret services stand to gain nothing by my liquidation and that, on the contrary, they would merely confirm the assertions of this record. But a moment later I tell myself that I should be denying the quintessence of these memoirs were I to believe in the logic, let alone the humanity, of the secret services. The most absurd ideas are chasing one another in my head. At one moment I am tempted to seek asylum from one secret service under the wings of another—almost as if the organizations threatening me were at the same time my only remaining haven of safety. At the next moment I dismiss the idea and ask myself if I am afraid only because of Johnny or also for myself. But is anybody ever afraid merely for himself? Is not everybody afraid because he does not want to believe in a life

without his own life? And yet it is not simply the thought that
Johnny would be left alone. Johnny alone—something in me
rebels against the thought being pursued to its conclusion. True,
I have made a careful Will, repeatedly amended and improved,
and I am sure I have forgotten nothing. Everything has been
thoroughly discussed with my lawyer and all unforeseen eventual-
ities have been guarded against. The document has been signed,
sealed, and deposited with a notary in due and proper form. But
all of a sudden, the notary's safe no longer seems a safe place to
me, and the notary himself, a pleasant and respectable man, seems
suspicious and possibly bribed by the enemy. The burglar did not
find anything in my wall-safe: the manuscript is in the vaults of
the bank. But even the cellars of the bank no longer seem a safe
place to me. If the papers were lost, if Johnny learned nothing
of their content—what would happen? As through a haze, I
hear Mr. Luckner's words; did he not mention the "secret-service
orphans," who are "looked after" by Intelligence, the children for
whom Intelligence is insidiously lying in wait? And is the secret
service not lying in wait for my son, for the boy it lost when
Johnny's real father disappeared behind the Korean lines, and I
adopted him? But even if all goes well, even if my Will and the
manuscript are found untouched—do they not both require an
oral commentary? Could Johnny understand either without my
interpretation?

During the past few days my eyes have strayed to Nora's
pictures with a clearer awareness than ever before. In all these
years I have trusted no one but her—and I have abused her
trust more than anybody else's. From my subconscious mind bursts
a long-suppressed desire to see her again, and perhaps to entrust
to her the manuscript of my book, and even my Will. My dreams
grow still bolder and I picture a meeting between her and Johnny,
a meeting which I might possibly bring about. But what do I
know of Nora's feelings now? Am I not weaving a pattern from
long-torn threads of the past? Am I not deceiving myself by
planning to meet Nora for Johnny's sake, while in reality all I
want is to see her again?

I know that this book, planned as a record and a warning, is
fast becoming a diary. Outside my windows lies a Christmas

landscape. I must return to that spring of 1955 when I was summoned to Dr. Lu Wang.

33

A Message from Dr. Lu Wang

I WAS ON the point of moving into my house on the Bisamberg when one day I received a strange message. A man with a foreign accent, and a very curious accent at that, rang me up: he did not introduce himself, but asked me to visit a certain movie house on the Opernring at a certain hour, and to collect a ticket kept for me at the box office in the name of Droste. He intended to get another ticket for himself in order to slip an urgent message into my pocket in the darkened auditorium. I did not doubt for a moment that I was dealing with a man well versed in secret-service methods: for who else would choose a darkened cinema for passing a letter which the post office would have transmitted without any difficulty? This very consideration induced me at first to decline the invitation and to ask for particulars. The man at the other end hesitated for a moment and seemed to wonder whether to identify himself; in the end he admitted to being the emissary of a man with whom I had been "at some school," who had "looked me up at a holiday resort," and with whom I had made "a long journey by air." This man—who I thought must be my friend Dr. Lu Wang—was in trouble, and was imploring me to receive his message.

By way of exception, and entirely against my practice, I took a gun with me, but my caution proved quite unnecessary. Everything happened just as the stranger had said. As arranged, a ticket for the second showing of the film had been deposited under my name at the movie house. I found myself sitting next to a little yellow man who slipped an envelope into my pocket, leaving immediately afterwards. When I got home I found that the envelope contained a few lines in the familiar hand of my Chinese friend.

These lines, though phrased in a calm and reassuring style, free from all hysteria, and indeed with a touch of bitter humor in one or two places, disturbed me profoundly. Dr. Lu Wang informed me that he was in a lunatic asylum near Vienna—the private mental nursing-home of Professor Wolfgang Amadeus Segantini—and that, though exceedingly well looked after and fed, he was being kept there against his will. At the same time, Dr. Lu Wang continued, he had no intention of escaping—partly because in a mad world a madhouse was a most appropriate residence for a sensible person, and partly because he was in comparative safety behind the walls of the institution. He was telling me all this lest I should think he was trying to make me his fellow-conspirator, or to entice me into a dangerous adventure; but my visit was of urgent and vital importance. However, he added, I must obey his instructions in every detail, since he was not allowed to receive visitors. After listing these instructions point by point Dr. Wang concluded his letter as follows: "If you will believe a man interned as a dangerous lunatic, the matter concerns not so much me as you, and it would therefore be madness—if you will forgive the unfortunate word—for you not to take up my invitation."

I did not hesitate for a moment. On the Sunday fixed by Dr. Lu Wang I went to the little town on the Danube where Professor Wolfgang Amadeus Segantini's private mental-home was situated. This institution, I seemed to remember, had been involved in one or two sinister affairs before. At an inn named by my Chinese friend I met one of the warders—no doubt an ally of his—a man with the physique of a wrestler and the head of a Figaro, who pocketed the fat bribe which Dr. Wang had suggested with the easy nonchalance of a barber accepting a suitable tip. He thereupon handed me a printed and duly rubber-stamped visitor's permit describing me, under a name I have since forgotten, as a relative of a patient named Oskar Maltezahn. Once I had passed the entrance gate, the warder explained, he would himself take charge of me—he was returning to the institution before me—and conduct me to my new relation Maltezahn. Dr.

Lu Wang would be near by, so that we should be able to exchange a few words and perhaps even have a long talk. In reply to my question why these elaborate maneuvers were necessary, the warder confirmed that the patient Lu Wang was not allowed to have visitors.

Professor Segantini's private mental-home was situated outside the little town, on a hill shaped exactly like a green bowler hat. From the road the institution looked like a monastery—an impression that was heightened by the pleasant little chapel, which had been built on to the block. But as one ascended the hill the friendly atmosphere gradually disappeared. First of all, around the crown of the hat, so to speak, there was a green wall of forbidding height and rough texture. No less sobering was the tall, broad-shouldered and black-bearded man in a doctor's white coat at the narrow door in the thick wall, who examined the visitors' permits and who— perhaps because he had dealt too long with dangerous patients— scrutinized even the most harmless visitor as though he were a candidate for permanent residence within the stone walls.

I must admit that I heaved a sigh of relief when, in response to a telephone call by the martial janitor, the warder appeared whom I had met at the inn by the river an hour before and who was evidently in Dr. Wang's confidence. He took charge of me to take me to the patient Maltezahn.

We crossed a well-tended park, the warder not deeming it necessary to address a single word to me. Two or three doctors passed us without so much as a second glance; four or five patients, accompanied by warders, eyed us with that understandable hostility which the alien intruder into the peaceful seclusion of the abnormal must always expect. Only one patient, a little old man of wizened appearance, was conversing with a Sunday visitor. The warder, still taciturn, conducted me past the big low building, which was basking peacefully in the biscuit-colored glow of the afternoon sun, and my frayed nerves were almost soothed when a disturbing sight abruptly roused me from my reverie. A man's leg, bare and hairy, was hanging out between the iron bars of a first-floor window—and, since there was nothing to be seen beyond that leg, one had the impression of some independent human object divorced from a body.

"At the end of the chestnut walk," my guide explained, stopping, "you will find Dr. Wang. Please do not move from the seat on which he is sitting. It is the only spot that isn't overlooked from the windows of the institution. I shall be near you with the patient Maltezahn." He spoke in a whisper, although nobody could possibly overhear us. "In case you are discovered run on down the walk as fast as you can, right to the end. There is a small door in the wall. It is unlocked."

"But surely I am a proper visitor?" I objected.

The warder shrugged his shoulders and motioned me to follow him.

At the beginning of the chestnut walk, into which we now turned, stood a seat, so hidden among the trees that one did not notice it till one was right in front of it. On it sat my friend Lu Wang. He was engaged in friendly, though apparently hectic, conversation with a gaunt man of dishevelled appearance, a man whose sooty-black shaven skull, prominent ears, and felt slippers made him look more like a convict than a patient. Dr. Wang's features and gestures, on the other hand, had not changed, but for that very reason I was doubly shocked to see him in his hospital clothes, with their faded blue and white stripes.

"Did he behave himself?" the warder asked my friend, even before I could greet him. He was pointing to the patient Maltezahn, whom he had evidently left under Dr. Wang's charge when he came down to the gate to meet me.

The Chinese gave a friendly nod.

The patient Maltezahn got up and said with a smile, revealing a toothless mouth:

"He has already given me one eye; he's going to give me the other in a minute."

"Of course," said Dr. Wang. "You shall have it any time you like, Maltezahn." Turning to me, while the warder led his mildly remonstrating patient to another seat, he added: "Maltezahn has started a collection of eyes. He will probably ask you presently to make him a present of yours."

I sat down next to Dr. Wang.

"For Heaven's sake," I said, "tell me what's happened."

"First of all," said Dr. Wang, "many thanks for answering my

call so promptly. Short as our time is, I hope to convince you that
I am not a lunatic—which is not so easy to prove in these surroundings as you may think. Once a man is inside a madhouse anything
he says seems rather mad, including his protestations that he isn't
mad at all. If one observes oneself carefully, which of course one
is apt to do in a high measure in this place, one realizes how many
of the statements we make every day can be interpreted as persecution mania, or megalomania, given no more than a little ill will or
suspicion. In these surroundings a man can't be too careful."

"I have no doubt whatever of your sanity, Dr. Wang," I said.

"That is most gratifying," said Dr. Wang, "for what I am going to confide to you is apt to test severely your faith in me." He
was talking rapidly, as if driven from within; he was talking more
rapidly and restlessly than I had ever heard him talk. "You may remember our conversation at the airport in Newfoundland. I told
you then that I was looking for allies, but I was not in a position
to answer any further questions from you. I was then on the point
of foiling a secret-service plot designed to whip up the already existing warlike atmosphere and, perhaps, trigger off an armed conflict of the gravest consequences. I was certain then, as I had long
suspected, that the secret services are the natural allies of the warmongers, since these will guarantee them unlimited funds and unlimited power for the duration of the war." He smiled. "You see, I
am right in the grip of persecution mania and megalomania. For
aren't you bound to regard it as a paranoic figment if I tell you
that I had been chosen to murder the Chinese Generalissimo in
Formosa in order to cause an international incident? And won't
you think I am suffering from megalomania if I tell you that by
the skilful sabotage of my assignment I have possibly prevented a
Third World War? You are horrified, my dear friend, but there is
no cause. The American Intelligence officers who cast me for the
role of murderer intended to present their own Government as
much as the enemy with a *fait accompli*. Intelligence, you know as
well as I do, is a State within the State. But human beings are so
crudely made that they have to experience in person the things
they already know in their mind. I had now experienced in person
what I had long realized: that a secret-service clique in the hands
of a few ambitious soldiers, or a few ambitious soldiers in the hands

of a secret-service clique, are capable of triggering off a conflict which no one can subsequently avert or halve. I decided to act. I collected around me a few agents with similar experiences—agents of both sides, mind you—you might call it a legion of belatedly-aroused consciences. I intended to publicize the experiences of the lot of us. Just then—it was in Vienna—Intelligence pounced on us. Of course, they could have made me disappear. I wouldn't have been the first victim nor the last. But the murder of a Chinese in a European capital would not have passed unnoticed; besides, they are still hoping that while he lives Lu Wang might betray the names of his friends." He looked around him. "In Dr. Segantini's institution there are several patients like myself—I might almost say that this beautiful place specializes in my kind of patient. Admittedly—and here's megalomania for you again—I occupy a special position, in that Intelligence has allotted to me a very special warder concerned exclusively with my person. This man, as I am bound to say without any persecution mania, is an extremely uncouth fellow; luckily he is away today to attend his sister's wedding. Which is why I have asked you to call this Sunday."

"But all this is monstrous, Dr. Wang," I said. "You give me full powers and I will get the best lawyer to take up your case."

Dr. Wang bowed slightly. The courteous gesture in the tight convict's clothes looked almost grotesque.

"Let me assure you again, my dear Droste," he said, "that this is not why I have bidden you to this strange rendezvous. So long as I am here my life is reasonably safe—and that's not a thought to be despised, since I hope to regain my freedom some day in order to work for the cause that happens to be close to my heart. I shall then surprise the world with a theory which culminates in the demand that the evil in us must be overcome by repressing it into our unconscious, instead of doing it—as is the fashion nowadays—the other way round. However"—he interrupted himself, "pleasant and profitable as it would be, we cannot indulge in speculative theories today."

"Indeed, no," I said. "I can see our warder watching us disapprovingly."

I had hardly finished the sentence when the restless patient Maltezahn jumped up from the seat under a horse-chestnut, where

he had been sitting for the past few minutes, and, before his warder
could restrain him, made for us. He was holding his right hand in
front of him, with his first and second fingers opened in the shape
of a horizontal V, as if aiming directly for my eyes. "He has promised me his eyes! He has promised me his eyes!" he was part shouting and part babbling. Before he could reach our seat his warder
had caught him and forcibly twisted his thin arms round his back—
but the incident made us realize that he would have to take his
patient, or rather, both his patients, back to the house in a few
minutes.

"Droste," said Dr. Wang, and his voice sounded almost solemn
—which was not in the least in line with the modest man's character
and usual manner of speech. "Listen to me carefully, Droste! You
may not know, or perhaps you only suspect, that I am exceedingly
well informed about your activities during the past few years. I did
not confide in you before because your motives, though leading to
the same goal, were very different from mine. You have badly
served the masters who paid your wages—our masters—but you
did not act from good convictions. I am the last person to blame
you for it. On the contrary, I feel I ought to apologize. I had
moral scruples about joining with you as an ally, although the
struggle I was engaged in did not justify fastidiousness."

"Won't you come to the point?" I asked, with growing interest
but also with growing impatience.

Dr. Wang would not be rushed.

"You confided to me in Washington," he said, "that you intended to write down your experiences in the secret service, and
perhaps publish them. I, for my part, have written down everything I know." Turning away from the seat where the warder sat
with the patient Maltezahn, Dr. Wang undid the collar of his convict's uniform and carefully detached a key from a narrow ribbon
he wore around his neck. "I managed to save this key," he
continued. "It opens my safe-deposit box at the Boulevard des
Italiens branch of the Crédit Lyonnais in Paris. I know that you
have seen and heard enough yourself, but I think the perusal of
my notes will greatly confirm you in your resolution to write your
memoirs—perhaps decisively. In case you don't hear from me

within a year I hereby authorize you to make whatever use you think fit of my papers. Have you understood me?"

I took the key.

"I understand you, Dr. Wang," I said, "and yet I don't understand you. Your past refusal to confide in me seems to me much more logical than your present frankness."

"I know, Droste," he replied, "that you have reached a point where there is nothing left but for you to speak out. And that, you see, is all I care about. I have a shrewd idea of what will happen to you once you take up your pen. You will begin in a humorous, frivolous, and vain mood—but you won't end in a humorous, frivolous, or vain mood. Do you remember my theories? A man becomes what he acts. Today I am trusting you only conditionally, but on the day that you complete your confessions I shall trust you implicitly." He smiled again; it was a serene smile. "That is, if I am still here to squeeze your hand." He reflected. "Just one other thing. Try to put an end to your fatal career! I've no right to preach, Droste, for I believed seriously that one could cheat the Devil while acting in his name. But, for good or ill, we become what we pretend to be. If you act as the Devil's agent, then you'll end up by pledging your loyalty to him; if you speak on his behalf, then you'll soon speak with his tongue; if you try to trap him, you'll be trapped yourself. In an argument with the Devil man is bound to be the loser. One can only defeat him by not understanding him." He seized my arm. "I am not a Christian, Droste. I don't know if the Devil fears the Cross. But I do know that he fears an open visor. Make an end! Don't conceal anything! Turn on the searchlight!"

He continued to speak, but I do not recall his words. A cold shiver ran down my spine as I sat there, under the leafy chestnut-trees in the park of Professor Wolfgang Amadeus Segantini's private mental-home, by the side of the strange Chinese in the striped convict's uniform, a few yards from the babbling patient Malte-zahn. On that day in the early spring of 1955 there rose up before me the memory of a hot summer day of many years before, and with it the memory of the black-and-white figure of Father Peter Zombory. It was almost as if he stood there himself in the shade of the chestnut-trees, his arms upraised, saying: "God created day and night; but dawn and dusk, twilight and gloaming He did not create: they arose without His doing, from the fatal intermingling of light and darkness, which God divided from one another on the first day of Creation, long before Man was made." Eight years had passed since the Father had uttered these words, and now the Chinese by my side had said much the same. The wheel had come full circle.

But what had I to do with all this? I had to ask the question. Rising, I said:

"I shall not abuse your trust, Dr. Wang. I shall collect the papers and keep them in safe custody, and hand them over to you again untouched. But you must not cast me for the part of the moral man: I should fail in it, miserably. If I decide to commit my recollections to paper I shall do so exclusively for the sake of my son, to whom I am answerable."

Dr. Wang also rose.

"It is irrelevant," he said, "for what reasons you begin to write . . ."

He had stressed the word "begin," and was trying to say something else—but it was too late. He was facing me, his eyes towards the building, or rather, towards the trees behind which the white monastery-like building was situated. Suddenly a terror which I am unable to describe was reflected on his normally calm and relaxed features.

"They're coming!" he said.

For a moment, I admit, it occurred to me that the man to whom I had been talking for the best part of an hour was perhaps, after all, not being wrongfully detained behind these walls. I turned my head.

Among the trees a group of men had appeared who might have got more dangerously close to us had they not acted in such a dangerous manner. In front ran a big thug of a man, broad-shouldered, broad-chested, fists clenched—from head to toe one of those hired toughs whom the secret services employ for the lowliest jobs. He was followed by two or three men in white coats, whom I had no time to look at closely. The moment the big thug shouted: "Get him! Get him!" I remembered the words of the warder and began to race down the walk towards the asylum wall as fast as my legs would carry me.

I did not turn my head. Only from the shouts which rang out behind me, from the confusion of voices in the peaceful park, did I conclude that our bribed warder was also, for the sake of appearances, taking part in the chase, and that even Maltezahn, unguarded for a moment in the general uproar, was galloping behind me with his stereotyped shout: "He promised me his eyes!"

Although I had not practiced any sport for many years I had once been a good runner and, fortunately, I did not seem to have quite lost my skill. I still had a good lead when I reached the little door in the wall, which the warder had mentioned. Indeed it was extremely fortunate that I had a lead, for the door was locked. I did not stop to think whether this was treachery, or simply negligence on the part of Dr. Wang's ally, or whether his complicity had just been discovered—I ran at the wall and jumped. My height and physical strength enabled me to haul myself up in one smooth movement. For a brief—but seemingly endless—moment I stood teetering on the top of the wall. Then I leaped down on the far side—into freedom.

Out here on the open hillside, dropping down towards the Danube, it was not so much skill and presence of mind as an irrational instinct of self-preservation which saved my life. After all, I was outside Dr. Segantini's sinister institution, on free territory subject to the law of the land, and I might have stopped, regained my breath, and reflected on what had passed.

But this I did not do. Instead, picking myself up quickly, I raced on. I probably ran ever faster downhill towards the river. A life-saving instinct drove me on. No sooner had I reached a point about half-way down the slope, when the little door in the thick wall opened and the thug appeared in it. Once more I acted instinctively, cleverly, in a cowardly manner, or certainly without false heroics: without another glance behind me I zigzagged down the hill towards a house I had spotted on the river bank. Behind me two shots rang out in quick succession.

I reached the house without being hit. Only then did I turn.

The thug had disappeared inside the wall. I had evidently moved away too far from the institution, too far into a freedom where the thug would not risk following me.

I brushed down my clothes, drew a deep breath, and looked back once more towards the asylum. In the evening haze which rose from the Danube the place wore an unreal air. I turned towards the village. I believe I was smiling. I thought: What rotten shots you are . . .

Epilogue

By DECEMBER 17, 1955, George Droste's memoirs had reached the point to which the reader has now followed them.

The panic within him had become unbearable. On the day he started the last chapter he had written a letter to Nora Güldendag, whose address a former Austrian diplomat, now resident in Sweden, had found out for him. His letter had been short and like a drowning man's cry for help. It had breathed an urgency that silenced all considerations of the person of the writer. Twenty-four hours before Droste finished the draft of his manuscript he received a telegram from Nora, advising him of her arrival in Vienna on December 18.

She arrived on the morning of the eighteenth and took a room at the Parkhotel Schönbrunn. She rang up Droste and asked him to lunch. He declined. He also declined to meet her in town for supper. He requested her to instruct the porter of her hotel to admit him, even at a late hour. Something in his voice made her agree to his strange request.

That evening he acted like a spy—a thing he had never done before. He dismissed his housekeeper. At ten o'clock he switched off every light in the house. Fifteen minutes later he rang for a taxi from his darkened study and ordered it to a villa near by. He crept out of his house, approached the villa by a roundabout route, and waited for the car. He had himself driven around and across the city for nearly an hour. Near the Palace of Schönbrunn he abruptly ordered the driver to stop. He entered the hotel by the back entrance, made sure he had not been followed, and did not step into the elevator until there was no one left in the lobby. It was almost midnight when he knocked at the door of the sitting-room which Nora had taken in order to be able to receive him at this unusual hour.

She wore a plain gray travelling suit. Her beautiful regular face had grown a little narrower and around her eyes the first signs of time's transience were appearing. She reminded Droste of the woman who had stood by the wine-red grand piano in the visitors' room at the convent.

He bent over her hand and said: "Thank you for coming."

"Your letter left me no choice," she said.

They sat down. He did not know how to begin. He must not talk to her as he had once talked to her, and he could not talk to her as if she were a stranger. It seemed unbelievable that they had once been one, but it seemed equally unbelievable that they were no longer one.

"Only one thing has not changed, Nora," he began with an embarrassed smile. "I still can't confide in anyone else. I want to be brief. I have written my memoirs." He motioned towards the briefcase which he had laid on the table. "They contain the most important points about my experiences during the past few years. They are intended for the public, but above all for Johnny."

"Who is Johnny?" she asked.

He told her about Johnny, about Korea, about his last years, and about his work. When he had finished she said without bitterness:

"I shouldn't have believed that you could be so human, George."

He said quickly: "In the event of my death, would you undertake the guardianship of Johnny?"

"I should be a stranger to him," she said.

"He is arriving here tomorrow," he said. "I could introduce you."

She did not answer at once. Then she said: "So you want me to read your memoirs."

He shook his head.

"I would ask you not to read them," he said.

She looked at him inquiringly.

"There is much mention of you in those papers," he said. "If I asked you to read the book you might misunderstand; in fact, you might take certain passages as an unsolicited letter to yourself. I have not written you any letters—except this last one, which I had to write. But I have brought you the manuscript because I want to ask you to keep it. I had it at first in the safe in my house, and then in the vault of a bank. I think it would be safer with you."

"I don't understand," she said.

"You know now my purpose in writing down my experiences of the past few years. In the vault of the bank the papers might be safe, but there would be no certainty that Johnny gets them. Only you can judge when he shall have them."

"You are afraid, George," said the woman.

He lifted his head. For the first time he recognized the voice he loved.

"Yes," he said. "I am afraid."

"Have you anything to go by . . . ?"

"Nothing definite." He got up and began to pace up and down. "I realize what I am asking of you, Nora," he said, changing the subject. "These papers are a dangerous possession. Everything I am asking you to do is dangerous. Nothing gives me the right to ask it." He stopped. "Nothing except a premonition that this may be a last request."

"I shall stay till Tuesday," she said.

A smile of relief passed over his features.

"I knew it," he said. "I have appointed you my executrix and Johnny's guardian. My Will is deposited with notary Dr. Martin

Tiefenbacher. You'll find his name and address in the folder."

She rose. "What time does Johnny arrive?" she asked.

"At ten in the morning." He glanced at his watch. "He's been on the train for several hours already."

"Will you bring him here for lunch?" she asked.

"Gladly."

He was facing her in silence, afraid that even the simplest, "How are you keeping?" might be misunderstood. He had called for help, but he had not done so for his own sake, and he was anxious that she should understand this.

"I'll go now," he said.

She gave him her hand.

"George," she said, "tomorrow your son will be here and we shan't be able to talk to each other alone. We don't want to talk to each other alone. But I should like to say that I feel just as guilty as you. I was indignant at St. Wolfgang when you accused me of severity. I thought I was entitled to be severe. I was not. During our good years I ought to have esteemed you less and loved you more."

She withdrew her hand which he was still holding.

The temptation to take her in his arms was great—as great as it had been at the time when they had been lying next to each other in the barn near the Hungarian frontier and when their fingers had crept toward each other.

He turned quickly and left.

He hurried through the empty hotel lobby. Snow was falling outside. He walked as far as the Hietzing bridge. He thought of the winter's night when he had left the house on the Bellaria. He thought of Johnny, whose train would just be crossing the frontier into Austria.

When Johnny Grant-Droste arrived in Vienna on the following morning he was met by a sobbing old woman and a man with short ice-gray hair. The old woman was Marie, George Droste's housekeeper; the ice-gray gentleman was Police Superintendent Dr. Hrovacka, George Droste's former classmate.

Marie, whom Droste had, out of hysterical caution, sent to his uncle at Korneuberg under some pretext or other, had returned to the house on the Bisamberg shortly before eight in the morning. She had found the complicated front-door lock broken open. Her shouts had remained unanswered. Her master's bedroom had been empty. His study, which she had entered next, had been in an unbelievable confusion. The safe behind the bookshelves had been forced open. On the floor, by the side of his likewise ransacked writing-desk, lay George Droste. The trickle of blood from his mouth down to his chin had long clotted. George Droste was dead.

The old housekeeper had notified the police. Half an hour later the homicide squad had arrived, accompanied by Superintendent Dr. Hrovacka. They had established that the murderer had used an ordinary pistol of a common make. Dr. Hrovacka had made a number of telephone calls which the old housekeeper had been unable to follow. But she had soon pulled herself together sufficiently to tell the Superintendent, in whom she had felt immediate confidence, of Johnny's imminent arrival.

The Superintendent first introduced himself to Johnny as a friend and former schoolmate of Droste's. The boy realized at once that his father was dead. Subsequently, he told Nora Güldendag that on seeing old Marie he had felt the same sensation as on seeing the postman who had brought the Grant family news of the death of his first father.

Johnny did not cry until they reached the house on the Bisamberg. Dozens of curious people were hanging around the house. Policemen, detectives, and other plain-clothes officers were busy in all the rooms. George Droste's body was still lying on the floor: the photographers had not yet finished with it. It had been provisionally covered with a pale-blue bathrobe. The sight of the body, or rather, of the bathrobe covering the body, robbed the boy of his brave self-control. He broke down, weeping.

Two hours later the Superintendent was called to the telephone. A woman's voice said she had just learned of the murder of George Droste and had some relevant information to give to the police. Her voice—the faint foreign accent discernible only to the sharp ear of the policeman—sounded choked with tears. She refused to give her name, but asked the Superintendent to get in touch with notary Dr. Tiefenbacher. Dr. Hrovacka invited her to call at his office at police headquarters. She replied that she would do so on condition that she would meet the newly arrived Johnny Droste there. The caller's accurate information astonished the policeman. He asked her to call at his office at three in the afternoon; he would give instructions for her to be admitted without delay.

The Superintendent took Johnny with him in his car. He had no children of his own, but he was fond of children and understood their mentality. He knew that what the boy needed most at the moment was something to occupy him: a sense that he was helping in the police investigation and hence a sense of his own importance.

A few minutes after Dr. Hrovacka and Johnny had arrived at the Rossauerlände a lady was announced.

Nora Güldendag walked up to Johnny, gave him her hand, and said: "I knew your father, Johnny. I loved him very much. He spoke a lot about you last night."

She exchanged a glance with Dr. Hrovacka. The Superintendent asked Johnny to wait in the next room for a few minutes. To give him something to do he asked him to pick from a pile of photographs those faces which might belong to the same criminals.

As soon as she was left alone with the Superintendent Nora introduced herself. Briefly she outlined her meeting with George Droste, her life with him, their parting, and their last meeting. She handed the Superintendent the letter which had summoned her from Stockholm to Vienna. She declared that Droste had appointed her his executrix and Johnny's guardian. She mentioned nothing about the manuscript which she had meanwhile dispatched to her bank in Stockholm.

Dr. Hrovacka was informed about the story of Nora Gülden-dag, the wife of the long-missing Legation Counsellor, even though he had not so far known of the connection between the widow of the diplomat and his former schoolfriend. He did not doubt Nora's account, especially as the notary had confirmed her statements.

"I am greatly indebted to you, madam," he said, in his jovial Austrian officialese. "Besides, I knew Droste well. We were at school together. Only a few months ago he was in this office, sitting on that very chair." He interrupted himself. "So Droste didn't mention any names, did he?"

"No," she said.

"And he gave you no reasons for his fear?"

"No."

The Superintendent gazed out of the window. Abruptly he said:

"You don't know what's happened to the memoirs, Frau Güldendag?"

"No, I don't, Herr Oberpolizeirat."

"Writing his memoirs, Droste was," said Dr. Hrovacka. "It's the memoirs they were after . . ."

"Who?" asked Nora.

"If only we knew that, madam! You see, he was working for several sides. That's going to complicate investigations enormously. Of course, if we had the papers . . ."

"Maybe the murderer has them," said Nora.

"The murderer hasn't got them, madam," said Dr. Hrovacka. "The murderer was informed about the smallest detail in Droste's life, but he didn't know what even"—he smiled at the last word—"what even the police knew—namely, that Droste did not keep his memoirs at his house. Surprising the things which the secret services don't know, madam."

"You are entirely ruling out the possibility of an ordinary crime?" asked Nora.

"Entirely."

"So you've got a clue . . . ?"

As on the day when Droste had been facing the Superintendent the siren of the Black Maria was heard from the courtyard.

The Superintendent got up. "I rather liked that fellow Droste," he said evasively. "Wouldn't have thought it of him when he sat behind me at school. But, of course, when all is said and done—he was a spy. Supposed to have been a real genius at his job, too. Perhaps he could have gone on nicely for a little longer if his conscience hadn't got the better of him. I always say: a man's conscience is like the police—they're never wanted until it's too late."

"You don't seem to have much hope, Herr Oberpolizeirat," said Nora. For an instant her anger was stronger than her sadness.

"I didn't say that at all," said Dr. Hrovacka. "The only thing is that the death of a spy is not the same as an ordinary death."

He stood facing the woman. He could see her grit her teeth without being able entirely to check her tears. With sympathy in his voice he said: "If by any chance you should hear something about those memoirs . . . we feel we ought to warn someone. There's somebody walking around with a briefcase full of dynamite. We should like to wind up the Droste business for good." He interrupted himself. "Speak to the boy. I shall ar-